Oscar Penn Fitzgerald

John B. McFerrin

A biography

Oscar Penn Fitzgerald

John B. McFerrin
A biography

ISBN/EAN: 9783337388645

Printed in Europe, USA, Canada, Australia, Japan

Cover: Foto ©Raphael Reischuk / pixelio.de

More available books at **www.hansebooks.com**

A BIOGRAPHY.

BY O. P. FITZGERALD, D.D.,

EDITOR OF THE CHRISTIAN ADVOCATE.

Fifth Thousand.

NASHVILLE, TENN.:
PUBLISHING HOUSE OF THE M. E. CHURCH, SOUTH.
J. D. BARBEE, AGENT.
1888.

NOTE.

CONSIDERATIONS sacred and imperative have induced the writer of this Biography, busied and burdened with official labors that engross his time and heavily tax his strength, to hasten in its preparation beyond his first intention. His supreme purpose has been to make such a book as would glorify God and do good, while fulfilling a friend's request and discharging a labor of love.

(3)

CONTENTS.

(5)

PROLOGUE.

TO a great figure perspective is helpful; to a small one it is fatal. Distance symmetrizes and smooths the one, but practically annihilates the other.

McFerrin will not lose by the perspective. He towered the peer of the greatest men of his day, and he will always hold a front place in the picture the Church historian will paint of the stirring times in which he lived and acted his part. The foot-prints of a giant will be seen by those who in coming generations shall trace his life, and at least the anatomy of a mighty frame will be left to posterity. Whether they will see the contour and color of life and feel the heart-throbs of the living man depends mainly on what is here written.

A phonograph is needed to bring back McFerrin's tones, as well as his words; the soul of the man flashed forth in inflections, cadences, and trumpetings that left the earth forever when he died. No one who once met him can ever forget him; one who never saw him can never fully know him as he was. The effects of his peculiar oratory may be described, but who can tell its secret? It is buried with him. He was altogether original. No homiletical professor will ever hold him up as a model; all his imitators will fail. Nature never duplicates its productions. Grace molds every regener-

(7)

ated soul into the image of Christ, but no man is ever modeled into the exact likeness of another.

McFerrin influenced multitudes, but begat no spiritual or natural son in his own image. As well expect the reproduction of the megatherium of the tertiary period in this year of our Lord 1888 as another man like McFerrin. His like will be seen no more among us, but his tracks were made in the plastic season of American Methodism, and when the moist clay of contemporaneous knowledge shall be hardened into historic stone the student of Church history will say there were giants in his day. And the student of comparative ecclesiology at that future time, finding even a fragment of the life or speech of this typical Methodist, will be helped in his effort to discover what sort of men were they who planted the gospel west of the Alleghanies, and under whose lead Southern Methodism gained nearly 600,000 members in the two decades extending from 1866 to 1886.

The preparation of this biography was undertaken at the request of Dr. McFerrin himself. Several years before his death he said to me: "There seems to be some expectation that my life shall be written after I am gone. I feel unworthy of such special remembrance after death; but should my life be written, my wish is that, if you outlive me, you should be the writer." In his last will and testament this request was repeated in a more formal manner, and his papers were accordingly placed in my hands.

Three of the requisite qualifications for the performance of my task I may claim: genuine affection for my honored friend, the intimacy of a long and unbroken friendship, and general agreement of opinion concerning the doctrines, polity, and usages of the Church of which we were fellow-members. It may be that some temperamental contrasts between my glorified friend and his biographer may not prove a disadvantage; the law of the affinity of opposites is no new thing to the thoughtful reader. If some were more alike they would be wider apart.

But my work is done, and whether well or ill done, it speaks for itself. It was written while the echoes of McFerrin's living voice were still sounding in my ears, and while from day to day, forgetting for the moment that he was gone, I listened for his familiar footfall. At times it has seemed to me that his fatherly presence was at hand, and that the lips that had so often spoken to me in words of wise counsel and kindly admonition whispered to me to be faithful to truth as well as to friendship as I penned these chapters. This has been my aim, knowing that I shall meet both my friend and my book at the judgment-day.

O. P. FITZGERALD.

Nashville, 1888.

NATIVITY AND ENVIRONMENT.

"BORN in a cane-brake and cradled in a sugar-trough" was the sententious account given of his nativity and early environment by the subject of these chapters.

In Rutherford County, Tennessee, on the 15th day of June, 1807, a boy-baby was born. He was of unusual size, healthy, but not pretty, except to the eyes that looked upon his large, uneven features in the transfiguring light of maternal love. That he was not weak-lunged or lymphatic in temperament was doubtless demonstrated very soon. That he liked to have his own way, and was apt to get it, was not less evident. But he was too sound in his bodily make-up to be cross, and too good a sleeper to wear out the young mother by keeping her awake o'nights. He was of Scotch-Irish blood. The best of this blood is very good—the worst is as bad as Satan would have it. Its calendar of militant saints is long and glorious; its muster-roll of great sinners is not short. The McFerrins were of this peculiar stock. The very name has the Celtic ring. One curious and expert in etymology might find in it the clannishness of a warlike, iron-handed race. The family came to America not, as did the defeated and broken-down Cavaliers, to get away from debt at home, or to repair their broken fortunes; or, as did the Puritans, to worship God as they pleased, and to make other people do likewise. They came because there was to them a fascination in the largeness and liberty of a new world. That there was a spice of adventure and danger in it was perhaps another attraction to these inquisitive and daring people whose God is the God of battles. They are great fighters. When a battle is going on you will find them on one side or the other. Neutrality is not possible to them. In the presence of a foe they kindle, they strike, they keep striking. Whether on the march, psalm-singing as they went, to battle for Kirk and country in the Old World, or to encounter the savage Indians and wild beasts amid the forests and cane-brakes of America, they are the same undaunted, unconquerable race.

Tennessee owes much to the Scotch-Irish pioneers who were among its first settlers. Robertson, Jackson, and Polk and Bell were of this lineage. They had their faults, but these faults were associated with splendid virtues. They would fight "at the drop of a hat;" they were horse-racers, they were adepts at an off-hand profanity remarkable for its emphasis and rhetorical ring; they were cock-fighters and card-players. On the other hand, they exhibited such magnificent courage that they have made heroism fashionable among their descendants unto this day. They had such a high standard of veracity that the slightest imputation of falsehood was cause for deadly combat. To give the lie was the same as to give a blow. Their personal honor was so ingrained and so fortified by family tradition and public sentiment that, whatever might be the bitter rivalries and fierce passions evoked by party strife, peculation or corruption in official life was scarcely known. They were a fiery, free-and-easy, sport-loving, gallant people.

When these hot-blooded, hard-headed men took to religion they did not go at it in any half-way style. In that day the Church and the world were farther apart than they are now. Whether God or Satan was chosen, the service was hearty. The Calvinistic theology dominated. It was no rose-water system. Its God hated sin with a perfect hatred and dealt sternly with sinners. The men and women molded by it were strong and steady, with heavy Rembrandt shadows in the background of their natures. Their belief in the divine sovereignty had fatalism enough in it to give them a power of endurance and a perseverance under difficulties that fitted them for the part they took in the subjugation of the wilderness and the founding of new States. The granite of their composition was hard; it only took a higher polish from the attrition under which a softer material would have crumbled. All honor to those grand old Calvinists! Their theology has been largely modified by a sunnier and, as we think, a truer view of God and the gospel; but it was the stock upon which was grafted the system which has borne the sweetest blooms and richest fruits in this western garden of the Lord. Though it fought Methodism at first with the fierceness of honest hatred of heresy, it gave to it much of what was best in its own system, and happily modified tendencies which, if left unchecked, might have led to disaster. Arminian and Calvinistic theology happily reacted on each other at that early day, and both are better for it now.

The women at that day were better housekeepers than theologians. They knew how to cook, wash, iron, weave, quilt, milk the cows, ride horseback, manage the garden, and cut and make all sorts of clothing. Of

course they knew all those little arts and winning ways
that are instinctive to their sex. But they had no time
or inclination for polemics. While their husbands,
brothers, and sons, in and out of the pulpit, were giving and taking hard knocks in doctrinal debate, they
kept the social life of the times sweet with their wom-
anly ministries, their patience, their tenderness, and
their charity. They were not lacking in strength
of character, but it was in their homes that they expended their life-force. Their affections were not
frittered away in the vapid conventionalities of fashionable city life. They were keepers at home. They
took time to read the Bible, to teach the catechism to
the children, white and black, and to go to church once
a month, more or less. They were free from most of
the diseases that result from luxury and irregular habits
of living, and were the healthy mothers of healthy
children. They possessed the elements that make heroines, and many of them were heroines without knowing it. They were unknown to the rostrum and to the
newspaper; they made no books, they wrote no poems;
they left no written record of their lives. But these
healthy, home-loving, sweet-souled women were none
the less efficient co-workers with the men of their time
in laying broad and deep the foundations of the institutions, civil and religious, that are the priceless inheritance of their posterity.

It was into this society and amid these conditions that
the large-framed, large-featured child whose life we are
to portray was born on that summer day eighty years ago.

A GENEALOGICAL GLANCE.

(To be skipped if you will.)

THE McFerrins emigrated from Ireland to America about 1750. They settled in York County, Pennsylvania. The family connection consisted of three brothers and their young families. The descendants of one of the three removed to the western part of that State. The Rev. Dr. McFerrin, an able and respected minister of the Presbyterian Church, lived for many years near Pittsburgh. William McFerrin, the grandfather of John B. McFerrin, removed to Augusta County, Virginia, in 1765, where he was married to Jane Laughlin. John Laughlin, the father of James, was married to Jane Matthews, and was reared within two miles of Belfast, Ireland. They emigrated to America in 1753, and settled in Lancaster County, Pennsylvania. His son James married a Miss Duncan, and the grandmother of John B. McFerrin was one of their numerous offspring. These Duncans indulged a pardonable pride in a family tradition that they were remotely connected with the once royal family of Scotland. (The most democratic of Americans are seldom indifferent to the fact of having a noble ancestry.)

The Laughlins and Duncans became numerous families, and intermarried with the Singletons, the Kings, the Sharps, the Prices, the Vances, the Berrys, the Youngs, the Porters, and many others.

The Laughlins were noted for their muscular strength and courage. These qualities were highly valued at

(15)

that day, and many striking incidents were related concerning these strong and dauntless people. One of these
was the grandmother of J. B. McFerrin. She was
small of stature, weighing only one hundred and ten
pounds, but was a woman of extraordinary bodily
strength. She became the mother of nine children, all
of whom lived to reach maturity and developed into remarkable physical vigor. Some of this Laughlin family became noted, also, for their intellectual power and
culture. There seem to be remarkable exceptions to
the law that unusual brain power is to be looked for in
connection with a vigorous *physique*, but the law holds
good in general. The sound mind is found with the
sound body. The human being is a unit, and all its
faculties and powers are correlated and interdependent.
It is not an unwise or heartless thing to inquire into the
physical as well as the moral soundness of the family
with which you may become allied by marriage. Passion will not pause to consider this question in most
cases, but rushes blindly on to secure its object, leaving
future generations to pay the penalty.

Martin McFerrin, who was captured by the Indians
when a lad and kept as a prisoner for several years, belonged to a branch of the family that removed from
Pennsylvania to Virginia and located near the present
site of the town of Fincastle. He was finally rescued,
and became a popular and influential man in Virginia,
representing his county for many years in the General
Assembly. From this branch of the family sprung a
numerous posterity, who are scattered through Kentucky,
Missouri, and Colorado. To this branch belonged Judge
William McFerran, of Glasgow, Kentucky, and his son,
the late Gen. McFerran, of the United States army.

(This way of spelling the family name was adopted in accordance with the American custom of naturalizing names, as we do the owners of them in our own way.)

The grandfather of John B. McFerrin at an early age entered the Army of the American Revolution. He was one of the bold and hardy band who, at the battle of King's Mountain, broke the backbone of the British invasion of the Carolinas, and prepared the way for the glorious end of the great struggle for liberty at Yorktown. It was the valor and unflinching fortitude of these men that beat back the heavy onsets of the British regulars, led by the brilliant and ill-fated Ferguson, who fell with his cause on that bloody day. This McFerrin followed the banners of Washington and Greene against the British, and under Col. Christy had also a taste of Indian warfare. When the war ended he married a blooming maiden and settled in Southwestern Virginia, locating a farm on the banks of the beautiful Holston River, about nine miles from the town of Abingdon. The soil was rich and the country new and romantic. He erected a comfortable dwelling in the old solid style, and it is still standing in a good state of preservation, though nearly a hundred years have elapsed since it was built.

Here the father of John B. McFerrin was born, and received the name of his maternal grandfather—James. The nine children, of whom mention has already been made, were all born on this Holston farm. In that new country educational advantages were limited. Families lived so far apart that schools were few, and in most cases the teachers were poorly paid, and of course were not distinguished for scholarship or skill. The pedagogue who could " cipher " as far as the Single Rule of

2

Three in Daboll's Arithmetic was a prodigy in the eyes
of many of his patrons, among whom he boarded around,
and by whom he was regarded as half-monitor and half-
mendicant.   It was a teacher of this type who threatened to flog a pupil for leaving the " t " out of the
word " which " in his copy-book!   Now and then a man
of a different sort would be found in these wilds teaching the children of the pioneers.   Educated Irishmen,
exiled for political offenses, or self-expatriated from
other causes, penetrated into these distant regions and
opened schools in which many distinguished men got
their first lessons in learning.   They were stern and ex-
acting pedagogues.   In the corner behind their desks
they kept a number of hickory or gum switches—not
for ornament, but for use.   The frequency and vigor
with which they wielded these disciplinary instruments
was in many cases made the measure of their popularity
with their patrons, who believed in no mild theory of
government, human or divine, and with whom obedience to rightful authority was the chiefest of virtues.
There was no little tyranny and brutality in some of
these schools, but somehow they managed to mold manly men and modest women.

The religious privileges of these Holston pioneers
were superior for the times.   The family resided near
the famous " Green Spring Meeting-house," erected by
the Presbyterians, where they had a regular ministry
and able preaching.   The Bible was their one book,
and it gave tone to their thought and shaped their lives.
They believed in election and predestination, in a real
heaven, and a real hell.   They believed in chastity,
debt-paying, reciprocal neighborliness, and in standing
up manfully for one's opinions and rights.   The Church

was the great conservator of the moral life of the community. Their children were baptized and faithfully catechised. Pastors and parents believed what they taught, and thus were able to impress upon the plastic mind of the young that faith in the supernatural, that reverence for sacred things, that sense of accountability to God that gave strength, stability, and dignity of character. The standard of morals was high. If classical scholars were few, grown men and women who were ignorant of the fundamental principles and facts of Christianity were fewer still. The Bible in their homes broadened and sweetened their lives, and was the torch that lighted the march of civilization in its westward course. May its light never be quenched in the homes of their children to the latest generation!

This grandfather was a farmer, and bred all his sons to the same calling; and all his daughters were married to farmers. He was a man of medium size, about five feet ten inches high, weighing about one hundred and sixty pounds. His florid complexion, blue eyes, and auburn hair attested his pedigree. He possessed good common sense, his general reading was considerable, and he was particularly well read in the Holy Scriptures, being a Presbyterian of liberal views. He lived to be ninety years old, and died in the State of Mississippi. William, the second son, was a man of great physical strength. In his old age he became very religious, was licensed to preach, and died in the faith. Burton L., the third son, after living many years in Tennessee, removed to Missouri, where he became an active and prominent member of the Methodist Church. He was roughly treated during the late war, and his son, an excellent young man, was murdered without provocation—one of

the many shocking and inevitable episodes of a conflict
in which the political blunders and evil passions of two
generations came to their disastrous culmination. Tab-
itha was married to Burton L. Smith, a devout Christian and an ardent Methodist. Eleanor D. was married
to Cullen Curlee, Esq., an excellent man. They became Baptists, and honored their Christian profession
by their godly lives. Mary was married to Poston Sto-
vall. She was a beautiful and cultured woman who
died in the bloom of young womanhood, leaving a small
family.

The father of John B. McFerrin was the first son
and second child of his parents. He was born in 1784,
and was married on his . twentieth birthday to Jane
Campbell Berry, who was two years younger than himself. She was the youngest of eight children, the daughter of John Berry and Jane Campbell. The Campbells
were an extensive family from Eastern Virginia, and
were related to Col. Campbell of King's Mountain ce-
lebrity. Jane Campbell Berry was also born on the
banks of the Holston River, at a place afterward known
as Berry's Iron Works, about three miles from the birth-
place of her husband. Her father was connected with
a large family, and possessed the remarkable physical
strength which was a family characteristic. He was a
zealous Presbyterian, and a ruling elder in the Church.
His wife's widowhood lasted more than thirty years.
She lived to be more than ninety years old, and was at
last buried in the same grave with the husband of her
youth. She reared eight children, who took respectable
positions in society. They were all married; the first-
born of each family was a son, and his name John Berry.
The Berry family of course became numerous, and are

scattered widely. They may be found in Virginia, Tennessee, Ohio, Missouri, Arkansas, Texas, and California.

Sallie was married to John Gilliland, and became the mother of a large family of sons and daughters. One of her sons, the Rev. Samuel Gilliland, became a useful minister in the Methodist Church, as did also one of her grandsons.

Two great-uncles of John B. McFerrin—James and Andrew—settled at an early day in East Tennessee, near the Virginia line, where they reared large families. some of whose descendants remain in Tennessee, while others removed to the South and West. In Oregon and Illinois are descendants of this branch of the McFerrin family.

A great-aunt married a Martin, from whom sprung the families of the Rev. Thomas Martin and the Rev. Patrick Martin; both were Methodist preachers, and both died in Robertson County, Tennessee.

This genealogical glance shows a prolific, sturdy stock, full of vitality, addicted to fighting, praying, and matrimony.

LOVE, EMIGRATION, AND WAR.

CLEAN-LIMBED, athletic, about five feet ten inches high, with ruddy and clear complexion, blue eyes, and reddish hair, when James McFerrin cast admiring glances upon the gentle and affectionate Jane Berry, he was not repulsed. They were born for each other—the bold and fiery soldier, and the quiet, trusting maiden. The wooing was in the good old country fashion—solitary walks on the hills, or along the banks of the sparkling Holston, or galloping over the rude highways with the mountain breezes in their lungs, the glory of nature around them and its voices mingling with the music of young love in their happy hearts. He wooed her in manly fashion and won her. They were married—he being twenty years old, and she eighteen. There is no record of the bridal festival; the bride's trousseau was not described by any newspaper reporter of that day; but we may be sure there was a joyful wedding at her home and an equally joyful "infair" at his, with abundant feasting, merry games, and shy jokes at the expense of the blushing, smiling couple. And we may believe also that a mother's tears, the crystal drops from love's sacred font, bedewed the fair young head in that glad yet solemn hour when the bride went out from the old home to meet what might fall to her lot in the wide, cold world.

A tide of emigration was then moving westward, as it is still moving now. The energetic young husband,

James McFerrin, caught the prevailing impulse. He had heard of Middle Tennessee—its rich lands, its noble forests abounding in wild game, its beautiful streams teeming with fish. He proposed to go and try their fortunes in this new field; and the young wife, as was her way, yielded to his wishes. They were soon ready and on the march. The journey was made on horse-back, his little stock of ready cash in his pocket, and their worldly goods taking up no more room than can be found in a portmanteau, or one of those packages in which a woman can stow away such incredible quanti-ties of things solid and things hollow, things square and things round, things tough and things brittle, things useful and things otherwise. That was a bridal tour for you! It is to be hoped that the season was mild and the weather fair. The route they took lay along the banks of the ever-beautiful Tennessee River, in sight now and then of the great Smoky Mountains, looking dim, distant, and weird through the gaps of the Cum-berland and Clinch ranges; and for whole days through almost unbroken forests where towered the majestic yellow poplar, the monarch of the Southern woods, with the oak, the hickory, the chestnut, and endless un-dergrowth and wild flowers of bewildering variety, from the snow-white dogwood blossoms to the glowing red Indian pink that lent its modest gayety to the scene. The world was before them, and love and hope were in their hearts. The hardships and dangers they encount-ered spiced their journey with a fresh fascination. She had confidence in her husband, and he relied on his own brave heart and stalwart arm.

Descending the steeps of the Cumberland Mountains, the young couple came to the waters of Stone's River.

Struck by the advantages and attractions of that region,
here they stopped and set about making a home in the wilderness. Bubbling springs and running streams abound-
ed, the virgin soil was rich, and the country was abundant in undeveloped resources. There were but few
settlers, and neighbors were few and far apart. The
first thing to be done was to build a house. It did not
take long to do it. The logs were cut and hewed, a day
was set for the " raising," the neighbors gathered in
force with their axes, saws, hammers, and before the
setting of the sun the walls were erected, the clapboard
roof put on, and all made ready for the daubing, floor-
ing, and chimney. These house-raisings were great occasions in the new settlements in those days. A dinner
of barbecued meats was usually one of its features, and
a pleasant one to hardy, healthy woodsmen, whose appetites did ample justice to the brown, crisp, and juicy
shoats, the fat and tender venison, the young lambs and
plump yearlings roasted over the glowing coals in the
trenches. It was not uncommon on such occasions to
have other and stronger drink than the sparkling spring
water and fresh, cold buttermilk. Total abstinence
from strong drink might have had here and there a
solitary adherent, but the drinking of ardent spirits was
a universal custom. A capacious jug of whisky from
the nearest store or still-house would be set in the midst,
and its corn-cob stopper withdrawn and replaced with
great frequency during the day. It was seldom that
anybody got drunk, but everybody became lively as the
jug got lighter, and now and then a weak-headed fellow
showed that he had taken more than he could decently
carry. House-raising was not easy work, but these
backwoodsmen had such abundant energy and mingled

so much good humor and fun with their labor that they did not mind it, and their redundant spirits were exhibited at the close of the day in trials of strength and agility in wrestling, running, and leaping. The "best man" in these contests was proud of his honors, and was only second to the best marksman with the rifle as a neighborhood hero.

In all these accomplishments James McFerrin was proficient. He could shoot, wrestle, run, or jump with the best; and he soon won the esteem and good-will of his neighbors. There was also a dignity of presence and a prompt and incisive way with him that inspired respect and confidence. The young couple from Virginia soon got a footing in their new home. The cane-brake was cleared, the farm was fenced, and the tasseled corn took the place of the wild pea-vine and the sweet honeysuckle; and they settled down to housekeeping, a healthy, hopeful, and happy pair. If they lacked the luxuries they might have enjoyed in an older community, they had large compensations in the freedom and freshness of their lives in their new home on the banks of Stone's River.

James McFerrin was a pretty good farmer and a better hunter. He was, as already intimated, an expert rifleman, and could bring down a bear or deer at long range, or knock a squirrel from the top of the tallest tree.

When a call was made for volunteers to fight the Indians, his bold and ardent nature made him one of the first to take the field. He was chosen captain of a company raised in his neighborhood, and learned what were the real hardships of soldier-life in a march to Natchez, Mississippi, to which point he was ordered. Soon after his return from this expedition to the South, trouble broke out with the Creek Indians, who were then close and dangerous neighbors, and he again entered the field. He exhibited notable courage and skill in this campaign, and won the confidence and special commendation of his fiery chieftain, Gen. Andrew Jackson, afterward President of the United States. The Creek War ended, and Capt. McFerrin resumed the peaceful life of a farmer. But the military spirit within him was not quenched. Military glory was the aim of all ambitious souls in those warlike times. The State militia was a very different thing then from what it became afterward; and so when Captain McFerrin rose to be Major, and then Colonel, these increasing honors showed that he was looked upon as a man among men.

The associations of military life were not favorable to religion. Profanity was looked upon almost as a soldierly accomplishment, and examples in high places were not wanting to give countenance to this and other sins that were regarded as venial. His early religious impressions, if not obliterated, were greatly weakened. The life he lived was not favorable to the acquisition of property. The loss of time in the militia musters, the purchase of costly uniforms, the claims of a generous hospitality—all made drafts upon the proceeds of the Stone's River farm; and so it happened that, as Col. McFerrin rose in reputation, he rather sunk in fortune. What cared he? Freedom, honor, manly sports, and robust health were the things he prized, and these he had. If others were willing to slave and stint and grab for money, let them do so; they were welcome to all they got. He preferred a grand militia parade to a finer house, an exciting hunting party to an extension of his farm, and the glory of being the bravest rather than the richest man of his neighborhood. Perhaps his choice was not wholly unwise. There are better things than money for a possession and to be transmitted to posterity. If this soldier had had a greater love of money his elder children would have been more liberally educated and exerted a wider influence upon the world— perhaps. Money has ruined more boys than it has really helped in life's battle.

A GREAT CHANGE.

THE Methodists had found their way to Middle Tennessee, and at this time—1819 and 1820—a great religious excitement pervaded that part of the State. Col. McFerrin had strong prejudices against the Methodist people, of whom he knew but little except by hearsay. They were not seldom made the subjects of his sarcastic remarks. In this he was no worse than others of that day, when the *odium theologicum* was bitter beyond what we can now realize. Methodism was a storm-rocked child in this land where it is now so great and strong. Though far from being a Christian, the doughty Colonel retained his early-taught belief in the Bible and respect for religion of the Presbyterian type.

A camp-meeting was held by the Methodists at Salem, not far from Col. McFerrin's. The name then truly described these peculiar gatherings—they were camp-meetings. A spacious bush arbor was constructed in the midst of the forest, usually near a cool spring of water; rude seats were provided; log-cabins or cloth tents were erected, and the people from far and near came in wagons, carry-alls, barouches, and gigs, on horseback and on foot. These crowds sometimes were numbered by thousands, attracted by curiosity or impelled by the mysterious impulse that sometimes moves the popular heart so strangely and unaccountably in times of religious excitement.

Col. McFerrin attended the Salem camp-meeting,

(28)

drawn thither with the crowd. The wave of spiritual excitement rolled high. The preaching was of a kind he had never heard before. That son of thunder, Thomas L. Douglass, was then in his prime. His direct and burning appeals to sinners were irresistible. There were others of the same spirit who, as soldiers of the militant Church, demanded immediate and unconditional surrender to Jesus Christ. The power of God was manifest. The stoutest sinners felt it, and many stubborn hearts were melted and subdued. An arrow reached the heart of Col. McFerrin. He felt that he must yield or fly. Awed, agitated, alarmed, the awakened, but still resisting, soldier mounted his horse and galloped homeward. But he found no relief in flight. The pains of hell had gotten hold on him. He was a convicted sinner, and in vain did he seek to banish the impression made upon his mind. "Now or never," said a voice within him. Reining in his horse, he paused in the road, and then and there decided the question of all questions. He surrendered to the Lord Jesus Christ, and the surrender was complete. His conversion was sudden and thorough—after the type of those marvelous times. He turned around and galloped back to the camp-ground, a changed man. He was not slow in telling what the Lord had done for his soul, and we may imagine the sensation produced by the conversion of this stout, fiddling, profane, hospitable, popular sinner. Who can estimate the consequences of his visit to Salem Camp-ground? It turned from its former channel a life that drew after it a series of influences that are still widening in their sweep, and which can be fully measured only when "the day" shall declare all things.

The converted soldier went home and told the wondering family of the great change that had come upon him, and on that night he held family prayer for the first time. The erection of that family altar was a decisive movement, commiting the new convert fully to his new life in the presence of the dear ones at home. If all heads of families would do likewise, how many homes, now spiritually barren, would bloom out in all the blessedness of family piety!

The conversion of the other members of the family quickly followed. The quiet, loving, faithful wife felt her heart strangely stirred, and the two older sons— John and William—knelt at her side as penitents. Soon they were all converted, and it was a joyful household.

Though his former predilections were all in favor of the Presbyterian Church, in which he was reared, Col. McFerrin, after due deliberation, united with the Methodists, and thenceforward never wavered in his devotion to Methodist doctrine, polity, and methods. When Methodism is thus grafted on good Presbyterian stock you have almost the ideal Christian character—the steadiness and solidity of the one type and the spontaneity and warmth of the other. (Perhaps this would work just as well in reverse order.)

Two weeks after the conversion of the mother and two sons they too joined the Methodist Church, being received into the "Society" by the Rev. James Sanford, a local minister, formerly a traveling preacher in the Virginia Conference.

Soon Col. McFerrin began to exercise his gifts " in public," exhorting and holding prayer-meetings among his neighbors. He laid aside his fiddle, and the places that knew him before knew him no more. Though the martial element in his nature was still there, hence

forth he is to be the soldier of Jesus Christ, and the only
enemies he will fight will be the devil and sin.   About
one year from his conversion he began to preach.   He
labored two years as a local preacher, and then joined
the Tennessee Conference, and traveled nearly twenty
years, filling various important positions as preacher in
charge, presiding elder, delegate to the General Conference, etc.   In his diary there is this record: "Up to the
15th of October, 1839, I have preached 2,088 sermons,
baptized 573 adult persons and 833 infants, and taken
into the Church 3,965 members."   A minute that he
kept on the last page of his pocket Bible showed that
he had read it through eighteen times on his knees.   He
died September 4, 1840.   The impression was on his
mind from the beginning of his sickness that he would
not recover.   "Twenty years ago," he said to one of his
sons, "God for Christ's sake pardoned my sins.   I then
dedicated myself to him in fervent prayer, and asked
that my life might be spared for twenty years, that I
might devote that time to his service and promote his
cause.   That time has just expired, and I think my
heavenly Father is going to take me to himself."   His
last hours were full of joy and triumph.   "When it was
evident to all and to himself that the hour of departure
was near, he had all his family gathered around him,
and addressed them one by one, suiting his exhortations
to their various ages and conditions; but when he came
to take leave of his wife and pronounce a blessing on
her the scene became indescribable.   He spoke of the
number of years during which they had sustained to
each other the relation of husband and wife, and referred to the children God had given them; talked of
the sorrows and joys which they had shared together,

exhorted her not to grieve, for the Lord would take care of her, and their separation would not be long. He then told her that, with God's permission, he would be her guardian angel through the valley of death." (Memoir by Dr. A. L. P. Green.) This was a touch of nature, and an example of the ruling passion strong in death—the brave, loving heart going out in tenderness and protection to the woman who had journeyed on by his side from the day that she, a blushing bride, had put her hand in his in pledge of union for life. "He then lay for a few moments with his eyes closed, and, with a smiling countenance, commenced singing with a loud voice,

'Jesus can make a dying bed
    Feel soft as downy pillows are,'

and continued in this frame of mind until he breathed his last. In answer to a prayer I often heard him offer to God he died in his senses, with Christ in his arms and glory in his soul." (Dr. Green's Memoir.)

THE BOY CHRISTIAN.

THE turning of the McFerrins to Methodism was no half-way movement. It took all the older members of the family—the impulsive, courageous father, the wise, steady, loving mother, and the two stout, growing boys. John was large and "forward" for his age. He began to walk when he was but seven months old —a sort of prophecy of his itinerant career. He grew rapidly, being equal in weight and stature to other boys two years older than himself. He was full of boyish life and loved fun. But, fortunately for him, there were such safeguards thrown about him at the time as were much needed by one of his temperament. He was kept busy, and that was a good thing. Perhaps he thought at times he had too much of this good thing; a healthy boy likes play, and feels cheated if he does not get it. John worked hard on the farm; he rode on all sorts of errands through the country; he went to mill; he did almost every thing, and throve on it, body and mind. Self-reliance was thus early developed in a nature always inclined to mark out its own course. The stout-limbed boy, with his large, uneven features and quick, energetic way, was his father's right hand on the farm, a *factotum* in the family service.

A wise thought it was in his father to call on John now and then to lead in family prayer. "This made me more careful," he said in after years, "of my conduct at home; for how could one pray in the family

3   (33)

when his spirit and conversation contradicted his profession?" In this connection he also said: "My father
watched over me with great vigilance, often conversed
with me as to my Christian experience, and always encouraged me in the work of my personal salvation.
Never, perhaps, was a son more indebted to a parent
for his affectionate, Christian watchfulness over a child
than I was to my beloved father."

These glimpses indicate the family life, and give a
beautiful picture of the home religion of the McFerrins.
Its mingled currents flowed sweetly together, and it was
made easier for each one to be true and earnest in the
Christian life.

About the same time John was called on to "pray in
public." To us now this would seem premature. Fourteen is a very early age for such a function as this.
But the boy's development was, as we have already
seen, unusually rapid, and the Spirit of the Lord was
upon him. It was not in his nature to hold a passive
attitude toward any thing that interested him, and already a hand was pointing him to the path he was to
travel through life. Those old Methodist preachers
had a way of trying the metal of their converts, and
many a rough diamond was thus found by them, and
afterward polished into brightness and beauty. And,
it may be asked, if a delicate young girl may "show off"
at a graduation, at concerts, or in solos in church-choirs,
why might not young McFerrin make a prayer when
called on "in meeting?"

The "old-field school" was then the people's university. To it John went part of the year, picking up in
snatches the elements of a partial English course. His
knowledge of farming, wood-craft, and human nature

was greater than his knowledge of books. He learned to read from the New Testament—a book not specially adapted for school use by beginners, and not found in any series of school-readers now used in our graded schools. The genealogical table in the first chapter of Matthew must have been puzzling to John, and it is likely that some of his teachers did not too easily handle such names as Onesiphorus and Diotrephes. How much of its language he retained, and how much of its spirit he absorbed, is not known; but that that well-thumbed copy of the New Testament made its impress upon the plastic mind of the boy we cannot doubt.

Among the memoranda of his life written in his last years is found this entry: "I never received any punishment at school, except that one teacher boxed my ears once when I was five years old." That was a brutal blow, we suspect. The memory of it was vivid seventy years afterward. The heavy-handed tyrant had no right to strike a five-year-old child that way. Do not box the ears of a child, O ye mothers, fathers, elder brothers, sisters, and teachers! You may forget it, but the hasty blow leaves a scar upon the tender soul that it carries to the grave. It is matter of surprise that he only got one blow at school in those days when the moral suasion methods of school discipline were scarcely thought of. It is also known that the use of the rod was a rare thing in the home of the McFerrins. The secret was this: The old Scotch idea of implicit obedience to parental authority was adopted as a matter of course, and the children were born and grew into moral consciousness in an atmosphere of obedience.

At the house of the Rev. Thomas King, in Madison County, Alabama, John boarded and went to school the greater part of a year, and made good use of the opportunity thus given. Returning home, the Rev. Mr. Field—a Presbyterian preacher of whom he always spoke gratefully—taught him for a season, the last of his school-life. The sum total of his acquisitions, he says, "amounted to a partial knowledge of the English language and a few of the sciences—reading, writing, arithmetic, English grammar, history, and a smattering of geography and astronomy. To this might be added what I had read of a miscellaneous character and studied at home during my leisure hours."

During this time John's religious life steadily developed. "My Bible," he says, "was my companion; it was taken to the secret place, and often on my knees did I pore over its sacred pages, and ask God to give me wisdom and understanding according to his revealed will. My class-meetings were attended with pleasure, and I found peculiar benefit in the use of this means of grace. Often was I made happy in communing with God and my brethren in the class and prayer-meetings; and now, after many years' experience, I take pleasure in recording my firm belief in the utility of these social meetings for worship and for mutual edification among Christians."

It was not long before he was called to lead in these social meetings, for which service he must have shown special adaptation. A class-leader at sixteen! This was fine schooling for the youth. In those class-meetings, among the plain, earnest Methodists on Stone's River, was given the direction to his ministry which it always maintained. Spirituality, insight into human nature, directness of appeal, and ready tact in dealing with the varied wants of the people, were its marked

features. The class-meeting is the best theological seminary for the equipment of a young preacher for the
practical duties of an overseer of the flock of Christ.
When the solid old fathers and saintly old mothers in Israel were willing to be led in class by this beardless boy,
just of the gawky age, it is evidence enough that they
saw in him wisdom beyond his years, and gave promise
of good things to come. That word about his Bible-
reading " in the place of secret prayer " is significant, and
we can read between the lines of the internal struggles,
the wrestlings, the partial falls, and the victories of the
youthful Christian just fairly born into the world of
thought and listening with awe to the Interior Voice
sounding a divine call within its holiest depths. The
thick forest was his oratory, the whispering winds answered to his sighs, and the overarching sky above
him typed to him the Infinite for which he yearned.
This is the period for morbidness, but he had no time
for that. He had time to work, to read and pray, and
"go to meeting," but none to mope and whine in self-
pity and mawkishness. His inner life was sound and
sweet. This was in 1821. Sixty-five years afterward
(in 1886), reverting to this period, he says:

" Two weeks after my conversion I united with the
Church. We had preaching generally every two weeks,
and prayer or class-meeting every week. Though a
lad, I was soon called on to lead in the prayer-meeting.
At first the cross was heavy, but I never refused to bear
it. In class-meeting I always spoke either voluntarily
or in answer to questions propounded by the preacher
or leader. In family prayer my father occasionally
called on me to lead. In all these exercises I was much
blessed, and realized new strength in my heart. I also,

at about the age of seventeen, went into a band with two others, and we had our meetings frequently. These band meetings were very profitable. We spoke freely and without reserve to each other, and received great encouragement, one from another. But of all the social meetings I enjoyed most the class-meeting. At a little past sixteen I was made leader of a very large class; indeed the whole membership in the Church present often met together, and we held what we called a general class-meeting. These meetings were greatly blessed, and did much in building up and enlarging the Society. We read the Scriptures, we sung, we prayed, we spoke often one to another, and the Lord hearkened and heard, and a book of remembrance was kept. Here I heard much of Christian experience, and learned to understand the wants of others. Here I learned to give words of exhortation and comfort, and here I learned to appreciate the trials and temptations connected with the life of a Christian. Fifty years have passed, to the time of this writing, and the precious seasons that I enjoyed then are still fresh in my memory. I regard class-meetings as among the greatest providential means of grace ever instituted in the Church. They did much to keep me in the path when young, and many encouragements I had by the experience of older and wiser Christians than myself. Class-meeting is about the best theological school ever organized by the Methodists. It was a sad day when it declined in the Methodist Church; and I hope and pray the time may come when it will be revived in the Church that has gathered so much rich fruit from this glorious institution.

J. B. McFERRIN."

March 8, 1883.

THE MARTIAL METEMPSYCHOSIS.

THE doctrine of the metempsychosis hints at a profound truth in its application to the great movements of human society. Moral forces do not die; they transmigrate. The soul of a seemingly spent movement enters a new body. When Judaism had taught its lesson, its vitalizing spirit passed into the new movement initiated in the wonders of the Pentecost. The soul that animated the body of the visible Church until its corruption culminated in the reign of Pope Leo X. found a new body when liberated by the Monk of Erfurt. The doctrine of the conservation of forces is as true in the moral as in the physical sphere. Tides of energy reach their limit in one direction, and then gathering again in mighty volume sweep with resistless power in a new path.

Herein may be found an explanation of the fact that early Tennessee Methodism was so pre-eminently a militant movement. The echoes of the guns of Yorktown were still in the air; heroes who fought at King's Mountain were still living; Revolutionary fires were yet burning hot in the hearts of a generation who freshly remembered the fears, the suspense, the agonies of the seven-years' struggle for liberty. The several Indian wars and the second war with Great Britain kept alive the martial ardor of the people. The literature of the day was ablaze with it; the " Star-spangled Banner " and similar lyrics were sung everywhere; Jackson, the hero of New Orleans, was the popular idol. The

(39)

military spirit pervaded the nation. Martial courage was the chiefest virtue of the people, cowardice the unpardonable sin.

Thus Methodism found a prepared people when it came to Tennessee. The unflinching heroism of its preachers, its aggressive methods, its hymnology resonant with the pæans of Christian soldiers in their victorious march to the conquest of the world—all combined to mold the converts and proselytes of early Methodism in Tennessee into the militancy that made it a disturbing, revolutionary, invincible force wherever its banner was unfurled and its doctrines promulgated. Men who had for conscience' sake broken through the meshes of ecclesiasticism, who had led a successful religious revolution, and who feared neither man nor devil, the Methodist preachers of that day reflected in their character and methods the very genius of that heroic time. The soul of the civil revolution seemed to animate the religious revival; the fires of 1776, refined into a holier flame, kindled anew in the West; the new nation that had been born into freedom amid blood and flame was being born again to God as the itinerant hosts moved westward, singing and shouting as they marched. It was a martial metempsychosis.

These early Methodist preachers in the West had little use for defensive weapons. They wielded the sword of the Spirit with a skill peculiar to them as men of one Book. They made no compromises with the world, the flesh, or the devil; they thundered against the strongholds of sin with the artillery of the law, and demanded unconditional surrender in the name of the Lord Jesus Christ. Their battle-song was, "Am I a soldier of the cross?"—a lyric that still rings along the lines.

The stimulus of a warlike time was not needed to give to the ministry of young McFerrin an aggressive character. He did dearly love a fight, and was sprung at once when the call of duty summoned him to battle for the truth. If he sometimes thought he saw the red flag when it was not visible to others, and charged with headlong energy where no enemy was, we need not be surprised. He started out as a preacher with the notion that this is an evil world that must be righted, a world in error that must be corrected, a rebellious world that must be subdued, by the gospel of Jesus Christ. On this line he started, and he followed it to the end. But his courage was happily balanced by caution; he was daring, but not rash. He knew his own resources, and measured quickly the difficulties to be overcome. He rarely failed to carry his point. He could reason in his own way, and persuade with winning force; but the bent of his nature led him to employ a method of his own. Selecting the most salient points in the errors he wished to combat, he bore down upon them with Scripture quotation usually apt, with playful touches of humor that made his hearers smile, but sent a barbed arrow through a joint in the enemy's mail; then he would deliver a succession of blows so rapid and so stunning that, under his final declamatory onset, victory was complete. This pugnacious method was followed by him with success even in dealing with congregations that were all on his own side. He would personate and catechise an imaginary antagonist, and then pierce him through and through, using the *reductio ad absurdam* with such effect that the error he attacked was ever after made to look more ridiculous and more hateful to his delighted auditors. Thus he was a man of war from his youth up; sword in hand, he was always ready for an encounter. Universalism sought but vainly to get a footing among the people of the West in that day when it was finding a lodgment in New England with other isms that came in with the reaction against ultra Augustinianism. This heresy found no mercy at the hands of McFerrin; upon it he exhausted all the sharpness of his wit, the drollness of his humor, and the vehemence of his invective. It was indeed a bold man who would confess himself a believer in it after he had thus riddled and gibbeted it. His Presbyterian pedigree did not prevent him from running full-tilt against the sharp angles of the Westminster Confession when they seemed to get in his way. If a good Baptist or other immersionist wanted to dispute about the mode of baptism, he was ready to wrestle with him at the shortest notice. If a brother preacher of his own Church showed signs of unsoundness in doctrine, or allowed metaphysical speculation to entice him into the region of misty and doubtful disputation, the first thing he knew McFerrin was after him, cudgel in hand, to drive him back into the beaten path. Fortunately for himself and for the Church, McFerrin's pugnacity was of the conservative sort; it did not incite him to break down or to break over the wall of orthodoxy, but rather to set himself for its defense, to restrain restless spirits within, and to repel all assailants from without. Had he been destructive rather than conservative in his spirit and purposes, he would have made some thrilling chapters in Methodist history. He possessed all the elements of an ecclesiastical or political revolutionist—boldness, shrewdness, the magnetism that attracts and the will-power that controls men. Had he taken the role of a reformer of the radical type, what a stir he would have made among the Methodists whom he had joined! Had he been a politician, what a commotion he would have made in the political arena! Tennessee would have rocked under his tread. If Andrew Johnson and John B. McFerrin had met "on the stump," when both were in the prime of their powers, the collision would have been indeed terrific. He was not inferior to that sharp-angled, forceful, audacious man of the people in his ability to impress the masses, and was his superior in the wit and tact that were such potent factors in the success of that other great commoner, Abraham Lincoln. What McFerrin would have been without religion is a speculation perhaps more curious than profitable. But if he had chosen the service of Satan rather than that of Jesus Christ, who can tell how greatly would have been changed the currents of history within the circle of his movement? As a soldier of fortune he would have made his mark on his time; as a soldier of Jesus Christ, under the Methodist system, his extraordinary powers reached their maximum of development, and his name will perhaps be spoken by men as long as that of any of his distinguished contemporaries who climbed to the high places of secular ambition.

The key of McFerrin's life is found in those characteristics of his times and in his own organic tendency. A sanctified pugnacity was its unifying principle. It will not be claimed by any that his pugnacity was always sanctified in the sense that he made no mistakes, that he never struck amiss, or that in all cases he knew when to put his sword back into its scabbard. He was very human, and when in the full tide of excitement—whether it was pathetic, humorous, or combative—the

play of his genius and the intensity of his feeling bore
him beyond the barriers where other men of weaker
natures and cooler passions paused.   In the heat of battle he thought of nothing but victory, and every lawful
weapon within reach was used by him.   He did not scru-
ple to employ the *argumentum ad hominem* when hard
pressed, and from force of habit he overthrew with it
many a brother, who was made to feel exceedingly uncomfortable under the storms of laughter raised at his
expense, while he found it impossible to get angry with
the victor who had struck him so hard and yet without
the least malicious intent.   When it is said that sanctified
pugnacity was the dominant trait in his character, and
the key to his career, the meaning is that he was a true
soldier of Jesus Christ, whose consecration was genuine.   He fought a good fight and kept the faith through
all the long and stormy years of a ministry of sixty years
in the Church of God.   .

McFerrin's nature was a harp of many strings tuned
by a hand divine, its dominant note the battle-call.   Its
discordant notes—and no life is wholly without them—
were the expression of the human infirmities that differ-
entiate every human life from that of the Divine Man,
whose banner he bore in the forefront of the fight with
a devotion that never cooled and a courage that never
failed.

GREEN AND McFERRIN.

IN the autumn of 1822 Rev. James McFerrin had removed to Alabama, and settled near the village of Bellefonte, in Limestone County, where he had charge of the circuit. His colleague was a young man whose name is now familiar to the whole Church—A. L. P. Green. He was a year older than John B. McFerrin—tall, well-proportioned, with chestnut hair slightly curling around a broad forehead, a blue eye that often twinkled in quiet merriment, but with an expression that betokened a thinker who could go deep into things. His motion was deliberate, but gave the impression that he would always be in time; his voice was full and musical, and held his hearers without apparent effort. It is likely that his preaching on the Limestone Circuit was crude enough, for he was very young, and had sprung up as a spontaneous growth in those days when preachers called of God went at once, like Amos from his sheep-cotes, to deliver the message of the Lord.

Aleck Green and John McFerrin were often thrown together this year, young Green making frequent visits to the family of his senior colleague. The young men were fine specimens of vigorous young manhood. They were just at the age when their whole natures were alive and aglow. Young Green, in the family of the McFerrins, could unbend from the severe gravity expected of the clergy, and indulge in the playfulness and mischief that never wholly deserted him. A wrestling-

(45)

match between the young men was prophetic of many
a hard but friendly tussle in after years. " I threw
Green the first fall," said McFerrin, " but he *downed*
me on the second trial. I wasn't anxious to try him
again." The genius of the two men is here indicated—
the impetuous temper of McFerrin that bore down his
adversary before he had time to think or brace himself
to meet it, and the cool, watchful, steady attitude of
Green that made him more likely to succeed in the second round than the first, and who won many a fight in
the councils of the Church that seemed hopeless at the
start. From this time the history of these two young men
ran in parallel lines and close together. They were fellow-soldiers and chieftains in a conquering army, inspir-
iting, balancing, supplementing each other. They were
rivals too, but in no bad sense. The friends of each
have said that with either one out of the way the other
would have been made a Bishop. This is perhaps true.
But it matters not. The office would have made neither
of them a greater man. They were *sui generis*, and
filled the places they were born for—Green, the wise
counselor whose head was steady in the midst of the
wildest storm; McFerrin, the man of action, the right
arm of executive energy. Their friends in after years
sometimes put them into sharper contrast and more an-
tagonistic attitudes toward each other than either would
have liked. When they met in heaven the friendship
that bloomed so sweetly among the North Alabama hills
in their youth was not marred in its blessedness by the
slight jostlings that took place when they were fighting
side by side in the Church militant.

The Methodist preachers were frequent visitors to the
McFerrin family, and John had the benefit of their so-

ciety and the inspiration of their enthusiasm for their sacred calling. "From these servants of the Church," he said, "I gained much valuable information on the doctrines of Christianity. I exercised myself in prayer and in exhortation, which proved beneficial to me if not to others. The class-meeting I led grew to a large and spiritual congregation in which many were converted."

At the age of seventeen young McFerrin was licensed to exhort by William McMahon, presiding elder —a strong man of a unique individuality, who doubtless left his impress upon the young exhorter. McMahon was a natural orator of no mean order, and a thinker withal. "How is it?" asked a studious and ambitious young·preacher who was traveling and preaching with him, "how is it, Brother McMahon, that though I read and study all the time, and you hardly ever look into a book, yet you beat me preaching?" "I have here," said McMahon, tapping his forehead, "what books are made of—*brains!*" McMahon was from Virginia, of Irish descent—a bold, rugged, deep-chested, muscular, hot-blooded man, whose courage was equal to any emergency, and whose faith ignored impossibilities. Day after day he could preach or exhort in the open air at the top of his voice, without apparent fatigue or hoarseness. He was a powerful preacher, but it is said that his special gift was exhortation. It was the custom in those days, when the preachers in apostolic fashion went forth in pairs, to follow the sermon at each service with an exhortation. It was then that McMahon rose to the full height of his power as an orator. His thought would kindle under the suggestions of the pulpit, his emotional nature would take fire, and, rising as the preacher sat down, he would pour forth a tide of eloquence that swept all before it. His appeals would startle the most apathetic; he would flash divine truth upon the guilty conscience as with an electric light, and then he would plead with the sinner with a pathos so melting that the hardest hearts would yield. His district embraced a vast territory, and with untiring energy he rode his rounds, stirring the masses of the people, winning the wanderers, and confirming the faithful. He was a " son of thunder," and yet had in him also the elements of a Barnabas—a mighty man of God in his day. The existing type of Methodism in all that region bears the indelible impress of the fervent, fearless, forceful men who first planted the Church among the forests and cane-brakes of Tennessee and North Alabama.

In those days the exhorter's license was the usual preliminary to the pulpit. Gifts and graces were tried in this way by the Church, and the neophyte thus felt his way along the untried path. It is not surprising that young McFerrin now began to look more earnestly toward the ministry. His own words will best tell what were his thoughts and feelings at this time:

" Now I began to think more seriously of preaching. Indeed, the subject had long lain with much weight on my mind. I strove against it. I had other plans and prospects in view, and these I did not like to abandon. And then the thought of the vast obligations of a minister of Christ, and my utter disqualification for so high and holy a calling, distressed me. Again and again I resolved to suppress the conviction and betake myself to an active life of business. Once I went so far, by the consent of my father, who did not then know my mind on the subject of preaching, as to make a contract to go into the store of a merchant, where I was to act as a

clerk and acquire a knowledge of the mercantile business. This project failed, and it was impressed on me
that it was providential, for continually it bore on my
mind, ' Woe is me if I preach not the gospel!' But how
could a stripling of eighteen, with a limited education,
take on himself the work of the gospel ministry? O
the deep anxiety of mind and the many struggles of
heart in settling the question whether, under all these
disadvantages, to go forward and make the trial, or to
plunge myself into worldly pursuits and acquire fame
or fortune as I might! At last I broke the subject to
my beloved father, and he quietly, yet decidedly, encouraged me to preach."

Only a preacher's heart can fully enter into the spirit
of that memorable interview between father and son.
Beneath the father's quiet manner was a joy too deep
for words in being called on to ratify the call of God.
That was a glad hour to him, and a solemn one to both.
The memory of it was vivid and precious when more
than half a hundred years had passed.

His name was brought before the " Society; " he was
duly recommended, and at the District Conference held
at Cambridge, Alabama, October 8, 1825, he was publicly examined, licensed to preach, and recommended for
admission on trial as a traveling preacher in the Tennessee Annual Conference.

4

ADMITTED INTO THE CONFERENCE.

THE session of the Tennessee Conference for 1825 was held at Shelbyville in the month of November. Young McFerrin determined to attend it. "It was," he says, "the first I ever attended. My feelings on leaving home I will not attempt to describe. As I rode away, and turned for the last lingering look, my eyes overflowed with tears and my bosom swelled with emotion. To leave my mother was a hard trial, and to bid farewell to brothers and sisters made the trial doubly hard. And then the fears entertained; it was very doubtful whether or not I would be received; and, if admitted, I doubted my ability to do the work."

A. L. P. Green was his companion in the journey to the seat of the Conference. Their way led across the spurs of the Cumberland Mountains. In that altitude, in the bracing keenness of the November air, with youth and health and hope, and the divine undersong in their souls, whatever may have been the heart-struggles of the two young preachers, theirs was not a gloomy ride to Shelbyville. No part of their talk by the way has come to us, but it would take but a few sentences to illumine these pages with the rosy light that bathes the mountain-tops in life's bright morning. It is likely that snatches of sacred song woke the echoes of the hills, and startled the squirrels that were frisking and feasting among the hickory and chestnut trees by the road-side; or, with subdued voices and moistening eyes, after the

(50)

fashion of the times, they exchanged "experiences," and made the forests through which they rode sacred as the temples of God.

They reached Shelbyville, and here for the first time young McFerrin saw a Methodist Bishop. Bishops Roberts and Soule were both present. "They were," he says, "men in the vigor of life. Their appearance made a deep impression on my mind. They were remarkably plain in their dress—wearing broad-brimmed hats, short breeches, and the old-fashioned Quaker or Methodist coats. They looked like patriarchs. Their preaching, too, affected me. Bishop Roberts preached in the forenoon on Sunday, and Bishop Soule in the afternoon. The fine voice, the wonderful pathos, and the natural oratory of Bishop Roberts greatly delighted me, while the profundity and great intellectual strength of Bishop Soule overwhelmed me."

The session of the Conference was stormy and long. The "radicals," as they were called, had made agitation in many places in Middle Tennessee. The passions of both parties were aroused, and in the Church trials that had taken place patience and forbearance had not been conspicuous. Several local preachers who had been expelled had appealed to the Annual Conference, with grievous complaints against some of the presiding elders and preachers in charge. So impartial were the rulings of the Bishops, and so just was the action of the Conference in dealing with these cases, that the tide of defection was stayed, and Tennessee Methodism hardly felt a movement that shook other parts of the Church like an earthquake. The head of Soule and the heart of Roberts were both needed for that crisis in the Tennessee Conference.

Young McFerrin, not yet admitted, did not hear the discussion in the Conference, but he was waiting with an anxious heart to know his fate. " The case," he says quaintly, "in which I felt the most interest was my own. I often asked myself the questions, ' Shall I be admitted? If so, where shall I be sent?' The Conference was well supplied, and there were many candidates for admission; but there was a call for men to go to Mississippi. I was willing to go anywhere, but felt myself incompetent to take charge of an important mission-field where the people needed instruction in the grand doctrines of Christianity. I needed the help of some one deeply experienced in the things of God and the work of the ministry to teach and lead me. I committed all to God and to my brethren. I was admitted on trial, and here began a work to which I resolved to consecrate my whole life."

He was appointed to Franklin Circuit as junior preacher, Finch P. Scruggs being preacher in charge and Alexander Sale supernumerary. William McMahon was the presiding elder. Franklin Circuit was then in the Huntsville District. Of the young itinerant's initiation we let him tell the story in his own language:

" The Conference adjourned on Saturday afternoon, and many of the preachers left immediately in crowds for their respective fields of toil. The Bishops remained with a few of the brethren who were going South. They preached again on the Sabbath, and rode a few miles in the afternoon to the house of a friend, intending to set out on Monday morning for Mississippi. Their route led them directly through my circuit, and I was anxious to have company, as the road was new and the distance at least three days' journey. I accordingly ordered my horse (I was stopping at the hotel by the special invitation of Col. Cannon, the proprietor, an intimate friend of my father, who was also his guest). When my horse was brought out he was rigged off with an old saddle and bridle not worth five dollars, instead of an entirely new and valuable outfit. Upon inquiry, the hostler said that on Saturday some man had gone into the stable and led out his own horse, and he doubtless had taken my saddle and bridle. The name of the thief was ascertained, and the hostler posted off twelve miles into the country in search of my goods. He found the man and recovered the property.

"On Monday morning, alone, I set out for my circuit. The feelings of my heart no one can imagine who has not had a similar experience. Young, going among strangers, and going as a *preacher*, going to fulfill the high commission of Heaven—how could I go? But I had given myself to God and to his work; my hand was on the plow, and I dared not look back. In the name of God I went forward with a sense of my responsibility and insufficiency. While riding alone, full of these solemn reflections, I was overtaken by the Rev. James W. Allen, who accompanied me two days on my journey. He was a young preacher of great promise, and an interesting traveling companion. The first night we reached the house of Mr. McGehee, a wealthy planter in Madison County, Alabama, where we were kindly received and hospitably entertained. He and his family were Methodists. The second night we reached Brother Allen's father's house, in Limestone County, Alabama. The next morning I set out alone for my circuit. At Brown's Ferry, on the Tennessee River, I came up with the Rev. Thomas J. Brown, who had been transferred to the Mississippi Conference, and was pushing on to overtake Bishops Soule and Roberts, who were a few miles ahead. At night we came up with the company at the residence of the Rev. Alexander Sale, near Courtland, Alabama. Here we tarried till morning, and witnessed the baptism of one of Brother Sale's children by Bishop Soule. I was now in the bounds of my circuit, but the Conference had been pro- tracted so long that the appointments were falling through. I however pushed ahead, and came up with the regular plan."

HIS FIRST CIRCUIT.

H IS first attempt at preaching on the circuit was at Tuscumbia, which was then a new and thriving village in Franklin County, Alabama. This experience is thus told by himself:

"There was no house of worship in the place. The various denominations occupied a small school-house, and worshiped together, or separately, as occasion might suggest. I learned on my arrival in town that the circuit preacher was expected to hold forth on the next day, which was the Sabbath. I felt easy for a time, for it was expected that my colleague, Brother Scruggs, would occupy the pulpit. But he came not. The morning came, the hour of service arrived, and with kind friends I went to *meeting*, supposing I would have to address the people. How my heart throbbed as we approached and saw the house crowded with a well-dressed, intelligent audience! To my great relief, as we drew near, I heard the voice of a minister who had risen to begin the service. My heart leaped for joy, and I turned away and took my stand on the outside of the building, and listened to the sermon. Before the minister (a Presbyterian) dismissed the congregation he announced that the new circuit preacher was to deliver a *sermon* in the same house that afternoon. The announcement struck me nearly blind. I had thought that I was relieved for that day. At three o'clock I appeared, and did the best I could for some thirty minutes. The text was, '*Who*

then can be saved?' Of the sermon I can say nothing,
only that it was delivered with fear and much trembling. Here began my career as a Methodist traveling
preacher. Our circuit embraced Franklin County and
a portion of Lawrence County, including the villages of
Tuscumbia, Russellville, and La Grange, with the adjacent country. We had some twenty or more appointments in four weeks, with more territory to be taken
into our work. The country was new, having been
purchased from the Indians only a few years before; yet
it was in many places settled by the best class of citizens—wealthy planters from the older States, who had
been attracted by the fertility of the soil in this fine cotton region. There was, however, some very rough and
uncultivated country through which we passed, where
we had coarse fare, small congregations, and miserable
houses in which to worship. In some instances we
preached in private houses. The people were hospitable and made us welcome, and this was better than luxuries without cheerful hearts.

"Nothing very remarkable occurred during the year.
My health was good, my colleagues and presiding elder
kind and courteous, and the people bore with my imper-
fections and inexperience, treating me as a son. I gave
myself to reading and study, and availed myself of all
the helps within my reach. I adopted as far as practi-
cable a regular and systematic plan. The Bible was my
daily companion; it was read carefully, and with reference to commentaries *whenever I could have access to
them.* [The italicized words are significant.] My sermons were studied with a good deal of care, and I strove
to observe some system in all my discourses. I was
rather a sober preacher, having not quite so much fire

and enthusiasm as many young men; yet my heart was in the work, and my zeal increased with my experience and practice. We had a very prosperous year; many precious souls were converted and added to the Church, and the cause of God was more thoroughly established. I formed many valuable acquaintances, and contracted friendships that will be renewed, I believe, in heaven."

He says he was at this time a "sober preacher." No doubt he tried to be so, and had reason to emphasize the effort. At that early day he would startle his congregations by those sudden sallies of wit, sarcasm, pathos, and nasal effects that made so many thousands laugh and cry and wonder in coming years. A "sober" preacher! Poor youth! he was trying to keep off of the rock of levity on which it was feared by his seniors he might split. How hard he held in, and how much he suffered while wearing the strait-jacket he needed, can not be told. This self-restraint was no inconsiderable part of the training of a raw but high-mettled youth who had so much to learn and so much will to curb.

Among the friends of this period he always spoke with special affection of the family of the good Alexander Sale. "No family," he says, "contributed more to my happiness and improvement than that of the Rev. A. Sale and his kind wife and affectionate children. Brother Sale was a man of sterling worth, sound sense, and genuine piety. He took much pains with me, and did much to help me forward in my studies and public exercises."

This year was erected the celebrated "Mountain Spring Camp-ground," near Courtland, Alabama—a place where hundreds of souls have been converted to Christ. In this neighborhood, besides the Sale family, many other excellent families resided.   Here was the home of Rev. Turner Saunders, Rev. Freeman Fitzgerald, the Harpers, the Garretts, and others.   The center of religious attraction for this region was Ebenezer Church; thither the tribes went up to worship in great numbers and with great fervor.

The foregoing touches from his own pen indicate the profound sense of responsibility and the unaffected diffidence felt by the young preacher in beginning the sacred work of the ministry of the gospel.   Self-reliant as he was, and independent as he was in his attitude and relations with his fellow-men, his humility toward God was always a marked trait in his disposition.   No young preacher ever entered upon his high vocation feeling more fully that his sufficiency was of God.   No flippant, irreverent, self-parading youth has in him the elements of a great preacher.   He will either seek a fitter sphere for himself in secular things, or he will sink down into the ranks of the nobodies that infest the holiest of avocations on earth.

HIS SECOND YEAR.

HAVING closed the labors of this first year, the young preacher visited his parents and had a grateful, joyful reunion with the loved home circle. The father rejoiced in the belief, after the year's trial, that he had advised wisely when consulted by his son concerning his call to the ministry; and though her words were few, the quiet mother looked upon her preacher-son through tears of joy, her loving heart swelling with maternal fondness and pride.

The next session of the Conference was held at Nashville. Young McFerrin attended in company with his father. Bishop Soule presided. No memorabilia of the session are at hand—so it must have been harmonious and pleasant. Young McFerrin was continued on trial, and appointed to the Lawrence Circuit with his friend, Alexander Sale, who had become "effective." Of this appointment and the year's work he says:

"This field of labor was immediately adjoining my first circuit, and embraced a portion of Lawrence County, and the whole of Morgan County, Alabama, and included the villages of Courtland, Decatur, and Somerville. Taken altogether, it was a pleasant appointment, yet it embraced some very rough and mountainous country. I was pleased with my work, and especially with my colleague, who proved himself to be my special friend. The year was one of considerable prosperity. Many souls were converted and added to the

Church, and we introduced preaching in some neighborhoods which before had been without the regular
means of grace. Decatur, then a young town, situated
on the south side of the Tennessee River, had never had
any regular preaching by the Methodists; so we took
it into our plan, and I trust made some steps toward
the permanent establishment of Methodism in that village, which has since grown to be a place of considerable importance.

"'Summer Seat Camp-ground,' a few miles south of
Decatur, was this year established. It became a place
celebrated for Methodist camp-meetings. We had several interesting camp-meetings in the bounds of the circuit during the year, where the power of God was displayed in the salvation of sinners. My colleague was a
strict disciplinarian. He was careful not only to preach
and visit from house to house, and hold class-meetings
regularly, but to maintain the honor of the Church by
a faithful administration of the rules of the 'Society.'

"A singular case occurred under his administration.
There lived an aged man in the circuit who had been
for many years an orderly member of the Church. He
had reared a family and buried his wife. The old gentleman, after a suitable time, sought to repair the loss he
had sustained, and becoming acquainted with an aged
widow lady in the neighborhood, he proposed the subject of marriage. He soon found that she was an acquaintance of his youth, and had formerly been his wife!
They were married when they were both young, but by
some means had become accidentally separated, and lost
all knowledge of each other, each supposing the other
to be dead. Each had married again and raised a family. Now, in their old age, they were brought together

again. As soon as the facts were all well authenticated they joined their destinies once more, and became man and wife without any formal or legal ceremony. A question then arose as to the morality and legality of the second union. Had they a right to recognize their first marriage contract, and live as man and wife without a second formal marriage ceremony? The question was brought before the Church and taken by reference to the Quarterly Conference, and the case was determined, if I remember correctly, that they were lawfully man and wife by virtue of their first marriage. My colleague dissented from the decision."

He and the wise and kind-hearted Sale were well matched. The pushing, rousing, persistent young itinerant was ballasted by the steady, benignant senior preacher. They preached, prayed, visited the people, pioneered new points, brought vast crowds together in great camp-meetings, and the work of the Lord prospered in their hands. With grateful pertinency he quoted the Psalmist's words in relation to the results of this year's work: " The little hills rejoice on every side, the valleys also are covered with corn; they shout for joy, they also sing."

AMONG THE INDIANS.

A T the Annual Conference which met at Tuscumbia, Alabama, McFerrin was admitted into full connection, and ordained deacon by Bishop Soule, who presided during this session of the body. "The services to me were very solemn and impressive. The vows taken deeply affected my heart, and I trust have never been erased"—thus he wrote when he was an old man. At the same Conference his father was ordained elder.

When his appointment was read out it must have been a surprise to the young preacher. He was sent as a missionary to the Cherokee Indians. It was a singular appointment for a youth not yet twenty years old. On what ground was it made? Was it to tame the too exuberant animal spirits of the youthful itinerant? This, we know, was not an unusual procedure in those days, when the leaders of the Methodist host were usually strict disciplinarians and suspicious of the least tendency toward "airiness" or levity. Both Bascom and Pierce had to run this gantlet at the start. It may have been thought that a campaign among the Cherokees would, if he survived it, rub off the sharpness of some of his angles, and act as a dose of humility. Or it may be that Bishop Soule and his advisers in the Cabinet saw in the young man a sagacity and prudence beyond his years, and thought the work among the Indians required a man of strong *physique* and daring spirit, and without family incumbrance.

(62)

It was a perilous appointment in every sense. The Cherokee Indians had passed through the usual experiences of the red men in dealing with the white people in America; they had been cheated out of their lands, and goaded to desperation by repeated wrongs; and when at last in their frenzy and despair they resorted to war they were overwhelmed by superior numbers, despite the savage cunning and valor that made it cost so dear to the victors. But the severity of their fate was mitigated by the benign influences of Christianity, to which this tribe seemed to be more responsive than most other Indians. This was not the first time nor the last in the history of these United States when the conservative power of the gospel of Jesus Christ has asserted itself in the alleviation of race difficulties and in happily modifying conditions otherwise invincibly difficult and embarrassing. It may be that the Cherokees were not more responsive to the gospel or more ready to assimilate with the civilization of the white race; but the conditions were more favorable to their evangelization. At any rate, the Christianization of this tribe presents one of the most romantic and thrilling chapters in the history of modern missions. The Cherokees intermarried more freely with the whites, and with exceptional results. The half-breed Cherokees were a fine race physically, exhibiting the best characteristics of both races. The men were tall and well formed, and the women, with their queenly carriage, brilliant dark eyes, clear complexion, expressive features, and vivacity tempered by a natural dignity peculiar to themselves, were remarkable for their beauty. The weak and strong points of both races are visible in their moral constitution. They are by turns generous, moody, brave, suspicious, true to friends, and implacable to foes, with a tragic element that flames out with terrific energy when least expected. All these characteristics are controlled or modified by the gospel of Jesus Christ which is to make a new heaven and a new earth, and which is destined to mold all kindreds, tribes, and tongues of men into the image of their risen and reigning Redeemer.

With what feelings the Cherokees first received the young missionary may be imagined. Timothy was not less than thirty-five years old when Paul admonished him to let no man despise his youth. The Indians, accustomed to associate wisdom with age, and prone to look upon all white men with more or less suspicion, doubtless subjected young McFerrin to a sharp scrutiny and unsparing criticism when he first appeared among them. He gives us a glimpse of the situation in this statement: " My station was Creek Path. It lay south of the Tennessee (now near Carter's Landing). My work embraced three regular preaching-places, besides a small school of Indian children. To this work I went with an anxious heart. I wanted to do good and bring souls to Christ, but I distrusted myself." And well he might, for it was a new and trying poitsion in which he was placed.

" My work," he continues, " was not arduous, but it was delicate and responsible. I taught the children diligently and preached faithfully, often making tours to different parts of the Cherokee Nation."

It may be taken for granted that the appliances and methods of that school for the Indian children were of the most primitive kind. And we run no risk in saying that this part of the missionary's work was that which was least suited to McFerrin's genius and tastes. He never had much to say about this experience in peda-

gogy among the Cherokees. It was not his way to neglect any work committed to him; but, with our knowledge of his temperament and preferences, we are inclined
to pity the little brown-faced boys and girls who learned
from him their A B C's, made " pot-hooks," and were
carried from their " a-b abs " onward into the higher
mysteries of education—such as reading, ciphering, and
history and geography in the mild form suited to their
undeveloped minds and to the resources of that first and
last institution of learning that had the direct benefit of
McFerrin's service as a teacher. Though ignorant of
his methods, we are safe in the assumption that he ex-
acted from his pupils the prompt obedience to which he
himself had been bred at home.

McFerrin's home was at the house of Edward Gunter, a half-breed. He was a man of considerable property, who spoke the English language fairly, and was
a fluent speaker in his native tongue. He was also an
earnest Christian, and exercised much influence among
his people. He was McFerrin's interpreter. Their
method was for them to stand side by side, and in short
sentences to address the audience—a method said to be
very difficult to unpracticed persons, but one to which
a deliberate speaker soon becomes accustomed, and by
which he can speak with ease to himself and with
effect upon his hearers. " Gunter and myself," said Mc-
Ferrin, " soon became so familiar with each other's
mode of speaking that we could make considerable
headway. *The words went with a kind of double force.*"
That is rather an original view of the matter. And do
we not get a hint here concerning McFerrin's life-long
habit of repeating his emphatic and weighty sentences?
He wanted the words to go with a kind of double force,

and so he acted as his own Gunter. " The effect," he continued, " was often visible, and a powerful impression was made on the multitudes. We saw many awakened and converted, and their after-lives demonstrated the genuineness of the work of grace upon their hearts. Untutored, and given to lives of idleness and crime, it was hardly to be expected that a reformation in manners would be sudden and thorough; yet many of the converts were so transformed by the power of grace that they really became new creatures in Christ Jesus. Many Cherokees died in the faith, giving glory to God.

" The work at this time was enlarging in the Cherokee Nation. The Tennessee Conference employed ten white missionaries, besides a number of native preachers. The field cultivated extended from the Alabama State line to the mountains of North Carolina. There were several large circuits, besides the station and mission-schools. Camp-meetings were common in several portions of the Nation, and hundreds were brought to God by the preaching of the word. In this work I took part, while I kept up the school. Some of the children made progress in their studies, and I had the pleasure of teaching a number of them to read understandingly the New Testament Scriptures. One of my pupils—Loony Campbell, a sprightly lad—died during the year. He gave evidence of piety, and left testimony that he was going to heaven.

" In the latter part of February I made a tour into Will's Valley, which lay east of the Raccoon Mountain, for the purpose of holding a meeting. Having brought the meeting to a close, I left on Monday, in company with Samuel Gunter and his sister Patsey. We crossed the mountain, and in the afternoon reached the Tennessee River at the mouth of Short Creek, a deep stream. Heavy rains had fallen, and the river was overflowing its banks in the lowlands. We found no canoe, and were at a loss how to cross the stream and make our way home. Night was approaching, and we could find no comfortable place for lodging. After consultation, I determined to take a log, lodged near the mouth of the creek, and work my way across the stream, and find a canoe on the margin of the river below. Half undressing, I addressed myself to my work. Little difficulty was found in dislodging my craft from its moorings, but I soon found it impossible to control the vessel. I was directly in the middle of the stream, rapidly descending, with no prospect of landing for six or eight miles. The log on which I floated was large and unwieldy, and I had neither paddle nor oar. What was to be done? Finally I came in sight of a canoe tied to the shore. I determined to abandon my craft. So, parting with what apparel I had retained for the voyage, and placing it on the log, I leaped into the stream and swam ashore. Chilled as I was, I made my way back, secured the canoe, and ascended the stream, where I refitted my clothing, swam our horses across the creek, and, half dressed, with cloak wrapped about me, we rode home in haste. Before we reached the landing below my craft had arrived—was espied by some boatmen, who recovered my clothes, supposing they had made a speculation in becoming the rightful owners of the property of some hapless voyager who had found a watery grave. But their joy was soon gone when on dry soil the proper claimant appeared, took the property, and went on his way rejoicing. This was my first and last ride on horseback without 'unmentionables.'

"During this year I had a great trial of my faith. Reading much and studying the sciences, my thoughts often wandered and Satan assaulted me sorely. I was tempted to infidelity or to atheism. I struggled and prayed, obtained temporary relief, and then Satan would come again with double force upon me. During the summer I visited a camp-meeting in the Franklin Circuit, where my father had charge. I preached and joined in the exercises of the altar, but my soul was cast down within me. My difficulties I had made known to nobody, yet I prayed earnestly for deliverance from the power of the Evil One. During the meeting my struggle became powerful, and final deliverance came. My soul was overwhelmed with love. Such expansive views of the love of God, the power of grace, and fullness of redemption I had never before realized. My doubts were gone, and from that day till the present I have been measurably free from temptations to unbelief. O it was a bright and glorious season!

"The camp-meeting was remarkable for its success. About one hundred and eighty souls professed saving faith in Christ. Many of the best citizens of the country were added to the Church, and Zion was greatly enlarged in her borders. It was a time of unusual power.

"At the close of this year the Conference convened at Murfreesboro, Tennessee. Here we met Bishop Soule again. The Conference was an interesting session. We had several Cherokee preachers present who took part in the missionary anniversary. This meeting was held in the upper room of the court-house. The congregation was large, the house crowded to its utmost capacity. Soon after the exercises began a great panic was produced by the report that the floor of the room was giving way. Consternation seized the audience, and many shrieked for help. The alarm was false, and after some effort the people were quieted and the meeting went on. At this meeting I delivered my first missionary address. The effort, I judge, was rather feeble, yet I did the best I could. I was very much excited.

"From this Conference I was returned to the Cherokee Nation, and was appointed to the Will's Valley Circuit and Creek Path. It was four hundred miles in circumference, extending from Gunter's Landing across the Sand Mountain to the mouth of Will's Creek, south of the Coosa River; east as far as the junction of Etowah and Oostanaula Rivers, where Rome now stands in the State of Georgia; then north, over the Pigeon Mountain, to the point of Lookout Mountain, where Chattanooga is now situated; thence across Lookout Mountain, down the Lookout Valley, into Will's Valley, and then across the Raccoon Mountain to the beginning point. This circuit I traveled round once in four weeks. The rides were long, the fare in most places hard, and the labor performed heavy. We often swam rivers, sometimes taking our horses beside a canoe; at other times we made rafts of light timber, and placing our saddles and baggage on these, we swam the watercourses, pulling the rafts after us, having for a tow-line a grape-vine gathered from the forest. Joseph Blackbird, a full-blood Indian, was my traveling companion. He was my interpreter. He was educated among the whites, so that he could read and speak English with some facility. This was one of the hardest years of my itinerancy, but in many respects it was pleasant. We saw many Indians converted to God, and took a number into the Church. I baptized at one time the mother, her daughter, and the grandchildren. Often did the wild woods ring with praise to Jesus for his pardoning mercy.

" The remarkable men converted among the Cherokees and added to the Methodist Church, during our missionary labors among that people, were Richard Riley, the Gunters, Trutte Fields, Young Wolf, Arch Campbell, John F. Boot, John Ross, the principal chief, etc.

" During my labors there I preached the gospel to some of the natives who had never before heard the tidings of salvation. Among the converts was an aged squaw nearly one hundred years old. I was the first preacher who ever visited the celebrated 'Dirt Town Valley.' Here the Indians erected a log church, and we established a congregation. In after years it became celebrated as a camp-ground among the whites who succeeded the Cherokees.

"Altogether, I trust my two years were profitably spent among the 'red men of the forest.' It had one effect upon my preaching—it led me to be more plain, pointed, and perspicuous in my style. Preaching through an interpreter produced these results. But my opportunity for study was limited during the last or second year, and then I was cut off in a measure from intelligent and congenial society.

" In reviewing these two years I feel thankful to God that it was my privilege to preach the gospel to the poor Indian."

PREACHES TO WHITE PEOPLE AGAIN.

AFTER his two years of service as missionary to the Indians McFerrin went up to the Tennessee Conference, held at Huntsville, Alabama, in the autumn of 1829. The two years' pastoral limit precluded his return to the Cherokees, but he never forgot them, and they never ceased to love him. He emphasizes the fact that he "passed the Conference examination" and was elected to elders' orders. That he dreaded the ordeal of that examination is quite apparent—and with good reason. It was no child's play. The fathers were not always highly cultured men after the pattern of the schools; but they knew the Bible, which was the principal text-book of the undergraduates, and on doctrine and discipline they were "posted" in every thing that a Methodist preacher ought to know, from the Arminian side of the "five points" to the intricacies of the most difficult questions that could complicate a trial in a Church court. McFerrin passed—and breathed more freely. His two years among the Indians did not fit him for a technical inquisition as would the Biblical school of Vanderbilt University or Drew Theological Seminary. But if he read less, and recited to himself alone, it is possible that he did more real thinking than many a theologue who is content to think only other men's thoughts and to repeat other men's words. The self-educated man is always at a disadvantage in some particulars; and most men of this class feel and deplore it all their lives. The poor creat-

ure whose mind is made a lumber-room of forms of
words held and delivered *memoriter* is doubly a failure,
having neither the ability to assimilate and use with
skill and vigor his scholastic acquisitions on the one
hand, nor to develop on the line of natural endowment
on the other. What classical culture might have done
for McFerrin is a question not without interest. It is
most likely that it would have made his intellectual life
broader and deeper, and given a higher polish to the solid
granite of his genius; it is also possible that in the proc-
ess much of the flavor of his originality and of the elements of his peculiar power may have been lost. Where
the blade is thin and of poor metal much whetting de-
stroys it; where it is heavy and of fine quality the
whetstone need not be feared.

Bishop Roberts, whom McFerrin held in the highest
veneration, performed the service of his ordination. It
was done at the private residence of Thomas Brandon,
the Bishop being too sick to preach and conduct the ordination service in the church. Of Bishop Roberts
little is left to the Church save the meager outlines of
his official work, but he was so reverend in presence, so
humble, so devout, so full of faith and the Holy Ghost
that where he passed it seemed that a breath of heaven
had come with him, and its aroma lingered long after
he had gone. His name was always spoken by Mc-
Ferrin with tenderness and reverence; and to the end of
his life, on recalling that solemn hour at the house of
Brandon, he remembered the awe and ecstasy that filled
his soul when the hands of the man of God were placed
on his yet youthful head and he was ordained an elder
in the Church of God, in the name of the Father, and
of the Son, and of the Holy Ghost.

He was appointed to the Limestone Circuit, in North Alabama, lying immediately south of Huntsville, and embracing a portion of Madison County, the whole of the County of Limestone, and one or two appointments in Giles County, Tennessee. Of his work here he may speak in his own words. The personal allusions, though in most cases of persons unknown to fame, preserve the names of some who deserve to live in the memory of the Church they helped to plant and which they nurtured in its infancy, and the incidents have the true flavor of the times:

" The country was finely settled with enterprising planters, Methodism was strong, and society good. The Rev. W. L. McAlister was my colleague, and the Rev. Joshua Boucher my presiding elder. Two more zealous, faithful, congenial spirits are seldom found.

" Brother McAlister and myself formed friendships this year which were never broken. He was a noble specimen of a Christian gentleman and a fine preacher He finally died in Texas a most triumphant death, being at that time a missionary to the Indians. Brother Boucher was an elderly man, but of buoyant spirits—a man of great native eloquence and much pulpit power. He also has gone to his reward. He long lived and labored in the cause of Christ in the Tennessee Conference, and especially in North Alabama.

" During this year we had a good work of grace, many souls were happily converted, and the Church prospered. We had several good camp-meetings. Camp-meetings in those days were numerously attended, and were productive of happy effects on the public mind.

" On this circuit there were many valuable men, min-

isters and laymen. Among the most estimable was the
Rev. David Thompson, a venerable minister. He was
a Scotchman by birth; he came to America when he
was young; was a teacher by profession, a man of much
learning and pulpit ability. He lived for many years in
the vicinity of Huntsville, where he exerted a happy influence on the public mind. He died during this year a
most peaceful and happy death.

"Mr. Thompson solemnized the rites of matrimony
in many of the best families in the country. On one
occasion he rode some ten miles through a snow-storm
to perform the marriage ceremony for two highly respectable young persons. When he arrived at the place
of the wedding he was very much overcome with cold.
Some one persuaded him to drink a glass of wine, which
he did, afterward seating himself by a warm fire. The
gentleman who handed him the wine, out of kindness, put
a dash of brandy into the glass without Mr. Thompson's
knowledge. The effect on his brain was sudden and
unexpected, so that when he arose to solemnize the rite
he found himself intoxicated. Yet, having his right
mind, a friend supported him, and he went through
without any blunder, but was profoundly mortified. He
reported the case to the Quarterly Conference. The
Conference excused him, in view of all the facts; but
he, not satisfied with the verdict, suspended himself for
three months, both from the ministry and sacraments of
the Church."

A STATIONED PREACHER.

THE next session of the Conference was held at Franklin, Tennessee. If there was any event of special interest or importance in connection with the occasion, McFerrin makes no mention of it. He does not even mention the name of the presiding Bishop. The presumption is that the session was peaceful; that the people of Franklin—the county-town of Williamson County, in the very heart of the richest and loveliest region of Middle Tennessee—were then, as now, famed for hospitality and comfortable living; and that his two busy and fruitful years on the Limestone Circuit had brought him into notice as a successful preacher and a rising man in the body. He was " read out " for Huntsville Station. This was decidedly an upward step for so young a preacher. How he took this appointment, and how he filled it, he himself may tell us:

" This was an important appointment. Huntsville was a beautiful town in the heart of a wealthy and intelligent community; the Methodist Church was strong in numbers, and had many members of intelligence. The young people were gay and fashionable. Altogether, it was regarded as rather a difficult charge to fill. I was young, had never filled a city appointment, and had gloomy apprehensions—great fear that I would fail and the cause would suffer in my hands. Besides, I was to follow an able minister, the Rev. W. P. Kendrick. With this state of feeling I proceeded to my

(75)

work depressed in spirit. I made the matter a subject of prayer to God, as I had always done in all my previous efforts to do good. I strove, moreover, to increase my religious enjoyments and to cultivate the graces of the Spirit, that I might grow to be a wiser and better man.

"When I reached Huntsville I was kindly met and cordially received by some personal friends I had made the previous year. An office was soon procured and a place for boarding selected, and I went to work in earnest.

"My congregations were large and attentive. I divided my time according to strict method. So many hours were devoted to study, so many to pastoral visiting, and so many to meals and recreation. I usually preached three times on the Sabbath—morning and evening to the whites, afternoon to the Negroes. One night in the week we had preaching, and one night public prayer-meeting. Besides these, we had class-meetings at different times in the week, in addition to funerals and visiting the sick.

"For several months during the spring I preached at sunrise on Sabbath mornings. My congregations at the sunrise appointments were frequently good and our meetings pleasant. One would suppose that here was work enough to employ our heads, hearts, and hands. Surely there was no time to idle away.

"But my health was good, and God helped me. We had some prosperity: several were added to the Church, and a number were brought to God. Some most valuable acquisitions to Methodism were made this year, and peace rested upon the congregation.

"The Church had been agitated by personal difficulties in previous years, especially the year immediately preceding. These had involved the preacher. Now they were in a measure healed, and it was hoped a foundation for prosperity in future was laid. So it proved.

"We set on foot a plan to build a new and more spacious church, which was accomplished the next year. To me it was a year of labor and trial, and in many respects a year of peace and Christian enjoyment. My personal associations were very pleasant. One of the most agreeable friends I had was Hon. and Rev. John M. Taylor. He was a local preacher of great worth and a man of fine intelligence. He had been a lawyer, and was a judge of the court, deeply pious, and of good report. His family was pleasant, and contributed much to my happiness. There were others who did much to promote my happiness and usefulness, whose names I remember with great pleasure—the Brandons, Mannings, Cains, Withers, Ewings, etc.—some poor, some rich; the salt of the earth.

"During this year we had a visit from the Rev. Henry B. Bascom, afterward Bishop Bascom. He attended a camp-meeting at Blue Springs, about four miles from Huntsville. He preached several sermons of great ability, but on Monday he delivered the celebrated sermon on "The Resurrection of Christ." The effect on the congregation was overwhelming. After years and years had passed away that sermon was fresh in the memory of hundreds. Perhaps Dr. Bascom never preached a more powerful sermon; the writer certainly never witnessed an effect so overpowering by any other sermon he ever heard.

"The effect of Dr. Bascom's presence at the camp-meeting had a very paralyzing influence on most of the preachers present. He was at every service; his praise was on every lip, and each preacher seemed to shrink from public gaze. The Rev. William McMahon was present. He was Dr. Bascom's old and long-tried friend. He brought the Doctor to the meeting; it was his own neighborhood, and he of course took but little part in the preaching, though himself an able and popular minister. The writer felt deep interest in the success of the meeting; many of his own congregation were present, and hence he had to bear the brunt of labor when the pulpit was not occupied by Bascom. He worked with zeal, and strove to address himself to his task with as much fortitude as possible."

There are modest but unmistakable intimations in the foregoing extracts that McFerrin's mental development was rapid and his extraordinary individuality making itself felt and recognized. There was uncommon metal in a man of his years who could preach in turn with Bascom while McMahon was on the ground. The Huntsville Station, that he had dreaded, tested but did not overtax his resources. Even thus early was begun his lifelong habit of being equal to the occasion, exhibiting that reserve force which is perhaps the surest mark of greatness. His methods of study and work are given by himself. He fails to tell us what books he read, but it would require no great shrewdness to make a pretty good guess about it. The Bible first and most of all; the works of Wesley, Fletcher, Clarke, Watson, and the Methodist standards generally; the *Arminian Magazine;* a sprinkling of the best books of Calvinistic writers, read inquiringly and dissentingly; " Dick's Philosophy of the Future State;" a few of the best standard authors in English literature in the departments of history, biography, and possibly some of the essayists. Did he then, or ever, read Shakespeare? His writings and his speech give no sign that he ever did so. The only poetry he ever quoted was from the sacred lyrists, save that at times, when he was in his most rollicking mood in debating, he would venture on a couplet or stanza of humorous doggerel that would upset at once his antagonist and the gravity of his audience. He read no novels or serial stories, such as now flood our literature; nor did he read any daily newspaper, that scatterer of the thought and robber of the time of this later generation. He digested and assimilated what he read, and was therefore better read than many who have gone over a hundred books to his one. Let it be said here, the indiscriminate and excessive reading indulged in by many persons in the ministry and out of it, in this age of cheap printing and freethinking, is worse than illiteracy itself. A literary junk-shop is worse than an empty room. Keen-sighted and wise John Wesley had in mind the dissipating and enfeebling effects of overreading and aimless reading when he advised his preachers to draw all their studies one way. The temptations to do otherwise were less in his and McFerrin's day than now. So let young preachers and all other Christian people who may read these pages take this kindly hint.

A RISING MAN.

McFERRIN was now recognized as a rising man in the Church. He rose by force of character and the quality and quantity of the work he did. He made the blunders inseparable from inexperience, and thus educated himself for better and still better service, as all other men who have risen in the world have had to do. It is said of him that when he was a boy-Christian, just after his conversion, his father would occasionally call on him to pray at family worship. He never hesitated, but was willing and ready to do the best he could. In the service of song in the family he would sing as if he were at a camp-meeting, but was now too high and again too low; his father often had to stop him and correct his blunders. This did not seem to discourage him; but, with a desire to improve, he continued to pray and sing when called on to do so. The oftener he was told of his blunders the harder he would try to avoid them. This characteristic exhibited itself now when he was making his way to the front among his brethren. He was not backward in taking part in the discussion of questions that came before the Church. On one occasion an exciting question was sprung, in which he took a prominent part. After the meeting adjourned, the old preacher with whom he had crossed swords said to him:

"Brother John, I am much older than you are, and I wish to give you some good advice. If you keep on

(80)

talking so much in Church deliberations you will soon talk yourself down."

" Well, if I do, I will talk myself up again," was the quick reply.

Never was a declaration of the sort more perfectly fulfilled. For nearly fifty years there was no question of interest to the Church in the discussion of which he did not take part. He got many a hard blow, and gave many a blow in return. It was impossible for him to keep quiet when a contest was going on. He was like that officer in the late war who on the day of battle was guided in his line of march by the sound of the enemy's guns, taking the nearest way to where the fighting was hottest. The three elements of a ready and effective debater were his—conscious strength, strong convictions, and undaunted courage. With the frame and untamed energy of an athlete, the vigor of his onset was a wonder to all and a delight to those who were on his side. His *vim* was splendid, exciting the admiration even of his antagonists. He took one side or the other with undoubting confidence, and put his whole soul into its advocacy or defense; he was no trimmer or compromiser, but a fighter who went in for victory and felt able to win it. His courage rose with the occasion; he was never at his best until he encountered some unexpected opposition. A rebuff that would have overwhelmed a timid man only roused him to greater exertion and evoked fresh resources. " What a man McFerrin is! " exclaimed George W. Brush on one occasion when, at the Louisville Conference, he had met and overcome formidable opposition in the consummation of some work he had in hand. " His resources are inexhaustible!" continued Brush, in a burst of admiration, as Mc-

6

Ferrin stood before the body a gladiator, master of the arena. Antagonism never intimidated, but only spurred him; apparently impending defeats were turned by him into most signal victories. Such a man could not be kept down. If by any blunder he stumbled, he was sure to be instantly on his feet and ready to renew the fight.

Had he been the only man of mark among his colleagues, McFerrin's rapid rise would not have been surprising. But belonging to the Tennessee Conference at that time were several men of extraordinary genius, and not a few who stood above the line of mediocrity. There was Robert Paine, the future Bishop, who had the dignity of a Roman Senator, the wisdom of a practical philosopher, the soul of a hero, a wit that was bright and keen, and at times an eloquence that was magnificent. There was Green, already rising before the Church in his grand proportions as a preacher of rare powers, an ecclesiastical statesman wise and strong, a conversationalist who in the social circle charmed those who were thrilled and won by his sermons from the pulpit, a massive, tactful man whose figure would have towered among the highest in any company. There was Fountain E. Pitts, a very magician among preachers, who sung like a seraph, whose marvelous discourses were oratorical cyclones set to music, and who at campmeetings and other great popular assemblies swayed the multitudes at will, producing effects that prove his title to be ranked with the greatest modern masters of popular eloquence. There was John W. Hanner, whose budding genius was exciting the admiration of the people, and whose silvery voice and almost matchless elocution took captive the hearts of the multitude, and who rose in pulpit power until his fame filled the Churches.

There was Thomas L. Douglass yet on the stage, a mighty man of God, one of the giant-like men whose tread shook these Western lands. There was Thomas Maddin, as clean as a snow-flake, as wise as a sage, whose preaching made truth as clear as sunlight, and whose ways were as winning as talent and goodness could make them. And there were others, still younger men, who became distinguished in Tennessee and elsewhere, and whose names are at this hour shining with steady luster among the lights of Methodist history in the West. Grand, gifted, holy men! Heroes, saints, martyrs, each one is worthy of a volume to himself; but the limits allowed in these pages permit only passing glances as the noble figures pass before us in the march of events. Their names are recorded in the book that shall be opened in the great day. Their monument is the great Church whose foundations they laid.

It was among such men as these that McFerrin was thrown in these early years of his ministry, and the stamp and power of leadership must have been seen and felt in him when they put and kept him in the front of the battle. But we shall miss the mark widely if we omit to mention that which was, after all, the chief factor in his success—absolute fidelity to all the trusts committed to him. He never slighted any work given him to do. He was willing to give to it the hard labor, the attention to details, the concentrated energy necessary to all real success. He was willing to pay the price, and the law of sowing and reaping worked its sure and gracious result for him. He was in a good sense a thrifty man; but it may be safely claimed that, during a ministry of more than sixty years, he never in a single instance was known to subordinate the interests of the Church to his own, to evade a responsibility, or to shirk a duty because it was laborious or difficult. It was this quality that won for him the confidence of the people at the start, and held it to the last. He possessed extraordinary popular gifts, and would have contested for the highest prizes on any arena; but it was this one golden talent of fidelity that ennobled and irradiated his whole career. He was not lacking in what might be called the arts of popularity; they were with him inborn and ineradicable. He could be grave in the pulpit, playful in the parlor, ready at repartee with an assailant, sympathetic with saints, and sociable with sinners, hail-fellow-well-met with casual acquaintances, and solemn and tender at the bedside of the sick and the dying. "What a politician he would have made!" exclaimed his friend, Gen. Clinton B. Fisk, after an hour with McFerrin in his office in 1880; "he could have had any thing he wanted." This was true enough, but he had what too many politicians lack—a Christian heart, a Christian conscience, and a Christian purpose in life, and so made a straight line from the day he took upon himself the vows of a minister of the gospel until he surrendered his commission with his life. The popular instinct is infallible; it recognizes a true man. It may be temporarily misled or confused; like the magnetic needle, it may at times be affected by disturbing forces, but it will at last point in the right direction. Let every young preacher, and every other young man who may read these chapters, take the lesson: honesty, trueness, fidelity come first in the conditions of real and lasting success in life. It is the core of genuine manhood, the fulcrum of the lever that moves men and communities onward and upward, the grace that elicits the commendation that will make the judgment-day a day of triumph to every true-hearted man and woman: " Well done, good and faithful servant; enter thou into the joy of thy Lord."

THE Methodist itinerants truly itinerated in those early days. It was no evidence of failure or cause of complaint for a preacher to be changed at the end of one year. Asbury and his colleagues had set the fashion that way. They were called traveling preachers, and it was no misnomer. The session of the Tennessee Conference the following year (1831) was held at Paris, a new and thriving town west of the Tennessee River. The journey from Huntsville to the seat of the Conference was a long one, and was made on horseback by McFerrin. Of that long ride we have only this item of information: " On the way I preached at Perryville, a little village on the Tennessee River." It was one of the many sermons dropped on the way-side by a man who was always ready to preach at shortest notice. In this respect he was like his great contemporary, Dr. Lovick Pierce, who never declined an invitation when able to preach. Preaching was a passion with them both. The preacher who does not love to preach may yet be called thereto, but needs to take a higher degree in preparation for his holy vocation.

The devout Bishop Roberts presided at this Conference. A revival—" a good work of grace," as McFerrin called it—blessed the session and hallowed it in his memory. There was usually a great stir whenever the Methodists met in Conference. Finding the people expectant, they left them rejoicing in the salvation of God.

In the election of delegates to the General Conference the name of John B. McFerrin appears as a reserve—no small token of confidence for a man only
twenty-four years old. A young Church legislator indeed! It so happened that he was not then required to
exercise legislative functions, but this vote was significant and prophetic; the elements of leadership had already appeared in the robust, ready, and resolute young
preacher.

The rapid rise of McFerrin as a preacher was made
apparent in the next appointment assigned him. He
was sent to Nashville, which was not the Nashville of
to-day, but was even then not only the capital of the
State of Tennessee, but remarkable for the number of
its distinguished men and the intelligence and refinement
of its society. The star of the self-taught young man,
divinely called, commissioned, and equipped for the work
of the ministry, was climbing upward in obedience to
the law enunciated by Bishop Bascom, that "a measure
of success always attends ministerial fidelity." We will
let McFerrin himself speak of his first ministry in Nashville:

"I was appointed, with the Rev. Lorenzo D. Overall,
to the city of Nashville. From Paris to Nashville we
had a very pleasant ride and good company. One of
my traveling companions was the Rev. Edward Drom-
goole Simms, who afterward was Professor at La
Grange College, and in the State University of Alabama. He was a young man of sweet spirit, and became very distinguished as a ripe scholar and successful
teacher. He died suddenly in the vigor of manhood.
His death was much lamented.

"On our arrival at Nashville Brother Overall and

myself called at the house of Joseph T. Elliston, Esq., who lived in the immediate neighborhood. Here a friendship began between Brother E. and myself which was never interrupted till he fell asleep in Jesus. At our first acquaintance he was somewhat advanced in years, a man of sound judgment and ripe experience. I have known but few men who possessed a greater amount of common sense or had a keener penetration than Joseph T. Elliston. He was wise in council, pure in intention, discreet in conversation, unfeigned in piety, and zealous in the cause of the Church of Christ. He was indeed a pillar in the Church in Nashville. His wife was every way his equal, filling her sphere in a style becoming a lady of wealth and position, and a Christian occupying a conspicuous place in the Church of God. They are both dead. Each died in the faith, and left the savor of a good name. Mr. Elliston was long sick. I visited him often, and always found him trusting in God and awaiting with joy the call of his Master. I preached his funeral discourse on the remarkable works of St. Paul: 'The last enemy that shall be destroyed is death.' He lived to see his youngest son a worthy member of the Church, who in a measure filled his father's place—a very difficult task to perform.

"We soon had a meeting of the official members, and found many men of sterling worth. Among the most active was Joseph Litton, an Irishman by birth, and long a merchant in Nashville. He was a man of age, with a large family of children. His daughters were all excellent women and ornaments to the Church. Mr. Litton was a good singer, a most active and successful steward and trustee, and did much for the cause of God in Nashville. He bore an important part in the Sunday-school, and was one of the best Church-financiers of his time. He possessed keen Irish wit and pleasant humor. He did much toward the erection of the Mc-Kendree Church. He died suddenly of apoplexy a few years subsequent to this time. I preached his funeral sermon to a vast crowd of weeping friends who mourned their loss. His wife too was a noble Christian woman. She fell asleep in Jesus in after years, while I was her pastor, and now sleeps among the pious dead.

"One of the most remarkable men of the Church in Nashville was John Price, an old merchant. He was very eccentric, full of oddities, and withal a man of fine sense and great zeal in the cause of his Master. Many amusing anecdotes were told of him. He died finally in Vicksburg, Mississippi, of cholera. His end was triumphant.

" Harry Hill too was in his glory in those days, a man of great financial skill and large liberality. He contributed largely to the finances of the Church, and oftentimes was very active in the exercises of public worship. His princely home was always open to the ministers of Christ. His wife was converted this year in our great revival, and proved herself to be a most valuable member of the Church. Simple in her manners and sincere in her profession, she had the esteem of all who knew her.

"Joel M. Smith was another excellent member of the Church, a man of consistent piety and uniform conduct. He lived to a good old age, and died full of faith. His funeral sermon I preached, before his interment, to a large audience, all of whom seemed to respect his memory as a good man and true.

"But time would fail me to record the names of many others who were faithful and sincere, and possessed many virtues. I must not forget to mention Mrs. Moore, the mother of W. H. Moore. She was a widow, had been left in poor circumstances, brought up her children to respectability, was a burning and shining light, and died in full hope of a glorious immortality. Her son, W. H. Moore, who lives at this writing, has maintained a good reputation as a Christian man. His fortunes have been various in worldly matters, but still he is true to his God. He was an active official in the Church when we entered upon our work.

"Brother Overall, who was my senior, was in charge. He was a pure, intelligent, faithful minister of the gospel. Both being single men, we occupied an office together on High Street, near the Episcopal Church. Here was our study and sleeping-apartment, and here we spent many pleasant and happy hours. Our relations were of the most agreeable character; we lived and loved as brothers; no jars, no unkind feelings, but only warm Christian affection. Brother Overall died soon after, and left a brilliant testimony in favor of the truth and power of Christianity. He died in Columbia, Tennessee, and lies buried on the margin of Duck River. His funeral sermon was preached by the Rev. Robert Paine—afterward Bishop Paine—at the ensuing Conference, and was attended by overwhelming manifestations of God's power and goodness.

"This was a year of great prosperity to the Church in Nashville. We had a most extensive revival of religion, and very many valuable members were added to the Church. Our labors were very arduous. The main church was on Spring (or Church) Street between Cherry and College Streets. In addition, we had a preaching-place on College Hill, one at New Hope, north of the Cumberland River, and one at the Nashville Camp-ground; besides regular preaching to the Africans, who had a church of their own. We alternated, and worked in all the help we could from the local preachers and visiting brethren. We had a camp-meeting this year at the Nashville Camp-ground; it was a meeting of great power, and many were converted. Here we had the aid for one or two days of the Rev. Edward Stevenson, of the Kentucky Conference. He preached with much power. Our meeting was transferred to the city, and progressed for weeks with great success.

"During this revival we had a visit from the Rev. Littleton Fowler, who joined our Conference, and was afterward sent to Texas among the first missionaries to that new field. He was a young man of zeal and piety, and was a very efficient laborer in a revival. He did great good in Texas, and died full of faith and the Holy Ghost.

" The extreme labor which I performed, and exposure, brought on a severe attack of fever, which detained me from active work for six weeks. My sufferings were painful, but my joy in Christ was great. I felt often-times that I was on the verge of heaven. Before I was taken sick I visited Columbia, and was present at quar-terly meeting, where my father was presiding elder. I preached several times, and the Lord was with me; pre-cious souls were converted—among others, two of the sisters of James K. Polk, afterward President of the United States. One became a Methodist, the other an Episcopalian.

" This year we determined to build a new and larger

central church. The work was commenced, and the next year McKendree was completed. We also projected a church on College Hill, which resulted in a neat brick edifice, which was succeeded by 'Andrew Church' a few years afterward, and then by Mulberry and Elm Street Churches.

"At the close of this year I was appointed Agent for La Grange College. My business was to travel, collect funds, and solicit patronage. This appointment was given especially in view of my health, which had not entirely been restored when the Conference convened. The work was laborious and somewhat responsible."

ANTITHETIC EXPERIENCES.

THE next Conference year (1832) was an eventful one to McFerrin, and quite antithetic in its experiences. Matrimony and a college agency came to him the same year—the one the summit of earthly happiness; the other—only college agents themselves know what it is.

The session of the Conference was held in Nashville, November, 1832. This was the first Conference at which Bishop James O. Andrew presided after his ordination to the episcopal office. "He conducted the Conference," according to McFerrin's notes, "to the satisfaction of all the preachers, and his pulpit ministrations impressed the public mind wonderfully. He was surely in those days a man of marked pulpit ability." This judgment of the heroic and saintly Andrew was that of the Church; his pulpit power was wonderful when at its highest. It was not his sound theology, though here he was unfailing; it was not his rare common sense; it was not his deep, mellow voice; it was not his fine person and dignity and devoutness of presence and deportment; it was not the fatherliness of his manner, blending authority with tenderness—it was not one nor all of these characteristics that elicited the special wonder and admiration of McFerrin. There was another factor that went toward the making up of the man who bore himself in the great struggle of 1844 with the fortitude of a martyr and the meekness of a

saint, and made the materials for a biographical picture
that the Church will not let die.   Reference is here
made to the "Life of Bishop Andrew," by the Rev.
George G. Smith, which is a unique and charming book
—unique in its plan and charming in the simplicity of
its style, and enriched by the letters in which the man
of God painted with his own hand in imperishable col-
ors the inner life of a preacher of righteousness.   It
was the afflatus of the Holy Ghost that explained his
wonderful power as a preacher.   Under that inspiration his thought took wing, his rhetoric took fire, his
soul melted into irresistible tenderness, and his oratory,
descending upon a congregation like a pentecostal gale,
swept all before it.   The plain, matter-of-fact preacher,
who cared nothing for the arts of the rhetorician, and
scorned the stage-tricks of the elocutionist, mightily convinced and mightily moved the people, because upon
him sat the tongue of flame.

The first quarter of this Conference year McFerrin,
by the appointment of Bishop Andrew, traveled the
Nashville District in place of the Rev. William McMahon, "who visited the South in behalf of La Grange
College."   By "the South," at that day, was meant
the older Southern States.   Tennessee was then a Western State; since then the West has changed its borders,
and stretched on and on until it has reached the Pacific
Ocean, and with a little deflection northward it has
made a leap across the waters to Alaska.   No record is
made as to the success of the eloquent McMahon's
Southern expedition in pursuit of money for Christian
education.

After making one "round" on the district, McFerrin
entered directly upon his duties as college agent—a pio-

neer in a service in which many noble successors have
toiled and groaned and wept and failed, the most onerous and perhaps the most thankless of any that can be
found in the line of unmistakable Christian duty. That
he magnified his mission and worked faithfully we may
be sure. " I traveled in Middle Tennessee and North
Alabama," he says, " and made small collections, amounting in all to a few thousand dollars. I did a vast amount
of preaching, attending a number of camp-meetings and
other popular assemblies." He was in his element at
these gatherings, for already he was showing himself a
master of assemblies. A few thousand dollars seems
now to be a small matter for building and equipping a
Christian college, but at that day this sum represented
an amount of work and a number of small contribu-
tions that only college agents could fully appreciate.
During this tour he had the pleasure of being with his
father, who was presiding elder of the Florence (or
Richland) District. "I was with him often, and had
many seasons of rejoicing in his society," he tells us.
Happy father, who was thus permitted to stand by the
side of his son on Zion's walls, and be the witness of
his zeal and to mark his growing power and widening
fame! Happy son, who to the blessedness of unalloyed
filial affection enjoyed the more sacred pleasure of fellowship in the ministry of the gospel! This allusion to
the many "seasons of rejoicing" they had together
makes us linger a moment on the page where it is recorded, which brightens with the touch.

This year McFerrin was married. This is his own
account of the important and joyful event:

" On the 18th of September, 1833, I was married to
Miss Almyra Avery Probart. This was, as I regarded it,

an important event in my history. She was the first and only lady I had ever addressed on the subject of marriage. When I entered the work of the ministry I was impressed with the importance of forming a character as a preacher before venturing into any matrimonial alliances. Hence I never suffered myself to become enamored of the charms of females, but pursued the even tenor of my way, treated all politely, and suffered my affections to be placed on none.

"Now, having preached nearly eight years, and meeting one whom I judged would make me a suitable companion, I proposed to her a union in holy wedlock. She was about twenty years of age. Her person was comely, her manners agreeable, her health and constitution good; her habits of industry, neatness, and economy such as I admired. She was an only child. Her father had died when she was very young. Her mother had married a second time, but had no other children. As to property, she had but little. Her father, William Y. Probart, was a North Carolinian, a nephew of Col. Avery. Left an orphan when young, he had wandered off to Tennessee, and was long a citizen of Nashville, where he was engaged in the clothing business. Here he married my wife's mother, Sarah Johnson, daughter of Oliver Johnson, long known in Nashville as a worthy citizen. Her father left a small estate, which my wife inherited. My own fortune was slim, but money was not my object. A wife who feared God, who would help me in my work, and one whom I would delight to honor, was what I desired. My selection was fortunate. We were married by the Rev. A. L. P. Green, and lived together for more than twenty years. She proved to be a wife indeed. She hindered me not in my work;

was active, industrious, of fine judgment, and did much in helping me in the support of my family. For my prosperity I was greatly indebted to her."

This was written long years after the faithful heart of his Almyra had ceased to beat, and is his final judgment and tribute to her memory. According to his own statement, which we are not disposed to question, he was most prudent and practical in the matter of marriage, in which so many ministers of the gospel are hasty and rash. His example is to be commended. There is another side to it, of course—not contradictory, but supplementary. The divine passion mastered him, as it masters all manly men on whom it takes hold. He was prudent, but his prudence happily coincided with his feelings. She made a good preacher's wife, but it was the man John B. McFerrin who wooed and won her in the good old way—love the attraction, and guided by the blessed providence that presides over every true marriage. The courtship—its rosy dawn, its delightful solicitudes, and its trembling joys, its progress, and its consummation, when the ardent, strong-limbed, fluent, popular young preacher obtained the thrilling affirmative answer to the most momentous of all questions concerning human relationship—all this might be imagined, but not written down for other eyes to read. Here is a slight post-nuptial touch that gives a glimpse of the young couple the first year of their married life—a poem in McFerrin's own handwriting addressed to his bride:

TO MY WIFE.

Here, Myra, may'st thou read my thoughts
 When I am far away from thee,
Gathered like autumn leaves that fall
 Upon a waveless sea.

7

Here may'st thou trace the sunny dreams
  That brightened o'er my manly brow;
Here may'st learn whence that dark shade
  Which makes me pensive now.

Here may'st thou see the smile of love
  When rapture woke beneath thy smile;
Here may'st thou mark the blanchèd cheek,
  While thou art sad the while.

No ripples o'er the silver lake
  Of Hope or sable Memory,
But glass with magic skill thy form—
  My heart is all in thee.

Thou art a mother in my grief,
  A sister in my hours of sadness,
Thou my child to wean me from
  My sorrow with thy gladness.

Thy smile to me is what the sun's
  Gay radiance to flowers may be,
Giving them life and health and strength—
  Thou art that sun to me.

Then when thou lookest within this book,
  On every page thou'lt find how dear
Thou art to me—my every thought
  For thee is treasured here.   JOHN.

Pulaski, Tenn., May 24, 1834.

The verses are inclosed within quotation marks, indi-
cating that the authorship belonged to another person,
or that McFerrin was half ashamed of the weakness of
expressing himself in rhyme. This is the only effusion
in that line that his biographer has discovered. The
facts that he had been married less than a year; that it
was at the season when the fresh beauty of May was
ripening into the summer glories of June; and that fair
Pulaski, in Giles County, Middle Tennessee, was the
place, will condone this one offense.

During the session of the Conference "a great excitement prevailed because of the falling of meteors, or, as it was popularly called, the 'falling of the stars.' The sight was grand, but," says McFerrin, "unfortunately I did not witness the phenomenon. Several laughable scenes took place among those who thought the world was coming to an end. Men prayed who were not in the habit of calling on God, but their piety was *meteoric.*" The writer of this biography distinctly remembers this marvelous spectacle, though he was but four years old at the time. It exceeded in its awful splendor every thing ever witnessed by him on earth, and he expects to see nothing to equal it until the trump of God shall announce the judgment of the last day. No description could give any adequate idea of it beyond what was flashed upon the mind in a single sentence which fell from the lips of that wonderfully rapid and brilliant declaimer, Dr. John E. Edwards, of the Virginia Conference: "It seemed as if a world in the midnight heavens had burst, and was flying in ten times ten thousand glittering fragments through the sky."

McFerrin was appointed to Pulaski, where he staid two happy and prosperous years, as may be inferred from his own account of his pastorate there:

"In Pulaski I was the only resident minister. Other ministers visited the place occasionally, but no other pastor resided in the town. My congregations were large and attentive, and we had two prosperous years. I had time to visit my flock, read, study, and prepare for pulpit work. Perhaps in no two years of my ministry did I make more progress than in the two spent in this pleasant town.

"I had two good presiding elders, Dr. Gilbert D. Tay-

lor and the Rev. F. A. Owen. The first year we boarded with Jacob Shall, and the second year with N. G.
Nye, Esq. We had very pleasant families and good
fare. My support was ample, and the means raised
without effort. Indeed, I seldom heard the subject of
money mentioned. The people of the world did a very
large part in sustaining me; and then the stewards were
active. Such men as Thomas Martin, Dr. Ralph Graves,
James McConnell, etc., never found it difficult to raise
means to support the Church.

" One of my best friends in Pulaski, not a member of
the Church, was William Flournoy, Esq., a lawyer of
influence. A few years afterward he died, I trust, a
Christian. He was a noble, generous-hearted man, and
was active in my support in Pulaski.

" In the autumn of 1834, at the close of my first year
in Pulaski, the Conference convened at Lebanon. Here
the Rev. Robert Paine—now Bishop Paine—delivered
a funeral sermon in memory of the Rev. L. D. Overall,
who died that year in Columbia, Tennessee. The sermon was one of the great efforts of the preacher. The
effect was overwhelming. This was the last Conference ever attended by Bishop McKendree."

The annual session of the Tennessee Conference for
1835 was held at Florence, Alabama. The event of
the session was the election of delegates to the General
Conference, which was to convene in Cincinnati, Ohio,
May, 1836. McFerrin was chosen among others. He
was appointed again to McKendree Church, Nashville.
At that time there was but one charge in that city, though
there were several preaching-places. He had supervision of the whole work, with the Rev. Reuben Jones, a
young man, as his colleague. " The year was prosper-

ous, and the cause of God advanced to some considerable degree," is his brief but satisfactory record.

He attended the General Conference. It was his first introduction to such an assembly, and there was in it no more open-eyed, inquisitive, sagacious observer than this stalwart, good-humored Tennessean. It was at this Conference that the Abolitionists made their first decided demonstration. The session was one of deep interest and suppressed excitement. The flames were already kindling that were to wrap the entire Church and country in a fierce conflagration. There were only a few who had the boldness to avow abolition sentiments, and they were rebuked by vote of the General Conference. But the anti-slavery excitement was strong; the moral convictions and aggressiveness of one party, and the inevitable resentment of the other, made a conflict that could have no peaceable settlement. Church and State were even then being carried by the propulsion of forces, seemingly beyond human control, toward the tragic scenes of the period when the blunders, vain compromises, and empirical devices of statesmen who meant well, but missed their aim, and Churchmen who too closely copied their fatal policy, were visited upon the heads of one generation, and the knots tied by folly were cut by the sword.

The spirit of the time will be best understood from a glance at McFerrin's own notes of that General Conference of 1836 at Cincinnati:

"Here was my first introduction to many of the noted and distinguished ministers of our Church. Among those who attracted my attention was Peter Cartwright. He took decided ground with the South, came into the convention of Southern delegates, expressed his preference for Southern preachers, and proposed to vote for any slave-holder for the office of Bishop the Southern preachers might mention. In 1844 he took strong grounds against the South, and became their enemy. So we might record of many others; but I mention him in particular, as he was so forward in effacing his sympathies for the Southern delegates, and as he may be noted as a specimen of many others. Thomas A. Morris and Beverly Waugh were elected Bishops. The Southern delegates voted for William Capers, of the South Carolina Conference.

" We all left Cincinnati hoping that, as the Abolitionists were so thoroughly rebuked, we should have no farther trouble with them, but their after history proved that our hopes were vain. Orange Scott, the leader, persevered; and though he himself was foiled, and afterward left the Church, the sentiments he inculcated gained ground, and finally swept the majority of the Northern Church, ministers and laymen.

"At this General Conference I first met that intellectual giant, Dr. Winans, of Mississippi. He was among the finest debaters I ever heard, and withal a meek, pious Christian minister—a man of lovely disposition and warm, generous heart. Here too I first saw that prince of preachers, the Rev. Dr. William Capers, and the celebrated Stephen George Rozell, of Baltimore. These were among the great men in our Zion in those days. Bishop Soule was in the days of his strength, and wielded a powerful influence in the Church. He was, I then thought and still think, *the great man* of the body. I was the youngest preacher except two in the General Conference. I was on the Committee on Boundaries."

After the General Conference adjourned he took boat

to Randolph, Tennessee, and then went by land twenty miles to visit his father, who lived in Tipton County. Here he met for the first time the Rev. John Early, of the Virginia Conference, then on a visit to some kinsfolk in West Tennessee, whom he described as a very active and energetic man, of great vivacity and firmness of purpose. This is a fair description, as far as it goes, of the future Bishop. His meeting with his parents, his wife, and all his brothers and sisters, made this visit delightfully memorable to McFerrin.

Returning to Nashville, he resumed his pastoral work, boarding with Mrs. Lanier, of whom he speaks as " an excellent Christian woman," and of whose two daughters—" Misses Lucy and Ann "—he speaks most gratefully. His recollection of individuals was extraordinary, scarcely surpassed by that of Henry Clay himself, who, it is said, never forgot a face or a name, and had shaken hands with every Whig and half the Democrats in Kentucky. During this pastorate were formed personal attachments that were unbroken through life. He knew by what handle to take hold of men of the most opposite kinds. It was to the last a puzzle with many how he could be equally popular with the demonstrative, shouting Methodists who sat in the "amen corner" at church, and the wild, rollicking horse-racer or "treating" politician. He was the people's man—and all sorts of people were drawn to him and held fast as friends. The very ecclesiastical combatants that he met and fought in the vigorous way prevalent in that day of pugnacious polemics, though they might reel under his heavy blows, or smart from the sting of his ready wit, had a secret liking for him, and allowed him a license of speech accorded to no other man.

AN UNEXPECTED TURN.

I N beautiful Columbia was held the session of the Annual Conference for 1836. Bishop Morris presided —a massive, fervent preacher, whose printed sermons had a great run for awhile, but have been superseded by later publications, which, though not sounder in doctrine or clearer in style, exhibit more of the qualities that attract modern readers.

The sickness of his wife called McFerrin home before the close of the Conference. A child was born unto them, but the little flower bloomed only to fade quickly. It lived only ten days. This first sorrow of his family life left a vivid impression on his mind, and the image of "the little stranger," as he called her, was never erased. "It was a sore trial," he says; "yet we resigned her to God, saying, 'The Lord gave, the Lord hath taken away; blessed be the name of the Lord.'"

Before leaving the seat of the Conference, he tells us that he had an interview with the Bishop, "stated his case," and asked him not to appoint him presiding elder, as he "feared its responsibilities, and preferred a circuit or station." The wise old Bishop made a prudent answer to his request. "He told me that he would do the best he could for me," says McFerrin. Doubtless he did. This is all that should be asked of a Bishop at any time, but every man has the right to "state his case." Ordinarily it is best to do this through the presiding elder; only for special reasons should another

(104)

channel be chosen for communication with the appointing power.

The very thing that he asked the Bishop not to do was done by him. He was appointed to the Florence District. He did not like this. "I felt sadly disappointed," he says. He was not the first nor the last Methodist preacher who has felt this pang—a pang doubly keen when the disappointment involves the comfort and the health of a wife. True soldiers of Jesus Christ, of whom the world is not worthy, these Western lands owe them a debt of gratitude that can never be paid. And when the calendar of true saints is known their wives, upon whom the heaviest sacrifices often fall, will be among them, a nimbus of glory encircling the head of each one of these meek and unselfish women who for their Master's sake lived homeless here that they might bring many souls to Jesus.

McFerrin groaned in spirit, but did not flinch. "I determined," he says, "to go to the field and cultivate it as best as I might. The field was large, embracing Franklin and Bear Creek Circuits and Tuscumbia Station, south of the Tennessee River; Florence, Alabama, and Cypress Circuit, in Alabama, on the north side; extending into Tennessee as far as Mount Pleasant, and reaching to Waynesboro and Savannah west.

"The preachers were Benjamin F. Weakley, Ashury Davidson, F. G. Ferguson, J. A. Bumpass, W. W. Phillips, John P. Sebastian, Jordan Moore, Samuel Watson, Jr., David J. Jones, Caleb B. Davis, W. B. Edwards, G. W. Martin, J. B. McNeal, and Robert Paine; C. D. Elliott and R. H. Rivers, of La Grange College; J. W. Kilpatrick was missionary to the colored people in the Courtland Valley. These brethren were all noble spirits, and worked with zeal and harmony. The year was very prosperous. We had many precious revivals. Our camp-meetings were seasons of rejoicing. I held ten or twelve this year, and went through the whole campaign without let or hinderance. I did not miss a single appointment. The preachers were all paid their disciplinary allowances, and the usual Conference collections were taken up. This country, especially North Alabama, was in a thriving and prosperous condition. La Grange College, which had been in operation for several years, was doing a good work in the education of the children of the Church. [This was written late in life]. After a lapse of many years it is now painfully pleasing to review the past. Where are the preachers who were with me on this district? B. F. Weakley, who was a doctor of medicine, a man of feeble health, located, married Miss Porter, daughter of the late Rev. Thomas D. Porter, raised a large family, and died near Nashville. He maintained his integrity. Asbury Davidson was transferred to the West Texas Conference, and died. He filled many important appointments. F. G. Ferguson was transferred to the Alabama Conference. He was faithful in all things, became a man of influence, and died a few years since secure in hope of a glorious immortality. J. A. Bumpass, who was a very promising young man, ran well for a season, located, turned politician, and died. W. W. Phillips became a doctor of medicine, and died years ago. He preserved himself in purity. J. P. Sebastian is a local preacher and a doctor of medicine. Jordan Moore is a member of the Conference; good and true. Samuel Watson is a Spiritualist. This I regret to say, for he was a clever man. Robert Paine is a Bishop, highly esteemed for talent and piety. The Rev. R. H. Rivers is an eminent minister and one of our best educators, a Doctor of Divinity. J. W. Kilpatrick, an aged minister, was faithful till death. C. D. Elliott located, and did a great work as an educator.

" The labors of the year having closed, in company with my wife and the Rev. Samuel Watson I went by private conveyance to the Conference, which convened at Somerville, West Tennessee. On the way I visited my father and family in Tipton County. We found a camp-meeting in progress near Covington. Here I preached several sermons. On the Sabbath I delivered a funeral discourse in memory of Mr. Robert Clark, a highly esteemed citizen and member of the Church whom I had known in Alabama in the days of my boyhood. The effect on the congregation was powerful. Sinners were awakened and Christians rejoiced. The camp-meeting resulted in many happy conversions and in the extension of the Church in that part of the Master's vineyard."

McFerrin at a camp-meeting always meant a stir. That funeral sermon was not exceptional in its effects. He had much of this kind of preaching to do. His popularity, thus indicated, was of a kind that took hold of the hearts of the people.

The visit to his parents was in keeping with his characteristic tender filial affection and dutifulness. If any man could claim the promise of the fifth commandment, he might surely do so. He honored his father and mother, and his days were literally long in the land. What of the dutiful children who die early, leaving gray-haired parents to go down in sorrow to the grave?

The promise must be dual, having both a literal and a spiritual fulfillment—literal under the Old Testament, and spiritual under the New, which points to a land of promise fairer than that which lay before the vision of Moses on Nebo's height.

RIDING THE CUMBERLAND DISTRICT.

THE session of the Tennessee Conference for 1837 was held at Somerville, in the heart of the rich cotton belt in West Tennessee. " The Conference session was pleasant, Bishop Andrew presiding," says McFerrin. " Here I had a pleasant sojourn with my brother, William M. McFerrin, and his family, who had a temporary home in Somerville. Here also were my father, mother, and the rest of the family." This was enough to make it pleasant—his friend, the wise, tender, courageous Andrew in the chair, and all the McFerrin family circle together.

He was " read out " as presiding elder of Cumberland District. " This district," he says, " lay north of the Cumberland River, extending from the lower end of Montgomery County, Tennessee, to the extreme eastern portion of Sumner County—embracing the towns of Clarksville, Springfield, Gallatin, and Cairo, and coming up to the margin of the river just opposite Nashville. The appointments were: Fountain Head, J. S. Davis; Sumner, John Kelley; Gallatin and Cairo, Thomas Maddin; White's Creek, William Jared; Red River, O. E. Ragland and F. T. Paine; Clarksville, John F. Hughes; Montgomery, William Moores; Mission to colored people on the Cumberland, John Rains. This was a small district when the number of appointments is considered, though it covered considerable territory. The work was very pleasant, and the preachers agreeable and faithful.

" The labors of God's servants were to some extent blessed; several revivals refreshed the Church, and souls were brought to Jesus. The camp-meeting season was very profitable. We held camp-meetings at Cairo, Salem, Fountain Head, Saunders's Chapel, all in Sumner County; at Cross Plains, Shaw's, and Settle's, all in Robertson County; and at Blooming Grove, White Bluff, and Asbury, all in Montgomery County.

" My family found a home at the house of Col. A. W. Johnson, near Nashville. The colonel was my wife's uncle, and had been her guardian. His wife was in feeble health, and desired the company of her niece. The good woman soon passed away, and my wife for a season supervised her children. Mrs. Johnson was a Miss Hobson, a lady of culture and piety. In person she was handsome and in manners agreeable."

A survivor and witness of the scenes that took place on his rounds on the Cumberland District could tell us why McFerrin emphasized these camp-meetings. They were mightily blessed of the Lord. The preachers by whom they were conducted were men of God, mighty in prayer, whose preaching of repentance toward God and faith in the Lord Jesus Christ was in demonstration of the Spirit and power, whose courage and sanctified tact were equal to any emergency. Entire neighborhoods and sections of country were taken by these invaders, who pitched their tents on the Cumberland hills. The attention of the thoughtless was arrested, the obduracy of the wicked was overcome, the prejudices of ignorance and bigotry were removed, the consciences of the assembled multitudes were aroused and their sensibilities stirred to the depths, and in the sweep of the religious excitement opposition broke down and many turned to

the Lord.   These were great occasions for great preachers.   The circumstances opened all the channels of their
souls for full tides of inspiration.   The expectant thousands exhibited no impatience if a sermon were long, so
it had point and power, and their responsiveness sent
back to the preacher refluent waves of feeling that bore
him upward to still greater heights of spiritual exaltation, and elicited yet more thrilling bursts of impassioned
appeal as he called them to immediate decision in view
of death, the judgment, and eternity.   The camp-meeting was to the preachers of that day what the hustings
were to the politicians.   Both alike were schools of oratory, and for every illustrious name that belongs to the
history of the State one can be found to match it in the
history of the Church.   A camp-meeting course for
young theologues now will have to come in as a post-
graduate privilege, but it would be invaluable to every
one of them who possesses the essential elements of a
popular speaker.

Thus the gospel was spread and Methodism established, the camp-meetings rapidly recruiting the Church,
and the godly discipline exercised by a zealous and faithful ministry conserving the gains, building on solid foundations an ecclesiastical organization that has blessed all
the land and been one of the chief factors in the development of what is best and most characteristic in the
life of this people.

The next year (1838) the Conference met again at
Huntsville, Alabama.   No Bishop being present, the
Rev. Fountain E. Pitts was elected President of the
Conference.   McFerrin was re-appointed to the Cum-
berland District, which was thus manned: Gallatin and
Cairo, Thomas Maddin; Fountain Head, Elisha Carr;

White's Creek, A. Chrisholm; Red River, J. S. Sherrill and J. M. Nolin; Clarksville Station, Samuel Watson; Montgomery, S. Brewer; Cumberland African Mission, John Rains. He tells us "nothing remarkable occurred this year"—which means that it was a year of peace. There was, it seems, one slight breeze of excitement growing out of a Church trial involving the character of a local elder—"a man of ability." He questioned the legality of one of the presiding elder's decisions, and the preacher in charge, a man of ability too, older than McFerrin, sustained him. " I maintained my ground," says McFerrin—a thing he had a habit of doing. Nobody ever charged that excessive pliancy was his failing. That the Bishop sustained his administration, and all the offended parties became reconciled to one another, justifies the belief that his action was legal and that his spirit was Christian. In his notes is this personal paragraph: "On the Sumner Circuit we had the Rev. R. C. Hatton. He was a man of fine pulpit ability. Years before he had become disaffected toward his Church on the question of its government, and withdrew from it and united with the Cumberland Presbyterians. But he was unhappy. He could not preach their peculiar doctrines. On reflection, he became satisfied with the Methodist economy, and returned to its communion. He was happy and useful, and died in the faith. He was the father of General Robert Hatton, who fell in the Virginia army during the late war between the North and the South. General Hatton was a brave man and a devoted Christian." This instructive glance at the times closes his record of his presiding eldership:

" This year closed my presiding eldership. Three

years I had served in this office—one on the Florence District, and two on the Cumberland District. They were years of labor and responsibility, but also of success and enjoyment. Hundreds had been converted and added to the Church each year; and, generally, the preachers were well sustained for the times. It was not customary in those days to give large amounts to the preachers. A single man was allowed one hundred dollars and his traveling expenses; if he filled a city or town station he was allowed his board and lodging. A married man was allowed one hundred dollars for himself, one hundred for his wife, and a few dollars for each of his small children. Besides, the stewards were at liberty to estimate something for his house-rent and table expenses. The presiding elder usually received but little on the score of table expenses. There were scarcely any parsonages in the South-west at this date.

"I had no children, and my expenses for board did not amount to much; so that for three years as presiding elder I received about six hundred dollars and a small pittance for board.

"I think I did not miss an appointment during the three years, and generally I preached a great deal between quarterly meetings—sometimes in towns for nearly a whole week without intermission. On the circuits I often preached on the week-days, traveling from one pastoral charge to another. The camp-meeting season was full of labor—from eight to twelve of these meetings during the summer and autumn. Open-air preaching was not so laborious after one's voice became accustomed to out-door speaking; but to preach once a day, exhort, hold prayer-meetings, and sing, sometimes nearly the whole night, tries one's physical strength.

8

But O these were seasons of refreshing to the spirit! During the three years several young men were licensed to preach and admitted into the Annual Conference. At some points on the fields I occupied it was necessary, occasionally, to preach on controverted points; especially on baptism—its mode, subjects, and design. While we did not court discussions, we never failed to try to defend the doctrines and usages of our Church, and to drive away 'strange and hurtful doctrines.' We had to encounter in some places infidelity and skepticism. This was done in the fear of God, and the results were very comforting to the people of God. Montgomery County and the town of Clarksville were infected with a class of open and avowed unbelievers. These were met, and from time to time the divine authenticity of the Scriptures was discussed and the sophisms of skeptics exposed. The progress of religion was steady and its triumph finally complete."

That was McFerrin—a peaceable, pugilistic, paradoxical polemic, who "occasionally found it necessary to preach on controverted points." The necessity for this sort of preaching is usually measured largely by the temperament of the preacher.

GEN. JACKSON AND THE PREACHERS.

THE session of the Tennessee Conference for 1838 was held at Nashville, Bishop Andrew presiding. The session was pleasant " in some respects," is McFerrin's guarded language. Some sectional jealousies had sprung up between the preachers in Middle and West Tennessee, and a little unpleasantness had grown out of the appointments made the previous year. " These things," he says, " created a little friction, but it all finally wore away, and the western portion of the State was set off with a part of the States of Mississippi and Kentucky, and the Memphis Conference was organized, which cured all troubles. The two Conferences were ever after as twin sisters." A touching episode of this Conference session was the visit of General Andrew Jackson to the body, thus described by McFerrin:

" During the session of this Conference General Jackson, ex-President of the United States, visited the city and expressed a desire to visit the Conference, as he had some old friends in the body. Joshua Boucher, Robert Paine, and myself were appointed a committee to wait on the General and escort him to the Conference-room. The scene was interesting and affecting. General Jackson was growing old, had become a Christian, and was a great friend to the Methodists. He was introduced to the Bishop and then to the Conference, and after a few pleasant words the body was called to prayer. Bishop Andrew offered a most fervent address to the

(115)

throne of grace, while the whole Conference responded with hearty *Amens*. The General then passed down the aisle of the church, when each preacher gave him the parting hand. When Cornelius Evans, a plain old farmer-looking preacher, grasped his hand, the General exclaimed, 'Mr. Evans!' and both burst into tears. Evans had been one of his brave soldiers in the Indian wars. They had not met for years. Both became soldiers of Jesus Christ, and now met in the Church of God. General Jackson recognized him instantly."

By invitation, the Conference in a body attended the inauguration of James K. Polk as Governor of Tennessee. Bishop Andrew made the closing prayer. Its appropriateness and fervency moved all hearts.

McFerrin was again elected one of the delegates to the General Conference. The delegation from Tennessee were: Robert Paine, Fountain E. Pitts, John B. McFerrin, Ambrose F. Driskill, and Samuel Moody.

For the third time McFerrin was appointed to McKendree Church, Nashville. "I entered upon my work at once," he says, "and lost no time during the winter and early spring. There had been an extensive revival the year previous, under the ministry of the Revs. F. E. Pitts, A. L. P. Green, and W. D. F. Sawrie. To nurture and train the young converts was an important and arduous work. I did all I could as a pastor; the Lord was with me, and we had prosperity."

In the month of April, 1840, with some of his codelegates, he left Nashville for Baltimore, the seat of the General Conference. He mentions with pleasure the fact that the Rev. Fountain E. Pitts and himself were the guests of Christian Keener, father of Bishop J. C. Keener. The future Bishop was not then a preacher, and McFerrin does not tell us whether he saw "Bishop timber" in the slender, auburn-haired, fair-faced young man. McFerrin was placed on the Committee on Boundaries, where he did good work. Phineas Rice, of New York, was chairman—"a man of genial spirit and great humor," who evidently excited the admiration of the like-minded Tennessean. "Our committee," says McFerrin in his notes, "was large and very agreeable. It recommended the formation of the Memphis Conference. This left Middle Tennessee and North Alabama the boundaries of the Tennessee Conference."

BECOMES AN EDITOR.

THIS General Conference of 1840, at Baltimore, brought a surprise and a great change in the life of McFerrin, transferring him from the pastorate to the editorial chair. It happened thus, he himself giving the facts:

"Four years previous this General Conference (1836) located a weekly paper at Nashville, called the *Southwestern Christian Advocate*, and elected the Rev. Thos. Stringfield, of the Holston Conference, editor. Mr· Stringfield, and a committee acting with him, bought out the *Western Methodist*, a paper that had been established in Nashville in the year 1833 by the Rev. Lewis Garrett and J. N. Maffitt. During Mr. Stringfield's term difficulties arose between him and Mr. Garrett, which were afflicting to Mr. Stringfield and injurious to the paper. The result was that, notwithstanding the editor was an able man, the enterprise failed in a measure, and the paper became seriously involved in debt. The General Conference was memorialized to grant aid for its pecuniary relief. This memorial I presented to the General Conference, and urged it before the Committee on the Book Concern. The committee reported in favor of $5,000 for relief. I moved to amend by striking out $5,000 and inserting $7,000. The amendment prevailed, and the amount was given. This was a great relief indeed, but still left the paper embarrassed. One condition on which the General Confe·en_e gave aid was that if the paper in one year did not promise success it was to be wound up and discontinued.

"Mr. Stringfield declined a re-election, and the Rev. Charles A. Davis, formerly of Baltimore, but then of New York, was elected editor. Mr. Davis, after time to reflect, declined coming to Nashville, and the Tennessee Conference had to elect an editor to fill his place. Much to my surprise, and to my deep regret, I was elected. I could not positively rebel, and yet I begged to be excused. The paper was still in debt, the subscription-list was small, and I was without much experience. Above all, I disliked to be thrown out of the pastoral work. My heart was in the ministry, and in that calling I wanted to live and to die. But the Conference said: 'Take it for one year; if it prove a success, well; if not, then we will bury the paper and allow you to return to the pastoral work.' Bishop Andrew said: 'Try it a year. I will take A. L. P. Green with me to the Memphis, Mississippi, and Alabama Conferences, and we will invoke their aid; if then it fails, you shall be released.' I went to work, but had not the slightest idea that I would remain at the same post of duty for eighteen years.

"I had finished my year at the McKendree, all in peace and with good results, and now surrendered my charge, little thinking that this would be my last work in that immediate line. Now, at this writing, nearly thirty-five years have elapsed, and I have been the whole time a General Conference officer."

On September 4 of this year (1840) his father died in Tipton County, Tennessee. These pathetic words show how deeply he felt it: "This to me was a sore af·

fliction. He and my mother and myself had all joined the Church the same day; he and I had preached together many years, and now in the vigor of life (only fifty-six years old) he fell a victim to disease, and 'ceased at once to work and live.' My love for him was very great." Truly it was so; his love for his father was the love of a son and the love of a fellow-soldier of Jesus Christ, a comrade in arms, a bond doubly tender and sacred. To the last there was a softening tone and not seldom a quiver of the lip when McFerrin spoke of his beloved father. It was a fitting coincidence that Bishop Andrew, by request of the Tennessee Annual Conference, preached his funeral sermon in Murfreesboro, where the session of 1840 was held—that town being the county-seat of Rutherford County, in which he had been converted, and where he began to preach the gospel.

A memorandum by McFerrin informs us that his "allowance" for this year was $700. On this, he says, they lived comfortably, but "had to practice economy" as housekeepers. A dollar was bigger and went farther then than now.

The feelings and aims with which he began his work as editor are worthy of study as portrayed by his own hand:

"Entering now on a new work, I had many serious thoughts as to my future. How shall I succeed as an editor? how will I be able to manage the finances of the establishment? were questions that time alone could solve. But having consented, though reluctantly, to take the work, I resolved to put forth my best energies. My salutatory was published November 7, 1840, and will be found in Vol. V., No. 1, of the *South-western Christian Advocate*."

His editorial work, begun as he tells us so reluctantly, extended over a period of eighteen years. He was placed in this position at first chiefly because a man was wanted who could publish a religious newspaper without going in debt. It is not strange that he was disinclined to take the *South-western Christian Advocate* upon his hands. It was in debt, and he had a holy hatred of debt all his life. It was a paradoxical fate that required him to wrestle so often with the debts of the Church. But it was perhaps the right thing that a man who was such a hater of debts should be called on to extinguish them. He put his heart into the work. His extraordinary physical and mental energy enabled him to perform the work of several men. He wrote editorials, he edited obituaries, he wrestled with the volunteer poets (whose name then as now was legion), he clipped and pasted selections, he acted as mailing-clerk, he canvassed for subscribers, he hired and paid the printers, he preached at camp-meetings and in revivals, and conducted theological controversies. "I preached a great deal in the city, in the country, at funerals, in revivals, and at camp-meetings," he said; "though called to conduct a paper, I was resolved never to surrender my office as a minister of the gospel."

These extraordinary labors were not in vain. The Church was inspired with renewed confidence; the new editor's zeal and courage were contagious. Bishop Andrew and the Rev. A. L. P. Green enlisted the brethren in the three patronizing Conferences, and Holston and Arkansas rallied to his support. The Publishing Committee, consisting of Thomas L. Douglass, A. L. P. Green, and John W. Hanner, heartily co-operated with the editor. The utmost economy was practiced. The editor's salary was $800 a year, and the clerks and all the employees worked at as low a rate as possible. This virtue of economy he never lost. If we admit that he carried it to excess, to it the Church is indebted beyond what it can ever know. He stopped the leaks that saved more than one sinking ship.

That he continued to preach at popular gatherings and to dispute with the enemies in the gate was quite natural. During the three years of his presiding eldership he had gotten in the way of doing such things, had fully awakened to that sense of power that no strong man lacks; as we know, he had a natural love for combat, and was never afraid of a "sanctified uproar." In his notes of this first year of editorial experience he tells us with evident complacency that he "had several warm discussions with the editors of the *Baptist Banner* and *Western Pioneer;*" and he informs us that he "also had occasion to review the teachings of Mr. Alexander Campbell and his adherents, and to defend Methodist doctrines and usages against the assaults of a number of enemies." " In all these controversies," he further adds, "the Methodists did not consider that their interests had suffered." Verily, he found occasion to review and defend! A man of his temperament never lacks such occasions. But let it not be forgotten that at this time the doctrine and polity of Methodism were still running the gantlet on the way to a conquered peace. McFerrin's love of fighting was, we may religiously concede, a part of his providential equipment for the sphere he was called to fill. A calmer, happier time came while he was yet living, and no man was then more sincerely irenic in spirit than this warrior of the earlier and stormier time. His pugnacity was never much abated, but it took a different direction in the brighter day for Christian unity that dawned before his chastened spirit was caught up to meet the saints of all ages in the world of eternal peace.

At the next session of the Annual Conference, held at Clarksville, Tennessee, in October, 1841, he was elected Secretary, as he had been for several previous sessions. Bishop Waugh presided—a well-balanced, good man, who did the work of a General Superintendent quietly and faithfully, never startling the Church by a flash of peculiar brilliancy, and never harming or disgracing it by any thing erratic in utterance or act. He was the kind of man to whom the General Conference has often turned in preference to men of more brilliant parts when a position of special responsibility was to be filled. He was a safe man. A safe man!— no higher eulogy or nobler epitaph could be coveted by any minister of the Lord Jesus Christ.

The first year of McFerrin's editorial service was regarded as quite a triumph. The Publishing Committee made a very favorable report. The Conference " resolved " that he had done well, and promised to be " more unwearied " in their exertions to promote the interest of the paper. The neat mechanical execution, editorial capability, and economical management were specially considered. " This hearty indorsement at the end of my first year's editorial life was very gratifying to my feelings," is his frank declaration.

He attended the second session of the Memphis Conference, which convened in the city of Memphis. He went by steam-boat, and overtook Bishop Waugh and others, who had been delayed on the way. They reached Memphis on Thursday, November 4, 1841, passing several wrecks of steam and flat boats by the way. In those days steam-boat travel was very uncertain; low water at certain seasons, fogs and high waters at other times, and delays by collecting and discharging freight, often retarded travelers. It was no uncommon thing to wait from twelve to twenty-four hours for a boat which was expected every hour. We believe McFerrin when he tells us, " This was trying to one's patience."

The Conference gave him a cordial greeting, and adopted the resolutions passed by the Tennessee Conference indorsing his work as editor and publisher.

" By vote," he says, " the Conference invited me to preach a funeral sermon in memory of one of the presiding elders, the Rev. John M. Holland, who had fallen at his post during the year. Mr. Holland was a noble preacher; he had long been a member of the Tennessee Conference, and was greatly esteemed. At the same Conference the Rev. Joseph Travis delivered a funeral discourse in memory of the Rev. Malcolm McPherson, another eminent man who had died during the year.

" Memphis at this time was a young but promising city. The streets were almost impassable in wet weather in consequence of the mud and quicksands. Still it grew rapidly, and soon became a very important city. The Rev. Fountain E. Pitts, a member of the Tennessee Conference, visited the Mississippi and Alabama Conferences in the interest of the paper. He had fine success; both Conferences renewed their pledges for our support. At the Mississippi Conference the Rev. Dr. William Winans submitted the resolution of approval and support. This was very pleasant to me, as I regarded Dr. Winans a man of great intellect and much candor.

"The Arkansas Conference, which met about this time, promised efficient aid. All these pledges greatly strengthened my purpose to sustain the paper."

During this year (1842) he had what he himself calls "a long and rather unpleasant discussion" with the editors of the *Baptist Banner* and *Pioneer*. First and last four distinguished Baptists entered the fight against him—Dr. Howell, the Rev. W. C. Crane, the Rev. Mr. Waller, and the Rev. Mr. Buck—and finally the Rev. Mr. Peck, of Illinois, took a hand on the same side. The controversy—involving the doctrines, usages, and polity of Methodism—was continued through several months, and was, as McFerrin tells us, at times angry and personal; "but," he adds, "I strove to keep my temper and maintain my ground upon fair and honorable terms. Sometimes I had to resort to wit and sarcasm to ward off their severe assaults; but in all things I endeavored to demean myself properly. The result was favorable to the cause of Methodism, especially in Tennessee."

That is the way he puts it. He had to fight for his Church; he had to use the wit and sarcasm with which he was so largely furnished. It is evident that those brawny Baptists struck him hard, and it is no less evident that he struck back with all his might. Who began the fray is left to the inference of the reader. That he rather enjoyed it, and felt that he came off victorious, seems also pretty clear. It is likely that from the other side there was a different version of the matter. Who ever heard of a contest of this sort in which both parties did not claim the victory? But it is safe to conclude that if McFerrin did not get the best of the argument, by his wit and sarcasm he got the

laugh on his opponents, and that his persistent pugnacity got him the last word. We give him our cordial
credence when he says that he strove to keep his temper, but his words have a semi-apologetical tone that
leads us to think that he himself had some misgivings
as to whether he had achieved perfect success in this
laudable endeavor. In this, as in innumerable instances
of a similar kind, it is probable that no little ink was
wasted on side-issues, verbal quirks and quibbles, and
the personalities that seemed to have a bitter taste in his
mouth long years after the fight was over. The gentle, scholarly, and eloquent Howell, his chief antagonist,
afterward became McFerrin's warm friend in Nashville;
and when he died, in the prime of his noble powers
and in the midst of a fruitful ministry, McFerrin was
among the mourners and took part in the funeral services. They have met on Mount Zion, where they see
the unveiled truth in the light of eternity, and where,
we venture to affirm, they both realize with ineffable
satisfaction that their little differences in belief on earth
were as nothing compared to the vital principles and
precious facts of the gospel which they held in common. The intimacy begun before Dr. Howell's translation, renewed in that fairer clime, will henceforth
know neither interruption nor end. Blessed be God for
the assurance that every believing heart that longs for
the unity of the Church of Christ, and dies without the
sight, will find it in the Church triumphant!

The militant McFerrins have their function in stormy
times in the Church below, but their hearts too will
thrill with ecstatic joy when they shall see the King in
his beauty, his throne encircled by the emerald arch that
symbolizes the blessed fact that the storms are all over!

This year (1842) his daughter Sarah Jane was born; a child that was a life-long joy to his heart, singularly like himself in physical features, and exhibiting many of his most marked moral characteristics, softened and refined by a sweet and attractive womanliness. Forty years afterward he traced these tender words: "She was the first child we had to live. She was a great comfort to me and my beloved wife. She was spared to us, but lost her mother when she was about twelve years old. She was trained by her grandmother and her step-mother, and graduated from the school of Dr. J. O. Church, in Columbia, Tennessee, when about seventeen years old. She afterward was married to Mr. James Anderson, and is now the mother of six children. She was always an obedient and affectionate child and greatly beloved." To see them together—the rugged and masterful champion of orthodox Methodism, and his softened counterpart in the person of this child of his early love—was beautiful. It was parental and filial affection in perpetual flower. They who tell us that such an affection as this will perish at death impeach the goodness of the gracious God who hath ordained and hallowed the sacred relations that make a Christian family on earth the truest type of the blessedness that awaits the whole family of the redeemed in that world where the home-longings of the soul shall be satisfied, and they who have loved shall meet to part no more. O Father in heaven, if this longing shall not be satisfied, then must these human hearts thou hast given us be wholly changed ere heaven could be heaven to us!

The Valley of the Mississippi was all aflame with revivals this year. McFerrin threw himself into these special labors with all his might. At quarterly meetings, camp-meetings, and on other occasions, he was ready for preaching; and the people were as glad to hear him as he was ready to preach. His coming was the signal for a popular rally. The Methodists recognized in him an undaunted and unconquerable champion of their faith, and all classes of people felt the attraction of his magnetism, smiled at his quaint sayings, were conscience-smitten by his pungent appeals, and wept at his pathos, which at times no heart could resist. In Nashville the word of God mightily prevailed. A great company of converts were received into the Methodist Church, Mc-Ferrin taking a most active part in all the work, vindicating the truth of his declaration: "Preaching was a work to which I felt God had called me, and I was determined to slack not in this holy vocation." It was well both for him and for the Church that he adhered through life to this wise determination. The man who is truly called of God to the ministry of the gospel is never absolved from the responsibility of that call, except by death or by positive providential disability. If he had allowed the editor to absorb the preacher, Mc-Ferrin would have been a less efficient editor and would have incurred the risk of losing the prophetic gift.

UNDER FULL HEADWAY.

THE seat of the Tennessee Conference for the session of 1842 was Athens, Alabama. The territory of the Conference at this time embraced Middle Tennessee and all that part of the State of Alabama watered by the Tennessee River, known as North Alabama.

McFerrin made the journey from Nashville on horseback, in company with the Rev. John W. Hanner and eight others. That was a lively party that thus rode together through that beautiful region in its autumnal glory. The long miles were made short by the relation of itinerant experience, anecdote, snatches of spiritual songs, and sallies of wit and humor within the bounds of ministerial decorum. As they went they preached. At Columbia, which place they reached on Friday evening, McFerrin preached. His subject was, " The Work of the Holy Spirit in the Salvation of the Believing Sinner." That was a gospel theme, and no doubt it was handled in orthodox fashion. The next morning he visited the grave of the Rev. L. D. Overall, his colleague in Nashville in 1834, who was buried near Columbia, whose memory he still cherished. Reaching Pulaski on Saturday, they had preaching on Saturday night and three times on Sunday. The power of God was manifest in the congregation. Remaining with a part of his company until Tuesday morning, McFerrin preached again on Monday night, and had "a time of great power," several persons being happily converted.

9   (129)

among them some of the most influential persons in the town. His pastorate in Pulaski in 1834 and 1835 had elicited a mutual affection between him and the people of that place, and his hearers were thus made more receptive of the message of God from his lips. "I loved that people dearly," he declares; and it is not strange that he retained a special regard for Pulaski, where he had spent two years of successful labor, hallowed by recollections of the wife of his youth, whose image came back to him whenever he thought of the place.

McFerrin was again made Secretary of the Conference. Bishop Andrew, who presided, was in the spirit of his work. His sermons and addresses made a profound impression upon the Conference and the community. The Conference was held in the court-house, while preaching was kept up morning, afternoon, and night in the Methodist church. That was the custom in that day, and it was a good one.

A pleasant episode of this Conference session was the visit of the Rev. E. S. Janes, Agent of the American Bible Society. His address to the Conference was "moving" in its effect upon that responsive audience. This note by McFerrin will not be without interest to the readers for whom it is transcribed: "Probably he [Janes] laid the foundation of his election to the office of Bishop in this visit to the Tennessee Conference. My impression is that I was the first person who ever suggested his name for the responsible position that he so long filled with credit to himself and with usefulness to the Church. He was elected Bishop in 1844, and died in 1876." McFerrin might have told more in this connection had not modesty or prudence forbidden. Bishop Janes owed his election largely to the votes of the Southern delegates to that stormy General Conference of 1844, that dated the stormiest era in the history of American Methodism; and there is reason to believe that the ardent McFerrin did more than any other man to place the miter upon the head of that compact, lucid, spiritual man who for thirty-two years honored the episcopal office and adorned the doctrine of Christ. There was always a warm regard for Bishop Janes among Southern Methodists, and at the time of his death his heart was turned toward them in fraternal yearnings.

An incident of this Conference session, as related by McFerrin, will illustrate both the temper of those bellicose times and a vital truth of the gospel—the truth that the Holy Spirit is the efficient agent in the conviction and conversion of sinners:

"About the time of the meeting of this Conference there was a great deal of discussion involving spiritual regeneration, justification by faith, and the efficacy of water baptism. The followers of Alexander Campbell were very bold in asserting that there was no remission of sins without immersion in water. They denied, many of them at least, that the Spirit directly wrought upon the heart of penitent sinners. In a word, they denied spiritual Christianity as we in the evangelical Churches understood it.

"On Sunday night of the Conference we had a wonderful demonstration of the doctrine of justification by faith. I preached in the 'Union Church,' as it was called, to a large congregation, while Dr. A. L. P. Green preached at the Methodist Church. In my congregation there was a young man, about twenty-five years of age, who was a deaf-mute. He was the

son of a Brother West, an aged Methodist of good
standing in the Church and in the country generally.
He had sent his son to a school for the education of his
class of unfortunate persons; and young West, being
very sprightly and studious, had made rapid improvement. He was a handsome young man, and gave indi-
cations of an excellent mind. Moreover, he had been
trained by pious parents, who taught all their children .
to fear God and work righteousness.

"I preached on the text, 'What shall I do to be
saved?' The audience was attentive, the preacher was
in the spirit of his Master, and a peculiar unction attended the word preached. At the close of the sermon
an invitation was given for penitents to present themselves at the place of prayer. Young West was the
first, or among the first, to rush forward and fall on his
knees. He seemed much engaged, and soon, after a
most fervent prayer offered by the Rev. Alexander Sale,
he was powerfully converted. He rose to his feet, his
face radiant, his gestures giving evidence of great joy.
He looked toward heaven, pointed upward, clasped his
hands, and embraced his friends. After a few moments
of rejoicing, he seized his hat, and with swift steps
moved toward the Methodist Church, where his father
and mother were worshiping. He entered the door, and
pressed through the crowd till he reached his mother,
when he embraced her, and made her understand in a
moment that he had found peace in believing. The
effect was overwhelming. In the Union Church there
seemed to be a power that shook the whole assembly,
and the congregation in the Methodist Church felt the
same divine influence, while the many friends of young
West rejoiced with him in his happy espousal to Christ.

" This occurrence produced a profound impression on skeptics and those who denied the power of the Holy Ghost in the soul's conversion to Christ. Sinners wondered, and were afraid. A good work of grace had commenced in the congregation at the Methodist Church, and this gave a new impetus to the revival. 'Believe on the Lord Jesus Christ, and thou shalt be saved,' was the theme of the preacher, and God verified his word in the conversion of this young man, who could not hear nor speak, but who could believe and feel the power of grace to save."

God is not limited in the exercise of his saving power by any thing save a resisting human will. A look, a gesture, a picture may be a channel of grace and salvation to a soul to whom the ordinary channels of gracious communication are closed. Blessed be the name of God our Father who loves all his children, and who provides compensations in this life for his weak and afflicted ones who will in the life to come enter upon the clearer light and larger life that will leave no painful mystery unrevealed and no longing unsatisfied!

Soon after the session of his own Conference, McFerrin swung out on a tour of Conference visitation. He went on horseback, still preaching as he went, and leaving a stir behind him. The first Conference he attended was the Memphis, which convened at Holly Springs, Mississippi, November 2, 1842. The journey took five days and a half. Bishop Andrew "was on hand," says McFerrin, and he felt that he had in him a wise and influential friend. This was the third session of the new Conference, and the year had been very successful. The increase in Church-members had been large—a considerable portion of it by immigration to

that new and fertile region. West Tennessee and
North Mississippi were inviting sections of the South-
west—the climate being mild, the soil productive, the
people industrious, and their condition prosperous. In
many places there had been great revivals, such as were
peculiar to that time, and thousands of souls had been
converted and brought into the Methodist Church.

The Conference at Holly Springs made a delightful
impression on McFerrin—from which it may be inferred
that he had "liberty" in preaching and plenty of it to
do, and that the brethren were not deaf or unresponsive
to his appeals for the *Christian Advocate.* He speaks
warmly of the hospitality of the Holly Springs people—
a virtue characteristic of our people and of those times,
and which is not likely to become extinct as long as they
read the New Testament and enjoy genuine religion.
The missionary anniversary was the most interesting
feature of the session, and especially so to McFerrin, as
it devolved on him to take the place of Bishop Andrew
on the platform. The Bishop, then in his prime, was
immensely popular, and no member of the body was
willing to take his place when it was known that he was
too much indisposed physically to fill his engagement.
A young Tennessee preacher—Philip P. Neely—consented to make the opening speech, the first of the kind
ever delivered by that silver-tongued pulpit orator,
whose eloquence in after years charmed the ears of delighted thousands in the principal cities of the South-
west. Of his effort it is said, "He made a handsome
speech;" and it may be safely concluded that whatever
may have been lacking in breadth or depth in so young
a speaker was largely compensated by the grace and
tact that never failed him. McFerrin followed. The

traditions of that speech long remained. He secured a larger collection than had ever before been made in the South-west. On this occasion was introduced the idea of contributing bales of cotton to the cause of Missions. Stirred by McFerrin's appeals, Mr. Willis Somerville, a spirited and high-toned Christian gentleman, arose and proposed to give a bale of cotton, to be sent to his commission merchant at Memphis, marked "MISSIONARY." Others followed, and twenty-one bales were contributed in a short time. Who has known a man who when he struck a lead like this could follow it up with more success than McFerrin?

On his return from Holly Springs he visited his widowed mother, and then met at Memphis Bishop Andrew and the Rev. L. Swormstedt, Book Agent, from Cincinnati. Shipping their horses to Vicksburg, Mississippi, he and the Bishop took boat for Helena, the seat of the Arkansas Conference. Bishop Roberts arrived on Friday, "having been delayed by sickness and slow boats." This was the last Conference that venerable man ever held. We have already seen how great was the veneration and affection entertained for him by McFerrin. In the same spirit is this note made by him in this connection:

"He [Bishop Roberts] came in the spirit of a true Bishop and as a beloved and loving patriarch. This was the last Conference he ever held. A more devoted, sweet-spirited, and sanctified Christian man and minister I never saw. I roomed with him and Bishop Andrew, and had the pleasure of waiting upon the venerable man. The impression he made on my mind and heart has never been erased. I kept his minutes, made out his returns, and read out the appointments of the preachers. The venerable man was full of love, cheerful and happy, and preached on the Sabbath at the earnest request of the brethren. The sermon was brief and simple and full of pathos. His subject was, 'The Christian Race.' His own race was run; at that Conference he closed his official duties as a Bishop. He had set out for Texas, but Bishop Andrew and others entered their protest and persuaded him to return home, where a few months afterward he closed a long and useful life.

" Bishop Roberts was a glorious preacher in his palmy days. He was simple and natural in his style and manner of delivery, and full of power and unction."

After this tribute to this simply grand and saintly man, McFerrin adds this bit of personal history: "Up to the time of this writing [1875] I have witnessed the beginning and the closing labors of several of our Bishops. I was with Bishops Andrew, Paine, Pierce, and Keener at the first Conferences over which each presided. I was present at the last Annual Conferences which each of the following Bishops attended—viz., Bishops McKendree, Roberts, Soule, and Andrew. All good men; all died in Christ."

BELLIGERENT AND MOVING.

FROM the Arkansas Conference, in company with Bishop Andrew and the Rev. L. Swormstedt, Mc-Ferrin took a steam-boat for Vicksburg *en route* for Jackson, the seat of the Mississippi Conference. On board the boat they met a Mormon preacher, with whom they had much conversation. The impression made on McFerrin's mind was that they were a fanatical and deluded people with corrupt and designing leaders. Their subsequent history has vindicated this judgment. Their cohesion under extraordinary pressure demonstrates the cunning of the Mormon chiefs and the zeal of the masses. Their peculiar industrial system has been the conservative feature of Mormonism. Every man among them must be a producer; idleness and vagabondage are excluded. Thus the people are thrifty, and furnish a striking illustration of this maxim in state-craft: a people who are provided with plenty and possessed of physical comfort will bear much misgovernment. Comfort is dearer than freedom to the average man save when lifted to a higher plane under the inspiration of a great idea that wakes the slumbering souls of the millions.

At Vicksburg the travelers found a hearty welcome at the home of the Rev. John Lane, then a presiding elder of the Mississippi Conference—"a man of wealth, deep piety, and great simplicity of manners," says McFerrin, in a sentence which paints a picture that charms

(137)

us. The Rev. Preston Cooper was carrying on a revival in the city, and the three remained a short time
and took part in the work. The forcefulness and ardor
of the Tennessee editor no doubt gave impetus to the
revival. He was a revivalist in virtue of the facts that
he was converted in a revival, had since lived in the
midst of revivals, was a believer in revivals, and belonged to a revival Church which was born in a revival,
and read the New Testament as a revival record from
the Pentecost to the closing invitation from the Spirit
and the Bride in the Apocalypse.

The Mississippi Conference opened at Jackson November 30, 1842, Bishop Andrew in the chair. On
Sunday the Bishop preached in the State-house to a very
large and intelligent audience. Jackson at this time was
rapidly growing, and was celebrated for its men of talent and its women of elegance and fashion. At the
missionary meeting on Monday night Bishop Andrew,
Dr. William Winans, and McFerrin were the speakers
—a powerful trio for the platform. The collection, in
money and cotton-bales, exceeded that taken at Holly
Springs; and, under the impulse of the occasion, the
brethren met two nights afterward and paid off an old
Church debt of large amount. "So true it is," said
McFerrin, "that the more persons give to the cause of
God the more they are willing to give." And it may
be added, the more they give the more they will be able
to give.

The good Bishop and McFerrin next started to Montgomery, the seat of the Alabama Conference—the former in his one-horse buggy and the latter on horseback.
That was a preaching journey. Accompanied by several of the preachers, they preached in Canton, Sharon,

Louisville, Starkville, and Columbus, Mississippi. At Columbus they spent the Sabbath and remained until Tuesday. The Bishop preached to a large congrega· tion on Sunday. On Sunday and Monday nights Mc-Ferrin preached two sermons by request—one on "The Deity, Personality, and Offices of the Holy Ghost," and the other on "Justification by Faith." The immediate cause of the request, he tells us, was the fact that "a Campbellite preacher from Tennessee had been in Columbus a short time previous, and made war upon the evangelical views of experimental religion and salvation by faith." No great persuasion was required to induce McFerrin to preach those sermons. The man who carries a loaded pistol is likely to have occasion to shoot. McFerrin went loaded in those days of fierce doctrinal conflict. The wrath of the "Disciples" was stirred by the sermons, and he was attacked in a lively manner by a writer in the secular papers of Columbus. He replied in the *South-western Christian Advocate.*

Resuming their journey, the Bishop and McFerrin took in their way Eutaw, Greensboro, Marion, and Valley Creek (afterward called Summerfield). The Sabbath was spent at Marion, where the Bishop preached in the morning and McFerrin at night. We smile as we read McFerrin's note of his sermon on that occasion. He discharged another chamber of his polemic pistol, which was loaded and ready. "A serious attack had been made on the Methodists a short time previous by a Calvinistic Presbyterian. I was privately requested to give the matter a little notice; consequently at night I preached on 'The Doctrine of Election.' I took with me into the pulpit the Westminster Confession of Faith, and in the course of my sermon I read from the

Confession and then from the Bible, and then noted the conflict between them. My congregation became very much excited. The Methodists seemed to be delighted, the Calvinists very much surprised, and some of them greatly offended." It is no wonder that they were offended. That is an exasperating way of conducting such a discussion. If unfairly done, it naturally irritates the other side; if fairly done, it makes them feel very uncomfortable. We are sure McFerrin tried to be fair. "The result," he says, "was good. Perhaps few sermons that I ever delivered made more stir or were longer remembered. The Methodists had been rather weak in Marion, and had been the subjects of persecution and proscription."

Leaving the Marion community in a ferment, and the Methodists exultant, the two resumed their journey, having with them the Rev. A. P. Harris, a young preacher of the Alabama Conference, described as "a good man and a great singer." He entertained his companions in travel with hymns and camp-meeting songs, making the forests vocal with praise to God. A little more than one year from this time he went up to join the songs of the glorified.

They reached Montgomery December 27, and that night McFerrin attended a meeting of a juvenile missionary society. Dr. Lovick Pierce and Dr. Jefferson Hamilton made addresses. McFerrin "added some remarks." If this was the first time those grand apostolic men heard him on the platform, they undoubtedly had a surprise. After the ponderous Biblical argumentation of Pierce and the conscience-searching of Hamilton, the audacious sallies, the flashing wit, and the simple pathos of the Tennessean were hugely enjoyed by the audience. That McFerrin enjoyed it is indicated by his note that "the Society gave a handsome entertainment."

The Alabama Conference convened December 28, 1842. Bishop Andrew was in his place, and the Revs. Seymour B. Sawyer and Thomas W. Dorman were elected Secretaries. Within two years Mr. Sawyer died. The year previous to his death he visited Nashville with his sick wife, in quest of health. McFerrin found them at a hotel, took them to his house, where Mrs. Sawyer in a few days died in full hope of a glorious immortality. "I am going to a world where there is no sin," was the solemn yet rapturous thought that was last on her dying lips.

The Alabama Conference continued more than a week; but on Monday morning, in company with a young preacher—George McClintock—McFerrin left Montgomery for Nashville. The horseback journey took ten days. A heavy snow-storm met him on the way, but he pressed forward, and at the end of ten days reached Nashville. He had traveled more than three thousand miles, mostly on horseback, and had been absent from home two months and a half. He had made "much interest for his paper," which by this time was getting out of debt, and had the promise of a large circulation. The country through which he had traveled was new to him; many new acquaintances were made by him and old friendships renewed. Reviewing this journey, he uses these words concerning his traveling companion: "Bishop Andrew, with whom I made most of the journey, I found to be a most delightful fellow-traveler. He was genial, easily satisfied, and never complained of coarse fare. He was always ready to preach when circumstances justified him in so doing.

His health was uniformly good, and he seldom missed an opportunity of doing good." That is a characteristic touch in which he says that the good Bishop "never complained of coarse fare." Methodist Bishops usually get the best that there is in these days, when Methodists are rich and numerous; but in that earlier time they had, like others, to endure hardness as good soldiers of Jesus Christ. There are other points in the foregoing description worthy of the special attention of preachers. Pause and re-read.

It must not be supposed that during this long absence the *South-western Christian Advocate* was a self-running sheet. The Rev. C. D. Elliott, then at the head of the far-famed Nashville Female Academy, supervised its weekly issues while the editor on horseback kept up a regular correspondence. In variety the paper could not compare with the weekly religious newspaper of to-day. Revival news, doctrinal and controversial essays, editorials not numerous but voluminous, original "poetry" generally very religious in tone and very greatly lacking in every other desirable element of verse, and the inevitable and sacred obituary department, made up its table of contents. From that day to this two things have never failed in the record of Methodism—the spiritual birth of new souls into the kingdom of grace and the happy translation of the holy dead to the kingdom of glory. McFerrin tells us that on reaching home he found much to do after so long an absence, but that he "went to work with a good will," and he had good health and a good constitution to bear him up in his labors. He adds this significant note: "Occasionally I had to controvert false doctrines and to defend Methodism. Those were days of much discussion and a good deal of angry disputation; but we held our own, and Methodism continued to prosper in the great South-west." False doctrines were as a red flag to him, and his readiness to "defend Methodism" was truly remarkable. The appearance of an assailant was the signal for fight. If he ever declined a challenge the fact is not recorded. That a warrior so quick to defend might sometimes be the aggressor is quite possible. Like many another stout but good-natured fighter, he somehow managed to have a contest on hand most of the time. If he ever grew tired of it, his friends never knew it; if he was ever vanquished, he did not know it. It may not be denied that there was a real necessity that he should controvert false doctrine and defend Methodism. The delusion called " Millerism "—one of those sporadic excitements concerning the second advent of the Lord Jesus Christ that from time to time have run a brief course—was raging like a wild fire in many parts of the country. In some places the followers of Miller abandoned all secular business, went into the fields or woods, lived in tents, prepared their ascension robes, and in some cases even went so far as to predict the very day and hour for the coming of the Lord. Other popular errors lifted their heads here and there and offered marks too fair to escape the blows of this vigilant watchman upon the walls. Methodism, though an aggressive, growing, prosperous organization, had not yet conquered a peace; but it commanded the respect of opposers and excited the wonder and admiration of friends and liberal-minded people of other Communions. And so we say the militant McFerrin was needed, and he must not be unduly blamed because he found that duty and inclination lay in the same direction. He had the magnanimity that could kindle with admiration at the prowess of an antagonist whose heavy blows had fallen on himself. This trait was illustrated in later years when, after a heated but courteous combat with Dr. A. G. Haygood before the Book Committee, on a question that always stirred him deeply, he exclaimed with undisguised admiration: " He hit me hard to-night. I taught the fellow to fight, and taught him so well that he can almost whip his teacher!" His sacred and enduring personal friendships with men whom he met in stern polemic strife showed that there was a knightly strain in his blood, and that the grace of God could temper the wrath of the most pugnacious of men. But he never forgot what he believed to be a foul blow; if he forgave it, it was a watchful and · discriminating sort of forgiveness that guarded against the repetition of the offense. He aimed to be just; if in any case he failed, it was an error not of intention but of temperament.

These were wonderful times in Tennessee Methodism. Over six thousand souls were added to the Church during this year within the bounds of the Conference. McFerrin, with Green, Paine, Pitts, Maddin, and other men of might and mark, led the hosts. But, Nehemiah-like, they builded with a trowel in one hand and a sword in the other. " We had various conflicts," says McFerrin. " The Campbellites, the Baptists, the Episcopalians, the Universalists, and others—all had to be met. And the *Christian Advocate* at Nashville was the greatest offender of all, because it was the organ of Methodism in the South-west, and boldly defended the doctrines and usages of the Church." They " had to be met," says our Methodist warrior, who from his editorial watchtower kept a sharp lookout for all sorts of enemies, and sallied forth with eager haste to meet them. To us at this distance from those stormy days it looks like running amuck when he enumerates Campbellites, Baptists, Episcopalians, Universalists, and others. Who were "the others?"

10

TRIPOD, PULPIT, AND PLATFORM.

THE Tennessee Conference met at Gallatin October 18, 1843. No Bishop being on hand, A. L. P. Green was elected President, and McFerrin Secretary, with J. W. Hanner as assistant. It was a notable occasion. A new and beautiful church was dedicated, the sermon being preached by the Rev. Fountain E. Pitts, the wonder of his contemporaries. That sermon was a marvelous one even for him. Bishop Soule arrived and took the chair the next morning. His visit was highly appreciated by the Tennessee Methodists, among whom, by the operation of a series of events which no human sagacity could have foreseen, he was destined to spend the last years of his grand and heroic life, and among whom he finally found his grave. During the past year that great preacher, Thomas L. Douglass, had died, and the Conference mourned for him as for a father. Rev. A. L. P. Green preached his funeral sermon amid the tears of the brethren, of whom some were his spiritual children, and all of whom had felt the impress of his lofty character and the inspiration of his evangelical eloquence. Another preacher—the Rev. Thomas L. Young, described as "a burning and shining light in the Church of God"—had died during the year, and Dr. Thomas Maddin preached his memorial sermon before the Conference.

At this session of the Conference delegates were elected to the ever-memorable General Conference to

(146)

be held in New York in May, 1844. Robert Paine, J. B. McFerrin, A. L. P. Green, and Thomas Maddin were chosen, with F. E. Pitts and J. W. Hanner as alternates. This was a strong delegation, and their influence was felt in the tremendous struggles of that body, whose action affected so powerfully the future history of American Methodism and the destinies of the nation.

The Rev. Dr. William Capers, then one of the Missionary Secretaries, was present at this Conference. McFerrin says the body was blessed with his presence and labors, and the words were doubtless well chosen. When under the full afflatus of the Holy Spirit in the pulpit, Dr. Capers combined the venerableness of an apostle with the glow of a seraph. On the missionary platform he was convincing and persuasive, producing not the immediate effects of ordinary popular oratory, but leaving lodged in the minds of his hearers the great basic principles that underlie the work of Missions and in their hearts the fragrance of his saintly spirit. No two good men could be more unlike each other than he and McFerrin. There was no positive repulsion, but they never got close together; their angles did not fit and interlock, as is sometimes the case with men of marked and diverse individuality.

The interests of the *South-western Christian Advocate* and his own love of motion and wholesome excitement led McFerrin to make another tour of Conferences this year. The reader will be pleased to have the notes of these journeyings in his own words:

"The Conference over, and a little business adjusted, I visited Paris, Tennessee, the seat of the Memphis Conference, Bishop Soule presiding. Dr. Capers was also present. The session was pleasant, and the brethren, by strong resolutions and material aid, sustained the *Advo-cate.* This Conference convened on the first day of November, but as I had to visit the Mississippi and Alabama Conferences, my stay was short. I made the trip in a buggy, accompanied by the Rev. S. S. Yarbrough.

"On the 24th of November, 1843, I left Nashville on board the 'Westwood,' a new steamer, Capt. Simon Bradford in charge. My point of destination was Bayou Sara, Louisiana; thence by rail to Woodville, Mississippi. The boat was fine and the accommodations excellent, but the weather was very unfavorable—rain, fog, and high water for the season, and a boat heavily laden. Loading and unloading in rainy weather was very disagreeable. And the fog! No one can fully appreciate a fog on the Mississippi River unless he has been in its midst. Our voyage was tedious, yet I managed to spend the time pleasantly. I read Dr. Olin's travels, wrote letters for the paper, perused the Bible, preached on board, and had agreeable company. At Bayou Sara I was detained twenty-six hours waiting for a railroad train to convey me a short distance to Woodville, Mississippi, the seat of the Conference. It was Saturday evening before I arrived at Woodville. The Conference had been in session since the Wednesday preceding. Bishop Soule was presiding. The Conference was very pleasant. Dr. Capers and Dr. Janes, both of whom were afterward elected Bishops, were present—one as Missionary Secretary, the other as Agent of the American Bible Society. These brethren added much to the interest of the Conference proceedings. The collections for the Bible cause, Missions, education, etc., were large and liberal. Woodville was in the heart of a fine cotton-producing country, and the inhabitants of the town and vicinity were intelligent and generous. Among the most princely Christians of the times was Mr. Edward McGehee, who resided near Woodville. He gave liberally to the cause of Christ, and stimulated others in their good deeds. The Conference still favored the *South-western Christian Advocate,* and treated the editor with marked attention and Christian courtesy.

"The session closed, in company with several of the preachers, I left Woodville on Saturday, on board the ' Brilliant,' and reached New Orleans on Sunday morning in time for service; heard Dr. Capers preach, and preached twice myself—afternoon and evening. My home at New Orleans was with my old Nashville friend, H. R. W. Hill.

"In company with Dr. Capers, I went from New Orleans, across the Lake and Gulf, to Mobile, Alabama. The voyage was rough, and most of those on board the ' Fashion' were seasick; but notwithstanding we were driven out to the Gulf I made the voyage without any inconvenience. This to my traveling companion was a wonder. He had been across the Atlantic, and suffered in this short Gulf voyage, and supposed I would have been forced to pay tribute to Neptune.

"Our visit to Mobile was exceedingly pleasant. Dr. Capers and I found a comfortable home at the house of the Rev. Jefferson Hamilton, one of the stationed preachers in the city. Here too I met Dr. Lovick Pierce, who had charge of one of the Mobile Churches, and Dr. Jesse Boring, the presiding elder of the district.

"Two missionary meetings were held during the Sabbath—one each for the children and young people. The first was in the afternoon at Dr. Pierce's Church, the other at night in Dr. Hamilton's Church. The speakers at the last meeting were Drs. Pierce, Capers, and myself. The occasion was one of great interest. To speak between two distinguished Doctors, such as Pierce and Capers, was no easy task. I made the best effort I could. Before I left Mobile I had presented to me a silver cup, with my daughter's name engraved, as a testimonial of regards of the managers.

" During my absence the paper was left in charge of the Rev. P. P. Neely, who was stationed at McKendree Church. At the Conferences I attended strong commendatory resolutions were passed."

From the time of his return from this tour until the middle of April following he was busy in closing up the accounts of the paper, preparing his report for the General Conference, and in conducting the editorial department.

It was a time of much anxiety and painful foreboding to prayerful and thoughtful Methodists in all parts of the country. As in earthquake countries a peculiar electric influence in the air forebodes to man and beast the approach of the dread convulsion of nature, so, as the time set for the General Conference drew near, the Church seemed surcharged with elements that portended disturbance and disaster. The institution of domestic slavery, which the framers of the Government had put into the Constitution, and which the fathers of the Church had not been able to control by any settled and successful policy, had long caused local irritation, which had now extended until the whole body was in a state of feverish excitability. The agitation, repressed at Cincinnati in 1840, was a smothered fire that soon broke out afresh. The Northern conscience was not allowed to sleep by the Abolitionists of all shades, from the furious fanatic who was ready for blood-shedding as the shortest and surest path to Negro emancipation to men like Olin and Fisk, who, though caught in the swirl of the agitated waters, never had any heart for the fraternal strife—only drifting with sad hearts with a current that was too mighty to be resisted by human power

Nobody could expect McFerrin to be silent under these conditions. "Several articles," he says, "were written with reference to the approaching General Conference, and much solicitude was felt as to the result of the deliberations of that body. I tried to believe, and so expressed myself, that the conservative element was strong enough to counteract the purposes of those who were unconditional and noted Abolitionists. We of the South deprecated the division of the Church. Still, we intended to contend for our constitutional and scriptural rights."

Certainly he was ready to contend for all his rights, at all times and under all circumstances. The "several articles" to which he refers took the moderate Southern view of the question at issue, and indicated that the writer was going to New York hoping for peace, but ready to fight rather than surrender any right or submit to any wrong. Here was the issue: The Northern conscience was in irreconcilable antagonism to what the South claimed to be "constitutional and scriptural rights." One fact should be noted here that ought to moderate the dogmatism of extremists on either side and plead for charity toward all the actors in these stormy scenes of 1844. The opinions of the parties to this strife might be mapped geographically. Beginning in New England, where the anti-slavery feeling was most intense, it shaded off as one progressed through the Middle

States over the mountains into the Valley of the Ohio. Leaving the Ohio, the contrary sentiment grew in intensity in a corresponding ratio, attaining its maximum in the extreme South-west. Whether we their successors will be fairer and broader than our fathers depends upon our ability to comprehend and apply the lessons of history. Great and good men as they were, they were but human, and they were controlled by their environment. There were exceptions to the statement that opinions concerning the questions under debate were determined by environment; and conspicuous among these broad-minded and philosophical men was Joshua Soule, the simple grandeur of whose character will stand out in bolder and still bolder relief when posterity shall look at him fully cleared of the mists of contemporaneous passion and misjudgment.

THE METHODIST CATACLYSM.

THE fateful General Conference of 1844 drew near. While the peach-trees were blooming and the oak-buds swelling, in the spring of that year, the delegates from all parts of the United States made their way to New York, the seat of the General Conference. McFerrin left Nashville April 11, in company with A. L. P. Green, on board the "Utica," Capt. Peppard, bound for Pittsburgh, Pennsylvania. Their boat was small but comfortable, the fare good, and the officers polite. The water being low in the Upper Ohio, and the craft not swift, the voyage to Pittsburgh took eleven days. Short pauses were made at Louisville and Cincinnati. No two more companionable men ever met on a journey by land or water. If all they said to each other and to their fellow-passengers during those eleven days and nights could be recalled, what a medley of theology, ecclesiastical politics, philosophy, wit, humor, and Christian experience would sparkle on this page! Green, in anecdote, had a perennial freshness that never cloyed, a quaint humor that gave his listeners quiet but pleasant surprises, and a philosophical turn of mind that penetrated to the very heart of many a puzzling problem. McFerrin's flow of animal spirits was well-nigh inexhaustible; his originality in thought and expression seemed doubly original when re-enforced by his unique manner of utterance, and the persons he met were provoked to talk or charmed to listen. . That trip down the

(153)

Cumberland and up the Ohio, though long, was not tedious to these two much-speaking delegates from Tennessee.   At Pittsburgh they met a number of delegates on their way to New York.   Sunday was spent in that smoky metropolis.   The Rev. Messrs. Holmes and Kinney, Methodist pastors in the place, were courteous and kind, and made their stay pleasant.

The General Conference opened its session in the Green Street Church, New York, May 1, 1844, and was the ninth delegated General Conference of the Methodist Episcopal Church.   McFerrin was assigned a home at Mr. Samuel Harper's during the session, with the Rev. Tobias Spicer, of the Troy Conference, as his room-mate—of whom he speaks kindly as " a man of age and respectable talents, and withal very amiable and pious."   Mr. Harper was a retired merchant, a man of means and large hospitality.   His wife was a charming Christian lady.   They both did all they could to make their Southern visitor comfortable, and won his lasting, grateful affection.   The trouble that darkened the ecclesiastical sky cast no shadow upon the social sweetness of this Christian home, though it is most probable that his Brother Spicer and his host and hostess were arrayed against the doughty editor from Tennessee.

Bishop Joshua Soule opened the Conference—with what conflicting hopes and fears it is not difficult to conjecture when we know how deeply he loved the whole Church, and that no man in all that august body understood more fully than himself the gravity of the occasion, or with the prescience of true ecclesiastical genius could forecast more fully the course of the cyclone that might be let loose by its action.

As a member of the body and a participant in its proceedings, McFerrin's impressions and opinions have a historical value that will justify the use of his own language in relation to it—a value still more enhanced by the fact that the words were written thirty-one years afterward and when his heart was warm with the feeling of fraternity that put him in the very forefront of the men who were then leading in the work of reconciliation among the two great branches of American Methodism:

" The body was large, consisting of clerical delegates from every Conference in the United States. Five Bishops were present—namely, Soule, Hedding, Andrew, Waugh, and Morris.

" In the organization of the Conference I was elected chairman of the Committee on Itinerancy. This was one of the standing committees, and was considered one of great importance. The committee consisted of thirty-three members. Of the Southern delegates there were on this committee William Patton, Edward Stevenson, E. F. Sevier, W. M. Wightman, William A. Smith, and others. The editors were appointed a committee to supervise the publication of the reports of the proceedings of the Conference, including the speeches delivered by the various members.

" I was one of this Committee of Publication, which added much to my other labors; yet I was in fine health, and could endure much work.

" It was somewhat remarkable that so many of the standing committees were headed by Southern men as chairmen. For instance, on Episcopacy, Robert Paine; on the Book Concern, William Winans; on Education, H. B. Bascom; on the Bible Cause, Lovick Pierce; and on Itinerancy, J. B. McFerrin.

" This session of the General Conference (1844) was the most memorable in the annals of American Methodism. The question of slavery had to some extent agitated the Church from its organization, threatening at times the peace, harmony, and even unity of Methodism. But the action of the General Conferences of 1836 and 1840, it was supposed, had put a quietus upon the subject, and it was hoped that in the future the different portions of the Church would have rest. The Southern Conferences had been in a measure proscribed; but they seemed to submit, especially as the Conferences of 1836 and 1840 had rebuked the Abolitionists, and had decided that slave-holding was no legal barrier to any office in the Methodist ministry in States not permitting emancipation. The whole Church in the South seemed to enjoy peace after the General Conference of 1840 had adjourned. Not so in New England. The spirit of abolition raged more furiously than ever; yet the South looked to the Bishops and to the conservative Conferences north of Mason and Dixon's line for protection, and felt secure till a short time before the meeting of this General Conference in 1844.

" Soon after the Conference had convened it was rumored that Francis A. Harding, of the Baltimore Conference, had appealed from the decision of his Conference, by which he had been suspended from the functions of the ministry for holding slaves which he had acquired by marriage. And it was further reported that Bishop Andrew, who resided in Georgia, had by inheritance and marriage become a slave-holder. These two cases occupied a large portion of the session, and resulted in the separation of the Church into two distinct organizations.

" The history of this event is written, and is familiar to most of American Methodists. I was with the South, of course, believing that the General Conference by the votes of the majority violated the provisions of the constitution of the Church and inflicted a great wrong on Harding, Bishop Andrew, and the whole Church in the slave States.

" To the delegates from the Southern Conferences the blow was sad and serious. They met soon after the resolutions *deposing* Bishop Andrew had been adopted by the majority, and I never witnessed such a meeting. For a season silence prevailed in the whole assembly, and this was succeeded by sobs and tears; every member present was distressed beyond measure. To separate from the Northern members, to divide the Church we loved, and to make a breach in the ranks of our glorious Methodism, was too much to be contemplated without feelings of the deepest grief. But what else could be done? What other method could be adopted? We could not return to our people with this illegal and proscriptive action upon us. To submit was in effect to abandon the Church in the South and to turn away from God's heritage. The enemies of Methodism in the South would rejoice; our people would no longer adhere to us, and we would be disbanded. We *protested.* Our protest was considered. A plan of separation was adopted, and the Southern delegates returned home to report the disaster and to do the best they could under all the disabilities laid upon them."

This statement is succinct and honest, and, from McFerrin's point of view, correct. The same facts have been given a different coloring by men equally well informed and no less honest than himself. Where is the truth? Not in the speeches of the great and good men who with all the vehemence of passionate sincerity contended with each other and for the right as they saw it; not in any partisan account of the struggle written while yet the scars of the combat remained. Majorities are apt to be overbearing, and minorities are apt to be suspicious and sensitive. Hard-headed Northerners and hot-headed Southerners came thus into collision, and, like chlorine and nitrogen, exploded in the concussion. McFerrin stood with the South, and had no perceptible misgivings as to the justice of its cause. His friend Janes took the other side as confidently and conscientiously. Their personal friendship' was never broken while they both lived. In the renewed fellowship and fuller light upon which they have since entered in the world of spirits they now see the truth that we are here so slow to learn and so quick to forget—that with good men radical differences of opinion may co-exist with gracious agreement in spirit.

The General Conference re-elected McFerrin editor of the *South-western Christian Advocate* without opposition. "This," he declares very naturally, "was gratifying after a struggle of nearly four years, and especially in view of the conflict going on in the General Conference on sectional questions."

On June 11, 1844, this memorable General Conference adjourned, and American Methodism, after plunging the Niagara of separation, entered upon its passage through the whirlpool of conflict that rushed and roared before it.

DISPUTING, PREACHING, TRAVELING.

McFERRIN and Green, after the close of the General Conference, returned homeward by Niagara Falls and the Northern Lakes. The scenery on the Hudson, the sublimity of the mighty cataract, the sweep around the lakes and the vast prairies, so engaged their delighted attention that the hardships and inconveniences of travel were forgotten. The companionship of Green would have enlivened a journey across the dreariest desert. The things they saw and the things they said would enliven as well as enlarge this narrative if either of them had put them on paper; but we have only a glimpse of the brother preachers on this journey, which was then a great undertaking, but which can now be made while the earth is making two of its diurnal revolutions on its axis. At Chicago McFerrin bought a pair of mud-boots, which he "found of great advantage in wading in the water and slush of the prairies." Those were the days when what was called stage-riding in Illinois was "to pull off your coat and throw it into the vehicle, shoulder a fence-rail, and walk alongside of it to be ready to help prize it out of the mud-holes." This bit of philosophizing was indulged in by McFerrin in the retrospect of this visit to Chicago. "Had we been possessed of foresight as well as after-sight, we could with a few hundred dollars have made purchase of real estate that within a few years would have made us millionaires. *So be it.* A great fortune is sometimes a

great calamity, not to say an absolute curse. Godliness
with contentment is great gain. If a man gain the
whole world, and lose his own soul, what advantageth
it him?" Had he by such a purchase become a million-
aire Methodist preacher, it is possible that the handling
of all that money would have destroyed the efficiency
of one of the most faithful servants the Church ever
had. Not many rich men seem to be called to this ministry, and very few indeed are called to get rich after they
enter into its sacred covenants.

By the time he had gotten back to Nashville McFerrin found that the storm of sectional conflict had burst
in all its fury. It was evident that a still fiercer battle
had to be fought between the North and the South.
Dr. Bond, the able editor of the *New York Christian
Advocate*—a Marylander by birth—took ground against
Bishop Andrew and against the separation of the Methodist Episcopal Church into two General Conferences.
Dr. Elliott, of the Cincinnati *Christian Advocate*,
though one of the committee of nine which submitted
the Plan of Separation, soon changed position and
wheeled into line with Dr. Bond, opposing a division of
the property of the Church as provided for therein.
This opened the war, and it flamed all over the length
and breadth of the Church. The *South-western Christian Advocate* had no circulation north of the Tennessee
line. In the States of Kentucky and Missouri both the
New York and Cincinnati *Advocates* circulated widely.
The ground being thus preoccupied, McFerrin anticipated much difficulty in introducing the Nashville paper
into territory north of it. But this was the thing he
wished to do, and he set about it at once. The red flag
was flying, and his place was at the front. It was soon

manifest that the course of the Southern delegates in
the late General Conference would be sustained almost
unanimously by the Southern Annual Conferences.
Primary meetings were held, resolutions of approval
were adopted, and the calling of a Convention recommended. The Annual Conferences convened in the
latter part of the summer and early in the autumn along
the Northern border. McFerrin attended the Kentucky
Conference, held at Bowling Green, at which Bishop
Janes presided. By an overwhelming vote this Conference adhered South, electing delegates to a General Convention to be held in Louisville, Kentucky, May 1, 1845.
Bishop Janes presided with great fairness, allowing all
questions at issue to be fully discussed. The leading
spirit in the Conference was Henry B. Bascom: with
him were Kavanaugh, Hinkle, Crouch, Brush, and others, who were men of might in the Church. Under
the stress of the existing circumstances, and the persua-
sions of McFerrin, the Conference resolved to sustain
the Nashville paper, and from that time forward its circulation greatly increased in Kentucky. Its moral influence was equal to an army of occupation.

McFerrin also attended the Missouri Conference,
which convened in the city of St. Louis, Bishop Morris
presiding. The question of the times was before that
body, of course. The Missouri Methodists were Southern in their feelings, but they had seen but one side of
the controversy, as the New York and Cincinnati organs
of the Church had hitherto been read by them almost
exclusively. The Missouri delegates in the General
Conference at New York had affiliated heartily with
their Southern brethren. W. W. Redman, James M.
Jamison, William Patton, and J. C. Berryman stood

11

firmly with them during the whole of that protracted struggle. After the adjournment of the General Conference Mr. Jamison, for some cause, changed his mind and threw the weight of his influence on the other side. Being a popular man, he created some interest, and seemed to be rallying a formidable party. He came to the Conference session confidently expecting to prevent the Missouri from going with the other Southern Conferences. Strong ties of personal friendship drew and held to him a number of the preachers who were disposed to sustain him in his war against the Southern movement. The business of the Conference was conducted in a most courteous and equitable manner by Bishop Morris. Ample opportunity was given for discussion. The debate was animated, the sturdy, fearless Missourians giving and taking heavy blows with the unflinching courage characteristic of them. The Southern sentiment was too strong to be successfully resisted. The Missouri Conference took position with Kentucky, approving the action of the delegates to the General Conference, and electing delegates to the proposed General Convention.

The Tennessee Conference convened this year at Columbia, Tennessee, October 4, 1844. Bishop Janes presided, and preached to the great satisfaction of the members of the body and visitors.

The action of the General Conference in the case of Bishop Andrew and F. A. Harding, and the subsequent proceedings in reference to the division of the Church funds and the organization of two General Conferences, were calmly considered. A committee of nine—consisting of F. E. Pitts, Joshua Boucher, F. G. Ferguson, G. W. Dye, P. P. Neely, W. D. F. Sawrie, John W.

Hanner, A. F. Driskill, and R. L. Andrews—was appointed to consider and report on the subject. In their report the committee unanimously approved the action of the Southern delegates at the General Conference, commended their own representatives, and recommended the election of delegates to the General Convention to be held in Louisville May 1, 1845. The delegates chosen were Robert Paine, J. B. McFerrin, A. L. P Green, F. E. Pitts, A. F. Driskill, John W. Hanner, Joshua Boucher, Thomas Maddin, F. G. Ferguson, and Robert L. Andrews. In earnest words the Conference deprecated the division of the Church, but affirmed its solemn conviction that nothing short of separation could save Methodism in the South, unless the Northern majority would " reconsider and repair the injury already done." That proviso was well meant, but the words were wasted. The action taken when the storm was rising would not be repealed when it was in full sweep over the land. If the leaders on both sides had been mere politicians maneuvering only for party success, a compromise might have been possible. But the paradox meets us, as we review the struggle, that the very goodness and sincerity of the actors on both sides made the breach irreparable. The North acted under the compulsion of a conscientious conviction that domestic slavery was an evil with which its ministry could have no complicity. The South acted under a sense of solemn and imperious necessity, believing (and most truly) that to yield to the demands of the North would be the annihilation of Methodism in the slave-holding States. The conditions that produced this peculiar and unhappy situation, in which a people so noted for the liberality of their views and the warmth of their affections were thrown into irreconcilable differences among themselves, were not of their own creation. The actors in that final struggle had to bear the brunt of other men's mistakes and to incur the risk that posterity might heap upon them the opprobrium due to criminals rather than the sympathy due to martyrs. They were godly, earnest men on both sides. That here and there was found among them an ecclesiastical politician who sought to trim his sails to catch the popular breeze we may concede; but they were few in number, and were rated at their real value by both sides in the end.

The Methodists in the North, in the meantime, were agitated to an equal degree. The editors and others on both sides, who were in the thick of the fight, naturally became more vehement and bitter as the controversy went forward. It is dangerous to some persons to spar for sport; in giving and returning blows they get more and more heated, and what begins in sport ends in a fight. So it is with men who begin a discussion such as that which was then going on. They began with sincere protestations of regret that any cause of difference existed, and with expressions of mutual esteem and affection; but the blows they dealt became harder and harder until, the barriers of Christian moderation once broken over, they astonished one another by the exhibition of a virulence hitherto unsuspected and incredible. If the warriors of the period of which we are now speaking could now read in paradise all that they then wrote and spoke, they would be astonished at themselves. There was bewilderment, misgiving, and sorrow, as well as wrath and bitterness, on both sides; but in such a crisis the currents of passion are usually so strong that all are swept before it—the conservative and the radical alike. So it was in this instance. A solid North seemed to confront a solid South, while there were tens of thousands on this side and on that whose only difference was the accidental one of geographical position. It was a hard time for men of quiet spirit and peaceful inclinations. The good Bishop Hedding will furnish an illustration. He "adhered" North, but he loved the whole Church, and his heart was sorely grieved at the necessity for taking sides. He presided at the session of the Philadelphia Conference in the spring of 1846. On the presentation of candidates for deacon's orders the following proceedings (as quoted from a contemporaneous record) took place:

"The Rev. Mr. Quigly proposed that each candidate should be asked whether he was a slave-holder, and whether he was engaged in any of the modern movements for promoting the abolition of slavery; and none dissenting, the question was severally asked as follows:

"Bishop Hedding: 'Are you a slave-holder?'

"To which all answered, 'No.'

"Bishop Hedding: 'Glory to the Conference! not one of their souls is stained with the blood of Africa.'

"The Bishop then informed the candidates that he was about to put a question the meaning of which, before put, he was in duty bound to explain as he understood it. By an 'Abolitionist,' in the sense he was about interrogatively to use it, he meant not one who was opposed to the holding of men in bondage for mere gain, for the purpose of growing rich by slave labor, to grind the face of the poor that the master might be exalted; but he meant those who uncharitably denounced men who happened to have been born in a slave-holding State, born in the possession or heritage of slaves, who treated them well; who nurtured the sick and the poor; who did not hold them for mere gain, but for good; who did the best they could under all circumstances. After this explanation the Bishop said that in asking them if they were Abolitionists he meant to ask if they were prepared to curse all who were slave-holders, under any and all circumstances.

"Bishop Hedding: 'Are you an Abolitionist?'

"To which all answered, 'No.'

"Bishop Hedding: 'Thank God! there is none of them willing to cut off the heads of our Southern brethren because they happen to hold slaves.'"

About this time Bishop Andrew published a letter to the Methodists of the South and South-west, which is so characteristic of the man and of the times that we make room for it here:

BISHOP ANDREW'S LETTER.

To the Methodists of the South and South-west:

Dear Brethren:—The position in which we are mutually placed by the organization of the Southern Conferences into the M. E. Church, South, will probably be a sufficient apology for the liberty I take in thus addressing you. The Southern Annual Conferences having all, without exception, ratified the acts of the late Louisville Convention, and elected delegates to represent them in the approaching General Conference at Petersburg, I may be allowed to congratulate you on the unexampled unanimity of sentiment and feeling with which this movement has been carried through, the peace which pervades the new Connection, and the security and equality of ecclesiastical rights thus effected. Southern Methodists now feel that their privileges are not held at the mercy of a wild and wayward fanaticism which makes its caprice and its power the rule of action, and which by mere courtesy allows slave-holders to continue members of the Church. Instead of the quadrennial struggle which in former times made the General Conference the arena of strife, and which continually threatened to put the ecclesiastical power in conflict with the laws of the

Southern States, and periled the gospel which it has ever been the peculiar mission of the Southern ministry to preach to the poor, we now look forward to peaceable sessions, where the appropriate work of the Christian ministry will alone claim attention, deliberation, and action.

Will you allow me to express the wish that, in behalf of the approaching General Conference—the first to be held under the new organization—frequent, fervent, and united prayer may go up to the throne of the heavenly grace that God may vouchsafe to the members composing that body the unction, rich and full and free, of the Holy Ghost, without whose light and aid nothing good can be effected? Send up to the mercy-seat from every family and Church altar, and from every closet throughout our extended Zion, mighty and believing prayer that Jesus, who bought the Church with his own blood, and who as the great Shepherd of souls careth for the flock, may be present in our midst; may preside in our counsels, to enlighten, direct, and restrain; that the deliberations of that body, which must be so influential for good or evil through all time to come to the Church of which it is the highest council, may in all their issues be for the manifestation of the truth and the advancement of the cause of God among men. The best ability and strength of the Church will be found in that assembly; yet our trust is not in an arm of flesh, but in the living God. His presence and blessing will give prosperity, will insure a successful result to all the measures for the weal of the Church which may be devised and instituted on that important occasion. And we are confident that the prayer of faith, presented most humbly but most earnestly, and in the all-prevailing name of Jesus, will secure to us the Divine guidance and blessing.

Indulge me with the liberty to add that it is most devoutly to be wished that the commencement of our history as an independent Church, under the exclusive jurisdiction of a Southern General Conference, may be marked as a memorable starting-point in a fresh and glorious career of holiness and usefulness. Let us labor and look for a large baptism of the Holy Ghost, such a deepening of the work of grace in the Church as has not heretofore been known. Let preachers and people pray for a mighty and sweeping revival of religion; seek it from God, through Christ, night and day, in solitary and united supplication, and never rest until our stations, circuits, and districts feel the hallowed influence of the promised Spirit of grace, and rejoice in the triumphant march of truth and holiness over the land. Then, and then only, shall we have old-fashioned, primitive, genuine Methodism, when believers are advancing in holiness, and sinners by scores and hundreds are turning to God. For this high and holy end all Church organizations should exist. Where this is not accomplished all else is vain; the body has no quickening spirit, no vital, heaven-kindled soul; the temple has no indwelling divinity. I beseech my brethren in the ministry to seek a fresh baptism of the Holy Ghost, to give themselves with redoubled energies to their one great work of calling sinners to repentance and building up believers in their most holy faith; to bestir themselves that the blood of souls be not found upon their garments. Let us gird ourselves afresh for the duties appropriate to our present circumstances, maintaining an unwavering loyalty to Christ and an unfaltering faith in God's promise, and looking with confidence to see the work of holiness increasing and spreading over these Southern lands.

And now that the God of peace may direct and sustain the whole Church, membership and ministry, in the blessed paths of peace and holiness, and save us all in his heavenly kingdom, is the devout prayer of yours, most affectionately,

JAMES O. ANDREW.

Oxford, April, 1846.

The Conference, by a very hearty vote, indorsed McFerrin's course as editor. He had borne himself so wisely and courageously in the great debate, and had managed the financial interests of the paper with such energy and skill, that this expression was no more than his due.

The election for President of the United States took place while the Conference was in session. Bishop Janes, Dr. Paine, A. L. P. Green, McFerrin, and a few others, dined with Mr. James K. Polk, the Democratic candidate, on the day of the election. He seemed perfectly calm, and entertained his guests as though nothing uncommon was on hand. At night, though the returns were coming in from the surrounding country, he went to Church and was perfectly collected, manifesting outwardly little concern as to what might be the result.

The session was long, harmonious, and remarkably spiritual in its tone. In the presence of the great issues before them, and looking to a future as yet all unknown to them, they were solemn and prayerful. The closing scene was one of great power. The brethren sung with spirit the hymn then popular, " He died at his post." Every heart was moved with its martial strains, and shouts of praise went up to God from these men in whose hearts glowed the spirit of heroes and martyrs The origin and tone of this lyric illustrate the times in which it was written. The Rev. Thomas Drummond was born in Manchester, England, January 27, 1806; came to this country in early life, and after his conversion joined the Methodist Episcopal Church; was licensed to preach, and admitted into the Pittsburgh Conference. After filling several appointments in that Conference he was transferred by Bishop Soule to the Missouri Conference, in 1835, and stationed in St. Louis. He had preached on Sunday, June 14, with his usual perspicuity and power, expressing with great pathos the joyful feelings which animate the possessor of strong Christian faith in view of heaven. He was attacked with cholera the same evening, and died the next day. Though suffering great pain, he died in triumph, saying, among other things, " Tell my brethren of the Pittsburgh Conference that I died at my post." Young, brilliant, and popular, his sudden death among strangers produced a profound impression, especially upon his old comrades of the Pittsburgh Conference, who were deeply moved when his message reached them,

reminding them that he thought of them in his dying moments, and wished them to know of his stead-
fastness to duty.   They wept for him as a brother beloved, and Dr. William Hunter, a member of the body,
who had much of the sentiment and music of poetry in
his soul, put the dying message of the young preacher
into this lyric, which became very popular with our song-
loving and heroic fathers.   There may have been better
poetry in some of Hunter's " Select Melodies;" but the
pathetic incident on which it was founded, and the stirring air to which it was sung, gave this production of his
muse a wide popularity while the facts were fresh in the
minds of the people, and the militant spirit animated its
self-denying and heroic ministry.   The music and fire of
the old times will come back to a gray-haired soldier of
the cross here and there as he reads the lines:

Away from his home and the friends of his youth
He hasted, the herald of mercy and truth;
For the love of his Lord, and to seek for the lost;
Soon, alas! was his fall—but he died at his post.

The stranger's eye wept that, in life's brightest bloom,
One gifted so highly should sink to the tomb;
For with ardor he led in the van of the host,
And he fell like a soldier—he died at his post.

He wept not himself that his warfare was done;
The battle was fought and the victory won;
But he whispered of those whom his heart clung to most,
" Tell my brethren, for me, that I died at my post."

He asked not a stone to be sculptured with verse;
He asked not that fame should his merits rehearse;
But he asked as a boon, when he gave up the ghost,
That his brethren might know that he died at his post.

Victorious his fall, for he rose as he fell,
With Jesus, his Master, in glory to dwell;

He has passed o'er the stream, and has reached the bright coast,
For he fell like a martyr—he died at his post.

And can we the words of his exit forget?
O no! they are fresh in our memory yet;
An example so brilliant shall never be lost;
We will fall in the work—we will die at our post.

So our fathers sung, so they lived, so they died. It is
not strange that, forty years afterward, McFerrin felt
his heart stirred with the old fires as he recalled the singing and the shouting at Gallatin.

This was a stormy year to McFerrin. He had a
memorable controversy on the subject of dancing by
Church-members, the particulars of which may be omitted here, but in reference to which, long years after, he
used these emphatic words: "I now here and again record my settled opinion that dancing is a pernicious practice, and should not be allowed in the Church. Persons
who will persist in dancing, after a fair trial to reform
them, should be cut off. *I never knew a devoted Christian who loved to dance or who indulged in the habit.*"
The Tennessee Conference, by a unanimous vote, sustained his course in this controversy.

His characteristic energy is indicated by the fact that,
immediately after the adjournment of the Tennessee
Conference, McFerrin accompanied Bishop Janes to the
Memphis and Mississippi Conferences—the first at Somerville, Tennessee, and the second at Port Gibson, Mississippi. The journey was pleasant, and his reception
by the brethren kind. His course as editor was warmly
approved, and the patronage of his paper greatly increased. How it was edited during these long absences
he does not tell us; so we infer that Dr. Elliott was still
helping him in that work.

On his return from Mississippi he had what he called
"a slight discussion" with the Rev. Dr. Tomlinson on
the question of the division of the Church. Tomlinson
was an eloquent preacher and a good writer, but in this
instance he became entangled in strange inconsistencies.
After making a strong speech in the Kentucky Conference favorable to the Southern view, he changed to the
other side, and his articles on that side were very severe.
There was a defect in his organization at some point,
and his life ended tragically. He became mentally de-
ranged, and died, it was said, by his own hand. His
erratic course may be explained by his mental infirmity,
then unsuspected by his robust and ready antagonist.
Had McFerrin known the fate that was impending
over the brilliant Tomlinson, the tone of this "slight
discussion" might have been modified.

From this time until the first of May [1845] the discussion was animated. McFerrin was in the very focus
of the fight. He had many a tilt with Dr. Bond, of the
New York Christian Advocate, and with Dr. Elliott, of
the *Western Christian Advocate*, at Cincinnati—both
men of ability, large attainments, and controversial skill.
Prior to 1844 these papers had a very large circulation
in the West. Notwithstanding their powerful influence,
the Southern cause was well sustained, and Kentucky
and Missouri were saved to that side. In both these
Conferences there were noble and talented men who
came to the front when wanted—Bascom, Kavanaugh,
Henkle, the Stevensons, Crouch, Ralston, Latta, Redman, Berryman, Patton, and others. It is noticeable
that in this conflict McFerrin took a graver tone, and
was more circumspect in his use of words than was
usual with him. The momentous issue sobered while

it nerved him. He struck straight, hard blows that were very effective, but it is evident that he tried to rise above the low plane of party feeling and to speak and write in view of the judgment and eternity. "In all this controversy," he wrote after most of the combatants on both sides were dead and buried, "I strove to do all parties justice, and I never willfully misrepresented any one, nor did any one intentional injustice." Bond and Elliott and Tomlinson may have thought differently at the time, but none will dispute his statement now. No honest man ever does "intentional injustice" in a controversy, but when the blood is hot in battle the temptation to take a nigh-cut to victory is so strong that the best of men who feel that duty constrains them to enter the arena of debate will do well to watch closely and pray much.

In the issue of his paper for April 11, 1845, McFerrin announced that it was out of debt. The strong man rejoiced with a pardonable exultation to be appreciated by only two classes of persons—those who have had the burden of debt lifted from them, and those who have vainly longed for such deliverance. "Owe no man any thing," was his rule. He was a Connectional debt-payer for his Church, and in his private business affairs he was most punctual. He guarded well this point at which too many are weak—and he had his reward.

AT THE LOUISVILLE CONVENTION.

THE Convention at which the Methodist Episcopal Church, South, was organized met at Louisville on the first day of May, 1845. McFerrin was in his place as a delegate at the opening—with what feelings no one who was not an actor in that notable historic assembly can now fully realize. Commiseration and admiration are mingled in the review of what they said and did—commiseration on account of the sad necessity under which they were constrained to act; admiration for the wisdom and heroism displayed by them in meeting the great crisis that directly involved the destiny of Methodism, and indirectly, to no small extent, that of the nation. A majority of the delegates were clear in the solemn conviction that separation or the practical annihilation of Methodism in the South were the only alternatives. They were praying men, and moved as under the eye of God. They knew the temper of their section of the Union. They loved the Church they had builded in the South with so much toil and self-sacrifice, and felt that its preservation was a paramount duty devolved upon them in the order of divine providence. But they were not the men to sever heartlessly the ties that bound them to their brethren in the North. Upon their minds rushed a flood of sacred memories common to all American Methodists. The asperities of recent controversy had not obliterated the personal friendships of brethren who, though divided in opinion, were yet

(174)

one in heart. The men who wept in heaviest sorrow at New York, when first they felt they must separate, were stirred still more deeply at Louisville when the time came for them to take decisive action. They did not falter. Separation was a foregone conclusion; the people had voted it, and to their representatives in convention assembled nothing was left but to formulate their wishes and launch the new ship upon a stormy sea. They were equal to the emergency, moving with deliberation, skill, and courage at every step. The passions that had been roused in the struggle of the late General Conference at New York, and in the contests along the border, were doubtless seething in the hearts of some of the delegates who had been in the thickest of the fight, and who came up to the Convention still smarting from its wounds. Here and there was one of those men of war who, like stormy petrels, seemed to be happiest in the midst of a gale like that which was now agitating the waters upon which the old Methodist ship was tossing. These men were men of like passions with us their descendants, who have fretted and fumed at one another with far less provocation. They were not wholly free from the alloy that has mixed itself with every council of the Church from that first one held at Jerusalem, under the presidency of the wise and conservative Apostle James, down to the last General, Annual, District, or Quarterly Conference of the Methodists of to-day. But they were a body of men who rose to the height of a great occasion, among whom were real intellectual giants. They were many of them men who had braved the hardships of the wilderness and wrestled with the dangers and difficulties of the frontier. They were men who had led the march of Methodism in its conquests southward and westward.   There were others who had proved themselves powerful athletes in the contests that had taken place on the floor of the General Conference the year before at New York.   But they were men of God, Christian ministers, in whom had been developed a depth of sensibility not found in any other calling.   They addressed themselves to the work before them with stern determination.   The crisis was too grave and the exigency too pressing for oratorical effusiveness or sentimentality on the floor of the Convention, but they spoke and voted with swelling hearts. If the secret history of the body could be written, it would reveal the fact that many a bed-chamber was a place of agonizing prayer, and many a pillow was wet with tears.   The conditions that made their movement compulsory were, as has been already said, largely inherited conditions.   Neither the majority nor the minority in 1844 can justly be held responsible for the separation of the Church.   The seeds of that separation were planted by the hands that planted Methodism in America, and the prophecy of it was written in the Federal Constitution and in the Constitutions of the several States.   That the catastrophe—if a catastrophe it was in its final results—was precipitated, and its consequences aggravated, by the infirmities and passions of the men of 1844 on both sides, may now be freely admitted by all without incurring the imputation of unfairness or impeaching the character of the dead who can not speak either in explanation or defense.

A glance at the *personnel* of the body will not be out of place here.   Many of these men have written their names in imperishable lines in the history of the Church, and no one will complain that these allusions to them are brief. The caliber and quality of this body, if its constituent elements were subjected to a close analysis, would entitle it to rank among the most august assemblies that have ever convened in America:

From Kentucky there was Bascom, kingly in person and eagle-like in the sweep and elevation of his thought; Edward Stevenson, a polished shaft and strong; Kavanaugh, a giant in the pulpit, a child in the guileless simplicity of his nature; Crouch, a powerful preacher and a trusted counselor; Brush, endowed with common sense, wit, and grace; McCown, scholarly, stately, and saintly; Ralston, devout, gentle, fervent, whose pen translated heavy theology into the language of the people; and William Gunn, who sung like an Asaph, and was as sturdy as a Covenanter.

Missouri sent up Andrew Monroe, a man whose modesty was equaled by his good sense, conscientious to the minutest point, not often heard on the floor, but much given to prayer in secret; Wesley Browning, a man who walked with God, and was loved and trusted by the people; William Patton, a leader of large mold and finely toned, eloquent, impulsive, generous, magnetic; Boyle, sagacious and brainy, yet guileless and sweet-souled; and Thomas Johnson, the apostle to the Indians, a man of affairs and a man of prayer.

From the high hills of the Holston country came Catlett—able, eccentric, earnest, hiding under his stern exterior a warm, loving nature; Stringfield, an "all-round man," strong as a writer, preacher, and polemic; Timothy Sullins, an Israelite without guile, simple-hearted, wise, grand; and Creed Fulton, the apostle and pioneer of Christian education.

From the Tennessee Conference there was Robert

12

Paine, a Church statesman, Christian educator, McKendree's biographer, a Bishop who *filled* the office; McFerrin, of whom inquire in these pages; Green, a Nestor in council and a Fabius in ecclesiastical strategy; Pitts, the traditions of whose extraordinary eloquence will linger with the descendants of the men and women who heard it while through hill and valley flow the waters of the Tennessee and the Cumberland; Maddin, a man of God, beloved of men; Ferguson, a straight-edged Methodist, able to lead, and leading wisely; and Andrews, wise and good and strong.

From North Carolina there was Bryant, whose preaching was high Christian thought set to music; Leigh, a prince in the pulpit, a weighty man in Church affairs, the peer of Fisk and Olin, and like-minded; Blake, sunny and saintly; Carson, a mighty evangelist who won many souls to Christ; and Doub, a self-taught Apollos, mighty in the Scriptures.

From the Memphis Conference there was Moses Brock, a rare genius—weird, wise, unworldly, given alternately to inspired moods and eccentric humors; Harris, "the father of the Conference," in speech classic, eloquent, logical, aglow with the touch of the live coal from the divine altar; McMahon, full of Methodist fervor, Irish wit, and vigorous, good sense; and Joyner and Davidson, true men and strong.

From Arkansas there was Harrell, the pioneer preacher, unconsciously heroic and grand; and Truslow and Custer, men of the same stamp.

From the Virginia Conference there was John Early, a militant saint and a mighty man in peace or war; Thomas Crowder, polished as a courtier and pure and unbending as a Puritan; William A. Smith, leonine of port, invincible in logic, a gladiator who in high debate always stood unconquered in the arena; Abram Penn, gifted and godly, whose early death cut short a career that would have carried him to the very highest honors the Church could bestow; Doggett, styled the Cicero of Southern Methodism, the intellectual fire in whose grand discourses kindled into a still brighter, holier flame when the Spirit descended upon him in pentecostal power; Cowles, a strong, pure, and polished minister of Christ; and Dibrell, grave and grand, whose preaching was like the roll of Sinaitic thunders.

From the Mississippi Conference there was Campbell, a man who knew men and was a leader of men; Drake, in whom genius and goodness were mingled like the veins in a shaft of finest variegated marble; Watkins, adorned with every grace of manner and trait of character that could entitle him to the name of a Christian gentleman, eloquent in the pulpit, and the delight of every social circle; Winans, a mighty thinker and a master of assemblies, a profound theologian and a wise master-builder, whose name Southern Methodists will not let die; and Jones, clear-brained, unselfish, observant, reflective, who lived to be the historian of Methodism in Mississippi and the connecting link between two generations of Methodists.

From Texas there was Robert Alexander, a mighty man of valor in the army of the Lord, in physical stature a head and shoulders above his brethren, a leader born; Fowler, eloquent, courageous, and steady; and Wilson, strong, brave, and sharp-edged.

From Georgia there was Lovick Pierce, who ranked second to no man in the love and veneration of American Methodists; Evans, a mighter singer, a Nehemiah in church-building, a revivalist whose many converts recruited the Church and peopled paradise; Longstreet, theologian, pedagogue, jurist, author, a marvel of versatility; Glenn, personified common sense; Anthony, an Ironsides modified by Methodism, brave as Luther, spiritual as Fletcher; Isaac Boring, incisive, large-brained, strong-willed; Paine, godly, self-forgetting, beloved in Georgia by white Methodists and black ones; and George F. Pierce, the Bishop that was to be, then a rising star whose fame now fills the Church.

From the Alabama Conference there was Jefferson Hamilton, strong in the pulpit, strong in the cabinet, strong in the field, strong everywhere, a rounded man, holy without asceticism, great without pretentiousness, humble without sanctimoniousness; Jesse Boring, whose pulpit oratory reached climaxes of almost unexampled power, splendidly gifted as a debater; Thomas H. Capers, a man of rare social gifts and effective popular eloquence; Thomas O. Summers, encyclopedic and unique, just rising into fame and entering upon his remarkable career as an editor, theologian, and author; and Greenberry Garrett, a man of large brain and glowing heart.

From South Carolina there was Capers, the future Bishop, a great preacher, founder of the Methodist Missions to the Negroes in the South, whose fame is the common heritage of all Methodists; Wightman, another Bishop *in futuro*, pure, broad, and strong, highly endowed and highly cultured; Walker, adorned with humility, firm of purpose, good and wise; Dunwoody, a rarely eccentric genius whose oddities never led him into sin or folly, keen-sighted, canny, original, trustworthy, a man of one Book, and a man of might; Bond English, sturdy, saintly, and sure at all times; Whitefoord

Smith, a brilliant rhetorician and eloquent preacher, with the heart of a poet and the tongue of an orator; Boyd, a safe, strong man; and Samuel W. Capers, worthy of the honored name he bore.

From Florida there were Smith and Benning, stalwart soldiers fresh from the field.

The sayings and doings of the body may be only glanced at·here. Dr. Lovick Pierce opened its deliberations by reading the second chapter of St. Paul's Epistle to the Philippians, and after singing the hymn beginning, "Come, Holy Spirit, heavenly dove," he offered a most fervent prayer for the blessing of God upon the proceedings of the Convention. The Rev. T. O. Summers was elected Secretary, and the Rev. T. N. Ralston assistant. Bishops Soule and Andrew, in response to a resolution of the body, agreed to preside during the session—Bishop Morris, for reasons satisfactory to himself and to his colleagues, declining so to do. Bishop Soule, on taking the chair, said:

BISHOP SOULE'S REMARKS.

I rise on the present occasion to offer a few remarks to this Convention of ministers under the influence of feelings more solemn and impressive than I recollect ever to have experienced before. The occasion is certainly one of no ordinary interest and solemnity. I am deeply impressed with a conviction of the important results of your deliberations and decisions in relation to that numerous body of Christians and Christian ministers you here represent, and to the country at large. And knowing as I do the relative condition of the vast community where your acts must be extensively felt, I can not but feel a deep interest in the business of the Convention, both as it respects yourselves and the millions who must be affected by your decisions. With such views and feelings, you will indulge me in an expression of confident hope that all your business will be conducted with the greatest deliberation, and with that purity of heart and moderation of temper suitable to yourselves, as a body of Christian ministers, and to the important concerns which have called you together in this city.

The opinion which I formed at the close of the late General Conference, that the proceedings of that body would result in a division of the Church, was not induced by the impulse of excitement, but was predicated of principles and facts after the most deliberate and mature consideration. That opinion I have freely expressed. And however deeply I have regretted such a result, believing it to be inevitable, my efforts have been made, not to prevent it, but rather that it might be attended with the least injury and the greatest amount of good which the case would admit. I was not alone in this opinion. A number of aged and influential ministers entertained the same views. And, indeed, it is not easy to conceive how any one, intimately acquainted with the facts in the case, and the relative position of the North and South, could arrive at any other conclusion. Nothing has transpired since the close of the General Conference to change the opinion I then formed; but subsequent events have rather confirmed it. In view of the certainty of the issue, and at the same time ardently desirous that the two great divisions of the Church might be in peace and harmony within their own respective bounds, and cultivate the spirit of Christian fellowship, brotherly kindness, and charity for each other, I can not but consider it an auspicious event that sixteen Annual Conferences, represented in this Convention, have acted with such extraordinary unanimity in the measures they have taken in the premises. In the Southern Conferences which I have attended I do not recollect that there has been a dissenting voice with respect to the *necessity* of a separate organization; and although their official acts in deciding the important question have been marked with that clearness and decision which should afford satisfactory evidence that they have acted under a solemn conviction of duty to Christ and to the people of their charge, they have been equally distinguished by moderation and candor. And, as far as I have been informed, all the other Conferences have pursued a similar course.

It is ardently to be desired that the same unanimity may prevail in the counsels of this Convention as distinguished, in such a remarkable manner, the views and deliberations and decisions of your constituents. When it is recollected that it is not only for yourselves and the present ministry and membership of the Conferences you represent that you are assembled on this occasion, but that millions of the present race, and generations yet unborn, may be affected in their most essential interest by the results of your deliberations, it will occur to you how important it is that you should "do all things as in the immediate presence of God." Let all your acts, dear brethren, be accompanied with much prayer for that *wisdom which is from above.*

While you are thus impressed with the importance and solemnity of the subject which has occasioned the Convention, and of the high responsibility under which you act, I am confident you will cultivate the spirit of Christian moderation and forbearance; and that in all your acts you will keep strictly within the limits and provisions of the "Plan of Separation" adopted by the General Conference with great unanimity and apparent Christian kindness. I can have no doubt of the firm adherence of the ministers and members of the Church in the Conferences you represent to the doctrines, rules, order of government, and forms of worship contained in our excellent Book of Discipline. For myself, I stand upon the basis of Methodism as contained in this book, and from it I intend never to be removed. I can not be insensible to the expression of your confidence in the resolution you have unanimously adopted, requesting me to preside over the Convention in conjunction with my colleagues. And after having weighed the subject with careful deliberation, I have resolved to accept your invitation and discharge the duties of the important trust to the best of my ability. My excellent colleague, Bishop Andrew, is of the same mind, and will cordially participate in the duties of the chair.

I am requested to state to the Convention that our worthy and excellent colleague, Bishop Morris, believes it to be his duty to decline a participation in the presidential duties. He assigns such reasons for so doing as are, in the judgment of his colleagues, perfectly satisfactory, and it is presumed they would be considered in the same light by the Convention. In conclusion, I trust that all things will be done in that spirit which will be approved of God, and devoutly pray that your acts may result in the advancement of the Redeemer's kingdom and the salvation of the souls of men.

The organization of the body for business was effected, and after feeling their way carefully at every step, the great question of separation was taken up. Mc-Ferrin was one of the working members of the Convention. He and the Revs. Leroy M. Lee and William M. Wightman were appointed a committee to report the proceedings—"a very onerous and responsible position," he said; but his co-workers were, like himself, diligent, and their work was fairly done. Their reports were published in the secular papers of Louisville and copied into the Church papers. There was some complaint that the reports made of the speeches were not full enough. McFerrin replied on the floor of the Convention that the resolution under which the committee on the publication of the proceedings acted only required a synopsis thereof; that, if members wanted their speeches published in full, they must write them out and pay for printing them; and then playfully threatened that if the brethren insisted on having their speeches reported at length, he " would try to give them —*rhetoric and all!* " The hit doubtless produced its intended effect. On May 5 Dr. Winans made a great speech on his resolution instructing the Committee on Organization " to inquire whether or not any thing has transpired during the past year to render it possible to maintain the unity of the Methodist Episcopal Church under the same General Conference jurisdiction without the ruin of Southern Methodism." The key-note of this remarkable speech, and of the whole Convention as well, was given in this opening sentence: "Only necessity can justify the meeting of this Convention; expediency could not." This strong statement was then made by this strong man: " He said that slavery was so interwoven with the texture of Southern society that it was impossible for any one to disentangle it, nor can any religious society avoid, if it would, connection with this institution. It is also true that public opinion rallies around this institution with great jealousy; and he who comes to the South, or lives in the slave-holding States, and arrays himself against slavery, disqualifies himself from exercising any influence whatever. He who would oppose slavery can have no influence in the South, civilly, politically, or ecclesiastically." And yet it had been but little more than a decade previous to this time since Virginia and Kentucky had both taken tentative steps looking to the abolition of slavery. The extraordinary change that had taken place was due to the passions that had been evoked by the agitation that had in the meantime prevailed. Dr. Winans saw clearly what was plain enough to all after the event. "He said that the North would never rest until slavery was driven from the Church, if the union be maintained. But," he continued, "we are admonished to pause. I would ask, For what? I can see no prospect of a retraction upon the part of the North." And then he exclaimed passionately: "I would be willing to wait twenty years, to lie down in my grave, if I could believe that finally the difficulty could be amicably settled!" Nobody who knew the great-brained, high-souled Winans could doubt that he spoke truly. And he voiced the conviction and feeling of the Convention. While this conviction of the necessity of separation was undoubtingly held by them, their reluctance to taking the final plunge expressed itself in this resolution offered by Dr. Drake, of Mississippi: "*Resolved,* That the Committee on Organization be, and they are hereby, instructed to inquire into the propriety of reporting reso-

lutions, in case a division should take place, leaving the
way open for reunion on terms which shall not compromise the interests of the Southern, and which shall meet
as far as may be the views of the Northern, portion of
the Church." This was also adopted.

Then this resolution was offered by Dr. William A.
Smith, of Virginia: "*Resolved, by the delegates of the
several Annual Conferences in the Southern and South-
western States, in General Convention assembled,*
That we can not sanction the action of the late General
Conference of the Methodist Episcopal Church, on the
subject of slavery, by remaining under the ecclesiastical
jurisdiction of this body without deep and lasting injury
to the interests of the Church and the country; we
therefore hereby instruct the Committee on Organization that, if, upon a careful examination of the whole
subject, they find that there is no reasonable ground to
hope that the Northern majority will recede from their
position, and give some safe guarantee for the future security of our civil and ecclesiastical rights, they report
in favor of a separation from the ecclesiastical jurisdiction of the said General Conference."

Of Dr. Smith's able speech of two hours' length only
this one point is given here: "The General Conference,"
he said, "had ceased to exert a conservative influence
upon the political union. The South could not remain
in the Connection without promoting the agitation and
excitement of the whole country upon the subject of
slavery. To keep up this state of things would soon
dissolve our political union. Our separation, therefore,
is highly important to the union of these States." That
was a plausible paradox from his point of view; ecclesiastical separation was necessary to political union!

Dr. Lovick Pierce said no Church ever provided any law for a prospective division; that the only law that could justify a Church in dividing into two ecclesiastical jurisdictions was *necessity*. This law, he contended, existed in the present controversy, in that we had reached a point where such legislation as would save the North would ruin the South, and such as would save the South would ruin the North.

In these words the great Georgia preacher formulated the statement which will be accepted as the judgment of posterity.

Dr. William Capers, "in a few able and eloquent remarks, advocated the resolution, and set forth with great earnestness the absolute, undeniable, irreversible *necessity* of an independent organization."

Then spoke George F. Pierce, who was in the blossoming-time of his genius and fame. He was bold, rhetorical, fiery, urging that separation, or independence, as he called it, was necessary for the preservation of the Negro missions. "Are those missions," he demanded, "which, like green spots in the wilderness, dot the face of those sunny lands, to be swept with ruin?" He had no prejudice against the North; but whether there be peace or war as to the principles of the government, powers of the episcopacy, and the like, he could never stand by and see the spiritual prospects of the Negro in the South put in jeopardy. He longed to see the day when Methodism, precious and blessed, should in the Southern country rise in the majesty of her strength and the tenderness of her love, and move abroad, untrammeled and free, in her godlike work of blessing and saving the souls of men of all conditions and in all circumstances of human life. He besought the Convention to interpose no let or barrier to her progress, but give free scope to her energies, that in her errands of love and compassion she might go to the bedside of the dying Negro and point his fading eye to the brightening glories of the cross and the immortality beyond.

Dr. Longstreet traversed the whole ground of controversy in a masterly legal argument, emphasizing the view that, instead of weakening the union of the States, the proposed " separation of the Church government" would strengthen it. In closing, he apostrophized Methodism in a way that struck a responsive chord in that body of Methodist preachers: " Let us, with our new organization, try to get back to primitive Methodism. I speak not of its externals, some of which never legitimately belonged to it, but of its inward graces. I speak of its former zeal, which glowed with equal fervor amidst the miasm of the lowland swamps and the healthy breezes of the mountains, which led the Methodist preacher to seek the lost sheep of the fold of Christ whithersoever they wandered. I speak of that Methodism that preached not only on stated days and at stated times, but which preached at all times and in all places—in the chapel, the hut, the kitchen, the grove, the wilderness—to fathers, mothers, husbands, wives, parents, children, masters, servants; which never entered a house without a word for the Lord, and never left it without praying a blessing upon it; which planted the standard of the cross on the spot which we occupy ere the elk and the buffalo had left it; which pushed on its labors until at times exhausted nature sunk under them. When I thus speak of Methodism let me not be understood as claiming for our sect all the religion there is in the world. Far from it; there is as pure religion in the other

Churches as in ours. I am no sectarian. If I possess one Christian virtue, it is love for all that love and serve the Lord Jesus Christ; but I confess I feel a kindling emotion, allied to the moral sublime, when I contemplate Methodism, personified in such men as our Nolly, whose funeral obsequies were performed by himself, whose dirge was sounded by the winter winds, whose winding-sheet was the snow-drift, and whose monument was the sturdy oak of the forest—found by the woodsman frozen on his knees, and buried in the attitude of prayer. Of myself I will not glory, of my Church I will not glory; but of such as these I might become a fool in glorying, and all Christians would pardon me, if not join me."

Dr. Paine reviewed the situation in a calm, cogent, candid way; and "sat down amidst loud cheering from every part of the assembly." It is amusing to notice that he defended his friend, Dr. Bascom, from the charge of "radicalism," and retorted on his assailant, Dr. Bond, by charging that his (Bond's) name stood "appended to a petition to the General Conference of 1824 for *lay delegation!*" These golden sentences closed his speech· " Methodism claims, and actually does possess, a self-adjusting energy. It adapts its economical rules and jurisdictional principles to the world as it finds it. It exists in monarchical governments, it is found in republics, it makes its lodgment in every latitude, in every zone; and everywhere it is the conservator of existing law, of order, of public peace. It is no friend of discord; but it goes forth to soothe the sorrows it can not prevent, to alleviate the burdens it can not remove, to gild the dying hours of the poor sufferer in life's pilgrimage, and to point his closing eye to the glories of immortality.''

H. H. Kavanaugh, of Kentucky, said epigrammatically that he and the border Conferences went with the South because the South went with the Discipline, and argued with great force to sustain that declaration. Addressing himself to his Southern brethren, in conclusion, he said: " While you maintain principle I will be found in your ranks; your people shall be my people; where you go I will go; where you die I will die; with you I will be buried, and with you I will rise in the morning of the great day, when truth and purity will meet their just reward."

F. E. Pitts, of Tennessee, spoke "with force and pathos," closing with a declaration of his firm purpose " to adhere to true Methodism as set forth in the Discipline and maintained by the Church in the South."

Moses Brock, of the Memphis Conference, said he represented " a border Conference, bounded on the north by the Ohio River, extending down the Mississippi River five hundred miles or more, including a fine country, chivalrous people, many Christians, and a great many Negroes "—a climax or anti-climax—which did he intend?

William McMahon said he had been listening three days longer than Job's friends held their peace, but now, he supposed, he must open his mouth. The reporter said: " He was so rapid in his flights of eloquence that I could not keep pace with him. His speech produced much merriment and applause."

Joseph Boyle, of Missouri, said that he had come to the Convention with cherished impressions that a separation was not necessary, but since he had witnessed the discussions, and heard the representations of the brethren from all parts of the South, he was fully satisfied that the separation was inevitable. He should therefore vote for the resolution, and felt it due to himself to make this avowal, believing that it was understood by the delegation from Missouri that though the necessity with them might not be so imperious, yet, making common cause with the South, it was the interest and duty of Missouri to go into the Southern organization.

When the vote was taken on the resolution setting up the new Church organization, it was adopted by 293 ayes to 3 noes. That it may be preserved in this connection it is herewith inserted:

"*Be it resolved by the delegates of the several Annual Conferences of the Methodist Episcopal Church in the slave-holding States, in General Convention assembled,* That it is right, expedient, and necessary to erect the Annual Conferences represented in this Convention into a distinct ecclesiastical Connection, separate from the jurisdiction of the General Conference of the Methodist Episcopal Church as at present constituted; and accordingly we, the delegates of said Annual Conferences, acting under the provisional Plan of Separation adopted by the General Conference of 1844, do solemnly declare the jurisdiction hitherto exercised over said Annual Conferences by the General Conference of the Methodist Episcopal Church *entirely dissolved;* and that said Annual Conferences shall be, and they hereby *are, constituted* a separate ecclesiastical Connection, under the provisional Plan of Separation aforesaid, and based upon the Discipline of the Methodist Episcopal Church, comprehending the doctrines and entire moral, ecclesiastical, and economical rules and regulations of said Discipline, except only in so far as verbal alterations may be necessary to a distinct organization, and to be known by the style and title of the *Methodist Epis-copal Church, South.*"

McFerrin was also made chairman of a committee to prepare and publish a history of the organization of the Methodist Episcopal Church, South. It was published at the office of the *South-western Christian Advocate,* the Rev. Moses Henkle, D.D., performing much of the literary labor of the publication. It was considered an important work, and was the text-book of subsequent publications relative to the separation of the Methodist Episcopal Church and the organization of the Southern branch thereof.

The Convention appointed McFerrin, in connection with the Rev. John Early, an agent to receive proposi-tions for the location of a Book Concern, or Publishing House, to report to the first General Conference of the Methodist Episcopal Church, South.

This sort of service indicated the estimate placed upon McFerrin as an able and willing worker. It was un-derstood that he was almost incapable of fatigue; that he knew the value of accuracy in details; that he was prompt, and had the art of making others so; that his judgment, conscience, and tact could be trusted in money matters; and that no personal interest or side issue would be allowed to divert him from the work of the Church. The only danger of such diversion of his time and energies grew out of his readiness to accept a challenge from some enemy of Methodism who wanted to fight, or to run off to a distant Annual Conference in search of subscribers and good-will for his paper. But not even his relish for polemics, or his editorial ardor, could tempt him to neglect any work he had consented to do. Absolute fidelity was his purpose and his practice.

The sectional conflict was renewed with fresh vigor and prosecuted with great heat after the adjournment of the Louisville Convention. The New York and Cincinnati organs opened their batteries upon the new organization. The Church property question intensified the feeling of the opposing parties. McFerrin was still in charge of the *South-western Advocate,* both as editor and financial manager. Shot for shot, he returned the fire of the big guns at New York and Cincinnati. At the request of the Kentucky Conference Dr. Henkle was appointed assistant editor. He entered upon his duties in the autumn of 1845, and continued in that relation several years. Of him and his work McFerrin says: "He was an able writer and a man of extensive information and much experience. His connection with me as assistant editor was very pleasant. We harmonized in our work, and he rendered much valuable service." This co-editorship was a fit. McFerrin was pugnacious, Henkle was cautious; McFerrin had a special turn for business, Henkle for books; McFerrin liked to travel, and had a genius for the platform, while Henkle liked the quiet of the *sanctum,* and would rather write than make speeches; McFerrin looked to the subscription-list and the cash account, Henkle never tired of the pen, the scissors, and proof-reading. They were happily complementary to each other.

Soon after Dr. Henkle's arrival in Nashville, and assumption of his editorial duties, McFerrin was again on the wing, visiting several Annual Conferences, preaching as he went, flashing forth his wit and pathos from the platform, of which neither his hearers nor himself ever tired, and extending the circulation of his paper. In Kentucky and Missouri particularly his visits were

13

beneficial to the publishing interests he represented and
to the Church, in the midst of the prevalent excitement. His eloquence was inspiring and his courage was
contagious. He confirmed the faithful and encouraged
the faint-hearted. The very presence of the athletic,
bold, buoyant editor of the Church organ acted as a
tonic to weak nerves and feeble faith. When he spoke,
doubt was dissipated, fears vanished. He had superflu-
ous energy enough to put a whole regiment of lymphatic
idlers in motion; audacity enough to say what he pleased,
with good judgment that tempered and kept it from
harming him or his cause; enthusiasm that swept every
thing before him; and tact that turned every incident
and accident to advantage.

The conflict was very fierce along the Ohio River,
and it was judged important by the brethren of Kentucky that they should have a paper on their border.
This was attempted in Cincinnati and Louisville, but resulted in pecuniary loss. The principal management of
this paper devolved on H. H. Kavanaugh, D.D. (afterward Bishop), and Dr. S. A. Latta. Kavanaugh was a
great preacher, and Latta's " Chain of Sacred Wonders "
—a book that enjoyed a considerable popularity in its
day—showed that he was fluent and fervent with the
pen. But neither of them seemed to have any providential call (if they had the gifts) for editing and publishing newspapers. Their venture in that line soon
failed, and the *South-western Christian Advocate* kept
the field and magnified its office as the exponent of the
principles of the Southern Church and its able and fearless defender along the border. A defender it was, but
with McFerrin as its inspiring genius its methods of defense were often very aggressive. No man understood

better or acted more continually upon the military axiom that the attacking force is most likely to win the battle. The momentum of assault counts. He always persuaded himself that he was not the aggressor, but after the fight begun he pressed his foe at every point. His grief at parting with his brethren of the North, whom he. sincerely loved, and for the necessity laid upon him to take a position at the front in the fight against them, was largely compensated by the pleasure he enjoyed in a tournament with a foe worthy of his steel. He was a sort of clerical *Cœur de Leon* who, being always ready for a fight, found a fight always waiting for him somewhere.

EDITING, FINANCIERING, FIGHTING.

THE Tennessee Conference met at Huntsville, Alabama, October 22, 1845. By episcopal appointment A. L. P. Green presided. Delegates were elected to the first General Conference of the Methodist Episcopal Church, South, to convene at Petersburg, Virginia, May 1, 1846. They were: J. B. McFerrin, Robert Paine, F. E. Pitts, A. L. P. Green, J. W. Hanner, A. F. Driskill, E. W. Sehon, S. S. Moody, and F. G. Ferguson. Dr. Sehon had belonged to the Ohio Conference, but because of the action of that body in reference to Bishop Soule and the Southern Conferences he, with Dr. S. A. Latta and G. W. Maley, "adhered South," and were received into the Tennessee Conference. Dr. Sehon was complimented with a seat in the General Conference, and all three were transferred to the Kentucky Conference. This was gracefully done. The Tennessee preachers withheld what has ever been considered a high honor from one of a number of strong, good men of their own body, that this stranger from Ohio should have brotherly recognition among them. Sehon was a courtly, sunny-faced, sunny-souled Christian gentleman, with the mien and bearing of a prince and the glowing soul of a Methodist preacher, whose presence gave a new charm to every pleasant circle he entered and brought comfort to every sorrowful home and heart with which he came in contact during the long and useful years of his life in Kentucky To

(196)

those who knew him the sight of his name on this page will illuminate it like a sunbeam. He was raised to high honor in the Church to which he came, constrained by principle, and amid the asperities of those stormy days he was the one man against whom malevolence itself brought no accusation, and in whose presence no bitter feeling could live.

McFerrin was soon on the wing again. If he liked to travel and preach and thunder on the platform, and canvass for his paper, he was surely a happy man; if he did all this from a sense of duty, he was surely a faithful one. Early in the year 1846 he visited the South, and attended the Alabama Conference, rousing the Alabamians by his remarkable sermons, his inimitable Conference talks, and his platform speeches that captivated the masses, excited the wonder of the wise, and brought showers of dollars into the treasury of the Church. He had become well known throughout the the South and South-west; his coming was looked for with interest, and his presence was like a breath of highly oxygenated air. When it was announced that he was to preach the people crowded to hear him; if he rose to speak on the Conference floor, the brethren leaned back in their seats with expectant faces, expecting that he would say something to think, laugh, and perhaps cry over, before he got through.

With Green, Pitts, and Hanner, on April 15, 1846, he started to Petersburg, Virginia, the seat of the first General Conference of the Methodist Episcopal Church, South. They chose a roundabout way to get there. They took passage to the mouth of the Ohio River on the "Sligo," a pleasant little steamer; from thence to Louisville, Kentucky, in time to take part in the first anniversary of the Missionary Society of the Methodist Episcopal Church, South. The Rev. John Lane, of Mississippi, conducted the opening religious services, and Green and McFerrin made the addresses. The Rev. Edward Stevenson, Corresponding Secretary, read an abstract of the annual report of the Board of Managers, the first of the new organization—the Methodist Episcopal Church, South. This report was very gratifying to McFerrin. "More than SIXTY-SEVEN THOUSAND DOLLARS," he wrote exultingly, "has been contributed during the past year in aid of the glorious enterprise of evangelizing the world; all the drafts in favor of the Missions will be promptly honored; and thus the experiment has fully proved that the South can and will sustain the cause of Missions, and will take a conspicuous place among her sister Churches in sending the gospel to the poor."

He made a note of the fact that on the Ripley Circuit, Kanawha District, the Rev. Samuel Black and his people adhered South, and was happy to say that the Southern cause was prospering on the border.

At Louisville they changed boats, and passing Cincinnati, McFerrin and Hanner went to Maysville with the Rev. W. M. Grubbs and Dr. Adamson, a noble layman, who continued to be McFerrin's life-long friend, who desired them to spend the Sabbath-day in that place. Here they were the guests of Col. Respass, a worthy citizen, a respectable lawyer, and a Methodist, in whose house Dr. Hanner became acquainted with Mrs. Coleman, the widowed daughter of their host. This lady afterward became the wife of Dr. Hanner. On Monday they rejoined their brother delegates, and reaching Wheeling, they took stage-coach for Cumberland, Maryland; here they took the railroad train for Baltimore, where they had a cordial reception, and McFerrin made one of his rousing missionary speeches. Then they went on to Washington, where they visited their fellow-Tennessean, President Polk; and thence *via* Richmond to Petersburg. A trip to Europe would now be a smaller matter than that journey from Nashville to Petersburg. The world shrinks as the Church of God enlarges in its resources and aims.

The General Conference was composed largely of the men who had the year before met in convention at Louisville. Among the new men, however, there were several of notable character: From Kentucky, C. B. Parsons, an elocutionist of magnetic quality, who could make even commonplaces seem lofty, and who was immensely popular in his day; Jonathan Stamper, a man of uncommon logical force and master of a ready wit that served him well on occasion; N. B. Lewis, a noble type of a Methodist preacher belonging to a family of preachers. From Holston there were Elbert F. Sevier and D. Fleming, strong, good men. From the Memphis Conference there was William M. McFerrin, brother of the subject of these chapters—a solid, plain man of hard, good sense and deep piety; and John T. Baskerville, a man of strong and noble character and cultured mind. From South Carolina there were Charles Betts and Nicholas Talley, men of fervent zeal for God and of great weight of character in that Conference. From Georgia there was William A. Parks, who was devout toward God as he was unbending toward men, a Regulus in courage and a Bernard in devotion. From Alabama there was the ornate and polished E. V. Le Vert. From the Arkansas Conference there was W. P. Ratcliffe, whose strong, symmetrical, handsome *physique* was a fit vehicle for his well-balanced mind and noble spirit. Among the reserves were some of the coming men of the Church, whose names were very familiar afterward: G. W. Langhorne, D. S. Doggett, of Virginia; James Reid, of North Carolina; Alexander Means and J. W. Talley, of Georgia; William Murrah and A. H. Mitchell, of Alabama.

With what wisdom and grace Bishops Soule and Andrew presided over the body; how grandly and graciously Bishop Soule announced his adhesion to the Methodist Episcopal Church, South, and the profound effect produced thereby; how the questions of a hymnal and a publishing house were debated; how William Capers and Robert Paine were elected Bishops, making, with the two former ones, a quartet not surpassed in the real elements of goodness and greatness; how provision was made for a *Quarterly Review*, and Dr. Bascom was made its editor; how book depositories were located at Richmond and Louisville; how John B. McFerrin and Moses M. Henkle were elected editors of the Nashville *Christian Advocate*, William M. Wightman and Thomas O. Summers of the *Charleston Christian Advocate*, and Leroy M. Lee of the *Richmond Christian Advocate;* how A. L. P. Green, H. B. Bascom, and Samuel A. Latta were appointed Commissioners to settle the property question pending with the Methodist Episcopal Church; how John Early was appointed Book Agent; how Dr. Lovick Pierce was elected a delegate to attend the General Conference of the Methodist Episcopal Church at Pittsburgh in 1848, "to express to that body the Christian cordiality and brotherly affection" of their Southern brethren; how Transylvania University was accepted by the General Conference, and Dr. Bascom and Dr. George F. Pierce were recommended as suitable persons for President and Vice-president; how the boundaries of the several Annual Conferences were fixed; how it was resolved to send two missionaries to China, to establish Missions among the Jews in our own cities whenever the door should be opened, and to establish a Mission in Africa at as early a date as Providence should indicate that the way was open; how co-operation with the American Bible Society was pledged; how it was recommended that where there were not churches expressly for the use of the colored people, proper provisions be made for their accommodation in the churches occupied by the whites; how the Discipline of the Church was left unchanged in substance, though its arrangement was somewhat altered; how the men that towered highest in the last year's Convention maintained their altitude in the General Conference; how John Early and John B. McFerrin seemed to be the financial balance-wheels of the one body, as they had been of the other—of how all this was done only this briefest outline can be given here. In the "History of Methodism," by Bishop H. N. McTyeire, the story is told lucidly, fairly, and fully.

In entering anew upon his editorial work, McFerrin reviewed his six years' experience therein, and indicated his spirit and purpose in an article characteristic of the man and of the time in which it was written:

TO THE FRIENDS AND PATRONS OF THE SOUTH-WESTERN CHRISTIAN ADVOCATE.

You have already learned through our columns that the connection heretofore existing between this paper and the General Concern at New York has been dissolved. Hereafter the *Advo-*

cate published at Nashville will be under the exclusive control of the General Conference of the Methodist Episcopal Church, South. It will be an organ of that branch of our common Zion, and will be expected to advocate the peculiar doctrines of Methodism, and to sustain the Discipline of that organization, to which the editors hold themselves responsible, not only as Christians and Christian ministers, but as conductors of a journal which is the property of the Church. Whenever we can not conscientiously discharge our duty as officers of the General Conference, as honest men we will feel bound to retire and allow the proper authorities to select such men as will promote the views and advance the interests of the Church whose servants we are, and for whose prosperity we feel bound to labor.

The writer has been in charge of this paper for nearly six years. He has, according to the best of his ability, discharged the high responsibilities resting upon him. He has seen the Church in her highest state of prosperity extending her borders from the shores of Canada to the wilds of Texas, while her Domestic and Foreign Missions have been greatly enlarged. He has seen the Church in her greatest conflict, and has witnessed with heart-felt sorrow the breach that has been made in the ranks of our Israel. To prevent this disaster he labored until resistance was useless; and when the blow was struck he felt that, with his Southern brethren in common, he was willing to sacrifice himself upon the altar of principle, and fall a victim in support of the rights of conscience which, in his judgment, were infringed by the exercise of a power unsustained by the law or constitution of the Church. Hence, since the memorable Conference of 1844, he has without wavering maintained the principles upon which he acted as a member of that body—principles publicly avowed, and well understood by the Conference when he was placed in the chair editorial of the *Southwestern Christian Advocate.*

And now that he has by re-election, at the late General Conference of the Methodist Episcopal Church, South, been placed in the highly responsible station of conducting one of its organs, he enters upon his labors with a sense of his obligations, feeling that his work is onerous, and that to God and his brethren he will be held amenable for the faithful performance of his duties. He, however, advances to his work with the greater confidence, from several considerations.

1. An experience of several years has satisfièd him that he will have the hearty good-will and cordial co-operation of his brethren in the ministry and membership. The kind indulgence of the former and the liberal support of the latter inspire him with confidence that in time to come there will be no want of zeal upon the part of those interested in sustaining any enterprise of the Church.

2. He gratulates himself upon the fact that he has in the person of his colleague an able and efficient coadjutor, who has already given to the readers of the *Advocate* demonstration of his ability to fill well the station to which he has been called. With a co-laborer of much experience he hopes, then, to make the Nashville *Christian Advocate* a paper worthy the continued patronage of an enlightened and generous public.

And now, friends and brethren, in entering anew upon our toils, we ask the continuance of your prayers, good wishes, and liberal support. We have no *new doctrines* to advance, no *new rules of discipline* to sustain, no untried system upon which we are about to experiment; we are Methodists, Episcopal Methodists— Methodists in doctrine and economy, such as were our fathers; Methodists of the Asburian and McKendreean school. We seek no changes, we ask no new modifications of our well-tried system. It has stood the test and proved itself to be an efficient plan, and we believe one in accordance with the teachings of God's holy word. We love Methodism—Methodism in its simplicity and godly sincerity—that Methodism which is "Christianity in earnest." Converted through Methodist influence, reared and nurtured by Methodists from our infancy in Christian experience, and having been long identified with her in her class-meetings, lovefeasts, and sacraments, and in her ministry, our love for her increases, and we desire that her reputation should remain untarnished and her escutcheon unstained.

It will be our highest pleasure to cultivate peace with all men, and more especially with our brethren from whom we have recently separated. We most earnestly desire that the Northern press should cease its hostility, and allow us to pursue our own course without molestation; but if we shall be compelled still to defend ourselves against the assaults of our *brethren*, we will strive to maintáin that spirit of charity which suffereth long and is kind, and only defend ourselves for the maintenance of truth.

J. B. McFerrin.

This "leader" exhibits in every part of it the pugnacious conservatism, or the conservative pugnacity, that characterized this man who always wanted peace, and was ready to fight for it when to him it seemed needful. "Let us alone," he says with kindly voice; but there is a warning gleam under his eyebrows, and the clinched hand and corded muscles of his arm show that if struck he will not be slow to return the blow.

THE NEW REGIME.

A S was inevitable, a heavy cannonade and a fierce fu-
sillade from the big guns and small-arms of the
North were opened upon the new organization of the
Methodist Episcopal Church, South. The proceedings
of the General Conference were assailed by the New
York and Western *Christian Advocates.* "Myself and
my colleague, as in duty bound," says McFerrin, "defended our Church, and maintained as best we could our
rights and the rights of Southern Methodists. Our success was all that could have been desired." How like him
is this language! He felt in duty bound to strike back,
and if he ever got the worst of any encounter he did
not know it. Editors Bond and Elliott may have felt
the same complacency at the result of the contest. Each
party seemed to be astonished at the acrimony exhibited
by the other, and not without reason. But it does not
follow that they were intentionally unfair or consciously
unchristian in spirit. "In all my controversy," wrote
McFerrin in 1875, "I never intentionally misrepresented
any of the facts involved; neither did I ever intentionally
pervert or misstate the argument of an opponent. I may
not always have been in the right, but I thought always
that I was the advocate of the truth and of what was
acceptable in the sight of God." This solemn assevera-
tion, made after nearly thirty years had come and gone
with their sober after-thought and chastening influence,
may stand.

In October, intent on newspaper success financially, and eager to see and enlarge his growing constituency, he sallied forth on a fresh Western tour, first visiting the Missouri Conference, which held its session at Hannibal, on the Mississippi River, above the city of St. Louis. Bishop Paine presided. It was his first Conference after his ordination. In the chair, in the pulpit, and in the cabinet he exhibited the high qualities that distinguished him during the whole of his long career as a Bishop. This note of McFerrin, written in connection with this occasion, has a happy significance: "As I was very earnest and active in his election to the office of General Superintendent, it gave me much pleasure that he began his work as a Bishop with so much ability and promise of usefulness in his new sphere. He very reluctantly accepted the office, but I doubt not God moved in his election." At the Conference McFerrin stirred the Missourians in the pulpit and on the platform in his usual style. At Palmyra, Glasgow, Fayette, and Booneville, he preached with great immediate effect, and left impressions of himself on his hearers that were never effaced. The energetic, courageous people of the West recognized a kindred spirit in this man, whose talks to them combined so much common sense, mother-wit, and audacity. In one of his letters of travel he moralizes thus on the junction of the Missouri and Mississippi Rivers: "I left St. Louis Tuesday evening at dark on board a fine little steamer. The next morning I awoke and found myself some distance above the junction of the Missouri and Mississippi Rivers. When I looked out upon the placid, clear stream, as it glided gracefully along, I could not realize that I was ascending the Mississippi. I had descended the Illinois and Missouri Riv-

ers; I had read of the marked difference between the
Upper and Lower Mississippi; but still the contrast was
so great that I could scarcely believe my own eyes. The
Mississippi, as I have been accustomed to see it, with its
turbid waters, its serpentine windings, its crumbling
banks, its immense volume boiling and dashing furiously
on, was so different from what I now beheld that I in-
voluntarily exclaimed: 'Surely, there is some mistake in
this matter.' Here was a river clear as the Cumberland, gentle as the Ohio, pure as the Niagara, dotted
with beautiful islands, moving smoothly on amidst the
wild woods and broad prairies, bearing upon its bosom
the productions of a vast country, the resources of which
are just beginning to be developed. But soon it is lost
in the mighty tide of the great Missouri, where its waters mingle with the muddy stream that rolls from the
base of the Rocky Mountains, sweeping through the
most extensive valley on the face of the globe. How
much like the race of man! Pure and unpolluted he
came from the hand of his Creator; but alas! mingling
with the turbid waters of sin his life is defiled, and like
the overswelling flood he carries death and destruction
in his course." If the figure in this extract is a little
strained, the description is good and the theology is sound.

A great revival in Nashville this year was joyfully
recorded in his paper. Fountain E. Pitts, the chief instrument in the work, reported over four hundred conversions, three hundred and eighty-five of whom joined
the Methodist Episcopal Church, South. "Our young
members," he added, "are very lively, and are delighted
with their class-meetings and prayer-meetings." L. C.
Bryan, a sweet-spirited, fervent man, was Pitts's colleague and helper. McFerrin took part in the work as

opportunity permitted, and rejoiced in the gracious results.

His home was gladdened this year by the birth of a
son, who was named for his two grandfathers, James
William, and who lived to manhood's estate. The
tragic death of this noble and beloved son was one of
the heaviest sorrows that fell to the father in his old
age. But no prescience of his fate cast any shadow upon
the brightness of the joy at his birth, or marred the
comfort derived from the promise of his youth and the
nobility of his manhood.

At the Tennessee Conference this year (1846) Bishops Soule and Andrew were both present, and alternated
in presiding. McFerrin was assistant Secretary, the
Rev. F. G. Ferguson being the principal. At this session of the body was organized the "Preachers' Relief
Fund," of which he was appointed one of the managers,
and to which he gave his labors in the very last year of
his life. The fact that Bishop Andrew ordained fifty-
five deacons and Bishop Soule twenty-six elders at this
session of the Conference is a proof of the vitality and
vigor of Methodism at that time within its territory.

At this Conference a resolution was adopted advising
young preachers to refrain from entering into matrimonial alliances until after they have been elected to elder's
orders—"in the general a wise suggestion," says McFerrin. "After many years' observation," he adds, "I am
satisfied that more preachers have finally failed from
premature matches than from any other cause." But
few readers among the preachers will dissent from the
opinion here expressed; but that clause, "in the general," will be a saving clause to many who disregarded the
suggestion, and many more who will do so in marrying.

In nothing are prudence and discretion more needed, and in nothing are they oftener ignored, than in this sacred matter that involves beyond any other one event in human life the temporal happiness and eternal salvation of the parties. This solemn affirmation of this acute observer and outspoken adviser is commended to whom it may concern.

The collection at the anniversary of the Missionary Society was $1,200—a fact McFerrin thought worth recording. At an early period in his ministry he became famous for collections; and if any man ever learned to enjoy the process of depleting the pockets of a willing or unwilling congregation for the Lord's treasury, he was the man.

In November, 1846, he attended the session of the Memphis Conference held in the city of Memphis. On account of "vexatious delays" he did not reach the city until Friday, though he left Nashville on Monday. He recorded only two facts concerning the Conference: Moses Brock was made President pending the arrival of Bishop Andrew, and the missionary collection was $1,200. The collection he never forgot.

During this trip he visited his mother, who then lived near Somerville, Tennessee. His filial affection grew deeper and tenderer as he grew in years and honors, and these periodical reunions were unspeakably delightful to them both. Next to the conscious favor of God, the affectionate pride of a mother in the success of her son is a powerful incentive to a man of noblest mold. During this visit to his beloved mother he met also his brothers, William M. McFerrin and James H. McFerrin, and his two sisters, Mrs. Gilliland and Mrs. Applewhite. His social nature continued sweet and wholesome

14

through all his active public career, for he never allowed ambition to swallow up or dwarf his natural
affection; and as fond as he undoubtedly was of the excitement of the rostrum and contact with crowds, home
was always to him the dearest spot on earth.

From Somerville he went to Natchez, the seat of the
Mississippi Conference. He was powerfully impressed
by " those great and good men," as he called them—Dr.
Winans, Dr. Drake, John Lane, Dr. Thornton, and
Judge Shattuck, who were there in the fullness of their
strength. Of the three first named mention is made
elsewhere in this volume. Dr. Thornton was indeed a
strong man of purest metal, of large nature and glowing
zeal. Judge Shattuck was worthy of the special mention
given him. School-master, preacher, lawyer, jurist, he
was versatile almost beyond precedent, and yet not vola-
tile or wayward. As an evangelist he was in his early
ministry a flame of fire; as a lawyer and jurist he was respected for his learning and revered for his integrity
and benignity; as a school-master he combined the discipline that commanded obedience with the fatherliness
that won the affection of his pupils. His sermons were
models in clearness of method and never-failing common sense; his prayers in the public congregation, as on
mighty waves of faith, bore the assembled worshipers
upward into the very presence of the King Eternal.
Born in Connecticut, he became an ardent Southerner
in his feelings when he came to know the South. In
Mississippi he combined, as perhaps no other man ever
did, the functions of preacher, politician, and lawyer, in
stormy times. He went to California at an early day,
and was the first Judge of the Superior Court of San
Francisco. He was a terror to shysters and all other

evil-doers that came before him; but his kindly face was welcomed on the bench by every litigant and every lawyer who had a good cause. Though he was Southern in his political ideas and affiliations, he cherished an undying love for New England, the place of his birth. At a Democratic convention held in Sacramento City about 1853, a delegate raised a laugh by alluding to him as "his Southern friend from Connecticut." Shattuck rose to his feet with a smile on his kindly face, and said: "I accept the designation which my friend has given me—a Southern man from Connecticut. There are no skies so beautiful to me as those that arched above my childhood's home, no hills so dear as those climbed by my boyish feet, and of all the streams that water the earth none looks so lovely to my eyes as the smooth-flowing Connecticut. I love New England, I love her people, I glory in their history, and I am specially grieved at any indication that they are departing from the faith of the fathers of this Government and setting up false gods." The applause that followed this friendly retort was a tribute to the manliness of the speaker no less than to the patriotic sentiment he uttered.

McFerrin recorded with pleasure the fact that his hostess at Natchez, the wife of the Rev. Berry Jones, was the daughter of Dr. Heman Bangs, of New York. His heart never failed to kindle when he met the name of a fraternal brother who lived on the other side of the sectional line.

With Dr. Henkle he undertook this year the publication of a monthly magazine called the *Lady's Companion*. It was an early literary blossom that did not come to full fruitage, but for a time it was popular and made money. Dr. Henkle, who did most of its editorial work,

was good-natured, sentimental, and devout, and its pages
reflected his spirit. McFerrin looked after its business
management. It was published with the approbation
of the Publishing Committee of the *Christian Advocate*, and with the approval of two of the Bishops. Its
profits were applied to the support of the superannuated
preachers and the widows and orphans' fund. McFerrin
concentrated his editorial work upon the *Christian
Advocate*, and on February 19, 1847, he was able to
make the joyful declaration that it had ten thousand
subscribers, and was out of debt. All who have any
practical knowledge of the difficulties that beset early
religious journalism will pardon this little "hurrah" from
the man by whose energy and skill this achievement was
made.

Some sharp disputes on Christian doctrine during this
year kept his controversial weapons from rusting, and
gave the comforting assurance that he was a faithful
watchman on Zion's walls. We let him tell how it happened:

"During the winter I had quite a sharp discussion, or
controversy, with Talbot Fanning, a preacher of the
Campbellite or 'Christian' order. Mr. Fanning I had
known from our younger days. He was a man of gifts
and respectable attainments. He taught school, and was
President for years of the 'Franklin College,' an institution situated in the country a few miles from Nashville. In his younger days Mr. Fanning was what was
called in this country a 'schismatic,' or a follower of
the celebrated Barton Stone. He was indeed an Arian
in belief. He was very bitter in his opposition to what
he called 'the sects.' He took pleasure especially in
ridiculing the Methodists and the doctrine of spiritual

and experimental religion. Being about the same age, and knowing him personally, I felt it to be my duty to rebuke him. This I did with some severity. We had a number of shots back and forth. Toward his later years he became much mellowed in his spirit and tone. He and I were friends, but we never came together in our doctrinal views. He died suddenly in 1874, and went to his reward. In my last interview with him, a few months before his death, when he was in good health, I remarked to him pleasantly and in good earnest: 'Brother Fanning, you have done good, I have no doubt, as a teacher, but as a preacher your life has been a failure.' He looked seriously at me, and then pleasantly remarked that he would see me some time on that subject and would pay me back. I never saw him again. He had many good qualities, but I thought he was far from teaching the truth as it is in Jesus.

"In the early part of this year I had a long discussion with one of our correspondents on *infant purity.* This discussion occupied some time, and I trust resulted in good. To deny man's natural depravity, and his incapacity to obey God's law before he is renewed, is absurd, contrary to the teachings of God's word, to human experience, and to the facts of human history. 'There is not a just man upon the earth, that doeth good and sinneth not.' (Eccles. vii. 20.) This same question," he added, " was discussed in the papers in after years. I have feared that in maintaining the right of children to Christian baptism and the zeal for Sunday-schools and moral training, there has been a tendency in the minds of many of our preachers and people toward Pelagianism. To be sure we should magnify the grace of God in the salvation of all infant children who die in childhood, or before coming to the years of discretion, but that in no wise changes the teachings of God's word, which affirms that 'all have sinned and come short of the glory of God.'"

At the Tennessee Conference, which met November 3, 1847, Bishops Soule and Paine were both present. On the first day McFerrin preached the annual sermon, to which he had been elected a year previous. His text was 1 Corinthians ii. 4, 5: "And my speech and my preaching was not with enticing words of man's wisdom, but in demonstration of the Spirit and of power: that your faith should not stand in the wisdom of men, but in the power of God." From such a text it is not difficult to infer what sort of a sermon he preached on that occasion. His hearers got Arminian theology undiluted, and the supernatural element of gospel preaching was affirmed with the emphasis of earnest conviction and illustrated from his own experience. In the copious baptism from on high that fell upon the Conference while he was preaching there was a fresh demonstration of the truth of his doctrine. A copy of the discourse was requested for publication, but he declined to furnish it—probably for the reason that he had not written it out, and would rather preach a hundred sermons than write one. He also made one of his characteristic addresses on the occasion of the missionary anniversary. At that time, and for several years, he was the treasurer of the Tennessee Conference Missionary Society.

In company with Bishop Soule and Dr. Edward Wadsworth, he attended the Memphis Conference, which convened at Jackson November 24, 1847. The journey was made in a one-horse barouche, taking five days, including Sunday, which was spent at Waverly, where Dr. Wadsworth preached. Dr. Wadsworth was the successor of Bishop Paine as President of La Grange College. He was worthy of this succession—a preacher of much clearness of thought and spiritual power, a scholar of varied learning who knew what he knew, a teacher who had the happy art of infusing moral influence while imparting knowledge, a man of thought who knew books, a man of prayer who knew God. Virginia, North Carolina, Alabama, and Tennessee all helped to mold and make him what he was, and his track can be traced by a radiant line wherever he went.

McFerrin's veneration for Bishop Soule was never diminished, but rather enhanced, by the familiar intercourse of many years. He gives us a pleasant picture of that grand man as he appeared on this journey: "Bishop Soule, though advanced in years and in feeble health, was a most agreeable traveling companion. He never murmured or complained; he was always cheerful, and always trying to make others happy. Altogether he was among the most affable and agreeable Christian gentlemen I ever knew. I am certain I never saw his superior in these respects."

In 1847 and 1848 McFerrin had what he called "an animated discussion" with the *Christian Record*, a Presbyterian paper edited by several Presbyterian clergymen. "That paper," he says, "made a heavy charge upon the doctrines of the Methodist Church, maintaining stoutly the doctrines of the Westminster Confession of Faith. I had the popular side in the argument. The principal contestant was my friend the Rev. Dr. Lapsley. He and I had been intimate for years. In this discussion we became somewhat heated, or rather my friend did. I tried to keep cool. [Of course he did, but the files show the battle-heat.] We afterward became as in former times, but more intimate. I often preached to his congregation. He was a strong Calvinist, but a good man. He died as he had lived—a worthy Christian gentleman."

During all this time the discussion was kept up with "our brethren of the North" concerning the separation of the Church in 1844. The Southern Methodists were denounced by some of the Northern editors as secessionists and schismatics. The Southerners maintained that the division was by mutual consent, and that the North —if any wrong was done—were the wrong-doers, for they were in the majority, and consequently able to control the action of the General Conference. And so the fire continued at long range, while here and there on the border the fight was hand to hand. The feeling of antagonism was intensified by the action of the General Conference of the Methodist Episcopal Church which met at Pittsburgh, Pennsylvania, where the Plan of Separation was nullified, and Dr. Lovick Pierce, fraternal messenger from the Southern Church, was rejected. The long and bitter controversy that followed makes one of the most painful chapters in the history of American Methodism. McFerrin's position as editor necessitated that he should take a prominent part in this controversy. He affirms that he "tried to preserve a good temper and write in the spirit of candor," and no one will now question his sincerity, whatever may have been thought and said by his antagonists at the time.

The *Christian Advocate*, at this juncture, was like a Gatling gun, revolving rapidly, and scattering its shot on all sides. McFerrin puts the case thus:

"I had a contest about this time with the editor of the

Cumberland Presbyterian, on the doctrine of the possibility of apostasy, and we were again assailed by the *Tennessee Baptist*.

"Indeed, the whole world seemed to be against us. Our doctrines were assailed, our government was criticised, and many of our leading men personally scandalized. And then the controversy with the Methodist Episcopal Church made our sheet in some of its aspects very militant. So it is, men oftentimes have to contend earnestly for the faith. It, however, should always be done in a Christian spirit. Professed Christians should never exhibit angry passions."

These battles will not be fought over again in these pages, but they will be dismissed with this personal affirmation by McFerrin, written after nearly all the combatants were dead, and when he himself was near the end: "In my long editorial life I had many discussions, mostly in defending the creed and polity of the Methodist Episcopal Church. In all these controversies I was sincere in my convictions and in my defense of my Church. Sometimes I indulged in severe remarks, because I thought the circumstances demanded or justified it. Hard arguments have always been considered fair if the words are soft." ·

In the month of March of the year 1848 his second son, John Anderson, was born in the city of Nashville. This son fulfilled his father's wish and prayer by becoming a minister of the gospel, and is now a worthy member of the Tennessee Conference of the Methodist Episcopal Church, South.

During the autumn and winter of this year (1848) he attended at Louisville a meeting of the Missionary Society of the Methodist Episcopal Church, South, and of the Commissioners appointed by the General Conference to settle questions of property between the North and the South; spent a Sunday in Cincinnati, where he preached twice (in the morning at the Southern Methodist Church, and at night at the Church of Dr. Thomas H. Stockton); attended the Kentucky Conference at Flemingsburg, where he heard "two great sermons" on Sunday—one from Bishop Capers, and another from Dr. Bascom—and where he himself preached on Sunday night, and made a speech on Monday night at the missionary meeting. He had a spell of sickness on his return home, but recovered in time to be present at the Tennessee Conference, which met at Clarksville October 26. He dressed his paper in new type, and paid a dividend of seventy-five dollars to each of the patronizing Conferences. At the Conference he heard the Rev. Dr. Noah Levings, Agent of the American Bible Society, whom he called "a great preacher and a grand platform speaker." Visiting his mother on the way, in December he went to Vicksburg, where the Mississippi Conference was in session. Here he met Dr. Levings again, and heard him preach his last sermon. He (Dr. Levings) spoke at the missionary meeting on Saturday night, made a Bible address on Monday night, left on a boat, reached Cincinnati sick of cholera, lingered a few days, and died. "He was a noble Christian minister" is McFerrin's estimate of him. Though rough and sharp in debate, McFerrin was unenvious and hearty in his admiration of the gifts and graces of his brethren.

CONVERSION OF PRESIDENT POLK.

THE story of the conversion of President James K. Polk, eleventh President of the United States, is to be told here. It is outwardly to be dated in 1849, but its genesis goes back farther than that. There are what are called sudden conversions, and there are gradual conversions, so called. But what seems to be a sudden conversion may go back to the first glimmer of spiritual perception and include every gracious influence that has ever touched the soul. The culminating experience may be very vivid to the consciousness, and may be the result of special conditions that crystallize the elements that were mingled in the life, and had been gathering in preparation for this final transforming touch.

At a camp-meeting held at McPeak's Camp-ground, near Columbia, Tennessee, in 1833, McFerrin preached one of his characteristic sermons. Among his hearers was a young lawyer who was rapidly rising to distinction as a public man. The plain common sense and earnest spirit of the sermon commended the truth to the judgment of the clear-headed and honest lawyer, and the Holy Spirit opened his heart to receive the message of God. The gracious impression was indelible. He went away from the camp-ground a convicted sinner, if not a converted man. The words of the sermon still rung in his inner ear, the prayers and songs of the worshiping multitude followed him, and as he rode homeward through the beech forests and fertile fields of

Maury County he was a changed man. Why did he
not make an open profession and unite with the Church?
He was a man of strong political convictions, and was
an ardent partisan, not slow to express his opinions nor
weak in their defense. It may be that he was one of
the many men of this stamp who, in the rush and rough
collisions of politics, defer positive action with regard
to the vital matter of religion for the quieter hour they
hope to find in a coming day. Ambition is hardening,
and delays are dangerous. Happy for them if they are
not swept to destruction by the fatal current to which
they thus yield themselves. The pushing of a political
career too often proves the ruin of a soul. A double
tragedy is enacted when, having broken over the moral
barriers that seemed to stand in the way of success, the
lower nature becomes altogether dominant, and both
body and soul are lost. The very temperament and gifts
that command success in politics are the sources of the
temptations that destroy politicians. The tide that floats .
them dashes them against the rocks. Mr. Polk was
Speaker of the House of Representatives; he was the
presidential candidate of the Democratic party in a canvass of intense excitement; he was President during
four eventful years, with a foreign war on his hands and
a vigilant and able opposition party to fight at every
step; and yet no whisper of detraction was ever breathed
against his personal character. As he was opposed to
that matchless party leader, Henry Clay, it was partisan
fashion to belittle him intellectually; all the wit and
sarcasm of the splendid old Whig party were expended
in drawing unfavorable contrasts between the two men
in this regard; but no one ever insinuated that Polk was
not a true man, pure in his private morals and above all

suspicion of official venality. Now that they are both
dead, all their countrymen are proud of the genius and
patriotism of Clay and of the purity and administrative
ability of his less brilliant but more successful compet-
itor. Mr. Polk was fortified by Christian principle.
Under the pressure of the heavy responsibilities of his
great office he leaned upon the arm of the gracious God
who came so close to him that Sunday, under the brush-
arbor in the hills of Tennessee, while the minister of
Christ preached to him the word of life. His mother
was a member of the Presbyterian Church, and his wife
was a worthy member of the same denomination. Mr.
Polk was a Methodist in sentiment. These facts probably explain his failure to make a formal profession of
his faith in Christ by uniting with the Church. The
thought of separating in Church affiliation from his beloved mother, and from the wife whose virtues and gifts
so adorned her high station as the wife of the chief
. ruler of a great nation, and whose affection was the joy
of his life, was painful to him. His domestic relations
drew him in one direction, and his religious convictions
and affinities in another. Thus pivoted, he let the years
go by, holding to his faith and purpose and hope as a
believer, but doubtless losing much both in the comforts
and joys of religious experience and in the influence he
would have exerted as an avowed disciple of the Lord
Jesus Christ and an active member of his Church.

On his return from Washington City, at the expira-
tion of his presidential term, Mr. Polk settled in Nashville, where he proposed to spend the evening of his
life. He had fixed the purpose in his heart of uniting
with the Methodist Church. This purpose was known
only to himself and his wife. When he was taken with

what proved to be his last illness he sent for McFerrin, revealed the matter to him, and requested to be baptized and received into the Methodist Church. And then, by request of the dying statesman, the memorials of the death and passion of our Lord were administered to him according to the solemn ritual of the Church; and he died, we may trust, in full hope of heaven. His remains were taken to McKendree Church, where the funeral services took place. A great concourse of people were present, and listened to the sermon which was preached by McFerrin from the same text on which was preached the one under which he was awakened and formed the purpose of becoming a Christian in 1833. This sermon will make the next chapter, and some will invest it with a threefold value because of its historic interest, its illustration of McFerrin's modes of thinking and written style, and the solace it will convey to sorrowing hearts in view of death and the grave.

THE CHRISTIAN'S HOPE.

A Sermon Delivered at the Funeral of ex-President James K. Polk, in the McKendree Church, Nashville, Tennessee, June 15, 1849

TEXT: " Blessed be the God and Father of our Lord Jesus Christ, which according to his abundant mercy hath begotten us again unto a lively hope by the resurrection ot Jesus Christ from the dead ; to an inheritance incorruptible, and undefiled, and hat fadeth not away, reserved in heaven for you, who are kept by the power of God through faith unto salvation ready to be revealed in the last time." (1 Pet. i. 3–5)

NOTWITHSTANDING the very intimate relation between Christ and his disciples for three years and more, they did not fully comprehend the nature and design of his mission. When, therefore, he was betrayed, and tried, and condemned, and crucified, and buried, the hopes of his followers seemed to perish : they were as sheep without a shepherd, a family without a head ; their buoyant hopes had been blasted, and, filled with sorrow, they determined to return to their former avocations. But when on the third morning Christ arose from the dead and showed himself to his disciples, and convinced them that it was he, and that he had overcome the power of death and was alive again, their hopes revived and they went forth with strong and unwavering faith in his Messiahship, and looked forward with pleasing anticipation to the glorious rest he had prepared for them in heaven.

It is supposed that in view of these facts St. Peter wrote the words of the text that we have selected as the foundation of the discourse at the present hour: " Blessed be the God and Father of our Lord Jesus Christ, who hath begotten us again unto a lively hope by the resurrection of Jesus Christ from the dead," etc.

Whatever may have been in the mind of the Apostle, or whatever may have stimulated him to pen these words, they certainly, in most appropriate, consoling terms, speak of the hope of the Christian ; and this shall be the theme of our discourse.

Hope! what is it? The term is very frequently employed, and

(223)

it is a term that is not infrequently misapplied. It really signifies
desire and expectation, and always has reference to something future But we oftentimes desire that which we do not expect to
attain, therefore we can not hope for it. We may expect that
which we do not desire; for this we do not hope. But when we
both desire and expect the realization of some future good, then
we hope for the attainment of that good. The Christian desires
the resurrection of the body, the immortality of the soul; he desires to live in the enjoyment of God's favor, and expects, when his
pilgrimage on earth shall end, to make one of the redeemed, and
hopes to share the enjoyment of the blessings of God in heaven.
But this hope, that it may give real comfort to the Christian,
must have ground upon which to rest.

Every Christian should be ready to give a reason of the hope
that is within him. What, therefore, are the grounds of hope to
the Christian? Why does he desire and expect the resurrection
of the body and everlasting life after death? Has he any reasonable ground on which to entertain these delightful views, these
glorious anticipations? We answer that he has a strong foundation, a sure base, on which to build these desires, these expectations.

He believes in the resurrection of the body, the certainty of the
resurrection of the body, in view of the fact that Jesus Christ rose
from the dead. If Christ be not risen, the dead will rise not; and
if the dead rise not, our preaching is vain and your faith is vain,
and we are yet in our sins and are found false witnesses before
God. But if Christ did rise from the dead, if he did take humanity to heaven, if he did carry his crucified and risen body to the
right hand of the Father, and thus became the first-fruits of them
that slept, then we have reason to believe that those who sleep in
Jesus God will bring with him. But questions preceding this arise
in our minds: Did Christ die? did the Son of God veil himself
in the body of the flesh, lead a life of toil and labor and usefulness and of great notoriety? and was he put to death? Did he
die on the cross as a malefactor? was he crucified? did he yield
up his spirit? was he buried in Joseph's tomb? did he come forth
from the tomb the third morning? does he live again? and is he
making intercession for his saints at the right hand of God?
These are important questions, and demand a sincere and satisfactory answer. We are not dependent upon the records of Matthew, Mark, Luke, and John alone for the history of the life and la-

bors and death of the Son of God. That Jesus of Nazareth was born nearly nineteen hundred years ago, in the days of the Cæsars, that he grew up to manhood, that he preached in the temple and in the synagogue and in the streets of Jerusalem, in the land of Judea and throughout Galilee, and wrought many notable miracles and attracted great attention of multitudes of people, both learned and illiterate, rich and poor, can not be doubted at all. We have just as authentic information of the history of the life of Christ and of the notoriety of the Nazarene, as he was called in the days of the Cæsars, as we have of any other event of importance in those ancient times. Jewish history and Roman history, and the traditions of the ancients that came from the fathers in the beginning of the first century, go to testify that Jesus, the son of Mary and the Son of God, lived and preached in the city of Jerusalem, and died within the outer walls of that great city.

His trial was official. He was brought before Pilate, the governor of the province; he was accused, witnesses were introduced, a formal investigation ensued. He was then sent to Herod, who was still king with subordinate power; by Herod he was examined, and then sent back to Pilate. Pilate, after testifying to his innocence and purity of character, affirmed that he found nothing in him worthy of death, yet consented to his execution, signed the death-warrant, and handed him over to the officers to be put to death according to the law. Above his head was written in Greek and Latin and Hebrew, "This is Jesus, the King of the Jews;" and when he was requested to alter the superscription and write "He said, I am the King of the Jews," Pilate answered, "What I have written, I have written." All this trial and this condemnation and this crucifixion and his burial were official transactions, known to the citizens of Jerusalem, and published abroad everywhere throughout the civilized world; and no man, Jew or Gentile, Christian or heathen, pretends to doubt the fact that these scenes of the suffering of the Son of God were endured in the days of Pilate by the son of Mary, the Saviour of the world.

From the grave he rose the third morning and was seen by the disciples, talked with them, ate with them, and at twelve different times appeared in his risen form in such manner as to remove all doubt as to his identity. His disciples went abroad, having seen the Christ, testifying to the world that God had raised him from the dead. Finally he was seen of Stephen, when he was stoned

15

to death; kneeling down, he looked up to heaven and said, "I see Jesus standing at the right hand of God," and committed his spirit into the hands of the risen Saviour. He was seen by Paul, the great Apostle of the Gentiles, who was caught up to the third heaven and saw things unlawful for man to utter, but affirmed that he saw the risen Saviour, who was living at the right hand of the Father. Again this risen Saviour lives in the heart of every genuine believer. Whosoever believes that Jesus is the Christ has the witness in himself, and can say with the ancient patriarch, "'I know that my Redeemer liveth.' I have the consciousness in my heart that the life I live is a life of faith, that it is no more I that liveth, but Christ that liveth in me."

Now, then, Christ having risen from the dead, and the question of his resurrection being forever settled in the mind of the genuine Christian, he believes that those who sleep in Jesus God will bring with him; that all they that are in their graves shall hear the voice of the Son of man and shall come forth; that this mortal shall put on immortality, and this corruptible incorruption, and death shall be swallowed up in victory, and bodies redeemed, like the crucified body of the Son of God, shall be admitted into everlasting habitations, there to join with the multitudes that sing unto Him that hath loved us and hath washed us from our sins in his own blood—to him be glory forever.

But we now proceed to look at the next grand pillar that supports the truth of this doctrine that constitutes the broad foundation on which the hope of the Christian rests: "Blessed be the God and Father of our Lord Jesus Christ, who hath begotten us again unto a lively hope." Here you perceive that there is something more to be wrought in the soul than the mere faith in the death and resurrection of the Son of God. The idea is that we are to be born again and conformed to the image of our risen Lord. All men will be raised at the last day, but some will come forth to a resurrection of damnation; it is only a special or peculiar class that will rise to a resurrection of life. Christ says, "Except a man be born again he can not see the kingdom of God." The text says, "We are begotten again unto a lively hope." Mr. Wesley translates it, "We are regenerated and made new creatures in Christ Jesus by the power of the Holy Ghost, thus becoming the sons of God." The idea of the Apostle is the tender relation existing between the father and child; we are to become children of God by the new birth, by the regenerating power of the Holy Ghost; we are to be changed in our moral nature, transformed into the likeness and image of Christ. Unless this change is wrought in the soul, and unless this glorious transformation is brought about in our moral and spiritual character, we have no well-grounded hope of future happiness. Man may desire to be happy, may desire to escape the sorrows of death, may desire to enter upon the joys of the glorified; but he has no well-grounded hope of entering into those joys until he is born again; born from above, born of the Spirit, adopted into the family of Christ, begotten again unto this lively hope. Wherever this change is really wrought in the soul, and man is brought into fellowship with the Father and with his Son Jesus Christ, he has the witness that he is born of God. Then he can adopt the language of the Apostle and say, " Blessed be the God and Father of our Lord Jesus Christ, who hath begotten us again unto a lively hope by the resurrection of Jesus Christ from the dead." Upon these two grand pillars rests the hope of the Christian—the resurrection of the Son of God, and the realization in our hearts that we have been raised to newness of life in him; the life we are now living is a life of faith in the Son of God. We come now to consider:

THE NATURE OF THIS HOPE.—It is called by the apostle "a lively hope;" not a dead, inactive, joyless hope, but a living, vital principle in the soul, imparting vigor to the mind, and creating exhilarating joy in the heart. The hope of the Christian, comprehending a desire for the joys of the celestial world and expecting the realization of the promise of the everlasting covenant, creates a lively emotion in the soul, which enables the Christian to know by happy experience that if the earthly house of this tabernacle were dissolved he has a building not made with hands, eternal in the heavens. Being conscious of his acceptance with God, he rejoices with joy unspeakable and full of glory.

The Christian religion does not consist in mere forms and ceremonies and outward observances; it is not a mere ritualism, but it is a religion of the heart. It sanctifies the affections, elevates the feelings, imparts joy to the soul because the believer is conscious of his acceptance with God; consequently he has in him a well of water springing up into everlasting life, and his joy in religion enables him to triumph in the God of his salvation and to count all things but loss for the excellency of the knowledge of Christ Jesus our Lord. In a word, it is what we call experience—a glorious realization in our hearts that God's Spirit bears witness with our spirit that we are the children of God; and thus being justified by faith we have peace with God through our Lord Jesus Christ, by whom we have access into this grace wherein we stand and rejoice in the hope of the glory of God; and not only so, but we glory in tribulation also, knowing that tribulation worketh patience, and patience experience, and experience hope, and ·hope maketh not ashamed, because the love of God is shed abroad in our hearts by the Holy Ghost which is given unto us—a joy unspeakable and full of glory.

THE OBJECT OF HOPE.—We hope for an inheritance. Here you see again the idea carried out by the inspired Apostle—the idea of sonship, of heirship.

A child of God inherits the promised good that awaits him in the future. It is not to be anticipated by those who have not been born again, but by the heirs of God according to the promise. The legitimate child inherits the estate of his father; so the child of God inherits the blessings that are promised. It is not given to hypocrites. It is not given to the unregenerate, or to those who are strangers and aliens from God, but is given to God's children, to those who have been born of the Spirit, to those who have been adopted into the family of God, to those who are heirs of the kingdom. This inheritance is described as "incorruptible, undefiled, and that fadeth not away." It is undefiled, and therefore it is incorruptible; and being undefiled and incorruptible, it shall never fade away. All the pleasures and treasures of earth are temporary, evanescent, passing away, withering as the grass, and all glory of man as the flower of grass; the grass withereth, and the flower falleth and returns to dust. So the pleasure of sin shall perish and fade and wither as the grass of the field, as leaves of the forest; because all things in this life are defiled, and the earth itself was cursed for man's sake; thorns and briers and noxious weeds it brings forth, and it is in the sweat of his face that he makes the bread upon which he lives, and then his brightest hopes go down to the dust like his own putrid flesh; but the inheritance of the saints in heaven, being pure, undefiled, unstained, incorrupt by sin, will know no depreciation, no decay, no death, no end. The soul will spring into immortal youth, and all the joys of paradise will be as an ever-blooming garden of Eden before it was cursed by sin. "There," as we ofttimes sing, "everlasting spring abides, and never-withering flowers." Every thing on the earth has been cursed because of man's sin. In paradise, before man violated God's law, all was pure, all was bright, all was beautiful; but sin entered and drove man out of his original Eden. All earth was cursed for his sake; and now, amidst toil and strife, many disappointments and losses, and a thousand cares, he must work his way through his earthly pilgrimage, and finally he drops into the tomb and is closed from life forever; but in heaven, that pure world, that city of our God, that home of the faithful, he shall live forever, free from turmoil and free from death. This is a reserved inheritance; it is kept for you; it is reserved and kept in store for those who are faithful; for those who are kept by the power of God through faith unto salvation, ready to be revealed at the last time.

This is the glorious inheritance of which the Apostle speaks, and shall be the crowning glory of all of God's children who have been made pure by the washing of regeneration and renewal of the Holy Ghost, who have continued steadfast to the end.

THE SOURCE OF THIS HOPE.—All this rich inheritance is of grace, of the mercy of God, of the abundant mercy of God—that mercy manifested in the gift of his Son, who himself counted not his own life dear to him, but according to the will of the Father, by his own voluntary action, laid down his life to redeem a sinful and ruined world. Sinners are saved by God's mercy. There is no salvation by good works—no inheritance enjoyed as a reward of our virtue separate and distinct from the great scheme of redemption. Man owes all to God, all to God through Jesus Christ, who is the gift of the Father's love; who suffered, the just for the unjust, that he might bring us to God. It is to this abundant mercy that we are indebted for that hope, that precious hope, that lively hope that stimulates us in the conflicts of life and enables us to rejoice in the prospect of a brighter and better home in heaven.

St. Peter, filled with a sense of God's goodness, and overwhelmed by his inspiration of mercy, introduces this passage by a note of praise: "Blessed be the God and Father of our Lord Jesus Christ!" Praise to his name! Honor and majesty and power and adoration be unto him whose mercy endureth forever, and who in his abundant goodness redeemed a lost and ruined race by the death of his only begotten Son! We should all join with the Apostle in the language of inspiration, and say: " Blessed be the God and Father of our Lord Jesus Christ, which according to his abundant mercy hath begotten us again unto a lively hope by the resurrection of Jesus Christ from the dead, to an inheritance incorruptible, undefiled, and that fadeth not away, reserved in heaven for you, who are kept by the power of God through faith unto salvation ready to be revealed at the last time."

And now we come to apply this subject to our friend and distinguished fellow-citizen whose remains lie before us incased and ready for interment.

Mr. Polk, as we have seen, seemed almost a man of destiny. His success in life was remarkable. He was modest, cultivated, high-toned in his morals, a man of untarnished reputation, and was loved and admired by all classes of his countrymen. Against his moral character no charge was ever brought. No man in the United States, filling the high offices that he has occupied, ever maintained a purer character for sound morality. His Christian principles were genuine; his belief in God and the inspiration of the Holy Scriptures was firm, unshaken. He always had the highest respect for the Christian religion, and always exhibited reverence for the house of God and the institutions of the gospel. He was a regular attendant at public worship, and observed the Christian Sabbath with great punctuality. In all his demeanor, during the time of his presidential administration, he maintained the character of a Christian gentleman and paid due respect to the institutions of our holy religion.

He was brought up by a Christian mother, who early trained him in the doctrines and duties of Christianity. She was a member of the Presbyterian Church. On one occasion she took her infant son to the church to have him dedicated to God in holy baptism, but through some misunderstanding between his father and the pastor in charge, in regard to the rules and regulations of the congregation, it was deferred, and he reached maturity without having received the ordinance of baptism.

He was a Wesleyan in sentiment, and believed in the doctrine and polity of the Methodist Episcopal Church. His wife, an intelligent Christian woman, was also a member of the Presbyterian Church; but it was understood by her, as well as by Mr. Polk himself, that he was a Methodist in his views, and from the year 1833 he determined that when he joined the Church he would connect himself with that organization.

On his return from Washington in 1849 he determined to make Nashville his permanent home, and for a time he was busily employed in fitting up his residence. His health was feeble, but he hoped that rest from political labors and the recreation of preparing his mansion for occupancy would soon restore him. But coming home through cholera atmosphere, he seemed to some extent affected by the poison of that malignant disease, and was soon brought to his room and to his bed. Early in his sickness he sent for Rev. Dr. Edgar—his wife's pastor, who had charge of the First Presbyterian Church in this city—and your speaker, and had a free religious conversation with them, and they joined him in prayer and supplication, and asked God in his providence to restore him to health; and in any event, whether for life or for death, that he might be taken under special guardianship of his heavenly Father and prepared for the great future, as well as for the responsibilities of the present life. Soon after, he sought a private interview with your speaker, and made known to him his desire and purpose to receive the ordinance of baptism, and to be admitted into the communion of the Methodist Episcopal Church, to receive the sacrament of the Lord's-supper, and thus identify himself with the Church of his choice. He said: " My mother is a Presbyterian, and I love her and respect her pastor; my wife is a Presbyterian, for whom I have the fondest affection as a Christian, and her pastor is a man whom I respect, and I respect the Presbyterian Church; but I am a Methodist, and desire to identify myself with the Methodist Church, and I have sent for you as my old friend, with whom I have long been acquainted, and desire that you shall administer the ordinance of baptism and receive me into the Church and give me the emblems of the broken body and shed blood of Jesus Christ." In due time his wishes were met, and in the presence of his family, and of the pastor of his mother and his wife, and other friends, he was baptized, admitted into the Church, and received the holy communion. His faith was strong, his confidence unbounded, and he was brought into fellowship with the Church after strong assurances of his belief in the Son of God, the Saviour of the world. He said to his brother William: " I am now about to join the Church a duty that I long since should have performed, and that long ago I made up my mind to perform, but in the hurry of the business of life and the political affairs of the country I postponed it till now. But I go forward in the name of my Lord and Saviour Jesus Christ, who I hope and believe has pardoned all my sins and washed me from all my iniquities." Upon this confession he was baptized and received into the Church, had his name enrolled upon the Church Register, and thus died in full fellowship with the McKendree Church of this city. Such in brief is the religious life and experience of the Honorable James K. Polk—a man whom we all loved, and whose death we all mourn this day, and whose departure will be regretted throughout the length and breadth of this great land.

During this year McFerrin had what he termed "a little discussion" with Dr. Patton, of the *Methodist Episcopalian*, published at Knoxville, Tennessee. Some one charged the Methodists with Toryism during the Revolutionary War, and he warmly repelled the accusation. He had also "a little turn" with the *Methodist Expositor* and the *Southern Methodist Pulpit*. These contests seemed to him necessary, and he mentions in connection with them that the *Christian Advocate* still lived and grew in favor with the people.

In the year 1875 McFerrin wrote down some memorabilia of his life during a period of great interest—from 1849 to 1878—extracts from which are given here.

The narrative is a little broken, being the crowding memories of a busy old man reviewing events in Church and State that were startlingly rapid in their evolution and tremendous in their consequences. The kind reader who follows him will get a contemporaneous glimpse of a vast, shifting panorama from a man who had eyes in his head and was not tongue-tied.

THE FIRST PERSON SINGULAR.

A T the Tennessee Conference for this year (1849) we had Bish. ops Soule and Capers as presiding officers. Bishop Soule, however, was in feeble health, and most of the labor was performed by Bishop Capers. He gave general satisfaction; indeed, he was one of the most accomplished gentlemen and eloquent preachers America ever produced. The Conference was a delightful season of refreshing. Sinners were converted and saints rejoiced.

Delegates to the General Conference, which was to meet in May, 1850, were elected. The following were chosen: J. B. McFerrin, F. E. Pitts, Thomas W. Randle, A. L. P. Green, M. M. Henkle, J. W Hanner, Edward Wadsworth, J. F. Hughes, G. W. Martin, and W. D. F. Sawrie.

At this Conference resolutions were adopted warmly commending the *Christian Advocate* and *Ladies' Companion*, and asking the General Conference to locate a Publishing House for the Church in the city of Nashville. The *Advocate* paid this year a handsome dividend to the several Conferences sustaining it.

On my return I left Nashville for Holly Springs, Mississippi, the seat of the Memphis Conference. I made the trip by water to Memphis, thence by stage to Holly Springs. Bishop Capers presided. The Conference was remarkably pleasant. The missionary anniversary was a success. Bishop Capers made a fine address. I followed. Collection over $1,000. Holly Springs at that time was a beautiful and growing town, full of hospitality, and entertained the Conference in fine style.

In the month of January of this year (1850) I visited the Alabama Conference, which convened at Columbus, Mississippi, on Wednesday, the 16th. Bishop Capers presided, assisted by Bishop Paine. I made the trip to Columbus on horseback—two hundred and forty miles—in company with Maj. H. P. Bostick and the Rev. E. H. Hatcher. The weather was unpleasant and the roads rough, yet we had a pleasant and safe trip.

In all my controversies I seldom came in contact with ministers or members of our own Church. Sometimes, however, it was necessary to have sharp contests even with brethren beloved. When such conflicts are necessary, they should be conducted in the spirit of Christian meekness. A man's personal religious enjoyment depends much on the spirit with which he meets the common conflicts of life and the manner in which he performs his work before the public. And surely the honor of our holy Christianity should lead all public men, and especially all ministers, to conduct themselves with great propriety. I always found that, to discharge my duties faithfully and successfully, much prayer was essential. Amidst all my duties I tried to keep up the spirit and practice of godliness. Family prayer I never neglected. Secret prayer was my daily habit; and as for preaching, I did much of that—not only on Sundays, but during the week, at funerals and at protracted meetings. Thank God! religion was to me a great comfort in all my trials and labors.

The session of the General Conference of 1850 was remarkable for its brevity, mainly on account of the prevalence of cholera in St. Louis. I was on the Committee on Itinerancy, and chairman of the Committee on Revisal. Amidst all the sickness I kept entirely well, having had during the whole time no symptoms of the disease prevailing in the city.

The election of Dr. Bascom to the office of Bishop was one of the important occurrences of the session. He was ordained after a great sermon delivered by himself. He lived to preside only at one Conference, and then fell in the prime and vigor of his manhood. Dr. Bascom was a great preacher and a man of masterly intellect. I was re-elected editor of the *Christian Advocate*, and Dr. Henkle was elected editor of the *Ladies' Companion*. On the 31st of May I made my introduction for a new term of four years, having edited the paper and managed its finances for ten years. Dr. Henkle now became sole editor of the *Ladies' Companion*, though it was still printed at the *Advocate* office.

Soon after the General Conference had adjourned a prospectus was issued for the publication of a paper at Memphis. This called forth an editorial on the multiplication of papers, which is found in the Nashville *Christian Advocate* of June 28. In that editorial I expressed myself freely, and delivered thoughts and made predictions of which I am not ashamed now after a lapse of twenty-five years. It was a sad mistake when the friends of the

Church in the South resolved to increase the number of their weekly journals to so large an extent. I say nothing against the worthy brethren who conduct these papers. They are good men and true; but it is simply absurd to suppose a newspaper can be made a first-class publication without capital. And I wish here and now to record the fact that I have always opposed the multiplication of papers in our Church, and also of schools and colleges under our supervision. An ably conducted religious journal is a great auxiliary to the pulpit, and a grand help in pushing forward the cause of Christ among men; but alas! oftentimes they become instruments of evil. After many years' experience, I am fully of opinion that the most important thing in conducting a religious paper is to know what to keep out of its columns. It requires sound judgment, good taste, and a knowledge of human nature, as well as learning and general intelligence, to make a good and popular paper.

In June and July of this year the cholera prevailed again in Nashville to an alarming extent. Many persons died, but it was most fatal among the colored people. Several citizens of prominence were its victims—among the rest our principal clerk and book-keeper, Col. John McClellan. He died on the 4th of July He was a noble man. Finely cultivated, with a heart warm with benevolence and a soul full of wit and good humor, he was a great favorite with those who knew him. Withal, he was a devout Christian and an ardent Methodist. I greatly deplored his loss.

In September, in company with Bishop Soule, I attended the Louisville Conference, at Greensburg, Kentucky, where we met Bishop Andrew. Bishop Soule was not in good health, though he stood the trip (stage-riding) very well indeed.

On the 8th of this month (September) Bishop Bascom died at the house of the Rev. E. Stevenson, Louisville, Kentucky. At the Greensburg Conference we met his brethren, who sorely lamented his death and gave us many particulars of his last illness and his victory over the fear of the last enemy.

The Tennessee Conference met this year at Athens, Alabama, Bishop Capers presiding. I was providentially hindered; the first that I had failed to attend since I was admitted on trial.

The autumn of this year was devoted to the interests of the *Christian Advocate*. In the meantime I preached a great deal and strove to cultivate personal piety.

The Louisville and Kentucky Conferences became satisfied that they could not sustain the *Louisville Christian Advocate* without pecuniary loss; hence it was proposed to merge it into the Nashville paper, and to call the consolidated sheet the *Nashville and Louisville Christian Advocate.* To this proposition the Book Agents and Publishing Committees of both papers agreed, and the union was made, which took effect January, 1851. The Louisville department was to have an editor who should act as a corresponding or associate editor. The paper was still to be published at Nashville, and I had charge of its finances. Those representing the Louisville department selected the Rev. C. B. Parsons as the Louisville editor. Enlarging our paper and procuring soon thereafter new type and a fine Hoe's power-press from New York, we began Vol. XV. under favorable auspices.

Dr. Parsons was a popular preacher, and it was hoped he would make a useful and successful editor. He had been, long before his conversion, a stage actor; but, having abandoned the stage, he entered the ministry and became a very popular preacher. He was a man of commanding talents and popular pulpit style; was a little fickle, and in after years he united with the Northern Methodist Church. He died a few years afterward. He still had a warm heart for the Southern Methodist Episcopal Church, and his family continued therein. I think Dr. Parsons was a good man, and I hope he died at peace with God. He and I were always on good terms. *Stability, firmness, settled principles* are great things in a Christian, and especially a Christian minister.

I now had eleven years' experience in conducting the paper editorially and financially. Five years I had had the help of Dr. Henkle, but the other six I had managed it alone; and while he aided me I gave a portion of my time to the *Ladies' Companion.*

When I was first elected editor we had no patronage worth naming north of Tennessee. When, however, we had gained Kentucky and Missouri, our brethren began to see the importance of having a paper on the border. Hence, as I have elsewhere said, the *Methodist Expositor* was set up in Cincinnati, then transferred to Louisville, and now, after a failure at Louisville, it was merged into the *Advocate* at Nashville. Now all this cost a great deal; but it was a pleasure to me to know that among these interests and failures the Nashville *Christian Advocate* was prosperous, and continued to increase its circulation. After reviewing the whole history of our publishing enterprises, and now after a lapse of many years, I am surprised at the success that attended our efforts. I was young (only thirty-three years of age) when assigned to the difficult and delicate work of conducting an important Church journal. I had no experience in this line, and the business of the office was financially embarrassed. Yet God gave us success. Our paper grew all the time in the number of subscribers, and I trust in influence. In the issue of February 13 I made another appeal, having started our new press and put on our new dress.

In June of this year, I preached, by request, the annual sermon at La Grange College, Alabama. I traveled from Nashville to La Grange in a buggy, in company with the Rev. Joseph Cross, who was then stationed at McKendree, in the city of Nashville. We were three days on our journey, and reached La Grange on Saturday evening, the 7th. On the 8th the sermon was delivered. The Rev. P. P. Neely preached in the afternoon, and Dr. Cross at night.

At this Commencement, quite to my surprise, the college conferred on me the honorary degree of D.D. This is a title to which I did not aspire. I felt myself unworthy the honor. The Rev. R. H. Rivers had the same degree conferred upon him at the same time. Randolph-Macon College, in Virginia, honored me with the same degree about the same period, neither college having any knowledge of what the other intended to do. I was much obliged to these two institutions for their good feeling and for the honors conferred; nevertheless, these favors in no wise impressed me that I merited such distinction. The calling and work of a *preacher of the gospel* I esteem the highest honor ever conferred upon mortal man.

My journey with Dr. Cross was very pleasant. He was intelligent, sprightly, and full of good humor. He impressed me that he was a Christian in experience and was striving to be one in practical life. I have no reason now to change my opinion, notwithstanding Dr. Cross afterward, and often, gave evidence of *fickleness* of mind.

In October of this year I visited the Louisville Conference at Elkton, Kentucky. Bishop Paine presided. The meeting was one of interest. From this Conference I returned, spent a few days at home, and proceeded to Lebanon, the seat of the Tennessee Conference. Bishop Paine presided. We had a good Conference, nothing unusual occurring more than a pleasant season.

In the month of November I visited the Memphis Conference at Paducah, Kentucky.

While we were rejoicing in our prosperity in the South, the great Church suit at New York was decided in our favor. This decision gave great satisfaction to the South, and insured to our Church the means of prosecuting its publishing interest. It for a time quieted the public mind, and seemed to put an end to the heated discussion of the questions at issue. The country needed rest.

On January 8, 1852, we issued the first sheet of our paper, No. 2—having omitted No. 1 for Christmas week—for the year 1852. Eleven years had passed since my connection with the establishment. We still had prosperity. About this time I had a discussion with a Baptist paper published in Louisville, Kentucky, on Methodist Church polity. The paper made the oft-repeated charge of the aristocratic and oppressive character of our Church government. I defended my Church, of course. This discussion was lively, and extended through several weeks. About those times there was a wonderful disposition to assail Methodist doctrines, Methodist government and usages.

In March we held a grand missionary meeting on the departure of the Rev. John Matthews as a missionary to California. During this year I dedicated the new Methodist Church in McMinnville, and also an elegant and spacious house of worship in Pulaski. This was a new house, built mainly through the instrumentality of Thomas Martin, long a prosperous and wealthy merchant in Pulaski. At many places I was in revivals of religion this year, and enjoyed the preaching of the word.

This year the Tennessee Conference met at Pulaski, Bishop Andrew presiding, assisted by Bishop Soule. The session opened on the 15th of October. The occasion was a season of refreshing to the preachers and time of revival in the Church. Souls were brought to Christ and a deep impression was made on the public mind. Dr. Rosser, of the Virginia Conference, was with us, and preached with zeal. During this year Dr. Latta, of Cincinnati, died. He was a man of fine talents, and his death was regarded as a great loss to the Church.

I had occasion to note this year the resignation of Bishop Hamline, of the Methodist Episcopal Church, North. This was the first instance of a Bishop resigning in the Methodist Episcopal Church. Bishop Hamline's views differed from those of the preachers of the Methodist Episcopal Church, South. His peculiar notions are set forth in his speech in the General Conference of 1844, where he represents the Bishop as a moderator, or a mere president or officer, who could be removed with or without a cause, at the will of the General Conference.

In January, 1853, we began a new volume of the *Advocate* under some apprehensions. Several new papers had been started, and I feared that the Church would suffer by too great a draw upon the people. Hence in February I wrote several articles on the publishing interests of our Connection. These articles were not well received in certain quarters. Local demands were pleaded and local prejudices were awakened. Nothing daunted, however, I stood my ground.

We all mourned the death of the Revs. E. H. Hatcher and B. R. Gant, two of our excellent brethren who finished their work in 1853. Gant was a noble Christian man. Hatcher was only about thirty-five years old, but was a man of superior gifts. Very few men of his age surpassed him in "gifts, grace, and usefulness." He is buried at Columbia, Tennessee. In the Memphis Conference, too, we lost two highly gifted preachers who took their start in the Tennessee Conference—the Rev. B. H. Hubbard, D.D., and the Rev. Wesley Warren, M.D.—both eminent preachers.

About this time we had a great excitement on the subject of temperance. I was at one time "Grand Worthy Patriarch" of the State of Tennessee. The temperance men not only advocated total abstinence, but the passage of a prohibitory law. I made many temperance speeches in various parts of the State, and the cause was very prosperous. But in the course of time the friends of the great reform gradually cooled in their zeal, and the Order waned. From time to time the friends rallied and made new fights. Much good was done. Some drunkards were reformed, and many young men were saved from plunging into hopeless dissipation. Altogether the evils of drunkenness can never be estimated, and every true philanthropist and every genuine patriot should stand against the flood of ruin that seems at times to sweep the land. Woe to the miserable drunkard, and woe to him that for gain putteth the bottle to his neighbor's mouth!

On the 4th of July I dedicated a new church called " Bethel," in the vicinity of Shelbyville, Tennessee. It was on the same ground where a "meeting-house" had long stood, and where much good had been accomplished. It was called "Warm Corner" because of the zeal of its members. Near by lived the Rev. William Mullens, once a traveling preacher, a man of zeal and great usefulness. In the evening I preached at Shelbyville, and reached home on Monday.

Church dedications, funeral sermons, and temperance speeches occupied much of my time. In the camp-meeting season I visited many of these popular gatherings, and labored with as much earnestness and zeal as my time would allow. My health was generally fine. I had a powerful constitution, and could work and travel, preach and write, visit the sick, and keep up the finances of the office, and experience but little weariness. I was seldom tired in those days; my physical vigor never flagged. We had a visit from Dr. Means, of Georgia, this year, which gave us much satisfaction. Nashville in those days was a place of great resort.

This year was one of great distress in the South, especially in New Orleans, on account of the yellow fever, which prevailed to an alarming extent. We lost some of our Nashville friends who had settled in New Orleans and Mississippi. Among these was H. R. W. Hill, long a resident of Tennessee, a prince in liberality and a life-long Methodist. He united with the Church when he was quite a young man. His excellent wife had preceded him to the grave. The cause of Missions about this time was exciting much interest. Bishop Soule had visited California and given the work a new impetus in that new field. Dr. Jenkins, from China, with a live Chinaman in his company, visited Nashville and many of the Conferences; and D. C. Kelley was set apart as a missionary to China. The collections were large, and the people enthusiastic at the prospect of success.

In September I left home for Versailles, the seat of the Kentucky Conference. On my way I called at Frankfort Kentucky, the capital of the State, and visited the cemetery where many of the sons of the "dark and bloody ground"—as Kentucky was once called—sleep in death. There rest the remains of Col. Dick Johnson, once Vice-president of the United States, famous for having killed the great Indian chief Tecumseh in a single-handed combat. There, too, are buried the remains of the great pioneer,

Daniel Boone, and his wife. I saw them re-interred some time previous while attending a Conference in Frankfort. I was indebted to Jacob Swigert, Esq., for many courtesies at Frankfort. Versailles is a pleasant town in the heart of a grand country, some twelve miles from Lexington. Bishop Capers presided at the Conference. Here I heard the Rev. H. H. Kavanaugh preach a funeral sermon in memory of the Rev. William Gunn. The effort was a great one, and the effect was wonderful. On Sunday I went to Lexington, with the Rev. W. C. Dandy and Dr. J. H. Linn, where Dr. L. and myself preached to large congregations. The missionary meeting was a time of great excitement. Dr. Jenkins and his Chinaman were on hand, and wherever John Chinaman went a crowd followed.

On my return I spent a day or two at Louisville, Kentucky, then, as now, the commercial center of the State. I visited the cemetery, and saw the grave of Bishop Bascom, and the resting-place of others. The grounds were beautiful.

In company with Dr. Parsons (my associate editor), Bishop Capers, and others, I went by steam-boat to Owensboro, the seat of the Louisville Conference, where I remained till it closed. The session was a very agreeable one. Bishop Capers preached with great power, and the word generally, as preached, seemed to be in the Holy Ghost and with much unction. Here I preached twice, and made a missionary address. God was with me in the pulpit.

From Owensboro Dr. Parsons and myself proceeded by the way of Smithland to Nashville by steam-boat. We met with many detentions because of low water, fog, etc., but reached Nashville on Saturday, and I found my family in health, after an absence of some three weeks.

On the Sunday after our arrival Dr. Parsons dedicated our new church in Edgefield, called "Hobson Chapel," in honor of Mrs. Hobson, the mother of Nicholas Hobson, who gave the lot on which to erect the building. In 1849 I had removed to the country, having bought a house and lot of land about a mile and a quarter from the Public Square. Here we erected a church, and Dr. Parsons, by request, came to dedicate it to the worship of God. The crowd on Sunday was large, and the Doctor was very successful. The remainder of the debt was fully provided for. The church at Hobson Chapel prospered until 1862. It suffered during the war, and was finally sold and a new and more commodious

16

house was erected, bearing the same name, where, at the time of this writing, there is a flourishing little congregation. The new house is farther from the city.

My object in moving out of the city was to provide a more rural home for my family and to provide especially for the comfort and moral training of my servants. My slaves were family servants. I never sold or bought one; but took those in my possession to keep families together and to properly settle my father's estate. I fed them well, clothed them comfortably, worked them moderately, and gave them full religious privileges. I feel that, under the circumstances, I did my duty, and when they were freed I felt that a great responsibility was removed from me. I was relieved, but my freedmen did no better. I would not have them back if I could, though they were worth at the time the war began at least ten thousand dollars in gold. The loss I never regretted. I think I did my duty by them.

The Tennessee Conference met at Franklin, Tennessee, October 12, 1853. Bishop Capers was to preside. He was not present at the opening, but appointed A. L. P. Green to preside till he should come. In those days a Bishop had the right to appoint a substitute in his absence, provided always that he selected a presiding elder. Dr. Green filled the chair well till the arrival of the Bishop, which I think was on Friday the 14th. This Conference was one of interest. Dr. Jenkins and his Chinaman were present, and David C. Kelley, son of the Rev. John Kelley, was elected and ordained both deacon and elder in view of his going to China as a missionary. The service was solemn, the more so because he was presented by his father; his mother also was present. David was an only son, and the only living child of his parents.

At this Conference delegates were elected to the ensuing General Conference, which was to meet at Columbus, Georgia, May 1, 1854. Eleven were chosen on the first ballot, an extraordinary occurrence. My brethren, as usual, honored me by placing my name at the head of the list—a distinction I did not deserve; but such was their kindness to one who duly appreciated their good feeling and partiality.

The Memphis Conference held its session for 1853 in November. I had the pleasure of meeting the brethren. Bishop Capers presided. I overtook the Bishop and Mrs. Capers at Tuscumbia, Alabama, lodged by the way. I made arrangements and got them off, and we had a most tiresome ride by stage to Holly Springs. Mississippi. There we left Mrs. Capers, and the Bishop and I, in a hack or carriage, traveled leisurely to Grenada, Mississippi, where the Conference convened. We consumed nearly two days in the journey. I found Bishop Capers to be one of the most pleasant and entertaining traveling companions it had been my good fortune to enjoy. Genial, intelligent, communicative, one never tired in his company.

The Conference was pleasant, and the missionary meeting was a success. Grenada was a pleasant town, situated on the margin of Yalabusha River, in the heart of a rich cotton country.

December 18, 1853, by request, I visited Murfreesboro, Tennessee, and preached a funeral sermon in memory of Mrs. Sarah Polk Phillips and Mrs. Joanna Jetton, daughters of Dr. W. R. Rucker. They were nieces of Mrs. President Polk. About three years before I had married both parties under one ceremony, and now in one funeral discourse the last tribute was paid to two excellent Christian women, both members of the Methodist Church.

On Christmas-day I preached a dedicatory sermon in the new church erected in Nashville for the benefit of the colored Methodist congregation. It was named "Capers Chapel," in honor of Bishop Capers. Bishop Soule was present, and after the sermon offered the house to God in prayer. He also made a present of a Bible and hymn-book to the congregation. Dr. R. Martin, a prominent layman, also presented the brethren with a copy of the Holy Scriptures. A number of white persons were present, and much interest was taken in the prosperity of the colored people. The same church has been deeded to the "Colored Methodist Episcopal Church in America." It was always a great pleasure for me to minister to the slaves. They were cared for by white preachers, who did much to elevate and save them from sin.

The next day after the dedication Bishop Soule set out for California *via* New Orleans. He was more than seventy years old. This was years before the railroad across the Rocky Mountains was constructed. Bishop Soule was an example of zeal and perseverance.

In January, 1854, began the eighteenth volume of the *Advocate*, and my fourteenth year in conducting the paper. From February till May I was busy with my work, getting every thing ready for the approaching General Conference. I preached nearly every Sabbath, made temperance addresses during the week, and wrote and read of nights. Several writers attempted to draw me into a discussion in reference to the propriety of establishing a Publishing House for the use and benefit of the Methodist Episcopal Church, South. I avoided the discussion, believing it would accomplish no good at the time. I had every thing ready by the first of May to make a full report to the General Conference. Many of the delegates passed through Nashville on their way to Columbus, Georgia, where the Conference was to convene. The condition of my family detained me for a few days. My beloved wife was in a situation which would not allow me to leave in company with the body of the delegates. Finally, by the persuasion of my wife, I left home with great reluctance. She was in the hands of a favorite physician, Dr. Robert Martin; the Rev. S. P. Whitten was an inmate of my family with his daughter, and my wife's mother was a member of the family. So she felt secure in the hands of friends and in the hand of God, and urged me to leave. I did go with a heavy heart, but apprehended no evil results. But alas! to leave home was to see my affectionate wife no more this side the spirit land. When I received the dispatch announcing her dangerous illness I was overcome with sorrow, and left on the first train for home. On my arrival I found that my dear wife was buried and the whole house was full of grief. The child, which was born four days before her death, was healthy and promising, and has lived to be grown. She bears the name of her mother. But little Bettie, her sister, three years and seven months old, and a fine child, was taken suddenly sick, and within ten weeks after the death of her mother went to meet her in the skies. She said before taken ill that she would die and go and see her mother. She was buried by her side. She was a lovely child, and her loss was much deplored.

Having left the General Conference, I did not return before the session ended. Before I left the question of the establishment of a Publishing House was discussed. I took ground in its favor, and made a long speech. After I left the question was decided in the affirmative, and the House located at Nashville. The Rev. E. Stevenson and the Rev. F. A. Owen were elected Book Agents; Dr. T. O. Summers was elected Book Editor and editor of the Sunday-school literature of the Church; the Rev. L. D. Huston was elected editor of the *Home Circle*, a monthly periodical which was to be published instead of the *Ladies' Companion*. I was re-elected editor of the *Christian Advocate;* the Louisville department was discontinued, and I alone had charge of the paper. The election took place in my absence, and the office was again conferred upon me without any solicitation on my part. I was also run for Bishop in my absence, and received several votes for Book Agent. The office of Bishop I never desired. It is a responsible station in the Methodist Episcopal Church, and involves duties that I never wanted to assume. Many spoke to me on the subject, and I was assured by friends that had I remained at the Conference I would have been elected; but that, owing to recent family afflictions which I was called upon to endure, it was thought better to retain me in the editorial chair. How much there was in this I do not know; but certain I am that I much preferred the office of editor to that of Bishop. I have a high appreciation of the office of Bishop in our Church, but I can truly say that I never felt that I was called of God to this position, and never felt disappointed or mortified that I was not chosen as one of our General Superintendents.

On the 15th of June I entered upon my work again. This was the fifth time I had been selected for this office. We had now a great work to perform. The *Advocate* in its finances was now to be placed in the hands of the Book Agents. This relieved me of a burden that I had borne for fourteen years. I had more time to devote to the literary department of the paper; but still to sustain the interests of the Church at this central point, and to maintain the honor of the Methodists in conducting its central organ, required much attention and unceasing labor. This new arrangement brought a number of brethren to Nashville: Dr. Stevenson and F. A. Owen, Dr. Summers, Dr. Huston; Dr. Sehon, Secretary of the Missionary Society; and finally Dr. Jefferson Hamilton, as Secretary of the Tract Society. With all these brethren I lived in the greatest harmony. Each respected each, and all loved one another.

During the summer of this year we had a visitation of cholera in Nashville, which produced much excitement, but I passed through it without any inconvenience. I attended to the sick, buried the dead, and continued to conduct the paper.

On the 4th of July, in company with the Rev. Adam S. Riggs, I visited Cornersville, Tennessee, where I dedicated a new church. During this trip we suffered much with heat and loss of sleep, being required to travel late at night to reach our appointment. The public conveyance on which we had depended failed, and we had to make private arrangements; hence the delay and the severity of the journey. About three o'clock in the afternoon our horse seemed to become exhausted from heat. We drove up to a spring by the wayside and cooled him as well as possible, and then pursued our journey. Six or eight persons who drank at that spring on that day were taken with cholera, and several of them died. To this day the spring is called the "Cholera Spring." I do not pretend to account for the fact, but it is certain the deaths occurred.

The remainder of the year was taken up in the discharge of my usual duties. My home was lonely, and the cares of my household increased. For my children I felt great concern, and spent as much time with them as possible. My revered mother-in-law, Mrs. Sarah New, a widow, gave me much aid. She was an excellent woman, was devoted to my children, and loved them as if they were her own. My servants did pretty well without a mistress to direct and manage, but the main support of my household was gone, and I felt the loss seriously. Who can estimate the loss of a mother? Whenever I see a family of young children without a mother my sympathies are enlisted, and I feel as though I wanted to extend to them a helping hand.

I had a warm debate about this time with the *Nashville Union*, on the theaters and circuses. See *Advocate* of those times.

On the 17th of this month (September) I dedicated the new church at Bethphage, in Sumner County, Tennessee.

I met the Kentucky Conference at Maysville October 20, where Bishop Early presided. The Bishop at that time gave great satisfaction in the chair and in the pulpit. He was prompt, and preached with unction.

The Tennessee Conference this year convened at Florence, Alabama, Bishops Soule and Paine both present. I was detained on account of the extreme illness of my brother, A. P. McFerrin, who was expected to die; but by good nursing, skillful practice, and the providence of God he survived, and was restored to good health. Here it was, on his sick-bed, that he consented to preach the gospel. He had long resisted the call of the Spirit and his convictions of duty, but now he yielded, and soon after his recovery applied for license to preach. He is now a traveling preacher. It was a sore trial to me to be absent from the Conference, but duty and affection kept me by the side of a sick brother whom I dearly loved.

Soon after I was permitted to visit the Holston Conference, which met at Cleveland, Tennessee. Here Bishop Pierce presided at his first Conference. He displayed tact and talent, and preached with great power. He evinced at once that there had been no mistake in his election and ordination to the office of a Bishop. The Rev. Samuel Patton, D.D., editor of the *Holston Christian Advocate*, had died before the meeting of the Conference. I was commissioned by the Book Agents to buy out the concern and consolidate the paper with the *Christian Advocate* at Nashville. After a tremendous struggle I succeeded in my mission, and the Holston paper was merged into the central organ of the Church. This, I think, was a wise move.

After this I visited Somerville, the seat of the Memphis Conference, and was commissioned by the Book Agents and Book Committee to make an effort to have the *Memphis Christian Advocate* transferred to Nashville, so as to have but one Church paper in the State. I made the effort, but did not succeed. The Memphis paper was continued, and the ensuing General Conference made an appropriation of four or five thousand dollars out of the funds of the Publishing House to relieve it of debts contracted in sustaining its publication.

In the latter part of 1854 the Book Agents resolved to reduce the price of the *Advocate* to $1.50, invariably cash in advance. This was wise for two reasons: 1. It increased the number of subscribers, and thereby became the medium of communication between the Publishing House and the members of the Church to a much larger extent. 2. As the terms were cash in advance, many bad debts were avoided. We had lost thousands by the credit system. This, however, gave great dissatisfaction to the conductors of some of the other papers, and a war on the Agents was commenced, which resulted in a sharp conflict between myself and brethren whom I greatly respected. I defended the Book Agents and their policy. Some brethren thought there was not a proper division of the funds of the Church between the different offices. Among others, I had a sharp discussion with H. N. Mc-Tyeire, editor of the New Orleans paper. He was sprightly, and at that early time gave promise of eminence in the Church. He has met the expectation of his warmest friends. He is now one of our prominent Bishops, and wields a large influence in the Church. I write him down at this day as a man of ability. He has a great power for good, and I pray he may prove an honor to the Church and a blessing to Methodism. I believe he will. May God sustain him and all our General Superintendents in their arduous and oftentimes thankless work! The Bishops are held to strict accountability, and not infrequently are judged unkindly. I am a friend to all our distinguished brethren occupying this high position, and hope none of them will ever bring a reproach upon the cause which they so ably defend.

VIEWS, DOINGS, JOURNEYINGS.

A ND here I wish to record my opinion of the officers of the
General Conference who were with me at the inauguration
of the Publishing House.

Dr. Edward Stevenson, the principal Book Agent, was a man
of age and experience as a minister of the gospel, and was a very
effective preacher. As a Book Agent he was honest, vigilant, and
indefatigable. He of course had but little experience in the man-
ufacture and sale of books, and consequently he labored under peculiar disadvantages in organizing a great concern like the Publishing House. He was in a measure dependent on others; but,
all in all, he was faithful, and did a great work for the Church.
Although I did not regard him as a very skillful financier, in his
integrity I had confidence. Dr. Stevenson was arrested and put
in prison by the Federal authorities because of his Southern pro-
clivities. Out of prison, he soon died—a good man and true.

The Rev. F. A. Owen was a genial, popular man, and a good
counselor. He was regarded as the Associate Agent, although he
had equal authority. He always deferred to his senior, and was
very modest in his suggestions. He never coveted the position,
and at one time resigned. He, however, was re-elected, and
served out his full time. He was loved and respected by all who
knew him.

Dr. Thomas O. Summers, who still lives at the time of this
writing, is in many respects a remarkable man. His early advantages were limited. He was brought up a mechanic, and had
not the advantages of early literary or scholastic training; but he
has been a student all his life. For close application, hard work,
a retentive memory, and the rapid acquisition of knowledge, he
has few superiors. He is decidedly the most indefatigable man
in the study of books and in his editorial life that I have ever seen.
Withal, he is a pure, sound-hearted Christian and a man of great
integrity of character. He loves the Church, and gives his whole
time and strength to advance the cause of his Master. He is an

(249)

able preacher and a sound expounder of the Holy Scriptures. He always lacked magnetism, and hence had not as much power with the people as many others of far inferior attainments. I regard him as a noble-hearted Christian and a man of wonderful knowledge.

L. D. Huston was a peculiar man. In person he was attractive, in voice and manner in the pulpit almost inimitable. He was a very elegant and eloquent speaker. As a writer he was chaste and beautiful; but he lacked industry. He was so fond of social life that it was difficult to confine him to his vocation as an editor. He was finally expelled from the Church for immorality. I thought he was not guilty of the charges and specifications on which he was excluded. In this I might have been in error; but I am of the same opinion now. The trouble in his case was that he had many evil reports following him. These had their effect upon the public mind, and weighed much in his trial. Poor man! I loved him much, and still hope that he may be saved. His wife was a charming Christian woman.

Dr. E. W. Schon, Missionary Secretary, was a noble specimen of a high-toned Christian gentleman. His person was commanding, his manner pleasing, his voice full and mellow, and his oratory popular. He had but one fault—he was a poor financier; but his soul was full of generosity. He did not know the worth of money. He was very sanguine, and hence he was often misled in his calculations.

Dr. Jefferson Hamilton was a great preacher and good man, but had no particular adaptation to the agency of books and tracts. The pulpit and pastoral work were his field of labor. There he was a host, and he died in the harness. His death was glorious. Few more successful preachers ever blessed our Church in modern times.

During this year the Rev. Alexander Campbell visited Nashville. He preached in McKendree Church, and lectured several times in the city on spirit-rappings and Universalism. Mr. Campbell was now an old man, but still had a great intellect. He had modified his former teachings very much. On the doctrines of the divinity of Christ, the Godhead, and the operation of the Holy Ghost he gave many of his own followers great dissatisfaction. He seemed, to Trinitarians, orthodox, and evinced a meek and Christian spirit. Bishop Soule heard his sermon on

"The Divinity of Christ, and the Deity, Personality, and Work of the Spirit," and expressed himself as agreeably surprised. Mr. Campbell was a great man, but many of his early teachings, I think, did much harm. Yet he seemed to be sincere, and closed his life, I trust, in peace with God and man. He was the founder of a sect that has become numerous; but as he had no creed, no confession, no articles of religion, his followers are not united, and have no common bond of union. They believe any thing or nothing as they choose. Mr. Campbell was much more orthodox than most of his followers.

About this time one of his preachers, the Rev. Jesse B. Ferguson, became one of the most attractive and popular ministers in the city. He drew large crowds, and was much admired. Alas for him! he became unsettled in his religious views, if he ever had any well-defined sentiments. He became a believer in spirit-rapping, embraced Universalism, and finally, I think, became a skeptic. He lost his influence, lost his church by fire, lost his congregation, and died in middle life. I often looked upon him with sadness, and mourned to see one so gifted, so popular, and calculated to do so much good waste his precious talents and fail to accomplish the good he might, if he only had had genuine principles in him and had been governed by proper motives and sound Christian sentiments. I always tremble for "star preachers," as they have been aptly called.

January 1, 1855, began a new volume. I visited the Georgia Conference, which was held at Atlanta. Bishop Capers and one other Bishop were present. This was my first visit to this Conference. I met a cordial reception, and procured many new subscribers to the *Advocate*. The missionary meeting was good—about $1,200 collected. It was my lot to be one of the speakers.

About this time McFerrin and Hunter (A. P. McFerrin) sold out their book-store to Stevenson and Owen, and they were both employed in the House, as they both had large experience in the book trade. During this month, too, Dr. Hamilton entered upon his duties as Secretary of the Tract Society. This enterprise, while it distributed many valuable books, in the end proved a serious financial loss to the House. The Doctor, as I have said elsewhere, was a great preacher and a good man, but he was too kind and too credulous to conduct a business that required rigid management.

February 8 of this year we announced the death of Bishop Capers. His death was unexpected and much lamented. In his palmy days he was one of the finest pulpit orators in America. He was the first to move in sending missionaries to the slaves of the South. His name is still precious to the Church.

About this time the temperance question ran high. Many of the friends of the cause were in favor of a prohibitory law, I among the rest. If nothing better, all wanted an optional law. I made many temperance addresses, and took an active part in the work of reform. During this month I visited Lebanon, Tennessee, where I made a speech on Saturday night, and preached twice on Sunday to large congregations. The Rev. W. C. Johnson was then stationed preacher in Lebanon.

In the months of February and March Dr. E. Stevenson, the Book Agent, was very sick in Louisville, Kentucky. He had not as yet removed his family to Nashville. The Rev. F. A. Owen and myself went by boat to visit him—quite a trip in those days. We were two or three days reaching Louisville—a journey that can now be completed in eight hours by railroad. We found Dr. Stevenson very ill, but improving a little. At his request I acted as Agent for him till he was able to remove to Nashville. He complimented me with a fine gold-headed cane, an elegant pencil, a gold pen, and a pair of gold-framed spectacles. The spectacles I did not much need, for up to that period my eye-sight continued good.

In April of this year the Bishops of our Church had a meeting in Nashville. It was also the time of the anniversary of the Missionary Board of our Church. Bishop Pierce preached a sermon on the death of Bishop Capers. It was a very fine discourse, and was published by request. The missionary meeting was a grand success. We collected about $2,250. I took the lead in the collection, and was assisted by Dr. A. L. P. Green, who in his palmy days was a good missionary speaker and a good solicitor. Bishop Pierce and Dr. Sehon made the speeches. The occasion was one of great interest. Three of the editors were also present: Dr. Myers, of Charleston; McTyeire, of New Orleans; and C. C. Gillespie, of Galveston. They were all comparatively young men, and all men of promise. McTyeire was afterward made Bishop. Myers was true, and died in 1876 much respected and greatly lamented. Gillespie apostatized, and died in 1876, near its close, or about the beginning of 1877. He made a wreck of himself. Poor fellow! he was a man in his day.

In the month of May of this year the General Assembly of the Presbyterian Church met in Nashville. It was an able body of ministers and laymen. Among the most distinguished preachers present were Dr. Boardman, of Philadelphia, and Dr. Thornwell, of South Carolina. During the session the Rev. Dr. Philip Lindsley died of apoplexy. He was a man of fine learning, and had been for many years before his death President of the Nashville University. His death was lamented in Nashville, where he was so well known.

About this time I visited Gallatin, where there was a gracious revival of religion. The Rev. A. F. Lawrence was the preacher, a good man and a successful minister of the gospel. He lately died in Christ. His death is lamented.

In the month of June I visited Charleston, South Carolina, as a member of the National Division Sons of Temperance. The meeting was an occasion of special interest. Some of the first men of the nation were present, and made addresses to large public assemblies. Judge O'Neal, of South Carolina, was present, and made an address. As Grand Worthy Patriarch of Tennessee I attended a number of mass-meetings during the year. Among other places, I visited Jackson, Tennessee, where we held a series of meetings with considerable success. Poor W. T. Haskell was present. He was one of the finest orators in the State, but had fallen by strong drink. Many efforts were made to save him. He took a new start at this meeting, but he lacked stability, and fell back into his old habits. He was a man of superior powers on the stump or platform. His excellent wife still survives, a warm Methodist and a highly cultivated lady. When Mr. Haskell was young he professed religion, united with the Church, and was firm and steady for a season; but finally law, politics, stump-speaking, and ungodly associations led him away. I have heard it stated that he was solemnly impressed when young that he was called to preach; but he resisted the call, and the train of evils alluded to followed. I have known other instances of the kind. It is a fearful thing to resist the Spirit of God and fail to do the work to which we are distinctly moved. On this journey I visited and spoke and preached in Trenton, Tennessee.

During this summer I visited Winchester, Tennessee, and dedicated a new church. I preached three sermons. The Rev. A. F. Driskill, the presiding elder, and Brother J. G. Rice, the stationed preacher, were present, and took an interest in the services.

In the latter part of the summer of this year I visited the towns of Athens, Courtland, and Huntsville, Alabama. These were favorite places with me, having spent much of my early ministerial life in North Alabama. I made a very pleasant tour, and preached a number of sermons. At Athens I visited the grave of my old friend and presiding elder, the Rev. Joshua Boucher, and the resting-place of the Rev. Albert G. Kelly, who both lie buried in the cemetery there.

August 31 of this year the Rev. Thomas Martin, of Robertson County, Tennessee, died; and, according to his request, I preached his funeral sermon. He was a good man, and left the savor of a good name. His son, the Rev. G. W. Martin, still lives at the time of this writing. Like his father, he is a man above reproach. They are kinsmen of my family. I preached a funeral sermon of another aged local preacher this year—the Rev. Alexander Rascoe—who had been preaching, as well as Mr. Martin, for more than fifty years. Father Rascoe died near Goodlettsville, some twelve miles from Nashville. It is a pleasant task to review the life and sketch the character of a good man who has long been a faithful follower of the Lord Jesus, and who closes his mortal career in hope of a glorious immortality.

In September, 1855, I preached a funeral sermon on the death of E. P. McGinty, editor of the *True Whig*, Nashville, Tennessee, and of Miss Catharine Louisa McGavock, daughter of Mr. John McGavock. They both died the same day. Mr. McGinty was the son-in-law of Mr. McGavock, and died at his house. A large concourse of people attended the funeral. Mr. McGinty was a talented, respectable Christian gentleman, and Miss McGavock was a fine-looking, amiable young lady—a Christian ready to die, and who departed this life in peace.

Soon after this I visited Walton's camp-meeting near Goodlettsville. The meeting was very profitable. There were many preachers present—among others, the Rev. F. E. Pitts and the Rev. Dr. A. L. P. Green. On Sunday morning fifteen infants and twelve adults were baptized at one time. The scene was very impressive. About this date I buried at Liberty Hill—the home of Col. Hill—the wife of the Rev. William Burr. She died near

Pulaski, and was brought to Williamson County for interment. She was a good woman, and belonged to one of the oldest Methodist families in Tennessee.

In the paper of October 11 will be found reflections on the meeting of an Annual Conference. The Tennessee Conference just now convened in Nashville. Bishops Soule and Kavanaugh were both present. Bishop Soule was feeble, and most of his work devolved on Bishop Kavanaugh. During the session Bishop Paine passed through Nashville and made a short sojourn. The Conference was an interesting occasion. We had many visiting brethren: The Book Agents, Stevenson and Owen; Dr. Schon, Missionary Secretary; Dr. Summers, Dr. Hamilton, and others. While the Conference was in session my neighbor, Hardy Bryan, died at the house in which I now live. I preached his funeral sermon to many sympathizing friends. He was a good man and a sound Methodist.

By special invitation I visited Knoxville, Tennessee, the last week in October. It was a grand temperance occasion. I made several addresses, and preached five sermons. When I arrived at the depot in Knoxville I found the Rev. W. G. Brownlow waiting to receive me. He conducted me to his dwelling, where I enjoyed his hospitality while I remained in the city. Mr. Brownlow was then a Southern Methodist preacher in good standing, was the editor of a paper, and was a strong temperance man. I was entertained handsomely at his home. His family treated me with great hospitality. Mr. Brownlow is a character. He still lives at this writing. Few men in this country have attained to greater notoriety. He was born in Virginia, and was brought up at a trade. He was a carpenter, I think. When young he professed conversion, and joined the Methodist Episcopal Church. He was the nephew of the Rev. Robertson Gannaway, long a worthy member of the Holston Conference. Mr. Brownlow was admitted on trial in the Holston Conference in the autumn of 1826, and was appointed this first year to Black Mountain Circuit, North Carolina. For several years he continued in the Conference, and had several debates, or conflicts, with the Baptists and with the Presbyterians. He soon made a noise in the world, and as early as 1832 was elected a delegate to the General Conference, which met in Philadelphia in May of that year. After a few years he became the editor of a secular paper, and went into politics. As a journalist he gained great notoriety. He was severe, fearless, and I may say reckless. From one position to another he went forward till he became Governor of Tennessee during the Civil War, and then was elected Senator to the United States Congress. He has from time to time had many friends and numerous enemies. He has been loved and hated as much, perhaps, as any one in the State. He has always been friendly with me and treated me with respect. He has some excellent traits of character, and in many respects he has led a life very ill suited to the calling of a minister of the gospel of Christ. He is now old and infirm—a member, as I understand, of the Methodist Episcopal Church (North), having gone off from the Methodist Episcopal Church, South, during the war He is a riddle. I hope he may end his life in peace. He has surely had much strife in his time. I think he is perhaps a better disposed man than many people judge him to be. He is said to be a good husband, a kind father, an excellent neighbor, and a generous and charitable citizen. Altogether, he is a remarkable man, and has had a curious career.

A BRIDAL TOUR, AND OTHER THINGS.

ON the evening of November 12, 1855, I was married to Miss Cynthia Tennessee McGavock, daughter of Mr. John McGavock, who lived a near neighbor to me. The ceremony was performed by the Rev. William C. Johnson, the pastor of Hobson Chapel, where the family held their Church-membership. It was just eighteen months after I had lost my first wife. The idea of marrying the second time, especially where there are children in the family, is a very serious one. Second marriages oftentimes end in misfortune. To marry a wife, and introduce her into a household where the remembrance of the departed mother is fresh, is a risk. All this and more I considered well, and made it a matter of sincere and solemn prayer. I had a family of four children. Their mother was an only child, and hence had no near relative to whom the children could be committed. I had but two sisters, and they lived at a distance, and had large families of their own. I was from home much of my time; my children needed a mother to watch over them. To marry a stranger I feared; so I selected one whom I had known from her young days, one whom my children knew well, and whom they approved. She was younger than I by several years, which might have been a serious objection, and yet I hoped that the match would prove a happy one. And so it did. And now, after more than twenty-one years, I feel that the hand of God led me. She has been a great help to me in my work. Industrious, vigilant, and a good manager, she relieved me of many cares. God has blessed me with two good wives, for which I am truly grateful. To both of them I was tenderly allied. I do not love the memory of the first the less because of my connection with the second, nor do I love the second the less because of my affection for the first. Both were worthy, and both alike had my sincere love. I have in all my married life been true and sincere in my affections, and have sacredly in my heart, as well as in my life, kept my marriage vows.

17   (257)

On the evening of our marriage, with my oldest daughter (Sarah Jane), we set out on the train for a visit to the North Carolina, Virginia, and South Carolina Conferences. After a pleasant journey we reached Wilmington, North Carolina, on Friday morning, an hour before daylight. A porter urged us to stop at a certain hotel, but when we reached the establishment we could find no room, and had to put in our time as well as we could till breakfast. We were treated very rudely by the proprietor. He first refused us a room, and then became enraged because we would not remain in his house. The Rev. Mr. Frost, the stationed preacher, found for us a charming home at the house of Brother Bawden, whose family made us welcome and treated us with marked attention. This was my first visit to the North Carolina Conference. Bishop Andrew was present and presided. The Conference gave us a hearty reception, and the visit was pleasant, and I trust profitable. I represented the interests of the paper and of the Publishing House. I also made a missionary address at the anniversary, besides preaching to a large congregation.

From Wilmington we proceeded to Baltimore and back to Washington City and to Richmond. My wife and daughter took much delight in visiting these old and famous Southern cities. We spent the Sabbath in Richmond, where I preached.

In the early part of the week we proceeded to Petersburg, where the Virginia Conference convened, Bishop Andrew presiding. Here we were entertained in a most hospitable manner by that great and good man, Mr. D'Arcy Paul—a man noted for his piety, liberality, hospitality, and good manners. His wife was a charming Christian woman. Both are now in heaven.

From Petersburg we went to Marion, South Carolina, the seat of the South Carolina Conference. Here we were entertained by Mrs. McIntire, an excellent Presbyterian lady. Bishop Early presided at this Conference. Dr. Sehon was also present. On Sunday evening Dr. Wightman, now Bishop, preached a funeral discourse in memory of Bishop Capers. The sermon was a great one, and the effect on the audience was wonderful. Bishop Capers was a native of South Carolina, and was long a member of the South Carolina Conference. He was greatly beloved and highly esteemed. The preacher was fully prepared, and the sermon was worthy of the occasion.

From Marion we went to Charleston, where we spent a day or

two with the family of Dr. E. H. Myers, who was then editor of the *Southern Christian Advocate.* Our visit ended, we returned to Nashville after an absence of nearly one month. Our return was greeted with pleasure by our families and friends, and my wife entered upon her new duties in life.

January 3, 1856, we began the twentieth volume of the *Advocate,* and I entered upon my sixteenth year of editorial life. During this month a discussion sprung up between Dr. D. R. McAnally, editor of the *St. Louis Christian Advocate,* and myself in regard to notices of the Publishing House and its publications. The Doctor, I thought—and he made the impression on the minds of many others to the same effect—was not friendly to the concern at Nashville, and consequently was unnecessarily severe in his criticisms upon the issues from the Church press. We had several articles pro and con., and wound up good friends. Dr. McAnally I regard as a good man, an able editor, a sound Methodist, and as one of my best friends. He has lived long and rendered valuable service to the Church.

And then, again, I had a little cross-firing with my old and long-tried friend, the Rev. William Hicks, of the Holston Conference. The Book Agents had bought out the *Holston Christian Advocate,* and it was understood that the influence of the preachers and members was to be given to the *Advocate* at Nashville. Mr. Hicks, after this, proposed to start, and did begin, the publication of the *Herald of Truth* at Henderson, in the bounds of the Holston Conference, and invoked the aid of the preachers. This I considered unfair, and consequently opposed the enterprise of Brother Hicks, or rather held that the Holston Conference was bound in good faith to give all their influence to the paper at Nashville. And here I wish to record, as perhaps I have done in other places, my protest against invoking Church patronage on private interest when that interest comes in conflict with the good of the Church. Every man has a right to write and publish in this free land, but he has no moral or religious right to injure the Church through its own agents. Brother Hicks is a good man, whom I dearly love, and is one of my warm friends.

All along through this year we had many discussions with our Northern brethren on the slavery question, and the relations of the two Churches, North and South, to the institution. We maintained the well-settled views of the Church on that question, while some of our friends North contended earnestly for its immediate abolition. The controversy oftentimes waxed warm, especially so as it involved other matters of importance.

Two unusual editorials appeared about this time, written by request. The first was an article against allowing one's self to grow old too soon, and the other was against remaining young too long. I bestowed some pains on both these articles, and they were highly approved. In the number of the *Advocate* of March 6 there is an article written by Dr. E. W. Sehon, called "A Model Paper," in which he passes a high encomium on our sheet. This was of course gratifying to one who put forth his best efforts to make a first-class Christian journal. Nothing should be charged to the account of vanity or egotism. To please men for good to their edification is commended by an apostle. Selfish or personal ambitious views are to be avoided, but to do good by securing the respect and confidence of men is not to be condemned.

Along during February and for several succeeding weeks I had a sharp controversy with some Presbyterian and Baptist editors and their correspondents. Indeed, our location at Nashville, our Publishing House, and the growth of Methodism seemed to excite jealousy and provoke opposition; hence I found it necessary to defend our Church, our doctrines, our polity, and our usages. All this I did with a good will, believing I was in the right. Angry controversy, strife, contention, bickering, are all unbecoming a Christian, and especially a Christian minister; but a manly defense of the truth is to be approved and commended. So I believed, and so I endeavored to conduct myself. I was conscientious.

Toward the close of this winter, which was marked for its severe coldness, the Rev. Thomas E. Bond, Sr., M.D., died in the city of New York. He was an able writer and a very popular and powerful editor. Though a Marylander, he, after fighting the Abolitionists for long years, took sides against Bishop Andrew and the South in the great conflict in 1844. He was a formidable opponent, and did much to mold public sentiment in the North, and especially in the middle Conferences. He and the paper which we controlled had many fierce battles, but he always treated me with due respect. He told some of my friends that he regarded the Nashville paper as his most formidable opponent, but at the same time passed a high eulogy on the manner in which it was conducted. He said its editor never misrepresented any one with whom he took issue. Dr. Bond was a great man; so was his son, Dr. Thomas E. Bond, Jr., who was a strong advocate of the rights of the South, and who died much lamented by the whole Church.

In the spring of 1856 there was a very important educational convention at Nashville, and also a meeting of the Bishops of our Church, the Missionary Board, the Book Committee, and managers of the Tract Society. The occasion was one of deep interest. Many of our distinguished ministers and educators were present.

May 29 was published an editorial on the progress of Methodism. This was written in answer to many bitter things uttered against our Church, as well as to strengthen our cause and encourage our brethren.

In the month of May the General Conference of the Methodist Episcopal Church (North) met in Indianapolis. We had a correspondent on the ground, who kept us well posted. He wrote many interesting letters, which were published in our columns. The writer was the Rev. W. C. Johnson, now editor of the *Western Methodist.*

Most of the members of the Northern General Conference about this time were extreme on the question of slavery, and many hard speeches were made. Some of the body, however, were temperate, and in a measure held the majority in check.

For some cause, or without a reason, the *Union and American,* a secular paper advocating the Democratic party, made an attack on political preachers, and before the matter ended a sharp controversy sprung up between the *Christian Advocate* and the aforesaid publication. In my defense of the preachers I published several editorials, which may be found in the *Advocate* of June 19 and July 31, 1856. To show the sentiments the *Advocate* maintained it is only necessary to refer to those issues.

By invitation I visited Washington, Georgia, where, on the night of the 3d of July, I preached to a large congregation. On the 4th I addressed a mass-meeting of the Sunday-schools of the town The crowd assembled in a beautiful grove in the outskirts of Washington; the audience was very large and the attention marked. A fine dinner was served, and the occasion passed off pleasantly and profitably. At night I preached again, and on the following Sunday I delivered a Commencement sermon at Madison to a large congregation. The sermon was at the instance of the Faculty of the flourishing Methodist female school in the beautiful town of Madison. The Rev. Messrs. Echols, Bass, and J. L. Pierce were all connected with the institution. My observation has led me to the conclusion that well-conducted schools for the education of girls exert a tremendous influence upon society. In thousands of instances women control the religious sentiments and Church relations of their male friends, and especially of their husbands. How important, then, that schools for girls and young women should be conducted on Christian principles!

In August, 1856, I visited Manchester, Coffee County, Tennessee, and made an address at the laying of the corner-stone of the Methodist Church. A subscription was raised for building the house.

During the autumn I visited the Kentucky Conference, at Winchester; the Tennessee Conference, at Huntsville, Alabama, and the Memphis Conference, at Jackson, Tennessee. At Huntsville a great revival followed the Conference, resulting in the conversion of some two hundred souls. At Jackson I preached at the Baptist Church. Notwithstanding my many controversies with the Baptists, I was very often invited to preach in their houses of worship.

January 1, 1857, we began the twenty-first volume of the *Christian Advocate.* January 8 a notice of the Rev. Samuel Gilliland is published. He was older than I, but we were converted on the same day, united with the Church together, were licensed to preach at the same time, and ordained deacons and elders together. He was a good man, an able preacher, and his death was greatly lamented. Our souls were knit together in love.

February 18 my mother-in-law (Mrs. Sarah New) died at my house. She had lived with my family for many years before my first wife's death, and continued with us till she died. She was an excellent Christian woman, one whom I greatly loved and respected. Her death was a sore trial to my children, especially to the youngest, who could not realize for a time that she was more than sleeping. On Christmas-day, 1856, my daughter Lulu was born. She still lives to bless her parents.

On the 22d of March I dedicated the new church at Springfield, and on the 28th the Methodist Church at Goodlettsville, twelve miles from Nashville.

There was a large collection of our Bishops and preachers in Nashville in April, and the 19th was a day of special pleasure. The pulpits were filled by our distinguished friends.

Early in May, with Bishop Early, Dr. A. L. P. Green, and Dr. Sehon, I visited Petersburg, Virginia, where was held the anniversary of the Missionary Society. Sunday was devoted to preaching and prayer-meetings—missionary. On Monday evening the missionary meetings proper began, and were continued several evenings. The results were good, for, besides a good spirit pervading the congregation, collections amounting to over $3,000 were realized.

From Petersburg I accompanied the Rev. Dr. Sehon to Clarksburg, Virginia, where, on the second Sunday in May, we formally dedicated an excellent new Methodist Church. I preached twice on the occasion, and Dr. Sehon once. Here his venerable mother lived. Here he was converted, and from this place went out as an itinerant Methodist preacher. Dr. Sehon had many friends and admirers at the place of his early home.

On the 27th of May the wife of Bishop Soule died near Nashville. 'Her funeral was largely attended by the friends of the Bishop and his family.

On June 14 I preached the Commencement sermon at Columbia, Tennessee, before the Faculty and students of the Tennessee Female College. June 21 I dedicated the new church at Bethel, Sumner County, Tennessee. Here Bishop Asbury often preached, and here the first Methodist Conference convened that ever assembled in Tennessee west of the mountains, and here on the day of dedication was exhibited Bishop Asbury's portable pulpit.

June 25 I buried Dr. Alexander Graham, of Sumner County, a young man comparatively, full of promise, but God called him home early. He left a wife and small family, but he died in hope.

The fourth Sunday in July I preached at Tullahoma, then a new town. Here I encountered Mr. Haile, a Baptist preacher, who made a furious attack upon all Pedobaptists, and especially upon the Methodists. His sermon was reviewed in the afternoon and at night, quite to the comfort of the Methodists. Mr. Haile promised to return to Tullahoma and respond, but I learn he never again appeared in the place.

We had frequent attacks from the Baptists during this summer. Dr. Hall, of England; Dr. Fuller, of Baltimore; and Mr. Spurgeon, of London, and many others, have greatly modified their views. Religious controversies are unpleasant, but they are sometimes essential. Erroneous and strange doctrines must be exposed and opposed.

The war on slavery continued, and it seemed that the Churches in the South were to have no rest on this vexed question. We took, as we believed, scriptural grounds on the subject, and defended the course pursued by the Southern Church.

The Tennessee Conference convened this year early in October at Murfreesboro. Bishop Early presided. The anniversary of the Missionary Society was held at two churches on Saturday evening. Dr. Green spoke at the Presbyterian Church, and the editor of the *Advocate* at the Methodist Church. The collections were liberal. On Monday twelve delegates were elected to the ensuing General Conference. The brethren honored me by placing my name at the head of the list. In the afternoon of that day I left for Nashville, that I might prepare for a visit to Arkansas in the interest of the Publishing House.

On my way I visited my mother, two brothers (William and James), and my two sisters, Mrs. Gilliland and Mrs. Applewhite. They all lived then near Marshall Institute, in Marshall County, Mississippi, and in Shelby County, Tennessee. My mother's children all met together during this visit. Several of her grandchildren were also present. It was a joyful meeting. I preached on Friday night at the Institute. Twelve or thirteen were converted, a revival being in progress. The Sunday following I preached in Memphis three times. On Monday I left for Jacksonport, the seat of the White River Conference. My journey was by water—down the Mississippi, up White River. Here I met Bishop Kavanaugh, who presided at the Conference. He was in fine trim, and during the Conference preached one of his great sermons. It was on Monday night. The effect was so wonderful that the people rose to their feet, stood on the seats, and actually climbed upon the backs of the seats. There was a great religious uproar. From Jacksonport I descended the river, and spent several days at Augusta, a pleasant town on the eastern bank of White River. There I preached several times, and saw signs of good. Monday I left for Little Rock, the seat of the Wachita

Conference, *via* Searcy, a pleasant village on the road. I was in a buggy with a little boy, Brother and Sister Whitworth in company in another vehicle. My buggy broke down about midday. Patched up a little, I progressed with fear, and finally down we came, utterly disabled, with no chance for repairs. We were in an unsettled country, some six or eight miles from Searcy. I was forced to go; had an appointment to preach that night in Searcy, and no place to lodge had we remained only in the wild woods. Loosing my horse from the buggy, I mounted him bareback, took the boy behind and my valise before. I rode into Searcy, and reached the town in full time to meet my engagement. My entrance into the village created some excitement, but the end of the day's journey was pleasant to me, especially as the bareback ride was any thing but easy and comfortable. But I had never found a difficulty that there was not a way out.

At Little Rock we had a fine Conference, notwithstanding the heavy rain that fell during the session. I lodged with Col. Absalom Fowler, a lawyer of distinction, whom I had known in Tennessee when we were both young. He was a man of good culture and of superior legal attainments. Our missionary meeting was a grand success. Dr. J. Hamilton, Bishop Kavanaugh and the writer all made short speeches. Here I met the Hon. Solon Boland, said to be the finest orator in the West. He was a Methodist, and a man full of generosity. Mr. Boland died comparatively young, and his loss was mourned by many. I came from Little Rock to White River in a stage-coach, thence by river to Memphis.

On my return I wrote and addressed through the *Advocate* a series of letters on the " Glory of Methodism " to Bishop Soule. They will be found in the *Advocate* of December 17, and on through the months of January and February. In these letters I gave my views of Methodism. Up to this time I have very slightly changed those views, if at all modified them.

December 20 Dr. A. L. P. Green, Dr. L. D. Huston, and myself attended the dedication of the new Methodist Church at Lebanon, Tennessee. The house had cost a large sum for those days, and was two thousand dollars in debt on the day of dedication. The plan was to have three sermons—morning, afternoon, and night—and lift a collection at the close of each sermon, hoping thus to pay off the entire debt. The day was beautiful, the

congregations large, and the spirit of the people good.   Dr. Huston preached the first sermon, and at the close the first collection
was taken, and to the surprise of everybody the whole sum was
contributed.   Then we had a happy people and a fine new house
out of debt.

From about this time till May, 1858, all hands were busy preparing for the General Conference, which was to meet in Nashville.   Several subjects were discussed.   Among the most important were the Publishing House and the support of the Bishops.

ROUGH TIMES.

O N the first day of May, 1858, the General Conference assembled at Nashville. The Hall of Representatives was offered and accepted, and the Conference assembled in that spacious room. The month of May was perhaps the most busy and laborious month of my life. I was conducting the *Advocate* as usual, edited the *Daily Advocate* during the session, was chairman of the Committee on Books and Periodicals—the most laborious committee of the Conference that session—and had my house full of visitors. But my strength was according to my day, and I did not fully comprehend my condition till the General Conference had adjourned. I then felt that I was well-nigh exhausted. A few days' rest, however, and I was myself again.

At this General Conference I was elected Book Agent, an office to which I did not aspire, and even tried to avoid. I was in favor of the election of the Rev. E. H. Myers; but he insisted that he could not accept the office, and urged that I should allow myself to be run for the position. The matter was submitted to my own delegation, and I begged my colleagues to vote for Dr. Myers and let me pass. The matter remained in that attitude till the hour of balloting arrived. Both were put in nomination, and on the first ballot I was elected by a considerable majority. This to me was a sore disappointment. I desired the election of Dr. Myers; but, knowing the difficulties connected with the operations of the institution, I reluctantly yielded to the wishes of the Conference, which were expressed by a decided vote. The House was seriously in debt, and there was not that full harmony in its support which was essential to its success. I gave up the editorial department of the paper with mingled emotions. I had been at its head for nearly eighteen years, most of that time alone. I had had success. The subscription-list had been run up from three or four thousand to above thirteen thousand; all its debts had been paid, and it was a source of revenue to the Church. I had many friends, and the excitement of an editorial life suited my temper. Hence, it had been an agreeable life to me, and I parted with the patrons and correspondents of the paper with regret. And yet it was a relief, after so many years of toil and labor, to be released from the responsibilities of duties involving so many interests of the Church. Having bid adieu to my readers, I entered upon my duties as Book Agent with a determination to succeed, if at all possible. It was a Herculean undertaking, but by God's help I proposed to address myself to the work. My time now was fully employed in supervising the publishing interests of the Church The Rev. H. N. McTycire was the editor of the *Christian Advocate*, Dr Summers of the *Quarterly Review* and Books, and Dr. L. D. Huston of the *Home Circle* and Sunday-school books. We had a large force in the composition-rooms, press-rooms, bindery, etc. These all had to be provided for, while in the book-store we had to keep a full supply of clerks and salesmen to transact the large business of the House. Still, I had time to preach, especially on Sundays, and never failed to do full work in this department as opportunity offered. I visited the Annual Conferences as far as possible, and made interest for the House wherever I could. The Rev. R. Abbey was elected Financial Secretary of the House. It was his business to form book and tract societies in the various Conferences, and to encourage the establishment of depositories in different sections of the Church. He succeeded in some places well; in other parts the scheme was not so much in favor. In his field, as well as in my department, all suggested by the General Conference, we worked to the utmost of our skill and ability. We had some success; indeed, I might say considerable success. Finally, in 1860, after a very heated canvass, Mr. Abraham Lincoln was elected President of the United States over Stephen A. Douglas, John Bell, and John C. Breckinridge. This event created much excitement in the country, especially in the South, as Mr. Lincoln was regarded as the Abolition candidate. The questions of slavery and abolition had been discussed till the whole country was in commotion. Politicians and statesmen in the Southern or slave States believed that slavery was doomed if Mr. Lincoln carried out the principles avowed in the Republican platform; and of this they had no doubt. They also saw, as they believed, that the doctrines of "State rights" would be assailed and the sovereignty of the

States destroyed. Hence arose a determined opposition to Mr. Lincoln. Then followed agitations in Congress, mass-meetings among the people, evincing a purpose to resist, then war, with all its horrors.

After Mr. Lincoln made his proclamation calling out troops I made a few speeches at the earnest solicitation of many friends. I never preached a political sermon. Tennessee seceded, but I went on with the duties of the Publishing House. We had a large business, and made handsome profits on our sales, and by February, 1862, I had reduced the liabilities of the House about $38,000. Fort Donelson fell, and Gen. Sidney Johnston, then in command, evacuated Bowling Green, Kentucky, and passing through Nashville, crossed the Tennessee River, leaving Middle Tennessee to the mercy of the Federal army. After consultation, I took my family south of the Federal lines, and halted finally at Cornersville, Giles County. I left because my friends thought it advisable, and because Gen. Johnston so counseled, as I was told. I understood that the prejudice against me in the North was very strong, because I was Book Agent, and because I was known to be a thorough Southern man in sentiment. After the war was over I was told that there was a strong desire to arrest me and to deal with me severely.

I left my house and furniture—most of it in the hands of others. I also left most of my servants, expecting, perhaps, soon to return home. After several months, some persons went to my home, captured twelve or thirteen of my servants, ran the blockade, and brought them to Giles County This was all without my knowledge or direction, and I was really sorry they were brought out. Some of my friends advised me to sell them, and rid myself of the trouble. I said: "No; I will find them homes. Should the war go against the South, they will be freed. In that case, I wish no one else to sustain the loss. I want no one's money without value received." And besides they were family servants, and I did not intend to dispose of them on any terms, unless they wished me to sell them. I had never bought or sold a slave, but those which I had were family servants. I had treated them humanely, and never intended to wrong them in any sense. In my heart I believed slavery to be an evil—more of an evil to the master than to the slave—but under the circumstances, and in view of the teachings of God's word, I did not believe it to be a sin

per se. After the war they all returned, and were free, but fared
not so well as when I had them at home and provided for all
their wants. And now, though I do not justify the means by
which they were emancipated, I am glad that I am free from the
responsibility of owning slaves. I did the best I could with them
and for them. I fed and clothed them well, gave them good
houses and plenty of fuel, worked them moderately, provided
medical treatment for them when sick, and gave them ample religious privileges. I strove to preserve their morals and to teach
them to fear God and work righteousness.

Going south I tarried a little by the way, but finally stopped at
Cornersville, Tennessee, where I was kindly received and entertained by my friends, Mr. Ange Cox and the Rev. James R. Mc-
Clure. Their families were especially generous in our entertainment, and I here wish to leave on record my grateful remembrance of the hospitality and generosity of these two families, particularly of J. R. McClure and of his excellent wife. Leaving
my family at Cornersville, I went to Atlanta, Georgia, to meet
the Bishops and Board of Missions at their annual meeting.
While here the Federals crossed the State and occupied all Alabama north of the Tennessee River. This cut me off from my
family. I had no chance to return to Middle Tennessee. It was
a sad and sorrowful day. There I was in Georgia, my wife and
children in Tennessee, from home, and full of anxiety because of
a separation from me. This was in the early spring of 1862. Our
General Conference was to have met in New Orleans April 1,
1862, but now all hope of convening was given up, and I was left
out of employment and out of hearing of my family. Seeing no
prospect of returning, I visited my relatives in West Tennessee;
went to Gen. Johnston's army at Corinth, Mississippi, where I remained a short time, visiting my friends among the soldiers, and
looking to the sick in the hospitals. This was soon after the battle
of Shiloh, where Gen. Sidney Johnston was killed. The Confederates gained a great victory on the first day of the battle, but
Gen. Johnston having fallen, and the triumph considered complete,
the Confederates did not follow up their victory, so that on the
second day, the Federals having been re-enforced, the Confederates lost what they had won, or at least the battle was drawn, and
each side took time to rest and prepare for another conflict. I
went to North Alabama, where I spent the summer in preaching

in Russell's Valley and about Guntersville and in Jones's Valley. I passed many days at the house of Maj. Green, a most hospitable gentleman, who resided a few miles above where Birmingham now stands. There was no town at that time where this young city is now growing so rapidly.

In the meantime my family returned to Nashville, and I could hear nothing from them. They could receive no communications from me, or if any thing was sent it was uncertain as to its reaching its destination. Thus we were ignorant of each other's whereabouts or of the condition of either party. While at Guntersville Rev J H. Gardner volunteered to run the blockade and see my family and bring me word, while I traveled his circuit and filled his appointments. He made a safe and expeditious trip, saw my family, brought some clothing, and reported all well. Mr. Gardner was an Ohio man. He had come to Tennessee some years before as a teacher. I had been his friend. He united with the Tennessee Conference, and was a very promising man. This act of kindness and heroism I shall ever remember with gratitude.

Gen. Bragg, who succeeded Gen. Johnston in the command of the Army of Tennessee, in the latter part of the summer made a raid into Kentucky *via* Cumberland Gap. This drew the Federal army out of Middle Tennessee south of Nashville, so that in October I returned to Cornersville, where the Tennessee Conference met on the 15th of the month. No Bishop being present, I was elected President of the Conference, and conducted the business to the end. We were in session five days. The attendance was tolerably full, though some of the brethren were too far north to reach the seat of the Conference.

After the Conference I met my family at Mr. Ab. Scales's, a few miles from College Grove, not having seen them since early in the spring The meeting was joyful. They went again to J. R McClure's, near Cornersville, where we remained most of the winter.

Gen. Bragg returned from Kentucky and occupied Murfreesboro, Tennessee, where, during the winter, there was a heavy battle. I was in Georgia at the time of the fight, but soon returned and visited and preached to the soldiers. In the course of the spring Gen. Bragg fell back to Shelbyville and Tullahoma. In April I visited Macon, Georgia, in company with the Rev. A. S. Riggs, where there was a meeting of the Bishops and Missionary

Board. Bishop Kavanaugh, however, was not present. He was in Kentucky, and Bishop Soule was in Nashville. At this meeting it was determined to send missionaries to the Confederate army. These were to be supported by the Missionary Society, and were to co-operate with the chaplains in the army.

At this meeting I was appointed by the Bishops in charge of all the Methodist missionary work in the Army of the Tennessee. The Rev. Dr. Myers, who was Assistant Treasurer, and resided in Augusta, was to push the collections at home and to act in concert with the preachers in raising money to support the men in the field.

On our return to Shelbyville, Tennessee, we found our mutual friend and brother, the Rev. S. S. Moody, a corpse. He had lingered long with consumption. I visited him often while he was sick, and always found him patient and trusting God. I preached his funeral sermon and laid him away to rest. He was a noble Christian minister, and had been for many years a popular and useful member of the Tennessee Conference, filling many important appointments. He said to me in our last conversation that he only reproached himself for want of courage to preach against popular sins. This, he said, arose from timidity, or fear of hurting some one's feelings, but said it was a duty from which a minister of the gospel should never shrink. His was a lovely character.

I entered immediately on my work in the army, and as rapidly as I could engaged as many preachers as I thought the Missionary Society could sustain. There was, however, no lack of men or means. Many faithful preachers were ready for the work, and the people were willing to contribute to sustain them. I began my work in Shelbyville. I was hailed with pleasure by the officers and soldiers, and especially the chaplains. Among my first sermons as a missionary I preached in the Presbyterian Church to a crowded house, made up of officers, privates, and citizens. Among my hearers was Gen. (Bishop) Polk. He lingered in the aisle after the benediction, gave me a very cordial greeting and bade me Godspeed in my vocation. He said he much preferred to be there as a minister of the gospel than in any other capacity. During my whole stay in the army I was treated with great courtesy by all classes. Not a single word was unkindly spoken to me by any one who knew me.

Gen. Bragg gave me authority to draw rations and forage, and issued an order that all the missionaries should be allowed a like privilege. For some time I remained about Shelbyville, Tullahoma, and the neighborhoods adjoining, preaching day and night. A great work of grace had commenced in many of the commands, and the chaplains and preachers in the neighborhood were actively engaged in the precious revival that was springing up in almost every direction. Preachers of the various denominations were united in the cause of Christ. A few extracts from my diary will indicate the state of the work.

On May 17 I preached at 10 o'clock in the Presbyterian Church; house crowded; mostly officers and soldiers; serious attention. At 3 o'clock I preached in Bate's Brigade; a very good time; revival in the brigade.

On May 19 I preached in Bushrod Johnson's Brigade; thirty to forty mourners; glorious work in this command.

On May 20 I preached at night in Gen. Polk's Brigade; many mourners; several conversions.

On May 21, at night, I preached in Gen. Wood's Brigade; forty to fifty mourners; fifteen or twenty conversions. Powerful work here.

On May 22 I made an address in Gen. Riddle's Brigade; a great work here; already more than one hundred conversions in this command. And so the work went forward.

June 15 I rode to Cornersville to visit my family. Here I was taken with the yellow jaundice, which rendered me unfit for duty.

Early in July Gen. Bragg retreated from Shelbyville to Chattanooga. I was sick at the time at Cornersville, and had no knowledge of his movement till he was across the Tennessee River. Sick as I was, I made my way on horseback south to the Tennessee River, crossed at Lamb's Ferry, and reached Courtland, Alabama, where I remained a short time, and then spent about two weeks with Dr. Smith at Mountain Home, recruiting my health. Having improved, I set out for Chattanooga, where I was to join the army. Preaching on Sand Mountain by the way, I reached Chattanooga and preached in Gen. Wright's Brigade on the night of August 14. He was camped a few miles from the city. There were five conversions that night, among them a captain of one of the companies.

18

August 16 I preached in Chattanooga to a large congregation at the Methodist Church. Here I met for the first time William E. Munsey. He was a young man, simple in manners and sweet in disposition, just beginning to take high rank as a preacher. From this till the 19th of September I was constantly engaged in preaching, visiting, and holding prayer-meetings in various parts of the army. At Chattanooga, Missionary Ridge, Harrison, Tyner's Station, and La Fayette, Georgia, many precious souls were converted during this revival.

On the 19th and 20th of September, 1863, the great battle was fought at Chickamauga, some fifteen miles from Chattanooga. The slaughter was tremendous on both sides, but the Confederates held the field, while the Federals retreated to Chattanooga. Had Gen. Bragg followed up his victory on the morning of the 21st, his triumph would have been complete. I remained on the battle-field eleven days, nursing the sick and ministering to the wounded. The sight was awful. Thousands of men killed and wounded. They lay thickly all around, shot in every possible manner, and the wounded dying every day. O what sufferings! Among the wounded were many Federal soldiers who had been captured in the fight. To these I ministered, prayed with them, and wrote letters by flag of truce to their friends in the North. They seemed to appreciate every act of kindness. In this battle my son James—who had just entered the army a few days before— was slightly wounded, and my nephew, J. P. McFerrin, was severely shot in the thigh by a minie-ball, which caused him great pain and disabled him for years to come. Many a noble soldier fell on this field to rise no more till the last trumpet shall sound. Here I talked to the wounded and prayed for the dying. Here I saw Capt. Otey just before he died; he expressed hope in God. Here Maj. Carr, of Rienzi, Mississippi, died of a wound, full of hope, full of joy. And many others went home to God.

After eleven days, in company with Capt. Gray, I passed through Georgia to Huntsville, Alabama, and thence to Cornersville, Tennessee, where I met my family, and where I remained a few days, and then recrossed the Tennessee, and by a long route reached Missionary Ridge, near Chattanooga, where Gen. Bragg's forces were in line, protected to some extent by breastworks. The Federals occupied Chattanooga. The two armies were in full view of each other for weeks. All along the foot of Missionary

Ridge we preached almost every night to crowded assemblies, and here many precious souls were brought to God. During this encampment I went on the summit of Lookout Mountain, and had a full view of both armies. The Federals occupied Chattanooga, and were camped along the Tennessee River on both sides of the stream. They had fortifications and strong batteries, and kept up almost a constant firing on the Confederates. The shells and balls were thrown into the lines of the Confederates, oftentimes creating excitement and anxiety. The Confederates occasionally returned the fire. The Confederates formed a long line on the west side of Missionary Ridge. This ridge took its name from a missionary station near its base, organized among the Indians in early times. The full view of both armies, numbering more than one hundred thousand men, was a grand sight, and filled the beholder with awe. After weeks of delay, and after Gen. Bragg had sent Gen. Longstreet to Knoxville, Gen. Grant made an attack on Bragg's army. Bragg's line of battle was so long and so thin that it was impossible for him to maintain his position against a superior force. After several hours' heavy firing Gen. Bragg retreated and abandoned the field. The loss of his army in killed and wounded was not so heavy as that sustained by Gen. Grant; yet he was overpowered by numbers and was compelled to retreat. This was a sad day with the Confederates. The army of Gen. Bragg never overcame the demoralization of that day. True they retreated in pretty good order, and for many months recruited around Dalton, Georgia, and under the leadership of Gen. Joseph E. Johnston, who superseded Gen. Bragg, were inspired with new courage. But the failure to follow up the victories at Shiloh, Murfreesboro, and Chickamauga, and the retreat from Missionary Ridge, dispirited the troops, and they afterward were not flushed with strong hopes of final success. A retreating army, with a constant decrease of numbers by sickness, death, and capture, is not likely to improve much in courage. And yet in the face of all these discouragements it was marvelous to note the spirit and pluck of the men.

The Confederate army went into winter quarters at Dalton. Here they remained until the month of May. During these many months the chaplains and missionaries were at work— preaching, visiting the sick, and distributing Bibles, tracts, and religious newspapers. Preaching was kept up in Dalton every night, except four, for nearly four months; and in the camps all around the city preaching and prayer-meetings occurred every night. The soldiers erected stands, improvised seats, and even built log churches, where they worshiped God in spirit and in truth. The result was glorious; thousands were happily converted and were prepared for the future that awaited them. Officers and men were alike brought under religious influence. Our custom was to admit persons into any Church they might choose, while in an army association we were all one. A good deal of my time was spent about Dalton, and yet I traveled up and down the lines, working wherever there was an urgent call.

In the month of February, 1864, I visited Kingston, Georgia, where I remained some twenty days, preaching to an artillery command that had gone back to rest and recruit their horses. I preached nineteen sermons. We had a glorious meeting. About sixty souls professed conversion. Among the converts were the sons of the Rev. S. W. Moore, D.D., and the Rev. Isaac E. Ebbert, D.D., friends of mine in the Memphis Conference; and also a son of a Presbyterian minister. Young Warner Moore afterward became a preacher, and at the time of this writing is a member of the Memphis Conference. Young Ebbert went home at the close of the war, and made a highly respectable citizen, and was a faithful member of the Methodist Episcopal Church, South. Three young men converted at this meeting afterward became preachers—one a Methodist (Moore), one a Presbyterian, and one a Baptist. During our meeting an Irishman from Grenada, Mississippi, became very much concerned about his soul. He was at the altar for prayer, and when an opportunity was given to unite with the Church he came forward. I asked his name. The answer was, "Patrick O'Sullivan." "To what Church do you desire to attach yourself?" I asked. He answered, "To the Holy Roman Catholic Church." I gave him a letter recommending him to the fatherly care of the priests of the Romish Church. Pat went through the war, and the last I heard of him he was at home in Grenada, Mississippi.

My head-quarters were with Dr. Avent, the surgeon in charge of the hospitals at Kingston. He was from Murfreesboro, Tennessee; was a noble Christian man and a member of our Church. He added much to my comfort while this meeting was going on. I also found a good resting-place at the home of Dr. Harris, in

Kingston, and at the pleasant residences of the Rev. Mr. Best and Col. Hawkins Price, in the vicinity. These families were more than kind.

In all my life, perhaps, I never witnessed more displays of God's power in the awakening and conversion of sinners than in these protracted meetings during the winter and spring of 1863-4. The preachers of the various denominations were alike zealous— Presbyterians, Baptists, Cumberland Presbyterians, Episcopalians, Methodists—all at work. Our army ministerial associations were pleasant, and at our meetings we had precious seasons of joy and rejoicing while recounting the victories of the cross of Christ. The preachers generally took fare with the soldiers, marched with them, camped with them, ate with them, and suffered and rejoiced with them.

About the last of April, 1864, I left the army and went to Montgomery, Alabama, to meet the Bishops and Board of Missions in Church council. On the way I visited Atlanta, Newnan, and La Grange, Georgia, and preached at all these places. At Atlanta a Mr. Steadman gave me a bolt of linen (blue). I had a suit made of it for summer wear. It was pleasant, but attracted much attention. I divided the bolt with a number of preachers, who had the bosoms of their shirts made of the article. It was well suited to army wear.

At La Grange, Georgia, I attended a quarterly meeting in company with the Rev. J. Blakely Smith. On Sunday I preached on the resurrection of the dead. A lady was present—Mrs. Judge Bull—who had lost a son in the battle of Manassas. She was noted for her intelligence and piety, but she had gone almost into despair because of the loss of her son; she went into retirement, and for a long time had staid away from Church until her · friends had become greatly concerned about her. Under the sermon on that day she was relieved from all her troubles, praised God aloud, and said he had sent the preacher there for her relief from sorrow. It was a time of great religious comfort in the congregation. Here I was entertained at the house of the Hon. Ben. Hill.

At Montgomery, on May 4, 1864, we met four of the Bishops— Andrew, Paine, Pierce, and Early. A number of the members of the Mission Board were also present. The meeting was interesting. The condition of the country and the Church was freely discussed. All resolved to sustain the work of religion in the army. Men were found willing to go with the soldiers and preach to them the word of life, and there was no lack of liberality in contributing funds. The hearts and the purses of the people were open.

While at Montgomery news came that the two armies had commenced hostilities a few miles from Dalton, in front of Rocky Face, a noted mountain north of the town. I delayed not, but left on the train immediately for the place of conflict. I met the Confederates at Resaca, and witnessed a severe skirmish in which many were killed and wounded on both sides. Here the Rev. Mr. McMullin, an aged Presbyterian minister who was a chaplain, led a regiment in an attack upon the line of the enemy. He was unarmed, but threw himself at the head of the column, followed by his son, a brave young soldier. They both fell in battle. The loss of the brave old preacher was much regretted, but all judged the act by which he lost his life as rash and needless. At this fight Col. Stanton, a chivalrous officer from Tennessee, was killed. He was a noble man and a special friend of mine. His body was brought off the field and buried during the night or the next morning. He did not fall into the hands of the enemy.

From this time till about the 10th of June there was almost constant fighting day and night. Gen. Joseph E. Johnston was still in command of the Confederate army, and Gen. Sherman was leading the Federal army. Gen. Johnston's effective forces were perhaps less in numbers by forty thousand than those of Gen. Sherman. When Gen. Johnston reached Kennesaw Mountain, north of Marietta, his forces fortified and arrested the progress of the Federals. Here and in this neighborhood there was a great deal of heavy skirmishing, and many lives were lost. At New Hope there was a ferocious fight, in which both armies lost many brave men. Near to this place Bishop (General) Polk was killed by a shell. He was on Pine Mountain, watching the movements of the enemy about a mile distant. Gen. Polk was a good man, a brave officer, and a skillful general; but I always questioned the propriety of his enlisting in the war as a soldier and general. He might have been equally useful as a minister of the gospel. So it was; he died a brave soldier, and his death was greatly lamented.

From Marietta the army fell back to Atlanta, where Gen. Johnston made a stand, keeping back Sherman and his army for some time; but finally he determined to evacuate the "Gate City," as Atlanta was called. This gave dissatisfaction at head-quarters. General Johnston was relieved, and Gen. Hood was made chief commander. This change was received with great displeasure by many of the troops, for I might say the whole army was attached to Gen. Johnston. Gen. Hood was a younger man, a brave and daring officer, and determined at once to make more rapid and aggressive movements. After several heavy skirmishes he re solved to flank Sherman by marching his army into Middle Tennessee and capturing Nashville, and thus cut off the supplies of Sherman's army. He soon had his line in motion, crossed the Chattahoochee, passed through Upper Georgia into Alabama, on to Tuscumbia and Florence, where he remained two weeks or more. During all this marching and fighting we kept up religious service whenever it was possible to collect the men together We preached in Atlanta, Macon, Perry, and intermediate points From May till September 9 the army was moving from Dalton to Jonesboro, and I might say every foot of ground was contested. Thousands in both armies were slain in battle or died of sickness along the line of march In the meantime I visited the hospitals, and preached with the missionaries and chaplains whenever it was possible to do so. During this period my health failed to some extent, and I went back with my sick son to Newnan and Perry, Georgia, where we both remained for a season until we recruited somewhat, and then we returned to the army and joined the forces as they moved toward Tennessee. At Newnan we were entertained by Maj Clark and family, and at Perry we found a delightful home at the house of the Rev. J. Rufus Felder.

In the march from Georgia to Nashville we had but few opportunities for religious services, except at Tuscumbia and Florence. Here for two weeks we had refreshing seasons. Large congregations assembled in the churches and in camp, and many souls were converted and Christians were made to rejoice. This seemed to be a preparation for the disasters that followed.

Leaving Florence November 21, 1864, the army marched rapidly till we reached Columbia, Tennessee. The people everywhere hailed the return of the Confederates with joy, and made many demonstrations of their great pleasure. Alas! it was a short season of rejoicing. Many of the brave men were march·

ing into the jaws of death; a slaughter-pen was just before them. Tarrying three days at Columbia, the army moved to Franklin, where occurred the most bloody battle of the war in proportion to the numbers engaged. Reaching the vicinity of Franklin on the evening of November 30, the fight began some time late in the afternoon and continued till a late hour in the night, when the Federals withdrew and retreated to Nashville. The slaughter was terrible on both sides. The Federals were strongly fortified, and the Confederates fought in an open field. They charged the breastworks several times, and hundreds were shot down while the muzzles of their muskets rested on the head-logs of the fortifications. By the rising of the sun the next morning I was passing through the heaps of slain soldiers, having spent the night at the field hospital, a mile distant from the main line of battle. The sight was sickening, heart-rending, horrible, awful. Such a scene I never before looked upon. I had witnessed more extensive fights, but here the dead lay in heaps. Many brave officers fell in this bloody fight. Among these may be mentioned Generals Cleburne, Gist, Streight, Adams, and Granberry; and others were wounded. My son was unhurt, for which I gave God thanks; but my heart was sad and my grief inexpressible at the loss of so many valuable lives. Never before had I been so fully impressed with the cruelty of war, notwithstanding I had witnessed many bloody fights. The dead buried and the wounded provided for as well as possible, the army moved on toward Nashville. Gen. Bate's Brigade turned off in the direction of Murfreesboro, and I accompanied his command. Murfreesboro was strongly fortified by the Federals. Troops were sent out to arrest the progress of Gen. Bate. A heavy skirmish occurred on Steward's Creek. After an hour or two of fighting both forces retired. Gen. Forrest coming to the assistance of Gen. Bate, and much of the railroad being destroyed between Murfreesboro and Nashville, Gen. Bate moved toward the latter place, where he joined Gen. Hood, who had formed a line on the south side of the city. After the fight at Steward's Creek I went in advance of the division alone. I had become so anxious to hear from my family, and hoping by some good providence to convey intelligence to them that James and I were still alive and in the neighborhood of home, that I could wait no longer. The ride was tiresome and hazardous. Many thoughts crowded into my mind, and I did not know what moment I might fall into the hands of the enemy; but I passed on, and reached my point of destination safely. Word was conveyed to my wife, who was on the north side of the Cumberland River. She ran the blockade, and met me at David McGavock's—her cousin—on the 7th of December. This was a joyful meeting after an absence from each other of fourteen long months. I asked for the children, but could not see them. We talked of war and home and many things, but could not see into the dim future. I told her where I had been, what I had done, how many good meetings we had had, how I had waited on the sick and carried rations to the soldiers, and how grateful the boys were. She listened with interest, and then, rising to her feet and standing on tiptoe, she said: "Husband, stay with them to the last!"

James obtained a furlough, and spent a few days with his mother. On the 14th he returned to the line of battle, and on the 15th the Federals moved out of the city and made an attack on Hood. I had gone down to the line that afternoon, and expected to return to David McGavock's that night or the next day; but the fight became fierce, and I spent a part of the night in riding to and fro, and a part in sleep at the house of W. L. Ewing. On the morning of the 16th the fight became general, and continued all day. Hood's ranks were broken, and he retreated toward Franklin. The confusion was great. The face of the earth had been covered with snow and ice for several days. Then there came a heavy rain; the snow and ice were melting, and the poor soldiers—many of them barefooted, or nearly so— moved back with bleeding feet and sad hearts, their hopes being blasted. They had expected when they left Georgia to make a successful campaign and regain their homes and see their friends, but now it was over, and their spirits sunk within them. My son was missing. His comrades who escaped reported him killed or captured. His regiment occupied the last position taken by the enemy, and his fellow-soldiers could give no satisfactory report of him. My wife, I heard, was still on the south side of the river when the Federal cavalry approached and cut off retreat in the direction of the children, so I was not certain of her fate, supposing it possible that she might have fallen into the hands of the enemy. In this state of uncertainty I turned my back on home, and with downcast spirits accompanied the retreating army. On we went in the rain, in the snow, swollen streams, and roads almost impassable. We passed Franklin, Columbia, Pulaski, and were pushing on to cross the Tennessee River, knowing that the Federals were in pursuit. The Rev. William Burr, W. Mooney, Felix R. Hill, and myself formed a party, and moved on in a squad together. Turning aside, south of Pulaski, to the home of Mrs. Jones, the widow of one of our preachers—a quiet and retired place—we spent the night. The next morning my horse was gone. He had been stolen, and I was left afoot. What shall be done? A citizen close by had a horse hid out. He could be bought for one hundred and fifty dollars, Tennessee money, but no Confederate money would be taken. I had Confederate, but no Tennessee funds. But Mrs. Jones offered to lend me the amount. The horse was brought in, and we were soon on the way, crossing the Tennessee River, which was very full, on a pontoon bridge.

In company with several friends in the quartermaster's department I went to Columbus, Mississippi, where I rested, and secured a new supply of clothing; remained three or four weeks waiting for the army to swing round by Corinth and Tupelo, Mississippi. I preached many sermons in Columbus, and received many evidences of hospitality. The Rev. A. S. Andrews, D.D., who was the pastor of the Methodist Church, gave me much attention. The ladies fitted me out with a new suit of brown jeans, which, though not fine, was comfortable, and came in "the nick of time." Long did I wait in painful anxiety to hear from my wife and son. A scout had promised to send me word. He was true. At last a note came: " Wife reached her children in safety; all well; James captured and taken to a Northern prison.—W." O the joy! O the relief to know that both were alive, and that no worse harm had befallen either of them!

In the meantime my stolen horse had been recovered, and with a small company I went to Columbus, Georgia, and on to Augusta. Here I remained, visiting the hospitals and preaching a few times, and making arrangements with the Rev. Dr. E. H. Myers—the Assistant Treasurer of our Missionary Society—for the payment of our army missionaries. Confederate money had gone down till it was worth but little; but it was all we had, and every thing to eat and wear cost heavily. At Augusta I met several chaplains and missionaries working in the hospitals and waiting till they could join the moving forces. Having accomplished what I could, I moved on across the State of South Carolina that I might meet the Confederate army as it moved into North Carolina, with the evident intention of uniting, if possible, with the army of Gen. Lee in Virginia. Gen. Joseph E. Johnston had been restored to the chief command, and the soldiers were flushed with the hope of a junction with the Virginia forces. Johnston's aim was to flank Sherman and make the junction with Lee as soon as possible; but in the midst of all these hopes news came to Gen. Johnston that Gen. Lee had surrendered to Gen. Grant. But one alternative was left. Gen. Johnston was compelled to surrender to Gen. Sherman or lose the remnant of his army, which had been reduced by sickness and death to a small force compared with the forces of the enemy. Gen. Johnston, having swept around by way of Raleigh, North Carolina, halted at Greensboro, entered into a treaty, and surrendered all his forces. The news of the surrender of the two favorite commanders fell like a pall of death upon the troops and upon the Southern country. But the war was ended, and the Confederate States and the Confederate army were conquered. While the terms of the surrender were being settled the Confederates were encamped in the neighborhood of Greensboro, where I preached several sermons to different commands. While I dwelt on such passages as " Here we have no continuing city, but we seek one to come," many hearts were moved. At the close of one sermon to a Texas brigade a fine-looking soldier stepped up to me, and taking me by the hand, said: " We thank you for your attention to the soldiers; we thank you for your sermons. All over now. I will never see you again. God bless you! Good-by!" Loosing his hand, he left a silver quarter in mine, and turned instantly away. He had drawn the day before one dollar and twenty-five cents in specie, and thus gave one-fifth of the amount. Noble spirit! I brought the quarter home and gave it to my wife, stating to her that that was the result of the war. She has that quarter at the time of this writing.

All the terms of the surrender settled, we soon made preparations for moving toward our home. Each soldier was *paroled*. Gen. Palmer, of Murfreesboro, put me on his staff, and hence I was allowed to keep my horse, and I accompanied the Tennessee troops led by the General. We crossed the mountains, most of the men on foot, and passing Asheville, North Carolina, we arrived at Greeneville, Tennessee. Here I camped out for my last night during the dreadful war. The march across the mountains was heavy, but the men bore up with great fortitude. The idea of getting home, though a conquered home, stimulated the brave fellows who had been in many hard-fought battles.

At Greeneville the horses and wagons were taken by the Federal officer having charge of that post. The General and his staff were allowed to retain theirs. This gave me the privilege of putting my horse on the train and having it shipped to Chattanooga. At Chattanooga an order was passed, or pretended to have been passed, that the officers were required to pay ten cents per mile freight on each horse from Chattanooga to Nashville, notwithstanding it was stipulated at Greeneville that the horses were to be shipped to Nashville. The officers of the army had, I supposed, full control of the road. No doubt it was believed that the Confederates could not raise the money to meet the charges, and therefore would lose their stock. But they found friends, and we borrowed the money and paid the freight in advance, fifteen dollars and ten cents for each horse—a round price—but we saved our horses, which were worth more to us than the cost of transportation.

We reached Nashville late at night, and found friends to take us in. It was now the 20th of May, 1865. My family were seven miles in the country, at the house of Mr. N. P. Gee. I could not leave the city without a pass, as sentinels were placed at every street leading to the country. As soon as the way was open I left and made my way to my family. I met them all except James, who was still a prisoner in Camp Douglas, Chicago. Our meeting was joyful. It had now been more than three years since we left home, and nearly two years since I had parted with some of the children. Through all the casualties of war we had all been spared; and though we had lost most of our property, our lives had been preserved. My family were boarding, and had seen some hard times during the great struggle. Sometimes in the neighborhood of Nashville and sometimes out, they scarcely knew where to call home. My dwelling-house adjoining Nashville, in Edgefield, as it was then called, on the east side of the Cumberland River, had been taken for a hospital or pest-house. My fences and out-houses were nearly all destroyed, and my beautiful grove of twenty acres was utterly laid waste. Now it was occupied by refugees and held by the Government as abandoned property They seized it, held it, and declared it abandoned. The house, of course, was in a dilapidated condition, but by an arrangement with the agent my brother, A. P. McFerrin, leased or rented the house, with the understanding that I was to occupy it. So soon as the refugees left it an old woman, who was following the army with beer and whisky, entered and took possession of the premises, where she kept a tippling-shop and a dance-house till she was removed by the military. Then my house was destroyed by fire, and the desolation of our home made complete. The house was burned on Sunday morning about daylight. I had an appointment to preach that day at " City Road." My sermon had been prepared from a chosen text: " Here have we no continuing city, but we seek one to come." Nowise disconcerted, I met a large congregation, delivered my sermon, and saw many of my old friends. I shed no tears over the ashes of my burned house, but rejoiced in hope of living in a house not made with hands, eternal in the heavens. Now for keeping house somewhere, that I could have my family around me once more. Mr. McGavock's house was also in the hands of the Federals. After some time and effort, it was surrendered to the owner, when the two families went in and began life anew. Horses gone, cattle gone, fences gone, timber gone, money gone, servants gone—the outlook was unpromising. Nothing daunted, however, we went to work to make a living, if not able to repair our fortunes. What real estate I had was in the hands of the Government, to be confiscated or restored at some future time—no telling which.

Not having possession of our property, we could not use it in any way for our own benefit. The Publishing House, too, was in the hands of the Government, and hence we could transact no business there. October came. The Tennessee Conference, that had not convened for two years, met at Tulip Street Church, Edgefield, Bishop Kavanaugh presiding. The house was in an unfinished condition, but it was our only chance, as McKendree was occupied by Northern preachers. The Conference closed, and the Bishop read me out as Book Agent—an agent without a house or goods to sell! Soon after the adjournment I went to Washington City. Mr. Lincoln had been assassinated, and Andrew Johnson elevated to the Presidency. The Confederates had surrendered, and it was doubtful what Congress might order, or what would be the policy of the Administration. It was soon made manifest, however, that Mr. Johnson intended, as far as possible, to favor the Southern people and restore the seceding States to the Union. He issued proclamations and announced the conditions on which Southern rebels should be pardoned, restored to citizenship, and have their property restored to them. My friends applied for me, and Gov. Brownlow, an inveterate Republican, joined in the request, and Mr. Johnson signed my paper. I was one of the first persons in the State of Tennessee so favored. Encouraged by this, I visited Washington in the interest of the Publishing House, and had a brief interview with Mr. Johnson. He requested me to make a brief statement of facts in writing, which I did, and left for home. It was but a few days till he sent an order to the post commander to restore the House to the authorities of the Church. I immediately, in connection with R. Abbey, took possession, and began to set things in order. We refitted the book-store and resumed the publication of the *Christian Advocate*.

On my way from Washington City, in company with the Hon. Milton Brown, of Jackson, Tennessee, I received a very serious hurt, that well-nigh proved to be fatal. At the Relay House, near Baltimore, we purposed changing cars for the West, having taken the train at Washington City in the evening about 8 o'clock. On arriving at the junction where we were to change cars the conductor failed, as I believed, to give the usual notice, and perceiving by lamp-light that we had reached the Relay House, I arose from my seat, and with baggage in hand asked the conductor if I could make the change. He had just rung his bell for starting, but said I could jump from the platform, and held his lantern and directed me how to make the jump. As I leaped from the car I careened and fell upon the platform beside the railroad, and was so shocked that I was unable to arise and walk to the office, a few feet from the place of the accident. A wood-sawyer happened to pass at the moment, raised me up, and bore me along to the station. I was severely hurt, but was not aware of the extent of the injury. Judge Brown, who was an old railroad President, made the conductor stop the train, and he got off in quiet, but supposed I had gone to Baltimore. Seeing my condition, he insisted that I should go to the hotel near at hand; but I thought it was only a shock, and that I would soon recover. Within a few moments the Western-bound train came up, and I was placed on the sleeper, where I spent about the most painfully-suffering night of my life. About sunrise the train reached Cumberland, Maryland. I requested to be taken from the train and carried to the hotel. I sent for a physician, who examined me carefully and said no bones were broken and no joints dislocated, but that my whole nervous system was shocked. He treated me kindly, and would receive nothing for his attention. The landlord, too, was kind, and would receive no pay for my entertainment. The colored boy who waited on my room was from Gallatin, Tennessee. He was very attentive, especially when he learned that I was from Tennessee. He waited on me faithfully, and gave me, when I left the hotel, a crutch that had been used by a wounded soldier. This I found to be an important help on my journey home and for weeks after my arrival at Nashville. The doctor, the hotel-keeper, and the young darky all have my gratitude, and I will never forget their kindness. The colored boy, of course, was compensated, but he had served me faithfully without much promise of reward. Having rested for two or three days, I was carried and put on the train, and after a painful journey reached home in a disabled condition. From this dreadful shock I did not fully recover for years. My nerves seemed to be unstrung or wrought up to the highest state of excitement. I lost flesh to the amount of sixty pounds. My liver was out of order, and my complexion sallow. Indeed, many of my friends predicted that my days were nearly numbered and that I would never be well again. But I had faith in God, and believed if I acted prudently I would recover. I was not afraid to die. No, blessed be God! my sky was clear and my hope unshaken; but I wanted to live for a season that I might put my family in condition to be above want. Several of my children were to be educated, a home was to be fitted up, financial matters were to be arranged, and provision generally had to be made; and besides, I did not feel that my work was done. So I kept in good heart, worked when able, rested when I could not work, and thus passed the winter, and made preparations as far as possible for the approaching General Conference. The Rev. R. Abbey still remained with me, and did much valuable service.

THE GENERAL CONFERENCE OF 1866.

THE General Conference convened in New Orleans in April, 1866. My brethren honored me again by placing me in the delegation. In due time I was at the seat of the Conference, and was in my place all the time, though in feeble condition. The session was important. The Conference appointed to meet in the same city in 1862 failed to convene because of the war. The conflict was now over, but the political elements of the country were in a fearful state of excitement, and the Church and the General Conference were not insensible of the fact. The body moved with caution and great circumspection; but, owing to the unsettled condition of affairs, the minds of many of the brethren seemed to be restless, and many changes and modifications in our Church polity were suggested. A few brethren seemed resolved to change many of the long-standing rules and usages of the Church. The debates were animated, but conservative measures finally prevailed to a large extent. Here lay representation was introduced. I favored its introduction, with certain restrictions and limitations. I was on the committee that framed the law as it now stands in the Discipline, with a slight modification. In the committee-room the discussion at one time became sharp; but the point in the committee and before the General Conference was carried—that the laity in the Annual Conferences should not be allowed to vote on "ministerial character or relations." So it passed, and so the Annual Conferences passed it, and it thus became a law governing the action of the Annual Conferences. The argument swaying the minds of a majority of the committee and the General Conference was that in the work of the itinerant ministry itinerants should be clothed with power to pass on the character and fix the relations of their fellow-laborers; or, according to the general tenor of Methodist law, every man should be tried by his peers. "Local men," said Bishop Soule, "have local views." At the General Conference in Memphis, in 1870, the word "relations"

(288)

was left out in the report of the Committee on Revisals. This I did not observe at the time the report was read and that part thereof adopted. I think changing the law at that time and in that manner was unconstitutional. The General Conference of 1866 had framed and passed the law by a constitutional majority, and sent it round to the Annual Conferences for concurrence. The Annual Conferences, by a constitutional majority, had concurred, and thus the new rule became the law of the Church, and I think it could not be altered without the vote of the constitutional majority in the General and Annual Conferences.

The General Conference of 1866, I think, made a mistake in extending the time of the pastorate from two to four years. I think this rule greatly embarrasses the Bishops in their work of stationing the preachers. Many men now think, when they are in good appointments, that to be changed before four years expire degrades them; and many who are in hard appointments think it oppressive for them to be kept four years on an inferior work. I, perhaps, will never see the old rule restored, but I wish the law was the same as in former times, not that I have any personal interest in the matter, but for the good of the whole Connection.

We had another great struggle at New Orleans on the publishing interests of the Church. The Publishing House had prospered up to the time the Federal troops reached Nashville. When they occupied the city, of course the business was suspended, and not long thereafter the Federal authorities took possession of the establishment, and held and used it in the interest of the Government and the army. Much of the stock and material had been used up, and the machinery greatly injured. Besides, the South had been greatly impoverished by the war, and the business of the House prostrated. The question arose whether, in view of all the surroundings, the House should be continued or sold out, and let the Church have its printing done by contract. The debates were long and spirited. I took part in the discussion, and favored the continuance of the House. This side prevailed, and it was resolved to make a strong effort to sustain the establishment. In view of my feeble health, I positively declined the nomination for re-election. My physical condition at that time would not allow me to entertain the thought of again entering upon a business so onerous and so important to the Church. A. H. Redford, D.D, was elected.

19

The missionary work at this General Conference was divided into two Boards—Foreign and Domestic. The Domestic Board was to take charge of all the home missionary work, and was to co-operate with the Annual Conferences and Bishops in supplying destitute places. This Board was located at Nashville. To the secretaryship of this Board I was elected without solicitation on my part. Indeed, I did not anticipate the appointment, and had no idea of being elected till a few moments before the vote was taken.

Four new Bishops were elected at this General Conference— namely: Revs. W. M. Wightman, of South Carolina; E. M. Marvin, of Missouri; D. S. Doggett, of Virginia; and H. N. McTyeire, of Alabama—all good men. Two of them at the time of this writing are in their graves, having finished their work. Bishop Wightman is feeble. Bishop McTyeire is yet in good health. In the election of Bishops quite a number of votes were cast for me, and I was assured by many friends that had my health been good I would certainly have been elected by a large vote. How far this was true I do not pretend to know. Nor is it a matter that gives me much concern. It is pleasant to have the love and confidence of your brethren, and it is lawful " to covet earnestly the best gifts," if they be desired for purposes of good. The office of Bishop in our Church is considered an honorable position, and is certainly an open door to great usefulness, provided one has the proper qualifications and is well adapted to the vocation; but it is a place of toil and many delicate responsibilities. Few men in our Connection have had better opportunities than myself of knowing the difficulties and thankless nature of the work of our General Superintendents; and I here record that, in view of all the " ups and downs," I feel very thankful that I was never put into the office. Moreover, I believe in the direction and control of Providence, and that God shapes the course of those who seek to follow the leadings of his Spirit. I have no regret, no mortification; have realized no disappointment in any of my connections with the work of the ministry. I have been placed in positions above what I considered my qualifications, and only console myself, first, that I never sought preferment; and, secondly, that in whatever place I have been found it was the order of my brethren and, I trust, the will of God. I have known many men to fail and lose their power for usefulness by being elevated to positions without ability to meet the demands upon them.

The General Conference over, I returned home, soon organized the Board of Domestic Missions, and entered upon my work. I visited the Annual Conferences, District Conferences, and as many popular meetings as I could. My health soon began to improve, and I came up slowly but surely. For a time I sat and preached, or leaning upon the pulpit or on my stick I did the best I could. I was allowed *ten per cent.* on the collections for Domestic Missions in each Conference. The remainder was under the control of the Annual Conferences. These Boards and the Bishops applied the money as they chose. With the ten per cent. I was to pay all my traveling expenses, my printing-bill, postage, stationery, room-rent—every thing; and my salary, too, was to come out of this fund. In the four years these expenses were all met, and a surplus of several thousand dollars was turned over to the general work. Dr. Sehon, for a time, and then Drs. Cunnyngham and Munsey conducted the affairs of the Foreign Board, which was located at Baltimore. Dr. Cunnyngham, however, only acted as a corresponding Secretary. The interests of the Foreign Board suffered from an unfortunate move of its Treasurer, W. T. Smithson. He invested eleven thousand dollars of the money in his hands as Treasurer in some sort of stocks, intending, he said, to double the sum for the benefit of the Board; but, unfortunately, he lost it all. He was never able to replace the money—since dead; a total loss. Why any one intrusted with funds of the Church should venture to make such a speculation is wonderful. He was a sanguine man, and I suppose intended well; but the mistake was sad. Another great trouble was that at the end of the war our Missionary Society found itself in debt some seventy or eighty thousand dollars. We had money in the treasury more than sufficient to meet all the liabilities of the Society, but it was worthless, being Confederate money and bonds. It devolved on the Secretary of the Foreign Board to raise the money to pay this old debt. This was a heavy undertaking, and had a tendency to crush the operations of the Board and discourage the Secretary. In the midst of this he resigned, and the office of Secretary was left vacant for a time—only Dr. Cunnyngham kept up the correspondence to some extent. Dr. W. E. Munsey was elected to fill the vacancy one year before the meeting of the General Conference.

THE GENERAL CONFERENCE OF 1870.

WHEN the General Conference came on at Memphis, in 1870, a strong and successful effort was made to consolidate the two Boards, and have but one Secretary. The movement called forth protracted discussions in the Committee on Missions and in the General Conference. I rather favored the continuance of the two Boards, for the reasons: (1) That the experiment had not been fairly tested; and (2) that our people in many places in the weaker Conferences needed help, and we had no Church Extension Society. I, however, quietly submitted to the decision of the General Conference that there should be but one Board. I was fully satisfied, however, that there should be two Secretaries. There was a heavy debt still hanging over the old Society. Our Mission in China was springing into new life, and there were pressing calls in other directions, as well as a growing work on the frontier, and I believed there was full work for two efficient Secretaries; nor have I till this day changed my opinion. Ideas of economy prevailed, and it was resolved to have but one Secretary and one Board. As I afterward more fully learned, the plans had already been matured, and it was understood that the two Boards consolidated into one should be located at Nashville, and Dr. Munsey was to be elected Secretary. For some reason, I can not tell what, this movement was not made known to me; perhaps it was out of respect to my feelings, or perhaps it was a matter of forgetfulness. At any rate, I only guessed or conjectured that some plan was on foot that I had not fully understood. Dr. Munsey was now Secretary of the Foreign Board, having been in office one year. He was in the midst of great popularity, and his friends believed he would make a successful Secretary and do much, especially toward paying off the old debt. I was no candidate, but I knew some of my friends intended to nominate me for the office. Had the brethren in the lead of the other movement mentioned the matter to me, I would have de-

(292)

clined the nomination altogether, and would have given Dr. Mun-sey my support, or I would have harmonized in the election of any one thought to be the most suitable person; but I never fa-vored any secret plans or combinations, and made up my mind to be still and abide the decision of my brethren and the direction of Providence. The motives of the brethren I did not question, the manner of procedure I did not approve; but I felt that all would end right so far as I was concerned. There were wide fields and plenty of work in every direction, and I had a longing desire to be in the pastoral work again. When the election came on four persons were nominated: Dr. Munsey, Dr. Sehon, Dr. Cunnyngham, and myself. The three brethren put in nomina-tion were all prominent, good men, and all my friends; but Dr. Munsey was considered the most prominent, and his election was confidently expected. On the first ballot Dr. Munsey received 46 votes; Dr. Cunnyngham, 31; Dr. Sehon, 4; and McFerrin, 74; some scattering; 156 votes cast. No election. On the second ballot Munsey received 50 votes; Cunnyngham, 14; L. Parker, 4; McFerrin, 87. Whole number of votes cast, 154; necessary to a choice, 78. This election, under the circumstances, was very grat-ifying to me. I had been taken out of the pastoral work while a young man. I had been kept in the editorial chair, the Book Agency, and the Missionary Secretaryship for many years, and I regarded this as a vindication of my course.

A new Board of Missions was formed, and located at Nash-ville—the whole to be under the guidance of one Secretary. Here was heavy work. The Missions, Foreign and Domestic, were to be sustained, and the remainder of the old debt—between thirty and forty thousand dollars—to be provided for. The finances of the Church were greatly reduced, the people well-nigh exhausted, and increasing demands were upon them. But it was no time to yield to despair. We went to work, the Church rallied, and be-fore the second year had expired the old debts were liquidated, and the Church relieved from a burdensome debt that for years had weighted down and clogged the wheels of our great mission-ary movement.

During the four years I visited nearly all the Annual Confer-ences, many District Conferences, and other popular meetings.

During all these years I preached many sermons, and took an active part in the spiritual progress of the Church. Our Missions in China were revived and strengthened, our border work was enlarged, and we began the great missionary enterprise in Mexico.

The payment of the old debt was regarded a great triumph. Thereby the honor of the Church was maintained and the creditors relieved. Dr. Carlton, one of the Book Agents of the Methodist Episcopal Church, had indorsed largely for our Society, and had paid the claims. He was re-imbursed and his credit saved.

At the General Conference Dr. J. C. Keener was elected Bishop, and became one of our active, working General Superintendents. He had much to do in establishing our Missions in Mexico.

MEASURES AND MEN.

IN May, 1874, the General Conference convened at Louisville, Kentucky. I was one of the delegates from my Conference, the brethren kindly placing my name at the head of the list. We had a strong delegation, clerical and lay. I was made chairman of the Committee on Temperance. We had some able discussions on the subject of intemperance and the propriety of more stringent rules on the sale and use of intoxicating liquors. The General Conference, however, determined that our General Rules, and the uniform administration of the law in accordance with said Rules, were fully sufficient testimony on the part of the Church against the evils of intemperance. The body of the members were in favor of adherence to the law. The General Conference was handsomely entertained at Louisville. The body met in a fine hall in the center of the city, and the people were liberal in their support of the delegates and visitors. My home was with Brother W. H. Frazer and family, and my room-mate was the Rev. William Burr, of the Tennessee Conference. We were finely entertained. Among the Tennessee delegation we had several brethren who soon passed away. The Rev. F. E. Pitts died during the Conference. He expired at the house of his relative, Mr. Hobbs, at Anchorage, about twelve miles from the city. I closed his eyes. He fell asleep in Jesus with the words " eternal life " upon his lips. His remains were brought to the city, and the General Conference in a body attended his funeral service at Walnut Street Church. His remains were then sent to Nashville, where they were received by a great crowd, and, after suitable ceremonies, he was laid away in Mount Olivet Cemetery.

Fountain E. Pitts was no ordinary man. He was a gifted preacher—a man of rare pulpit ability, and one of the finest camp-meeting preachers we ever had in the West. He had some peculiarities that in a measure curtailed his usefulness; but, all in all, few men in his day won more souls to Christ. I loved him much, and mourn his death to this day. He was an ardent friend, and one who clung to me even in death. He asked me to be with him to the last, and I saw him as he gently fell asleep, and committed his spirit to God.

At this Conference we were honored with fraternal messengers from the Methodist Episcopal Church, in the persons of the Rev. Drs. Hunt and Fowler and Gen. Clinton B. Fisk. Their addresses before the General Conference were able and in a Christian spirit, and were warmly received. Suitable responses were made, and the whole proceeding was marked by the spirit of sound Christian feeling and proper courtesy. Many hearts were warmed at the prospect of the restoration of brotherly love between the two great Methodist bodies in the United States. From that day the fraternal feeling has been increasing, with now and then some friction. It will finally prevail and pervade the whole Church, as I humbly hope.

Dr. A. L. P. Green was a member of this General Conference, as he had been a member of every one, except in 1840, from the year 1832. His health was very feeble, and he left Louisville before the General Conference closed, and went home to linger a few weeks, and then he died. He passed away July 15, 1874. He had been nearly fifty years in the ministry. He was one year my senior in age and in the ministry. We had been intimate for half a century. He was an able man and a successful preacher. He and I were about the same size and in the strength of manhood; more together than any two preachers of the Tennessee Conference; and yet we were differently constituted in mind and temperament. Dr. Green was calm, self-possessed, thoughtful, and prudent, wise in council, and had great power with men. His great forte was preaching and in the social circle. He liked to preach, and did a great deal of it. Few men in this country preached oftener in fifty years than did A. L. P. Green, and his ministrations were effective. He brought thousands into the Church. His last days were quiet and peaceful, and he died lamented by thousands. I was from home when he passed away, and regretted that I was not at his funeral. He had some views that were contrary to my own. He was not a strict constructionist, but more latitudinarian than myself. Perhaps he was right, and I in error; yet our friendship and mutual love endured. We worked together nearly fifty years in the same Conference. When he was called away I missed him much, and miss him till this day. Rev. Thomas Maddin, D.D., also died about the same time of the departure of Pitts and Green. Thus in a few weeks three great and good men passed away. They all sleep at Mount Olivet.

At this General Conference I was re-elected Missionary Secretary, and continued as heretofore in the active work of the office. I was very desirous to have an assistant, and after several trials the General Conference allowed the Board to select one. Dr. Haygood was chosen. He was also Secretary of the Sunday-school department, and performed this additional work without cost to the Board. He continued for some three years, when he resigned his position, and Dr. D. C. Kelley came to my help in his stead. They both did much valuable service, and relieved me of a part of the burden that was upon me.

In July of this year I visited Round Lake Camp-meeting, in the State of New York. It was a meeting in the interest of fraternity. Many branches of the Wesleyan Methodists were represented. We had brethren from Europe and Australia, from Canada and various parts of the United States. Bishops Kavanaugh and Doggett were present from our Church, with many others of our ministers. It was a meeting of great interest, and much was done here to set on foot true fraternal feelings between many of the Methodist families. It was a season of special grace to many, and was a blessing to me. My spiritual strength was renewed. The meeting was under the supervision of Bishop E. S. Janes, of the Methodist Episcopal Church. He had a committee to co-operate with him. Bishop Janes was a good and great man, full of faith and Christian love. He was always friendly to the South. By the votes of the Southern delegates, in 1844, he was elected to the office of Bishop.

From Round Lake I went to New York City, where I preached twice on the Sabbath. Thence to Boston and back home, *via* Philadelphia, Baltimore, Washington City, Lynchburg, and Chattanooga. I had the company of two of my daughters, my wife's niece, and the Rev. J. R. Plummer and daughter. Altogether the trip was very pleasant, and, I trust, not unprofitable. On my return I spent one day at the District Conference of our Church at Bristol, Tennessee.

The Board of Missions recommended that I should visit Colorado, Oregon, and California, in company with Bishop Pierce.

Accordingly, in the latter part of August, we set out. Our first point of destination was Denver, Colorado. Here the Bishop held an Annual Conference August 27-29. The journey across the plains was deeply interesting to me. Passing Kansas City, Missouri, we swept along for hundreds of miles through the great desert, where nothing was to be seen but dreary sand wastes, without scarcely any sign of life, either vegetable or animal. Denver is a beautiful city located in full view of the Rocky Mountains. Our Church, at the time of our visit, was small and feeble, but had the promise of improvement. It has since made progress. Leaving Denver, we crossed the Rocky Mountains, and reached Wheatland, California, in time to spend a few days at the camp-meeting near that town. Here I met my cousin, the Rev. B. H. Berry, a local preacher in our Church. He was a native of Tennessee, but had removed to Arkansas, and thence to California, and we had not met since we were young men. Our meeting was joyful. He had a family of eighteen living children, most of them grown and doing well. His eldest son, Campbell P., I found to be a prominent citizen, a member of the Legislature, and a member of our Church. He afterward was a delegate to our General Conference at Atlanta, and is now, at the time of this writing, a member of the United States Congress.

Our journey across the Rocky Mountains was very interesting to me. The vast plains surprised me. To see hundreds of miles of comparatively smooth and level lands was more than I expected. But ever and anon we passed rugged elevations and wild scenery that looked like the lurking-places of wild and ferocious beasts. It is really marvelous how the emigrants passed these barren wastes with their teams of oxen and wagons in their journeyings to the land of gold. Many perished by the way, and thousands spent "all their living" and returned bankrupt, while a few remained to grow rich and many to live in poverty and die in a strange land. The unwritten history of the "California fever" would fill volumes if it could only be collected and published to the world. The written history will be read with much interest in time to come.

At the camp-meeting at Wheatland I preached and labored with the penitents until Monday or Tuesday, and baptized two by immersion who were converted at the meeting. It is a fact worth recording that on Saturday, while Bishop Pierce was preaching, a lady was converted, and on Sunday, during my sermon, a young man was brought to Christ and experienced the forgiveness of sins. The meeting over, we left the neighborhood of Wheatland, and set out on our journey to Oregon. We went by railroad to Redding, where we took the stage for Roseburg. We passed the towns of Maryville, Yuba City, Chico, California, and various villages in the northern part of the State, and in Oregon. Jacksonville and Ashland we found to be pleasant towns situated in the valley of Rogue River. Here in this valley we passed as beautiful farming lands as can be found in almost any country in the far and fertile West. The trouble is want of a market. When railroads shall penetrate that country it will be sought for as a delightful region. Altogether, the travel in the stage-coach from California to Oregon taxed me more heavily than any journey that I remember in my long experience of travel. Two whole days and nearly three whole nights, going sometimes at a speed of ten miles an hour—up the mountains, down the mountains, cooped up in a stage, crowded for room, and not an hour of rest—wellnigh exhausted me. When we reached Roseburg, the third morning, and seated ourselves on the cars, I really thought I never enjoyed so great a luxury as a railroad. From Roseburg we journeyed by rail to Salem, the capital of the State. Here we found a beautiful and thriving little city. We dined, and then proceeded some twelve miles to the place of holding the Columbia Conference. It was a camp-ground called "Dixie." The Conference had appointed to hold its session in Salem, but from some cause not justifiable, I judged, it had been changed, and Dixie was the place of meeting. We had a very good time, all things considered, and I trust good was done. The business of the Conference was not pleasant in some of its aspects. The preacher appointed the previous year to Salem had been guilty of certain indiscretions; was tried, and suspended. His unfortunate course prostrated our cause in Salem, where we had erected a small, neat church, and gathered a promising little congregation. I fear we will never regain what was lost by indiscretion.

One of the troubles we have always encountered in planting the Church on the frontier is the want of the right sort of men. Unfortunate appointments have been made, and time and means and opportunities have been lost; but in despite of all these we have made, and are making, some advance.

The Willamette Valley is a beautiful and fertile country lying on both sides of the Willamette River. The stream rises in the mountains, and runs northward, emptying its waters in the Columbia River, with an open gate into the broad Pacific. Portland is a growing city not far from the mouth of this river. We visited Portland, and by invitation took passage on a pleasant little steamer down to the Columbia, and up that beautiful stream to the falls known as Spokane. On our return to Portland the Bishop preached at night to a large congregation in the Methodist Episcopal Church. We then visited Corvallis, Albany, Eugene City, and other places, and preached to appreciative congregations. We had fine views of Mount Hood and other places of interest. At Salem we lodged in the house once occupied by Jason Lee, a missionary to the Flathead Indians. At Roseburg, on our return, we spent two days and nights preaching and visiting. Here we had a church, congregation, parsonage, and a growing prospect for good. We enjoyed here the hospitality of Dr. Hamilton and his family. Then, by dividing our time, we made our way back to California, preaching at Canyon and Ashland by the way. Thus, by stopping on the return trip, we made the journey without much fatigue, and were ready to begin work as soon as we reached California.

The mountain region between California and Oregon is wild, grand, wonderful. The most interesting point is Mount Shasta, that lifts its head fourteen thousand feet above the level of the sea. Its top is covered with perpetual snow. We passed it early in the day. The sun was out, shedding his golden beams on the highest peaks. The clouds that shrouded its brow were gilded by the glorious morning light, and the whole mountain seemed to be wrapped in splendor. I could not hold my peace, but shouted aloud, "Grand! glorious!"

We visited various places, and preached sundry times at Linden Camp-meeting, Los Nietos, Carpenteria, Los Angeles, and attended two Annual Conferences—the Pacific, at Stockton, and the Los Angeles, at Carpenteria. All in all, our visit was delightful, and I trust fruit followed. The Bishop toiled day and night, and ceased not in his labors till he had completed his round. Wonderful man! His zeal and labors know no bounds within the extent of his ability. He counts not his life dear to himself so that he may finish his work. He has brought on himself premature old age and physical weakness by his excessive labors in the pulpit and by long and wearisome journeyings. I wish here to record that, after forty years' intimate friendship with Bishop Pierce, I regard him as combining as many elements of a great gospel preacher as any man I ever knew. I think I never knew his superior, if his equal. Besides, he is a man of large common sense, sound judgment, marked discretion, and one of the most unselfish men I ever met. He is full of charity, and has a heart that sympathizes with the suffering and sorrowful. Having finished our work, we left San Francisco, and reached Nashville on the evening of the sixth day. We made the whole trip without taking a sleeper, and reached home without much fatigue.

Our Church on the Pacific Coast has had many hard struggles, but still it lives, and will live, if the great body of the Church will sustain our brethren in that interesting field. I am fully satisfied in my own mind that a sufficient effort has not been made in that direction. While I am in accord with all live Christians in the effort to convert the heathen, I think more ought to be done for our home frontier work. Our missionary work has not always been wisely managed. We have had failures in men and failures in the management of finances; but still much good has been accomplished, and our brethren need more help. The outposts should be well fortified.

On my return from California in November, 1874, I found my family all living and in common health. A few days' rest, and I was off again to the Conferences, and for four years more (from May, 1874) I devoted all my energies to our missionary interest. First and last I visited every Conference in the Connection, except Montana. I made speeches, addressed Sunday-schools, spoke to the Conferences, attended anniversaries, preached sermons, and was busy all the time. We had a degree of success—kept the Board out of debt and established new Missions. During my term of service we greatly enlarged our field in China, established our Missions in the City of Mexico, on the border between Texas and Mexico, in Brazil, and kept up the work among the Indians, the Germans, and among the whites on our borders.

When the General Conference met at Atlanta, May 1, 1878, I had all my reports ready, and recommended the organization of a Woman's Missionary Society. Here ended my work as Missionary Secretary. Twelve years of toil and trave' and I hope not fruitless effort. We began in 1866 in debt to the amount of some $80,000, wrecked and ruined by the war, with a membership of about 400,000 whites. We kept up the organization, paid all our old debts, and lived to see the new Board on sound and safe footing. No one, perhaps, as well as myself knew the difficulties I had to overcome. Our people were just out of a disastrous war, their property gone, their spirits in a great measure broken; their minds and hearts full, and intensely moved against the world at large because they considered the world was against them on account of their connection with slavery—a connection which they themselves did not make. Never before did I feel so forcibly the power of these words, "Charity begins at home;" "The Greeks are at your doors." But we fought it through, and lived to witness a brighter day for ourselves and the heathen world abroad.

RUNNING NOTES.

THE General Conference convened at Atlanta, Georgia, May 1, 1878. As usual, my brethren elected me a delegate. My colleagues and I were present in time. The Conference was full, and much interest was felt in the proceedings. We were to have delegates from the Methodist Episcopal Church, from Canada, from the Methodist Protestant Church, and from four of the Colored Methodist Churches. Besides, we were to have a great and absorbing question to solve. The Publishing House at Nashville had become seriously involved, and it was questionable whether it could be safely continued or whether it should be wound up and the publishing enterprise abandoned altogether by the Church. I was placed on that committee and elected chairman. I tried to be relieved from serving on the committee altogether, but my brethren insisted, and would not allow me to decline. The committee was well selected. Several business men, laymen of eminent qualifications, were chosen, and some of the best financial minds among the preachers. The work of the committee was onerous, complicated, and very delicate. The reports of the Agent were accompanied by a history of the financial management of the House for many years and the report of an expert, who had been employed some time previously to examine into the condition of the business. These papers were all referred to the committee. It consisted of about seventy members. To preside over such a body, meeting generally in the afternoon, and, having a tangled and mysterious subject to handle, was no light task. Besides, the Agent was often present, trying to explain the condition of the business. After patient and impartial investigation our reports were made, and adopted by the General Conference, as seen in the Journal for 1878, and in the Discipline of the same year. In the discussions in the committee and before the General Conference there was much earnestness, and at times some warmth. [Here are omitted some pages in reference to a matter adjudicated by the Church].

Before the election for Book Agent came on I was earnestly besought by many brethren to allow my name to be presented as a candidate for the office. I refused; they insisted. Finally, at the urgent request of Bishop Pierce and others, I said if the General Conference would authorize the Book Agent and the Book Committee to employ a Business Manager who should be required to work under the supervision of the Agent and Committee, and who should devote all his time to the interest of the House, and if it is the wish of the Bishops, and something like the unanimous desire of the General Conference, I might perhaps be induced to accept the appointment; but I would do it with great reluctance.

The election came off. No nomination was made. Many of my friends understood that I could not consent to accept the position, and many names had been mentioned. On the first ballot two hundred and twenty-six votes were cast for twenty-nine different persons. I received eighty-two. On the second ballot, out of two hundred and fourteen votes, I received one hundred and forty, and by the persuasion of friends I agreed to serve; but I felt that I had consented to bear a heavy burden, if indeed it could be carried at all. Some said I would succeed; others said, "No, *never.*" Some said I was very unwise to undertake so hopeless a task; others encouraged me, and thought I would save the sinking concern. And here I was, between hope and fear.

The General Conference was an occasion of much interest in many respects. Fraternal delegates from the Methodist Episcopal Church, the Methodist Protestant Church, the Methodist Church in Canada, and the African Methodist Episcopal Church were present. Dr. Foss and Dr. Douglass both made fine addresses, two colored men made excellent speeches, and Dr. Clark, of the Methodist Protestant Church, also delivered a noble address. All the fraternal messengers did well, and the impression on the public mind was excellent.

I was domiciled at the Kimball House, where I had excellent fare and good associations. Bishop Pierce, his father, and several others of my friends were at the same House, which made it very pleasant when done with the labors and toils of the day. The work, however, was very heavy, especially of presiding in the committee. All things, however, were sifted, and finally reports of the committee were adopted, as they appear in the Journal of the General Conference for 1878.

For further proceedings of that body I refer to the Journal and to the *Daily Christian Advocate*, published during the session. The Conference over, I returned home, and found my sick wife much improved and the family in usual health.

No time was to be lost. The first day of June I was to take charge of the Publishing House. The Book Committee had a meeting, and organized by electing Judge James Whitworth President, and Dr. W. H. Morgan Secretary. We proceeded at once to inquire into the condition of affairs, and found them bad enough. We halted, inquired, turned matters over, looked at every side, and finally, after a trial of the capacity of the House, adopted the plan of relief known as the "Bond Scheme." For all these movements I refer to the reports of the Agent and Book Committee, and to our record book, where all our proceedings are carefully kept.

During nearly two full years my time was devoted to raising three hundred thousand dollars. I visited many of the Annual and District Conferences and several prominent cities in the South, and had the efficient aid of the Rev. R. A. Young, who was a successful canvasser. In all my toils I neglected not my ministerial calling, but preached many times, and occasionally had the blessing of God upon my labors. Separation from my family and absence from home were heavy trials, but still all was endured for the sake of the cause committed to my care.

In November, 1880, I met one of the greatest afflictions of my life. I was in Texas, working for the Publishing House. When I reached Dallas, in company with Bishop Pierce, on the night of the 16th I received a telegraphic dispatch that my son James had that day been killed by a railroad accident at Birmingham, Alabama. The shock was more than I could well bear, and had not God's grace sustained me I should have sunk under it; but he helped me, blessed be his name! The next morning, in a heavy snow-storm, I turned my face toward home, and made the long journey with a heavy heart and cast-down spirits. The body of my son had been brought home and had been kept unburied till my arrival. Then the last sad rites were performed, and he was laid away to rest till the morning of the resurrection. He was a noble man. No father, perhaps, ever loved a son more than I

20

loved him; and while I try to be fully resigned to God's will, I still mourn my loss—a loss this world will never repair. His good wife had been dead more than five years, and his only child (Annie) was, with him, an inmate of my family. She still lives in my house at the time of this writing, and will have a home there as long as I live and she may desire to remain. My son was a Christian, and had been from early life. He professed saving faith when he was about ten years of age.

In the year 1881 I visited Europe. I went by the appointment of the Bishops as a delegate to the Ecumenical Conference, which was held in London, England, commencing September 7, 1881. My whole journey was one of interest. At New York a fraternal meeting was held in Old John Street Church, the cradle of American Methodism. This meeting was convened on the evening of August 5, and was attended by delegates on the way to London and a large number of the citizens of New York. The Rev. Dr. Buckley presided. The Rev. Dr. Crawford, of New York, delivered an address of welcome, to which, by request, I responded. Others followed. The occasion was one of interest, and excited much talk among the Methodists in all parts of the land. It was regarded as an omen of good, an indication of what was to follow at the meeting in London. On the 6th of August we sailed from New York on board the fine steam-ship "City of Berlin." We had over two hundred cabin passengers, many of them delegates to the Conference. My daughter Lou. was with me. My room-mates were the Rev. David Morton, of Louisville, Kentucky, and the Rev. L. S. Burkhead, of North Carolina. The company was very agreeable, and the voyage delightful. We had good weather and a smooth sea most of the way. I escaped sea-sickness almost entirely. We had preaching and speaking on board the ship, and our time was delightfully employed. We landed at Queenstown, Ireland, on Sunday night, the 14th, about 10 o'clock. Here we took boat for Cork, about twelve miles from the harbor, situated on the River Lee. We arrived at Cork about 12 o'clock at night, and found comfortable lodgings at a hotel.

Monday we spent in sight-seeing; visited Blarney Castle, six miles distant, and had a fine view of the adjacent country. Tuesday we set out on our tour through Ireland. We visited Bandon, Glengariff, Kenmare, Dunluce Castle, the Lakes of Killarney, Dublin, the Giant's Causeway, Portrush, Londonderry, Belfast, and intermediate points. Here, in Ireland, we witnessed the extremes of wealth and poverty, intelligence and ignorance. Dublin is a grand old city, and Belfast is a most prosperous place. The country is beautiful, and the climate is fine. Altogether, I regard Ireland as one of the loveliest lands I ever visited. I preached in Dublin, and made the acquaintance of several interesting members of the Wesleyan Connection.

At Portrush, not far from the Giant's Causeway, stands a monument to the memory of Dr. Adam Clarke, the great Methodist commentator, who was born only a few miles from the place. I preached in Edinburgh, Scotland, and took some time in viewing this grand old city. John Knox and Walter Scott seem to be more sacredly held in memory by the great body of the people than any other two names, though hundreds of their former great men and distinguished women are held in fond recollection. The history of Scotland is more thrilling than any romance. The history of Scotland and Ireland fills as many pages in modern history as any other portion of the globe of the same extent of territory and number of population.

I passed near the home of my ancestors, and found that many of the name still remain in the Old Country, though they generally spell the name McFerran. We visited Paris, the most beautiful city in the world, I suppose, where we spent several days. I preached in the city, and visited many of the places of notoriety. For notes on this tour I must refer to the *Christian Advocate*, which contains several of my letters descriptive of our journeyings.

The Ecumenical Conference opened on the 7th of September, in City Road Chapel. For a detailed account of this great meeting I must refer to the volume containing its history. I was one of the editors bringing out the book. To me the meeting was a grand occasion, an epoch in my history. I preached several times in London; visited Newcastle-on-Tyne, where I preached and made a number of speeches at a supplementary Ecumenical Conference. I returned to London, where I preached again, and delivered a lecture on American Methodism, especially in the South. London is a great city, and England is a great country. Europe is a grand portion of the civilized world; but to a native of the New World there is no land like North America. Its extent of territory, variety of soil, climate, and productions, its free institutions and growing prospects, are all attractive.

With this patriotic outburst these autobiographical notes come to an end. As we look at McFerrin in the chapters that follow, from different angles and through our own glasses, the picture of him, we trust, will be rounded into unity.

TWO ORATORS ON THEIR METTLE.

McFERRIN was a visitor to the Georgia Conference in the autumn of 1854. He was then at the zenith of his power as a preacher and platform orator. There was great curiosity among the young preachers to see and hear him. He created a *furor* of enthusiasm. The crowd followed him from place to place when he spoke. He was to them a wonder and a delight. He had a characteristic tilt with Dr. E. H. Myers. The subject was the relation of the Nashville *Christian Advocate* to the local, or Conference, organs, and the special point at issue was the price of the General Conference paper. The debate waxed warm. Myers had plenty of facts and arguments, and knew how to use them. He presented his side of the question clearly and strongly, and seemed to have made out his case. McFerrin rose to reply, and began his speech by a sly witticism that made a ripple of merriment all over the house, in which even the grave and saintly Bishop Capers—who sat in the president's chair, with his silken, white hair, and great, luminous eyes—could not refrain from joining. Then the Tennessee editor grappled with the question in his own way, seizing an expression dropped by his adversary and giving it such a ludicrous twist that everybody had to laugh; then stating some facts with rapid enunciation and telling emphasis, and then swooping down upon Myers with a *reductio ad absurdum* so triumphant in manner that it provoked the Georgian into an interruption. Alas for him or any

other man who did that! Quick as lightning McFerrin
hurled back a shaft of his sarcastic wit that electrified
the assembly, and then he followed it up with a sort of
elocutionary bayonet-charge that carried the enemy's
works in complete triumph. In vain did Myers try to
explain and expostulate, and call him back to the facts
and to the argument. McFerrin poured in upon him
the full torrent of his ridicule, his nasal buglings rising
higher and higher until the whole Conference was in an
uproar of merriment. "He has tomahawked Myers,
scalped him, and is dancing a war-dance over his remains!" exclaimed a preacher, red in the face from excessive laughter. That was the verdict of the Conference at the time, but on a sober review of the case the
larger part of the brethren believed that the facts and
the weight of argument were on Myers's side. But
what chance had facts or logic against this Tennessean
of irresistible wit and sublime audacity? Myers was
chafed, not to say disgusted, at the result of the encounter; but he was too noble and too truly Christian to
harbor malice, and in after days no two men in all the
Church felt for each other a truer respect and good-will
than the rival editors who fought that forensic duel at
Atlanta in 1854. Myers was solid gold, whose fineness
was only revealed by the fires. The *hauteur* on his face
repelled strangers, but the great, true, loving heart won
and held forever every one who once got close enough
to him to feel its brotherly throbbings. He had rather
the gift of usefulness than popularity, until his martyr
death from yellow fever in Savannah in 1874 so revealed his lofty character that in him was furnished another illustration of the aphorism that "the world first
crucifies and then canonizes saints."

This encounter whetted the appetites of the Georgians for more of McFerrin, and when he spoke at the Sunday-school anniversary the next night the house was jammed. And such a speech! It combined the sweep and freedom of the hustings, the wild energy of the West, the subtle touches of a master in the forum, and the pathos and unction of a camp-meeting sermon. The people laughed, cried, and shouted. The excellent young brother who followed him with a written speech erred in speaking at all. No written speech had any chance of success after that extemporaneous triumph, and there were not a dozen platform orators in all the land who could have safely taken hold of that audience where McFerrin left them. "A minnow wiggling along in the wake of a whale!" whispered a preacher, as the young brother read out the rounded periods of a paper that was much praised when it was put into print. Never put a man who reads to follow one who speaks. Never read at all if you can help it.

The next night was the missionary anniversary, which was then the climax of the interest of an Annual Conference. There was speaking at two churches—McFerrin and Bishop George F. Pierce at the one, and two other well-known and eloquent speakers at the other. It is needless to say that McFerrin and Pierce drew the crowd. The spacious church was crowded almost to suffocation. McFerrin spoke first. He began by a playful allusion to Georgia as "the land of orators and Bishops," declaring that he felt no great weight of responsibility for the occasion, as he would be followed by their own matchless and well-beloved Bishop. Then he turned himself loose, so to speak, and made what was perhaps the greatest speech of his life. It was on a

higher key than the one of the night previous, and was
a vindication of the power of the gospel to save all sorts
of men.   He quoted and expounded text after text of
Scripture on this line, showed what were the Divine resources that guaranteed the fulfillment of the Divine
promise of the world's salvation, and illustrated first
from the facts of history and then from his own observation and experience as a missionary among the Indians.   When he described the conversion of an aged
Indian woman, her face radiant with the joy that filled
her soul, her gray hair streaming behind her as she lifted
her tearful eyes to heaven, and stretching her arms upward and exclaimed in rapture, "Jesulonica! Jesulonica!" ("Jesus my Saviour"), the emotions of the vast audience broke over all restraint, and he sat down in a
tempest of shouts and sobs, saying, " Bishop Pierce will
now make an appeal and take up a collection."

The Georgians, as soon as they recovered themselves
somewhat, showed manifest uneasiness.   Who could
follow that address?   What more could be said that
would not be an anticlimax?   "What will George
Pierce do?" anxiously whispered one to another.   He
answered the question by rising to his feet, glancing
over the dense crowd of human beings in front of him
and at the packed galleries above, and then, smiling as
he straightened his form of matchless, manly beauty to
its full height, he said: " My Brother McFerrin is rather
more ungenerous than usual to-night.   After making the
best speech of his life, and saying all that ought to be
said in the best way, he coolly tells you that *I* will make
the appeal and take up the collection!   The appeal has
already been made, and you are ready for the collection.
You have had a grand speech, and now let us have a

grand collection. Be liberal to-night, brethren, for it is a liberal gospel, backed by the promise of the infinite God who gave to his Son all power in heaven and earth, and through him to his Church, whose mission will be consummated in the universal diffusion of the truth as it is in Jesus, and in the universal establishment of his authority among men." Starting thus, with easy and graceful movement of thought and utterance, he dwelt on this one point—the liberality of the provisions of the gospel and the infinite resources of its Author, guaranteeing its perpetuity and final triumph, his form dilating with the mighty conception; his voice swelling into majesty, yet losing none of its music; his face shining like an alabaster vase with a lighted candle inside—it was a literal transfiguration. It was superhuman eloquence, for it was the afflatus of the Holy Ghost filling and firing the soul of a genius whose entire consecration invited his coming, and whose physical organism furnished a fitting vehicle for expressing the mind and heart of God to men. Does this description seem overwrought? No man or woman who heard that marvelous burst of sacred eloquence would think so. The effect was overwhelming. The people scarcely waited for the collectors; they emptied their pockets with joyful alacrity; it rained bank-notes from the galleries; Heber's hallowed missionary hymn was started, and with the last victorious stanza the great congregation broke into shouts, while Tennessee and Georgia were embracing each other in the chancel. Their friendship for each other was for many long years like that of Jonathan and David. Their hearts were fused, and flowed together that night in the white heat of a baptism of fire as they stood together on the missionary platform. There has been, there will

be, no separation of souls thus blended in the exalted
fellowship of the gospel. The crowd flocked to hear
McFerrin preach on Sunday afternoon. Floor, aisles,
vestibule, and galleries were all occupied to the last inch.
The Tennessee preacher had magnetized the Conference and all Atlanta, and all were eager to hear him. In
the pulpit and on the steps and in the chancel were the
fathers of the old Georgia Conference—Lovick Pierce,
prince of expository preachers, who proclaimed the law
of God with the authority of a prophet, from whose
lips the glad tidings of the gospel distilled as the dew,
and who led thousands of the Lord's people along the
shining way of holiness; Samuel Anthony, an Elijah in
heroic fidelity as a messenger of God, a Jeremiah who,
weeping with a breaking heart over sinners, broke their
hearts and made them responsive to the offer of salvation
in Christ, a mighty preacher, firm and true as steel, and
tender like his Master; William J. Parks, with a natural
courage exalted by grace into the truest Christian heroism, a man of power upon whom strong men leaned,
and whom the common people trusted implicitly and followed; James E. Evans, a revivalist whose pathos in sermon and song broke thousands of hearts to be healed by
the touch of Christ, who was a church-builder and financier, whose benign and massive personality would have
made him eminent in any company; William M. Crumley,
a revivalist whose serene face only wore a brighter smile
in the midst of the greatest excitements kindled by the
mysterious power of his quiet and simple speech, a living
demonstration of the supernatural power of the gospel;
John W. Glenn, whose massive head, burly frame, short
neck, heavy eyebrows, and positive ways typed the common sense, sturdiness, power, and persistence that made

him a leader of the people; Walter R. Branham, who
in a playful alphabetical classification of the preachers
of the Conference by a man of the world was marked
"A" as the first in the polish that makes a gentleman
and the grace that makes a saint, a Philip Sidney blended with a John Fletcher; Edward H. Myers, scholar
and thinker, with the ardor of a reformer and the tenderness of an evangelist; Alfred T. Mann, whose sermons shone with intellectual light and not seldom burned
with the intenser spiritual glow that charmed all classes
of hearers and edified the believing—these, and others
scarcely less noted and equally worthy of praise, were
there filling the front seats and chancel, and even the
pulpit steps, to hear McFerrin's sermon at 3 o'clock in
the afternoon. The text was Colossians iii. 2: " Set
your affections on things above, not on things on the
earth." It was a strange sermon—strange in its quality
and in its effect. It was so simple that a child could have
understood every word of it; not a single rhetorical
flourish was in it, nor a flight of fancy, nor the least display of learning. The things that are above and those
that are on the earth were put in contrast in a way that
brought the thought of the text home to the hearts of
the people with directness and skill, yet so quietly and
simply that nobody was conscious that he was listening
to a great sermon until he found himself with all the
vast audience strangely moved and melted. " This has
been to me the saddest and gladdest year of my life,"
he exclaimed, at the close, while the tears were raining
upon a thousand faces around him. " My heart has been
broken by sorrow and comforted by grace. Earth has
been darkened, but heaven is nearer, sweeter, and brighter. Glory be to God! If I were to follow the impulse

that now swells in my heart, I would stop my sermon right here, and out of the depths of my adoring soul I would say, Halleluiah to the Lamb! Yes, I will say it. Halleluiah! halleluiah!" Then the fountains of the great deep were broken up. Dr. Pierce, whose heart and lips had made a special response to McFerrin's tender allusion to his dead wife, answered back, "Halleluiah!" The word was caught up from every part of the house, the people by one common impulse rising to their feet and shouting "Halleluiah!" as with one voice again and again in a mighty burst of joy.

If great effects are the credentials of a great orator, then McFerrin was one. This scene at Atlanta was not exceptional in his history, though it is perhaps true that his marvelous pulpit power never rose to a higher point than it did that day. What was the secret of that power? We can give no better answer than that which was given in the whispered comment of a gray-haired preacher, whose eyes were still wet with tears as he left the church: "That was Holy Ghost preaching."

WITH THE VIRGINIANS IN 1858.

IN the autumn of 1858 the good Bishop Kavanaugh
presided at the session of the Virginia Conference,
held in hospitable Portsmouth, washed by the waves of
the blue Chesapeake. That is a good place to visit at
that season of the year. If there were nothing else, the
deliciousness of the Chesapeake oysters would make
Norfolk and Portsmouth—twin cities by the sea—delightful to all who relish that bivalve, which comes to
perfection in those waters, and which those tide-water
Virginians cook in a way that reaches the very poetry
of the culinary art. With the rotund and rubicund Kavanaugh in the chair, overflowing as usual with good humor, and radiating the sunshine of his great, loving heart,
the brethren invigorated by the sea-breezes, rejoicing in
the exuberant animal spirits consequent upon good fare
and good consciences after a good year's work, it was a
memorably pleasant reunion. The weather was beautiful, the Conference was full, and large congregations of
friendly spectators crowded the auditorium. Dr. Mc-
Ferrin was in attendance as a representative of the Publishing House and other Connectional interests of the
Church. On Friday forenoon the Bishop introduced
him to the body. Among other things he presented a
paper proposing some Connectional enterprise, soliciting
the approval and co-operation of the Virginia Conference. After explaining and advocating the measure
proposed, he took his seat. There was a brief silence.

(317)

The Virginians are good and ready talkers, but they are not lacking in dignity and decorum. The silence was broken by Dr. Leroy M. Lee, the editor of the *Richmond Christian Advocate*, who was a logical and effective speaker as well as a writer of great ability, especially in polemics. On this occasion he seemed to hesitate, approaching the matter in hand slowly and cautiously, exhibiting evident signs of doubt as to the expediency of favorable action on the part of the Conference. "But, Mr. President," he continued, "this is a Connectional enterprise, and demands the thoughtful consideration of this body. True, we have under consideration several local Conference schemes which demand the serious and thoughtful attention of this body; but these Conference enterprises must, in a measure, yield to the Connectional interests of the whole Church. To insure the success of the measure presented in the paper submitted by our friend, Dr. McFerrin, it must have the hearty co-operation of the Virginia Conference. The Virginia Conference, you know, Mr. President, is the oldest, the wisest, and the most influential body in our general Church, and without its aid this or any similar enterprise would likely fail. I therefore move that the plan proposed in the paper of Dr. McFerrin be adopted, and that we give it our sanction and support." Having thus spoken, he sat down.

McFerrin arose, smiling and with mischief in his eye, and said: "Mr. President, I am truly thankful to Dr. Lee for the resolution proposing the adoption of the measure before us, but am still more indebted for his accompanying speech. We of the West are duly impressed with the necessity of having the co-operation of the Virginia Conference in every important measure.

The Virginia Conference belongs to the Old Dominion, the land of Presidents, statesmen, orators, and divines. She is located east of the lofty mountains that divide our great country east and west. I do not forget, sir, that there is not a ray of light that falls on the broad Valley of the Mississippi that does not first illumine the East [laughter]; indeed, all the light we have comes from the East [more laughter]. All the daughters of this mother of Conferences appreciate the importance, influence, intelligence, and power of the Virginia Conference. We place, we think, a due estimate upon the learning, eloquence, and power of her preachers, and cherish with pleasure the memory of the fathers. Without multiplying words, Mr. President, I bow humbly to this great body [bowing low as he spoke], and concede with pleasure that the Virginia Conference is the *most greatest* body of ministers connected with the Methodist Episcopal Church, South." [Renewed laughter].

That last good-natured hit, delivered in his inimitable manner, immensely amused the well-bred Virginians, and brought down the house, almost the entire assembly applauding, the good-natured Bishop joining in the merriment. But there was at least one man in the Conference who resisted and resented the pleasant uproar. The Rev. George W. Langhorne, a man of excellent character and real ability, of solemn mien and precise ways, rose amid the excitement, and said: "Mr. President, I wish you would call the Conference to order. The Church of God is not a place for such demonstrations as this. We are not in a theater or opera house, but in the church of God, and it becomes us to be sober." In a short time all became quiet, and amid profound silence McFerrin rose and said with assumed gravity, again bowing obsequiously: "I beg Brother Langhorne's pardon. I intended no disrespect to the Conference or audience, nor did I intend to exhibit any lack of reverence for the house of God. I have a profound respect for the temple of the Most High and the teachings of God's blessed word, which says there is a time to mourn and a time to laugh; we are told to weep with those that weep, and to rejoice with them that do rejoice. Conforming to these directions, I have made it my rule through life to cry at funerals and to laugh at weddings."

The uproar was renewed, and became unmanageable. McFerrin's paper was adopted without a dissenting vote. Perhaps Brother Langhorne groaned in spirit, but no farther attempt was made to check the exuberance of the irrepressible Tennessean. From that time forward McFerrin was always a welcome visitor to the Virginia Conference. When he came the brethren expected a stir, and they were not disappointed. Their risible muscles were sure to be titilated and their lachrymal glands excited by a humor that never lost its flavor, and a pathos that no body of Christian people could ever resist.

AFTER MANY DAYS.

A FAITHFUL servant of God who lives to a ripe old age is sometimes permitted to antedate in part one of the experiences that will be an element of the eternal felicity that awaits him in the life to come. He is permitted to see the fruits of his labors. Often he makes discoveries on this line that give him pleasant surprises and fore-gleams of gladder and grander revelations hereafter.

Dr. McFerrin's last years were thus blessed in an unusual degree. He had preached so long, traveled so widely, and touched so many lives in so many ways, that, as he neared the end, his ears were saluted on all sides by these echoes of the past. The faithful words that he had spoken in the earlier years of his ministry came back to him freighted with comfort to his own soul. "I was converted under your ministry when I was a boy," said a gray-haired saint in one place as he greeted him affectionately. "You took me into the Church when I was a girl, and I am still journeying on heavenward," said a venerated mother in Israel, in another. "You took both of my parents into the Church; they died in the faith, and all their children are members of the Church," said a brother, who was a strong pillar in the Church. "The *Christian Advocate* has been in our family ever since you first became its editor, and next to the Bible it has molded my opinions and influenced my life," said another. Such words as these greeted him constantly wherever he went. It was a rare thing for him to preach anywhere in Tennessee without some occurrence of the kind. In the very last year of his life an aged Methodist lady in Sumner County told him that she was converted to God while he was singing a song at a camp-meeting fifty years before. "I remember," she said, "the hour, the words of the song, and the tune." Among the preachers he met not a few of the ablest and best claimed him as their spiritual father. These were grateful reminders along all the pathway of threescore years and more, and the echoes were like the notes of a prolonged strain of music. It is a blessed thing now in this life, and typical of the fuller blessedness of the life to come, that the discords drop out of the memory and only the music remains. From the unhindered operation of this law will come the perfect concord and unbroken blessedness of the heavenly world.

One of these incidents occurred during a visit of Dr. McFerrin to the Indian Territory in the year 1871, when he was Missionary Secretary. It is narrated by Bishop McTyeire, who was an eye-witness. Arriving at Fort Gibson, the Bishop and the Doctor found that they had to stay until the next morning, and then to take the four-horse line to their destination, one hundred and forty miles.

"A lady of St. Louis," says the Bishop, "who was of our company—Mrs. Dr. M.—had a letter of introduction to Mr. L., a merchant of the place. Knowing ones advised us that Mr. L. sometimes entertained travelers, and that it would be to our interest to stop there, if possible, for it was the best place in Fort Gibson. Halting at the door, where every thing was shut up and still, we were met by a lady who, with polite reluctance, admitted us. The hotel was small and full, and we were not easily put off. Dr. McFerrin and myself and two ladies were soon inside. The light of the room showed the lady of the house to be a half-breed Indian. Mrs. Dameron, at St. Louis, had supplied us with abundant lunch, and we agreed to do without supper, in view of bed and breakfast. A scene awaited us not down in the bill, and all the better for its surprise to all parties. Our Missionary Secretary was once, in his boyhood ministry, a missionary to the Cherokees in North Alabama and Georgia. That was a good while ago—away back in 1829 and 1830. He carelessly remarked, in an interrogative tone, ' We are in the Creek Nation, I reckon?'

"'No, sir; you are in the *Cherokee* Nation,' the lady replied. Dr. McFerrin thought he discovered in the reply something of the Cherokee pride of nationality, for the Cherokees hold themselves to be the nobility of the Indian race. He continued:

"'Where did you come from, Madam? You were not raised in this country?'

"'I came from Alabama.

"'From what part of Alabama did you come, Madam?'

"'From Gunter's Landing. My name was Catherine Gunter.'"

The reader may imagine these questions and answers as *increasing* in interest, and with what emotion the next inquiry was made:

"'Katie Gunter, do you know me?'

"'No, sir; I don't know you.'

"'Don't you remember John B. McFerrin?'

"For a moment she sat as one that had been stunned; another moment, she put her hand on his knee and looked intently into his face; then, in an abandon of joy, she threw her arms around his neck and wept.

"The Doctor's eyes were not dry, and he was a most unresisting victim of this delightful recognition. For forty-one years they had not met. He had preached and taught a missionary school in her home; he knew her parents, brothers, sisters, all.

"Very soon there was a stir in the kitchen, and weary travelers were invited to hot coffee. The ladies declared that the bed-sheets were snowy white; the breakfast was good enough for a king, and not a cent was anybody allowed to pay at parting the next morning.

"Weary as I was that night, I was interested by the conversation that followed. All the Gunter family were gone over—Sam, and Ned, and Patsy, and Betsy, etc.; the Ross family, both John (the chief) and 'little Jack' Ross, and others. What various histories and destinies! and nearly all ending in—'he died.' It was touching to hear our hostess now and then speak of the 'Old Nation.' What would she think, how would she feel, if she could revisit Guntersville, and Chattanooga, and Will's Valley, and Etowah, now? Some of the histories were very sad; one, at least, was triumphant: 'What became of *her?*' asked the missionary of forty years ago, naming a pious Indian woman who was one of his members, and famous for shouting. 'Did she keep it up after coming to this country?' 'O yes,' was the reply; 'she shouted as long as she lived, and she died a-shouting.'

"Affectionate inquiries were made after other missionaries in the 'Old Nation.' Greenberry Garrett was called in this connection. His Indian name was Ta-nu-cah, which means *gar-fish*, taken from the first syllable of his name. My hostess was glad to hear that I had seen him in his comfortable home at Summerfield, Alabama, so late as November of last year. Oo-skil-le-lah was Ambrose Driskill. His name was given him, our Cherokee friend said, because when a young man his hair curled, and that his hair yet curled; but the poll of forty years ago was considerably thinned out in these last days and hard times.

" Our hymn-book (last edition) was on the table, and other Methodist books. We were in a Methodist house. The husband was introduced to us, a white man of reputation as the leading merchant in the place. The son and two daughters were also introduced, refined and cultivated people, with whom it was a pleasure to converse and to sojourn. The son is a prosperous young merchant, bearing strongly his mother's likeness.

" This meeting of Dr. McFerrin with his Cherokee friend made one think of *that day*, and of the joy with which a saved spirit will recognize a benefactor long lost sight of, but not forgotten. We meet with our fellow-beings—talk, do business, teach, preach, converse with them for a longer or shorter time. We part. But there is, in the hereafter, a place and time where we shall meet every one of them of every race again. Shall it be with joy or grief? Are we prepared for it in the case of every soul of man with whom we have had to do?"

After many days all that has been sown shall be reaped. This will be heaven or it will be hell to each one of us.

EVERY great man has a great memory. It may be a verbal memory, or it may be a memory for facts, for dates, or for names and faces. This last is the politician's gift. That extraordinary party leader, Henry Clay, it is said, never forgot a name or a face. Every friendly voter in his Congressional District felt that he was a personal friend to the great man who so magnetized millions of his countrymen that his *dictum* was their political creed and his defeat the chiefest national calamity they dreaded. His rival, Andrew Jackson, was similarly endowed for popular leadership; he never forgot his friends, and so drew them to himself that they were ready to speak, vote, fight, and die for him. Had Clay been a soldier, with a fair field for the display of his ability as a leader of men, and as a strategist and tactician, he would have ranked with the greatest captains of all the ages. Jackson never lost a battle. McFerrin's personal acquaintance, perhaps, exceeded that of any man of his generation. His massive and unique personality so impressed the people that they never forgot him, and his gift of recalling faces and names prevented him from forgetting them. He was the great commoner of Southern Methodism—the people's man, the man they all knew, the man they all believed in, the man whose sayings they repeated, and whose lead they were ready to follow. He was a genealogical encyclopedia for Tennessee. One day, shortly after I became

editor of the *Christian Advocate*, wishing to learn something of the writer of a letter to the paper, I took it to
him and asked, "Do you know this man?" "What's
the name?" he demanded, in his high interrogative nasal
tone. I repeated the name. His face brightened all
over as he said: "Yes, I know him, and I know his
family connections. I took his grandfather into the
Church; I officiated at the marriage of his sister Mar-
garet, and at the burial of his mother;" and then followed detail of the family connections, amazing alike in
its minuteness and its extent. I never ceased to wonder at this marvelous faculty as exhibited by him. A
notable instance is related by the scholarly and excellent
Rev. Dr. J. M. Wright, of the Tennessee Conference.
Dr. McFerrin spent a night at his father's house when
he was a boy of six or seven years of age. He never
saw him again until he was over seventeen years old,
when, on a visit to Nashville, he went into his office and
found him seated at his desk writing. "Good-morn-
ing," said the youth, and instantly the Doctor recognized
him, and exclaimed: "Why, this is James Wright!
How are you, my son?" The youth was astonished.

"Do you know me, Doctor?" some one would ask,
after his sight had failed. "What did you say your
name was?" he would reply; and getting the name, he
would instantly recall the person, his residence, his kindred, and all about him. Of the multitudes he received
into the Church he rarely forgot one, not only recollect-
ing the name, but the time, place, and attendant circumstances. One joined the Church under his ministry at a
quarterly meeting at Salem; another was convicted at a
camp-meeting by a sermon from a certain text, and converted amid singing and shoutings never to be forgotten;

and yet others at this place and that, all over the land. In his later years his journeyings were attended with reunions with his spiritual children and old friends, so many and so tender that his way was lighted by smiles and greeted with tears. The hand that had been given to the grandfather or grandmother in token of fellowship when received into the Church, and which had smoothed the dying-pillow of a father or mother, was grasped with the warmth of an affection almost filial. He was the patriarch of the Methodist tribe in all Tennessee and beyond, the repository of their history, and the *nexus* that held three generations—the fathers and mothers, their children, and their children's children—in a sacred continuity of family and Church life. His coming was the signal for a sort of general reunion. Kindling with the local recollections, he would revivify the old times; and recalling the names of the holy dead, his voice would tremble with emotion, while through the responsive crowds would sweep great surges of feeling that none could resist. The old men would press their way to where he stood, grasp his hand, or fall upon his neck, weeping, as they thought of the days when the aged preacher and themselves were young, and of the beloved dead who had since then gone home to God.

This wonderful recollection of persons was not confined to Methodists. It embraced all sorts of people with whom he was in any way brought into contact, "He knows more about our Presbyterian people in Tennessee than I do," said a leading minister of that denomination. Of the history of the public men of the State his knowledge was extensive and accurate, and his personal acquaintance with them familiar. From the days of Andrew Jackson, Felix Grundy, and James K. Polk

to those of John Bell and Andrew Johnson, and further
on to Isham G. Harris, James D. Porter, and William
B. Bate, he knew the leaders of all the political parties,
and had for every one he met a hearty salutation, an admonition, or a pleasantry, or both, so skillfully put together that the one was made an efficient vehicle for the
other. He had the confidence of them all, and though
many of them belonged not to his religious Communion,
there was scarcely one of them who in his old age
would have hesitated to assign him the first place among
the ministers of Christ in his State—not the first in
scholarship or general culture, but the first in the strength
of his individuality, in the weight of character and influence, and in the universal veneration and affection accorded to him. He had so many touches of nature that
it made everybody feel akin to him. He was a privi-
leged character. Christians of other denominations took
his keen, yet not unkindly, thrusts in good part. The
satire with which he lashed the follies he saw among
his own people was rather relished for its pungency
than resented for its severity. And it was often noticed
that the hardest sinners would take more reproof from him
than from anybody else. So strikingly was this true
that the question was raised whether the good-will of
this class was purchased by any compromise of ministerial fidelity on his part. No imputation of this sort
could justly be made against him. A plainer, more faithful preacher of righteousness could not be found. He
spared no form of error or species of folly in the Church,
and no wickedness outside of it. When he filled the
pulpit the people expected that all sorts of wrong-doing
would be denounced and satirized, and they were seldom
disappointed. But the breadth of his sympathies and

his knowledge of human nature enabled him to correct
wrong where another would only have irritated the offender, and to draw the subject of his rebukes to the
preacher while he turned him from his evil way. This
is a rare gift, lacking in many men of purest metal, who
for their fidelity pay the price of unpopularity with the
very beneficiaries of their labors. Let no man of this
class envy the gift denied to them. They escape its consequent peril—the temptation to blunt the sharp edge of
truth that may offend—and verily they will find that for
all human applause lost by them because of faithful discharge of duty the Lord whom they serve will bestow
compensations so large and so lasting that nothing will
be left for them to regret and nothing to desire. In
one case it was intimated that McFerrin, in conducting
a funeral service in memory of an old friend, allowed
his remarks to take a latitudinarian sweep which he
would not have been slow to condemn in another.
When I mentioned the matter to him he was thought-
fully silent for a few moments, and then said, gently:
"He was an old friend and a noble man. I tried to be
tender toward the dead, yet faithful to the living." And
then he gave me an outline of what he said on the occasion, which, if his memory was correct, certainly vindicated him fully. But it remains true that friendship
may prove a snare to even the truest and bravest servant
of God. Let each one, therefore, watch and pray lest
he enter into the temptation which may come thus dis-
guised.

THE YOUNG PEOPLE'S HERO.

THE unfailing popularity of McFerrin with the young people furnishes a subject for curious psychological study. It might be thought that between the strong, angular, masterful preacher and the hearts of children there was a great gulf. But it was not so. The fact is, there is a natural sympathy between all honest, healthy, hearty men and young life. Was there ever a good man or a good woman who did not love children? No child-hater could possibly be a Christian. Such a soul could have no kinship with Him who took little children in his arms, put his hands upon them, and blessed them. No child-hater was ever called to the ministry of the gospel. The hand that feeds Jesus' lambs must have the skill which only true tenderness can impart. McFerrin had this mark of a true under-shepherd. He loved children and young people. His own exuberant physical life put him in sympathy with the buoyancy and brightness of childhood and youth. He had heard in his inner soul a voice that said, " Feed my lambs." His simplicity attracted them. A fondness for innocent mischief was inherent in him, and he could smile at their little pranks and enter into their little joys and griefs. The boy element never left him. If, in the judgment of men of more sedate temper, it broke out too strongly at times, it was all his life an element of ministerial success to him. The young people never tired of him. They would flock to hear him

(331)

speak in public, and hung about him to hear him talk in private. He was their hero.. His bold, masterful way pleased them. The imagination of the young kindles at any exhibition of unusual power, whether by a champion wrestler, a bear-hunter, a soldier, or a preacher. The man of whose polemic triumphs they heard their parents speak with pride was regarded with admiring affection by the young people. And then what a treat it was to them when he stood before them and gave loose rein to his rollicking fun and flashed gospel truth into their minds in statements singularly simple and lucid, and illustrated it in a way they could never forget! Sometimes the fun he created in speaking to an assembly of young people would become so uproarious that devout and timid souls would groan in spirit, wishing he would put more restraint upon himself at that point. His indescribable and inimitable intonations, his facial contortions—apparently involuntary and unconscious—his personal hits at some one present who offered a tempting mark for his sarcastic or humorous shots, his interjected exclamations and apostrophes that tingled like electric shocks, often made his addresses to the young people occasions of extraordinary excitement. But he usually managed to control the storm he raised, and before he ended his talk the boisterous laughter subsided, and the little faces and those of the older persons present would be wet with tears as he told of his own experience as a boy-disciple, or illustrated some truth by an incident whose pathos broke up the great deep of their hearts. In these talks to children he spoke of Jesus so simply and sweetly that the smallest child understood him, and he rarely failed to drop the right seed into the little hearts to which his tact had found the way of access. One instance

comes to mind here. At a session of the Kentucky
Conference, at Richmond, in that State, a children's
mass-meeting was held on Sunday afternoon. It was indeed a children's mass-meeting; the church was packed
in every inch of space. It had been announced that Dr.
McFerrin would make a speech and sing a song in the
Indian language. Expectation sparkled in every eye as
the boys and girls sat and looked upon the rugged and
remarkable old man who sat within the chancel with his
eyes half closed and his head leaning on his left hand.
After the melodious J. H. Rand, presiding elder, sung
some songs with the children and offered a prayer, Dr.
Morris Evans, then pastor of the Richmond Methodist
Church, introduced Dr. McFerrin. A stenographic report of the speech he made would be a literary curiosity. It was every thing by turns that a speech could be
within the limits of an hour. The hearers wondered
and laughed and cried. They winced under his cate-
chetical probings; they relaxed under the sallies of his
broad humor until decorum seemed to be in danger of
being totally lost. The Indian song, or Cherokee version of the old camp-meeting hymn, " I'm bound for the
land of Canaan," was strangely thrilling as he trump-
eted forth the curious syllables to the old tune whose
melody was familiar to tens of thousands fifty years ago.
At the last, by a route such as no one else could have
followed, he came to the great matter of personal salvation, and pressed it home upon the consciences and hearts
of the tearful children in the question, " Do you love
Jesus? " He had condensed the gospel into that simple
interrogatory, and brought his magnetized little hearers face to face with the solemn issue upon which hung
their destiny. The fun was forgotten, the accessories of

the occasion fell away from it, and every soul, young and old, wrestled with the crucial test that was made so solemn that none could be unconcerned, and so clear that none could evade it.

Such scenes as this, were common in his ministry throughout its entire course. He never grew old in spirit. It was wise in him thus to keep in sympathy with the young. The reflex influence upon himself of the young life with which he was thus brought into contact opened within his own heart a fountain of perpetual youth whose waters fertilized his life and made it all abloom with the fadeless flowers of sympathy, tenderness, and affection, whose roots are watered by the river that makes glad the city of God.

HIS ANTAGONISMS.

HIS antagonisms! Do the words bring a jar now that he is dead? It can not be helped. Such a man, living in such times as those in which he lived, and doing the work he did, must needs have had many jars in his life. He was a fighter by nature. What he did not like he must needs oppose. He would have been a crusader had he lived in the thirteenth century. Had he lived a century earlier than that, what he would have been God only knows—a monk burying himself alive to keep out of temptation, or a chieftain of some sort raiding his enemies, or hunting friends needing a champion to fight for them. He came upon the stage of action at a time when the Church he joined was in its most militant state. He was put early in the front, where he had to fight or flee. To the last he was kept there, and his latest sun went down while the battle-smoke was still in the air.

It may have been a weakness in him that he found it difficult to separate the man whom he antagonized from his cause. It was Bond and Elliott, opposing editors, who felt the sting of his sarcasms in the turbulent times about 1844. No word of disparagement or sweeping condemnation of the Northern brethren as a body is on record from him. In the contention that took place along the border it was Tomlinson's personal mistakes and inconsistencies that drew his hottest fire, rather than the measures he supported. The *argumentum ad hom-*

(335)

inem was his strength and his weakness—his strength, in that he wielded it with a power that was usually irresistible; his weakness, in that, unsuspected by himself, it often left a barbed arrow in the hearts of men whom he sincerely esteemed. Men who care but little for being overmatched in argument wince and writhe when they are laughed at. Satire is as dangerous as it is effective. It is deadly when skillfully directed against a foe, but it often wounds the hand that uses it. No words can describe the power of McFerrin's sarcasm. The lightning-like flash, the indescribable drollery of tone and gesture, the air of easy triumph that proclaimed him victor even when the facts and arguments had gone against him, sent many a discomfited combatant from the arena with a grudge in his heart. They said he was unfair and ungenerous, and watched for an opportunity to adjust accounts with him. But in most cases time did its healing work; the victims of his forensic excoriation saw other sides of his character; they found that the arrow that stung them so keenly was not poisoned with malice; and seeing others treated by him in like manner, they joined in the general laugh and forgot their own smartings. No man ever surpassed him in general popularity, but here and there in the wide circle of his movement were men—and good men too—who could never forget that they had met him and felt the touch of the lion's paw.

Several instances come to mind at this point in which he had long and exasperated personal controversies in his latter days. The detail of these conflicts is purposely omitted. The man with whom he had the longest and hardest wrestlings passed before him to the tribunal of the righteous Judge from whom no secrets are hid. All the tangible questions between them were adjudicated by the Church. There let them rest. As to what, if any thing, lay back of them; as to the undercurrents, if any, that were invisible to all but the all-seeing God; as to the self-delusion, if any, that obscured moral perception; as to the degree of alloy in the motive that could only be judged by us from the data that were accessible to human judgment—all this is left to the adjudication of the pitying Father of us all who knoweth our frame and who remembereth that we are dust, and to the interceding grace of our great High-priest, whose blood hath full atonement made for our sins, and who is touched with the feeling of our infirmities. The collision he had with another man of brilliant genius, who was master of a wit that was sparkling, and a satire that burned like caustic, might perhaps be traceable in its ultimate causes to similarity of temper on the middle plane of their natures, and to circumstances that developed an antagonism that would have melted away in the glow of personal association had they been thrown together where comradeship would have excluded rivalry, and where the angularities that thrust them apart when they met in the public arena would have been smoothed away in the hallowed association of fellow-laborers who see each other's tenderer and brighter side. Had this been so, the Richmond journalist who tilted with Tertullus might have been the writer of this biography, and put into it touches of color that could have been given by no other hand. Two other cases of alienation more or less complete recur to mind at this point, one of which was the result of temperamental antipathy, and the other of circumstances that gave him and thousands of others infinite pain.

22

Was he hard and unforgiving? Not consciously. But by virtue of his sagacity, courage, and force of will, he was much accustomed to having his own way; and it was his misfortune that his pugnacity outlasted his maximum of power. His sight and hearing partially failed, but his readiness for combat did not diminish. He kept a sharp watch to the last for innovators on Old Methodism as he understood it, and in the Board of Missions he was ready to break a lance with anybody who crossed his views. A smile would pass around the Board when, not hearing distinctly what was said or embraced in a motion, he would demand in his imperious tone, his whole manner showing fight: "What was that?" And when he did come in collision with some notion or motion that crossed his life-long prejudices, he bore down upon the opposing speaker with a vehemence that was surprising to new members and amusing to old ones. Once he stalked in about the middle of a forenoon session, having been detained with the Book Committee, which was also in session at the time, and seeming to think that something must be going wrong in his absence, he planted himself in the middle of the room, and demanded, "What is it you are doing?" in a tone so defiant that there was a general burst of laughter. A man of this sort will not escape antagonisms. He is born to them; they are involved in his mission to the world; they make the brightest and the darkest pages in his life-history. The trueness that was at the core of McFerrin's soul is evidenced by a fact that should be mentioned here. In the latter part of his life he was thrown into close contact with brother ministers of the Tennessee Conference, with whom in former years he had been brought into sharp collision. They exhibited Christian

politeness in their social intercourse, and that was all.
But it came to pass that issues arose involving vital principles and great Church interests; and at once these men,
recognizing each other fully for the first time, drew close
to one another in a fellowship that grew stronger and
stronger to the last. As in musical composition there
are minor discords that lead to a grand burst of harmony,
so it happens that the petty irritations and antipathies of
good men lead to delightful surprises when, lifted to the
highest plane of their being in such crises, they find that
at that altitude they are pitched on the same key. In
the exaltation that awaits all true disciples of Christ at
the manifestation of the sons of God, will not this be the
secret of their perfect and unending concord? "Mc-
Ferrin was never a friend of mine," said a high-souled,
generous man, who thought he had cause of complaint
against him; "but he was a true man; he was a good
man." That is the verdict of the vast multitude of persons who knew him. The names of those that dissent
could be counted on the fingers of the hand that writes
this sentence. A good man he was; a perfect man he
was not. That title belongs only to Him whom he followed in singleness of purpose during a ministry of more
than sixty years seldom equaled in the abundance of its
labors and in the fruits that were visible even before the
fearless heart ceased to beat and the busy hands were
folded to rest.

WITH THE BOYS IN GRAY.

DR. McFERRIN always kindled at any reference to his experience as a missionary in the army. The soldiers who met and heard him in camp and on the field kindled at the mention of his name. The boys in gray had a warm place in their hearts for him to the last. The tie that binds fellow-soldiers is strong and enduring in proportion to the dangers and hardships they have encountered together. The survivors even of a wreck at sea or a railroad disaster feel that, having come so close to death together, there is a secret bond of sympathy between them ever after. He who is unmoved by such a feeling is not a man, but a clod. The boys in blue, who were the victors in our Civil War, have perpetuated their organization in the Grand Army of the Republic, and maintained its *esprit de corps* by annual reunions, oratory, song, and martial parades. Membership in the organization is considered almost equal to a patent of nobility by the men who bore the banners of the Union, and who were on the winning side in that tremendous conflict whose echoes grow fainter and fainter as the years bear the nation on its way to whatever is in store for it in the future. If such is the sentiment of the victors, what must be that of the vanquished, with whom all the thrilling memories of the struggle are associated with the ineffable pathos of defeat? To the worn warriors of Lee Appomattox was a sacrament of sorrow, and all the true men who came out of the fiery furnace of the war alive feel for one an-

(340)

other a fraternal regard that has manifested itself on all possible occasions. A mere civilian has had but a small chance of success against a soldier who limped around on a lame leg or displayed an empty sleeve on the hustings. The men who led the Confederate armies during the war led the reconstructed States afterward. The manhood that proved itself in battle and on the march asserted itself in the untried and difficult conditions of that period during which the recuperative energies of the Southern people were so severely tested and so grandly demonstrated.

The preachers of the South, like those of the North, took the field at the start, and kept it to the end of the war. Not a few of them on either side took up carnal weapons and pressed into the thickest of the fight. There were among them those who discharged a double function, acting as chaplain and colonel of a regiment or captain of a company at the same time. Some of these were rare spirits, who prayed with fervor and fought with distinguished valor, while there were many sad examples to warn us that it is a dangerous thing for a man who has been called of God to save men by the preaching of the gospel to take up arms to kill men.

Dr. McFerrin's own notes have already told us how he left Nashville and got into the army, and given us a running account of his army life. Ten thousand living men could bear witness to the faithfulness and remarkable success of his work as a missionary to the soldiers. Among his papers was a faded, ragged sheet, which he had preserved with scrupulous care during all the eventful times from the day of its date to the day of his death. It was his commission as an " acting chaplain," and is in these words:

HEAD-QUARTERS ARMY OF TENNESSEE, May 15, 1863.

The Rev. Dr. John B. McFerrin, Methodist Church, an Acting Chaplain C. S. A., is recognized in that capacity, and will be entitled to all the privileges and advantages of that position.

BRAXTON BRAGG, *General Commanding;*
J. E. JOHNSTON, *General.*

Privileges and advantages! That sounds almost like a jest from the grim and exact Gen. Bragg, who never wasted words with tongue or pen. The privileges of a chaplain were to draw rations when there were any to be drawn, to preach to the soldiers, to. march and sleep with them, to nurse the sick and pray with the dying, on the field or in the hospitals, to bury the dead, and, if he felt so disposed, to take a hand in the fighting. The advantages! What were they? Only a surviving chaplain himself could tell. The signature of Gen. "Joe" Johnston in different ink was in the nature of a renewal of the commission, which took place after the bloody but brilliant victory at Chickamauga and the disaster at Missionary Ridge, where the lucky Grant found the unlucky Bragg. "Gen. Bragg was a fine soldier," said McFerrin—"a soldier who did the best fighting and reaped the least advantage from it in proportion of any officer we had. Yes, he was a fine soldier, and I respected him highly; but he was not a lucky man." For Gen. Johnston he had the highest admiration as a military genius. Of Hood, the heroic and ill-starred victim of invincible disabilities, upon whose devoted head was visited the blame for disasters which the most desperate valor strove in vain to avert, he always spoke with respect and generous kindness.

Dr. McFerrin was respected by the officers and loved by the men to an extraordinary degree. The magnetism of his presence made a stir in the camp at his coming, and he left it in a glow when he went away. The strange power that always attended his preaching was felt wherever he spoke to the soldiers. They wept and prayed, and pledged themselves to Christian living.

The Rev. S. M. Cherry, of the Tennessee Conference, a worthy fellow-laborer, a participant and eye-witness, gives a graphic sketch of Dr. McFerrin's army experience:

REV. S. M. CHERRY'S SKETCH.

Dr. McFerrin was with the Army of Tennessee much of the time from January, 1863, to April 23, 1865. After the battle of Murfreesboro, or Stone's River, we met for the first time in the army (January 7, 1863), at Shelbyville, Tennessee. I had been with Gens. Zollicoffer, J. E. Rains, and E. Kirby Smith in East Tennessee and Eastern Kentucky, in 1861-2, and had not seen the Doctor for more than a year, perhaps not since the Conference of 1861. I was truly glad to meet him and so many of our preachers of the Tennessee Conference after so long a separation. Three days after he sold me the finest little mare I ever owned. The next day, I note from my Journal, I "attended class-meeting for the first time during the eighteen months of camp life," and among those named as present was James McFerrin, the elder son of the Doctor, whom I often saw in the army as a faithful soldier.

On Sunday, March 22, Gen. Robert Vance, a devout member of our Church, went with me to hear Dr. McFerrin preach. His theme was "The Evidences of Christ's Divinity." The congregation was large, many officers attending the service, and the sermon was strong, scriptural, and full of life and power. In the afternoon he rode with me over to Bate's Brigade, and preached for us from Isa. lv. 6, 7—"Seek the Lord while he may be found," etc.—a most suitable sermon for the soldiers. After the service in camp we went together to the home of the Rev. Samuel S. Moody, near Shelbyville, and spent the night. Brother Moody was slowly, yet surely, going from his model family and beloved brethren to the grave. He was one of the sweetest spirits in our Conference, and was greatly honored and much loved by his brethren. He was my first and highly esteemed presiding elder. Dr. McFerrin was with him much the last few weeks he lingered among us.

He died in great peace May 6, and his funeral sermon was preached by his friend of many years, Dr. McFerrin.

While our army was encamped around Shelbyville, in 1863, the first meetings of our " Chaplains' Association " were held. Dr. McFerrin and other army missionaries attended, and of course he was always ready to speak a word in season. Dr. J. H. McNeilly, pastor of Moore Memorial Presbyterian Church, Nashville, one of our most efficient army chaplains, remembers distinctly a young chaplain's first contact with Dr. McFerrin in discussion. The zealous, sprightly young brother mistook some remark of the Doctor as a reflection on his denomination. In reply, he was sharp, severe, and scathing. The Doctor eyed the brother complacently, yet his look was quizzical. When the young man sat down the Doctor arose, and assured him kindly that no such reflection was intended. But the irate brother was not satisfied, and seemed to think that he had the better of his senior, and wanted to follow up the advantage gained by a decided discomfiture of the Doctor, whom he evidently thought rather demoralized by his first assault. He did not accept the statement as satisfactory, as others seemed to do, but renewed his attack with great vigor. Those who knew the Doctor's great ability in discussion were well prepared to enjoy the sequel. The fiery young chaplain was scarcely seated before the Doctor was standing squarely and solidly before him, and with searching gaze looked him full in the face and said: " My young brother, we have too big a fight on hand just now for any such foolishness as denominational distinctions and differences. But if you want to fight on such a line as this, just wait till we win in the fight now on hand, and we all unite in the army and at home and whip out the devil and his hosts; and then if you wish to attack me on the line you indicate, I am at your service, and *will just lay you across my lap and spank you good.*" The good humor of the Doctor and the Association's approval was so hearty that the young chaplain was more than willing to subside.

Dr. McFerrin's great power in the army was manifested during the remarkable religious revival which began in the Army of Tennessee in Middle Tennessee late in 1862, and continued until the close of the war in 1865 in North Carolina. The first buddings of this gracious awakening we witnessed in our brigade at a protracted meeting conducted by Chaplains Allen Tribble, J. G.

Bolton, E. C. Wexler, Capt. Brady of the Thirty-ninth Georgia Regiment, and myself, at Normandy and Manchester, Tennessee, late in November and early in December, 1862. The revival kindled into a still brighter flame around Shelbyville and Fairfield in the spring and early summer of 1863; but its full power was not realized till we were encamped around Dalton, Georgia, in 1864.

At Brown's Brigade, on the 12th of June, 1863, while in camp near Fairfield, I heard Dr. McFerrin preach to a very large and attentive congregation of serious soldiers, on " Repentance." At the close of his sermon he called for penitents, and eighteen came forward for prayer. Three nights later I preached to the same brigade, and witnessed three conversions. Chaplains John A. Ellis, A. W. Smith, T. H. Deavenport, J. W. Johnson, of the Tennessee Conference, and the Rev. Mr. Chapman (Presbyterian) were active laborers in this and other meetings during the revival.

The attack at Hoover's Gap, on St. John's Day, June 24th, while some of the soldiers and citizens were attending a Masonic celebration at Bellbuckle, resulted in serious loss to Bate's Brigade, and some casualties in Brown's, and broke up our protracted meeting there, which gave promise of gracious results; but we renewed the meeting a few weeks later at Tyner's Station, near Chattanooga, where we continued with increasing interest till the coming of the terrible conflict on the tortuous Chickamauga. Then, at the base of Missionary Ridge, the revival flame was kindled again, and many soldiers there declared their purpose to lead new lives who soon laid down their lives in battle on the slopes of the same Missionary Ridge late in the bleak November.

Dr. McFerrin was very faithful and devoted in looking after the wounded, I remember, at the ghastly and gory field hospitals of Chickamauga, September 19 to 22, 1863. His nephew, the Rev. John P. McFerrin, who had recently been licensed to preach, was very seriously wounded in that battle, and was disabled for a long while.

The Doctor showed his spirit of firmness and decision in a way that was very pleasant, to one man at least, while we were at the base of Missionary Ridge, fronting Rosecrans's army in Chattanooga, just before the battle at the former place. The Soldiers' Tract Association of the Methodist Episcopal Church, South, established a South-west Department at Macon, Georgia, to supply the soldiers of the Southern and Western armies with religious reading, and began the publication of *The Army and Navy Herald* in October, 1863, with the Rev. R. J. Harp, of Louisiana, as Superintendent; Rev. William F. Camp, General Collecting Agent; and the Rev. J. W. Burke, Treasurer. Dr. Camp came to our army in order to get Gen. Bragg to appoint a distributing agent for the Army of Tennessee, who should remain with the army and receive all Bibles, Testaments, hymn-books, tracts, papers, and other material furnished by the Association, and distribute the same to the chaplains, missionaries, and others, who would furnish their commands with such religious reading. Gen. Bragg was willing to appoint the man if Dr. Camp would find one suitable and properly recommended. Dr. McFerrin's experience in the army and all over the South, and his knowledge of men and affairs, suggested him to Dr. Camp as the man to aid him best in the selection of the distributing agent. The Doctor said: "Yes, I know the man you need; come with me." They went at once to Bate's Brigade, and asked for a chaplain who entered the army in 1861 and was now serving in that capacity his third year. When he came out of his tent, clad in common gray, looking much like an ordinary soldier who had been on the dusty march and roughing it generally during the heavy campaign of the summer, every expression of the well-dressed Doctor from the rear seemed to say: "Why, Dr. McFerrin, is that your man? He will not do at all." Col. R. and Gen. Bate both objected to the appointment, the latter firmly yet kindly saying, "We need him in the field." But the decision of Dr. McFerrin, who intimated that he had no change to make in his selection, was potent enough to prevail with Gen. Bragg, and Dr. C. and Gen. B. and Col. R. yielded to the inevitable. Result: this writer was distributing agent of religious reading for the Army of Tennessee from November, 1863, to April, 1865. All of that time I had very favorable opportunities of seeing and hearing much of Dr. McFerrin while he labored so faithfully and successfully for the spiritual welfare of our soldiers.

While I saw much of Missionaries William Burr, W. Mooney, R. P. Ransom, and C. W. Miller, and heard them and the Rev. C. C. Mayhew preach often in and around Dalton, and knew well their zeal and devotion "in labors more abundant," and was also a witness to the fidelity and heroism of chaplains too numerous to name, yet I saw and heard more of Dr. McFerrin in the great revival around Dalton than of any other minister of the gospel.

Four times in one week I heard him preach—December 22 to December 28, 1863. His texts were very appropriate to the place, time, and occasion. The first sermon I heard him preach there and then was from the text, "Seek ye first the kingdom of God and his righteousness." The next night he preached from the text, "Come unto me, all ye that labor and are heavy laden, and I will give you rest." He so preached the need of seeking the kingdom of God *first* in point of *importance* as well as *first in time* (I note from my Journal) that quite a number of soldiers came forward to seek salvation. The second sermon so directed those desiring salvation to come to Jesus that they came in confidence, and confessed his power to save from sin and to give rest to their burdened souls.

Nowhere else in life have I ever witnessed so wonderful a revival as that at Dalton from December, 1863, to May, 1864. At no other time or place did I ever hear Dr. McFerrin preach with such power and success as to our soldiers in camp. He came to them with a heart full of sympathy, and showed them by every token that he was one of them, ready to eat and sleep with them, and in every way to "endure hardness as a good soldier of the Lord Jesus Christ." His plain, matter-of-fact way of speaking to the soldiers was remarkably adapted to win their confidence, and he so preached Christ that he won the soldiers to faith in the great Captain of our salvation. Several thousand soldiers were publicly seeking religion around our rude camp altars near Dalton, in the spring of 1864. I suppose a thousand made profession of saving faith in Christ in the month of April alone. Dr. McFerrin was instant in season and out of season, did the work of an evangelist, and made full proof of his ministry to the soldiers. I doubt not that scores, if not hundreds, of soldiers dated their conviction and conversion to the ministry of Dr. John B. McFerrin in the army.

While Baptists, Presbyterians, Cumberland Presbyterians, and Methodists looked to Dr. McFerrin as a leader in the great revival and other ministerial work in the army, yet, if there was other delicate and difficult work to do, such as all would shrink from undertaking, Dr. McFerrin was selected for that duty. As an illustration: Chaplains were scarce in some of the commands—notably some from Arkansas and other Western States. Such needed attention from missionaries especially. An earnest effort was made to furnish all such commands with chaplains. Like all other well-meant measures, there was danger of overdoing the work. Bishop Paine, if I mistake not, ordained or appointed a man calling himself Casteel, or Castile, and he was rightly named, for he was hard and slippery; but he was assigned to duty in an Arkansas regiment. Conscription was the order of the day, and Casteel wanted an easy place, and he thought the chaplaincy the nicest for him in the army. But he had scarcely settled down in the army at Dalton before ugly rumors reached us of his character and conduct at Rome, Georgia. The chaplains were zealous to protect the reputation of their body from reproach. A consultation was held, and the result was that Dr. McFerrin was appointed a committee of one to see the new chaplain and to notify him of the reports from Rome. The Doctor did not shirk the delicate task, but frankly told him that it had been whispered to some of the preachers that he had stolen some hundreds of dollars on his way from Aberdeen to the army at Rome. Casteel candidly confessed that he took the money, but begged Dr. McFerrin not to mention it, for fear it might reach his regiment and "*injure his influence with the boys.*" The Doctor made no promise of secrecy, not even to save his *influence*, but returned and made his report. Casteel was full of expedients. He at once made out for himself a "leave of absence," and an order for "free transportation" to the rear. When presented to Major John S. Bransford, Chief of Transportation, the Major—who now lives in Nashville, as he did before the war—detected that the signatures were not genuine, and ordered the chaplain's arrest. The fellow was sent to the guard-house, where he feigned sickness, and was sent to the hospital, and thence made his escape. I have never heard any thing more of Casteel, save that he stole a watch from Dr. G——, of Aberdeen, Mississippi, while sharing his hospitality, just before Bishop Paine sent him to the army. But Dr. McFerrin heard much of him, and of "injuring his influence" from us during the last year of the war. During the entire four years of my army life I never met but the one impostor among the preachers in the army.

Your readers will learn from another source, I doubt not, that Dr. McFerrin was with the Army of Tennessee, and preached to the soldiers an appropriate discourse the Sunday of the surrender of that army at Greensboro, North Carolina, April 23, 1865.

Being with the division of Gen. Dibrell, which acted as escort for Jefferson Davis and Cabinet from Greensboro to Charlotte, before the surrender, I did not hear the Doctor, but preached the same day for Ferguson's Brigade at Rock Hill, South Carolina, and again at night, and assisted Chaplains Monk and McCheaver in the administration of the sacrament of the Lord's-supper to the soldiers after the surrender.

After the army left Middle Tennessee in December, 1864, we returned, *via* North Alabama, to Corinth, Mississippi; thence by railroad and steam-boat to Meridian, Selma, Montgomery, Columbus, and Macon, to Augusta; thence we marched across South Carolina, and took the train again to reach Smithfield, North Carolina, where our troops were engaged for the last time in April. There, in the old North State, I saw Dr. McFerrin, and heard him preach twice on the first Sunday in April at the Methodist Church in Charlotte for the pastor, Brother Stacey; and we slept together that night for the last time. In the morning his theme was "Growth in Grace;" at night, "Heaven," from Rev. vii. 13–17. We were then in the "great tribulation" of which he discoursed. Who that knew Dr. McFerrin well doubts that he is now with those "who have washed their robes and made them white in the blood of the Lamb, and are before the throne of God, and serve him day and night in his temple?"

Another minister, whose graphic pen has delighted thousands, old and young—the Rev. R. G. Porter, of the North Mississippi Conference—gives us this account:

REV. R. G. PORTER'S ACCOUNT.

The first I saw of him in this capacity was at Dalton, Georgia, the winter before the memorable Georgia campaign. At the time he came to us there was a deep and most wonderful revival of religion sweeping all over that army. Thousands of men were happily converted. I have never witnessed a deeper or more wonderful work of grace in my life. The brigade to which I belonged, and of which I was chaplain, was doing outpost duty on the Cleveland road that winter. For this reason I was not much with Dr. McFerrin, though he came out frequently and preached to my command. His coming and his preaching were always hailed with joy. His style and manner were admirably adapted to that kind

of life and to the work going on. He had a way of walking right
inside of a soldier's heart and taking possession at once. There
was nothing stiff or formal in either the style or manner of Dr.
McFerrin, in the pulpit or out of it. He was a man of the people—"one of the boys," as the soldiers put it. A fancy chaplain
or a "stuck up" missionary was an abomination to the average
soldier. Dr. McFerrin went round among the men like a father
among his sons, or rather like a brother among his brothers. His
quick wit and sharp repartee attracted the men to him, and made
him the center of attraction wherever he went. Dr. McFerrin's
wit was the quickest and his repartee the sharpest, but there was
no acid in it. This was his way of showing his friendship, his love
for men. He could be funny and pathetic by turns more easily
and naturally than any other man I ever knew. This trait came
out fully in camp life. It was beautiful to see how happy the soldiers were in his society. If they were eating, he would walk up
and "pitch in," as the men phrased it, as if he had been brought
up in camp on soldiers' fare—often only "hard tack" and water.

The Doctor was a hardy and a hearty man. He could recline
on a blanket, support his head on one hand, and converse with
the "boys" as any other soldier would do. He got close to the
men, and did not compromise his character as a Christian minister, either in the fact or manner of his approach.

Dr. McFerrin's plain, simple, earnest, strong preaching was admirably suited to those times. The soldiers, away from home
and exposed to hardship and imminent danger, wanted pure gospel preaching. The great mass of them had no patience whatever
with what they called *blatherskite*, or *buncombe*. This kind of solemn trifling was an abomination to them. Dr. McFerrin spoke to
the soldiers in their own tongue. He understood, and knew how
to use to the best effect, camp phrases and army terms. Some of
them took on new meanings as he used them. The language of
the camp became the vehicle to convey religious thought.

An Alabama Captain, somewhat advanced in years, was a
great admirer of Dr. McFerrin. They had known each other in
North Alabama long before the war. When it was known that
Dr. McFerrin was going to preach, this Captain took the rounds
and bragged on "John," as he called him, and drummed up an
immense concourse to hear him. The Captain was not religious.
The old Doctor was at his best that day. The tide of emotion

ran high; wave after wave of feeling had swept over the thousands of men present, and still the waves were coming. The Captain lost control of himself, forgot where he was, sprung to his feet, clapped his hands, and shouted: "Go it, John! you'll get every one of 'em!" This burst of enthusiasm increased the excitement. That was a mighty day in our camp. The slain of the Lord were many. The Alabama Captain was among the converts. O what a mighty commoner John B. McFerrin was! "The common people heard him," as they heard our blessed Lord, "gladly."

Another occasion will never be forgotten by hundreds of men. It was in the Public Square in Marietta, Georgia, while we were fighting on the Kennesaw line. It was a moonlight night. We had no light but that of the moon. The men were seated and thickly packed on the greensward in the court-yard. Dr. McFerrin preached. His subject was "The Characteristics of Job's Faith." The text: "The Lord gave, and the Lord hath taken away; blessed be the name of the Lord." His divisions were: (1) Job believed God to be the giver of all good—the Lord gave; (2) Job believed God to be the disposer of human events—the Lord hath taken away; and (3) this faith led Job to bless God under adverse as well as prosperous circumstances—blessed be the name of the Lord. That was a mighty sermon—not mighty in word, nor mighty in thought, but mighty in the presence and power of the Holy Ghost. It fell like rain on the dry and parched ground. The men, weary and worn with constant marching and fighting, went away refreshed as from a well-spring of joy. The very air that night seemed electric with the presence of God.

The foregoing was written by Mr. Porter in 1887, and he added the words: "Ere this the grand old man has met in the other world a great number of dead Confederates who greet him on the plains of glory, and call him 'my brother.' They were won to Christ by the message of life and love that fell from his lips."

The Rev. Warner Moore, of the Memphis Conference—one of the soldiers converted under Dr. McFerrin's ministry, and whom he mentions in his notes—furnishes these touching recollections of his spiritual father in the army:

REV. WARNER MOORE'S RECOLLECTIONS.

My first knowledge of Dr. McFerrin in the army was in the winter of 1862-3. My brigade (Stewart's) was on outpost duty at Guy's Gap, between Shelbyville and Murfreesboro. Dr. McFerrin would occasionally come out and preach to us.

In the spring of 1863 the boys built a large brush arbor in a field belonging to Dr. Hughes, and there the Doctor held the first of those wonderful meetings which were so blessed of God in the salvation of precious souls. His sermons during the winter had aroused the professed Christians among the soldiers to a sense of their obligation to labor for the conversion of their wicked comrades. When the protracted effort began he gathered this element about him, and used them just as we use the Church in a revival to-day. He made no distinction as to denominations. He was not a Methodist then in any sectarian sense. He was a minister of Jesus Christ, and these were his fellow-servants, and he called them to be co-workers with him in the work of the Master.

Day after day he preached to the masses of eager, anxious soldiers, and night after night there were heard the songs and prayers of awakened Christians and the shouts of those who had found the Saviour precious to their believing hearts. Between the services the Doctor could be seen riding from regiment to regiment, or sitting with groups of the men, talking in his cheerful and happy way on any subject that was brought forward, but always coming back to the important question of personal salvation.

If there was a sick soldier in a tent, the man of God would find him, and there would be such comfort brought to the body as he could provide or persuade others to provide, and there would be a song, a prayer, and either rejoicing in hope or else tears of penitence, according to the spiritual status of the subject.

On the march men hailed his appearance with joy. The lagging steps grew more elastic, the drooping form more erect, a smile came to every face, and the eye of the tired soldier sparkled as "Uncle John" rode alongside the column with words of greeting and of encouragement. Sometimes a would-be wit would loosen his tongue and begin to chaff the "parson" on his appearance or his "bomb-proof" relation to the army. Before that conversation ended the man who began it wished his tongue had cleaved to the roof of his mouth before he had uttered a word. Repartee came to no other man as happily and from no other as gracefully as Dr. McFerrin, and the most waggish "Reb" would always be discomfited when he measured words with this soldier-preacher. Many a man was silenced amid shouts of laughter from his comrades, and many a man carried to his soldier's grave or to the end of the war a nickname received in one of these efforts to "joke the preacher."

But the Doctor did not always ride. Oftentimes he was seen trudging along through the dust or mud with the marching column. On these occasions, if you would look ahead or to the rear you would see a barefooted, sick, or tired soldier riding the Doctor's horse. There was a tender heart in his breast for the callow boys who had rushed into a life for which they were unfitted, and many a poor boy got home to mother instead of rotting in a Northern prison, because this tender-hearted man gave up his horse, and walked until the weary limbs were rested and the boy was able to keep up with the retreating column. As to riding when he saw a gray head bending with weariness and burdened with gun and knapsack, it was not in him. And so it was that sometimes he would give one man a ride, and then he would mount and ride a few hundred yards, and down again to put another sick or broken-down man on his horse. More than once this writer has been ordered to dismount, with the explanation that a sick man had his horse, and he was tired.

When the long day's tramp was done and the scanty supper eaten, if you heard a hymn and saw men rising up from around the camp-fires and flocking toward the singer, if you followed you would see the light from the pile of cedar rails falling on the rugged face of Dr. McFerrin, and you would hear that voice of wonderful pathos and power raised in prayer. He prayed for the men, for the country, for the success of our armies. He prayed for the homes in the far-off States, for the dear old fathers and mothers; the loving, waiting, anxious wives; the blessed little ones that were lisping their little prayers for father's safe return from the war; and as he prayed, men would sob and weep, and join in the prayer, and then go and lie down on their blankets or on the ground, feeling safer and happier for their faith in that man's God.

23

He was not a fighter. He was truly a non-combatant. But he never shunned the field of battle. He seemed to have no fear. Calm and cool as if he trod the aisles of God's own house, he moved amid the falling shot and screaming shell. Down upon his knees to hear the last whisper of a dying man; praying for some despairing sinner, and telling of the Saviour's desire to save to the uttermost; twisting a handkerchief to check the flow of blood from a wounded leg or arm; lifting a wounded man in his arms, and bearing him to a place of safety or to the surgeon; in the lull of the battle moving among the men with words of cheer; so glad to meet the unwounded, so sorry to hear of the dead; so full of sympathy for those whose dear ones had been stricken down beside them; perchance, if time served, a prayer; and then, when the storm broke again, and the men began to fall, back to his arduous duties, his labor of love. And after the battle, when the wounded had been sent away to the hospitals, and the dead had been buried, he came to us like a father, and drew lessons from the facts of life or death to turn men's minds to God and make them feel the need of a personal Saviour.

But it was in the late winter or early spring of 1864 that Dr. McFerrin reaped the great harvest from the seed he had sown. Men had learned to love him. His name was a key to their hearts. His face was familiar. The tones of his voice were well known. The brave men respected the man who would face every danger without fear, and they loved the man who had faced these dangers for them. The men whom he had carried in his arms, to whose parched lips he had held the canteen of water, were back from the hospital and back from the furlough. They hailed his coming with delight. They talked of his good deeds, of how he looked and how he talked until the raw recruit knew him on sight, and needed not to be told whose voice he heard when he spoke to him. All around Dalton, Georgia, wherever there was a brigade encamped there was a meeting, and men were converted. He was as iron; he was tireless. He seemed to feel that thousands who must die in the next campaign were, if saved at all, to be saved now. And so he preached and prayed and sung, and thousands heard and repented and believed, and in heaven to-day are greeting him as the happy instrument in their salvation.

Down at Kingston, Georgia, was a battalion of artillery in winter quarters. Dr. McFerrin went to them. He began to preach, and the men who cared to listen to no other preacher went out to hear " Uncle John." It was a perfect Pentecost. In a few days the whole moral tone of that battalion was changed. Instead of two or three Christian men in each company there were now only two or three hardened sinners, who wondered and sneered and chafed at the change. There were prayers in every cabin, and happy was the mess with which the preacher lodged at night. There were two or three prayer-meetings every week. Every man who could talk a little was begged to preach or exhort.

From that meeting went forth three preachers of the gospel. One was a Methodist, one a Baptist, and one a Presbyterian; but all of them loved Dr. McFerrin as a spiritual father. Two of the three went on before the grand old man, and were ready to welcome him on the other shore. One, the Methodist, is still in the field working for the Master.

An incident at the close of the Kingston meeting shows the catholicity of the man. He opened the doors of the *Churches*. A half-dozen scribes wrote certificates that "A. B. had professed conversion at Kingston, Georgia, and wished to join such a Church." These certificates he signed, and gave to the men to be sent home to the pastors. The third man who came forward wanted to join the Roman Catholic Church, and he received a certificate to that effect. How grand it would be if every Roman Catholic were as soundly converted as Pat S.!

His sermons had a most wonderful power. Men were convinced by the simple utterance of the text. He preached from the text, " Marvel not that I said unto thee, Ye must be born again," and no man marveled. It seemed the most natural and simple thing in the world, and hundreds of men needed not the fiery exhortation that followed to induce them to seek the new birth. Again, it was " He that believeth shall be saved," and men believed and were saved, and sat full of triumphant faith until they could rush forward and clasp the preacher in their arms, and tell him the sweet tidings of their salvation. And he never forgot these men. Years after the war closed they would meet him on the train or on the street, and he would tell them what regiment or company they belonged to, and every incident of their army acquaintance would be recalled. Sometimes he would tell of circumstances the men themselves had forgotten. No wonder the whole Army of Tennessee loved this man! No wonder the name of John B. McFerrin is so precious to the children of these men among whom he moved as an angel of God, and to whom he brought the light of God!

In his visits to the sick and wounded in the hospitals he made no distinction between the boys in gray and the boys in blue. Many a Union prisoner was comforted and cheered by his ministrations, and bore to their Northern homes warm affection for him in their hearts, or died invoking blessings upon his head with their last breath. In this he was not singular; if there was a chaplain on either side who drew a line of distinction at the couches of the sick and the dying, the fact is not recorded. The Christianity that thus asserted its heavenly power to mitigate the horrors of war will, we can not doubt, in its full development and consummated mission, make all war impossible. That eruption from the hell of human passion can have no place on this earth when the Prince of Peace shall have established his dominion from sea to sea.

DR. McFERRIN AS BOOK AGENT.

DR. McFERRIN'S first term as Book Agent was cut short by the war. In his way he tells us how it was done in a former chapter. He was magnifying his office as an economizer, and making haste slowly and surely when struck by that cyclone. It would be an easy task to criticise his methods and to prove that perfect wisdom did not mark his management of the business of the Publishing House. The fact is, the whole matter of conducting such an enterprise was new to our people, and he had to educate both himself and the Church therefor. A more sanguine man might have gone faster, and there were many men in the Church who had read more books than he had. But the instinct that put him in this place was not at fault. There was no other man who was so certain to avoid extravagance and dangerous risks in attempting too much. There was no other man in all the Church in whom the people more fully confided. They looked to him for an honest, conservative, successful management of the financial interests of their Connectional Publishing House. And they depended on him also to use the influence of his office to guard the orthodoxy of the literature of the Church. With McFerrin in the Book Agency, and Summers in the editorship, nobody feared that heresy could break in over the courageous resistance of the one, or creep in by eluding the unremitting vigilance of the other. This was no small advantage. It was more im-

(357)

portant that the Church should start right than that it should move rapidly in such an enterprise. The debt of gratitude it owes to these two men on this score is large. The stream they set flowing, if small, was pure and sweet; if hereafter, as the volume increases, its waters become muddy, it will not be their fault.

The same sure instinct again turned the General Conference to McFerrin in the crisis of 1878. By a series of disasters the Publishing House was involved in a debt amounting to $356,000. The empirical devices usually resorted to in such emergencies had all been exhausted. The people were dispirited, the boldest were disheartened, the wisest were at their wit's end. Not a few were ready to abandon the enterprise altogether, proposing to sell out for whatever price could be obtained, and henceforth publish only by contract. Every expedient was suggested but one—no voice hinted of repudiation. All felt that the debt must be paid to the last cent. But how? was the question. What new device is possible? What can be done to restore confidence, to awaken hope, and to rouse the paralyzed energies of a great Church? The same thought occurred simultaneously to many—put McFerrin back into the Book Agency; the people all know him and believe in him. Put him back there, and one of two things will happen—the whole business will be wound up squarely, or it will be continued on a proper basis. When the matter was mentioned to him he held back, saying he was getting too old for such a task, and presenting other reasons why he ought to be excused therefrom. But the conviction was so strong and so general that the crisis demanded his services that it was evident he would be elected unless he peremptorily declined to accept the office. This he dared not do. And so he was elected. When the result of the ballot was announced, the strong old man wept. The tears he shed on the occasion might have had a twofold cause—a solemn and oppressive feeling of responsibility, and a grateful recognition of the confidence which such a vote implied. The high tension attending elections of this sort not unfrequently results in an exhibition like this. Tears bring relief to the overtaxed nerves. But there was more than sentiment in the weeping of the veteran servant of the Church. He knew, at least in part, the magnitude of the work before him. Had he known all that was coming from 1878 to 1887, his tears might have flowed still more freely. Had he looked still farther ahead, he would probably have realized the words written by an inspired singer and recorded in the Book wherein may be found all the best things: "They that sow in tears shall reap in joy."

When the General Conference had adjourned, and the new men chosen to conduct the publishing interests of the Church met in Nashville, the prospect was not a bright one. With Dr. McFerrin as Book Agent, Dr. Thomas O. Summers as Book Editor, Dr. O. P. Fitzgerald as editor of the *Christian Advocate*, and Dr. W. G. E. Cunnyngham as Sunday-school Editor, the new *regime* began. The creditors of the Publishing House were uneasy, some of them clamorous. The circulation of the *Christian Advocate* had run down to about seven thousand names. But everybody breathed more freely. A change of some sort was coming, and almost any possible change was preferable to the hopeless stagnation that had prevailed.

The new Book Committee were called together by

the Book Agent. It was a remarkable body of men. Its chairman was Judge James Whitworth, who was never a Jackson man in his politics, being an old-line Whig, but who was grandly Jacksonian in his pluck, persistence, and integrity of character, as watchful of Church trusts as he was of his own, and adopted business methods in doing Church business. Never was a sick child nursed more assiduously by a mother than was the crippled Publishing House cared for by this prompt, incisive, well-trained lawyer and banker. Next may be named Dr. William H. Morgan, a massive man every way, with front-head large enough to see all round a question, back-head enough to drive him forward to his aim, and top-head enough to make him hold to a conviction as long as he has breath. Then comes Dr. William Morrow, a man whose business sagacity and energy are equaled by his open-handed liberality, whose pleasure in dispensing money in doing good equals his genius in its acquisition; and Mr. Thomas D. Fite, a specimen of superb physical manhood, with a great Methodist heart and excellent business talents; and Nat. Baxter, Jr., a man who combines in a remarkable degree the penetration of a lawyer, the ability of a true financier, and the quick and rare grasp that takes in the various views of a body of men, and puts them into one motion that harmonizes them; and Dempsey Weaver, a banker whose financial ability did not surpass the generosity that made him the benefactor of every good cause and the goodness that made him the friend of all the needy; and Samuel J. Keith, a successful business man who brought to the Book Committee the same fidelity and large common sense that characterized him in the prosecution of his own affairs; and Col. D. T.

Reynolds, a Tennessee farmer of excellent judgment, liberal-minded, and zealous for the Church; and Mr. John A. Carter, a big-brained, great-hearted Louisville merchant, accustomed to large plans, yet possessing a genius for details; and last, but not least, among the lay members of the committee, Judge Edward H. East, a lawyer who holds no second place at the bar of his State—keen, quick, logical, eloquent, witty, as occasion may demand—whose services were invaluable, especially in the earlier and more difficult period of the Committee's work. Then come the clerical members: Dr. R. A. Young, a man who can handle money as well as theology and literature, a man who can preach sermons, write books, and keep books; Dr. Allen S. Andrews, a strong man, whose administrative capacity has proved itself equal to the pastorate of a city Church, the presidency of a Methodist college, or the guardianship of a publishing house; Dr. A. G. Haygood, a brilliant, brave, and brainy man who is making his mark on his generation. Of this committee Dr. McFerrin said: " It is not surpassed in ability by the Cabinet of the President of the United States." The Bishops of the Church were all advisory members, and their wisdom, experience, and wide knowledge of the wants, wishes, and resources of the Church were found very helpful in all emergencies. From California was called Mr. Lewis D. Palmer, to be the Business Manager of the Publishing House—described as " a man with a telescopic mind and a microscopic eye," a man who made logarithms the recreation of his leisure hours when a student, and who has the rare power of unraveling the tangled skeins of complicated accounts, and who did a work in that line for the Church that entitles him to its lasting gratitude.

In this brief enumeration of the forces that were now at work for the rescue of the Publishing House and the honor of Southern Methodism the name of Mr. Samuel K. Welburn can not properly be omitted—a man who by special adaptation to the work, long experience, and unremitting diligence, became a sort of *factotum*, knowing all about types, presses, books, every thing almost connected with the business of the concern—a walking encyclopedia of Publishing House matters.

A scheme for bonding the enormous debt was devised, which was the chief means of working out the salvation of the Publishing House. The honor of proposing this scheme has been attributed to two different members of the Board, one of whom is dead, and the other still living and working for the Church. As the entire Board had the good sense to adopt it and the good fortune to make it grandly successful, let them all share the credit of it now. Special honor will be awarded to whom it is due when every man shall be rewarded according to his work—that is, according to its motive and its measure.

The next chapter will give some account of the manner in which Dr. McFerrin worked on the plan thus adopted.

McFERRIN'S GREAT BOND CAMPAIGN.

TO sell the Publishing House bonds was the next thing, and it was not an easy thing to do. The depressed condition of the institution, the disheartened state of the Church, and the many openings for the profitable investment of money in the South, made it seem very improbable that business men would be eager to buy McFerrin's four per cents. But it was felt that they must be sold, and he started out to do it. The details of the scheme were explained through the Church press, and the faithful were urged to rally with their subscriptions. Nashville Methodists, including the Agent and the members of the Book Committee, started the movement in a liberal way, and by the time the autumn sessions of the Annual Conferences began Dr. McFerrin was ready to start on his great bond campaign. He had the assistance of Dr. R. A. Young, who had been requested by the Book Committee to lend his efficient help on a line of service wherein he had achieved uniform success. The speeches made by McFerrin as he went from Conference to Conference and from city to city touched skillfully every responsive chord in the hearts of the men and women who heard them. Starting at the lowest point, he told them that it was a good business investment, that four per cent. was fair interest on money, that the United States Government paid no more; that the security was as good as—yea, better than—that of Government bonds, for human governments might perish, but the

Church would never fail; that the Southern Methodist Church had paid the heavy debt incurred in the prosecution of its missionary work during the war; and that her honor was safe in the keeping of her children, nearly a million strong. Then he would draw a picture of the consequences of the failure of the scheme: the debt can not be paid, the mortgages are foreclosed, the Publishing House is to be sold, and the day of the sale has come. The Bishops, the General Conference officers, the preachers, the people—men, women, and children—are gathered on the Public Square in Nashville, in front of the Publishing House, to witness the sad and shameful scene—the sale of the honor and good name of the Southern Methodist Church! Who bids? Going! going!—about this time there are evident signs of deep feeling in the audience, and when at last, with moistened eyes and quivering lips he shrieks out with startling vehemence the words, "May I die before that day!" they are ready to act, and his bonds are subscribed for as fast as the quick-fingered secretaries can write down the names. Now and then the attendant circumstances would be inauspicious, and he would have to make a still harder pull, but he would prove equal to the emergency. One of his illustrations, in closing an appeal, was like this: "In my boyhood, when Tennessee was first being settled, I remember the exciting scenes that took place at the house-raisings. The hewn logs were lifted into their places, one after another, until the walls were raised all round, and last of all the ridgepole was to be elevated to its place. The women look on while the men push and pull and strain to the utmost; the top is almost gained, but the weight is too great, the ascent stops—steady! steady! the log will not move upward another inch; nay, it is ready to topple back and down upon the workmen. The cry comes, 'Women, help!' The women throw their weight and strength upon the skids, and with one more mighty effort the great piece of timber reaches its place, and the work of the day is done! Women of Southern Methodism, help now, or the Church you love may be dishonored, and the cause of your Saviour suffer!" This appeal, made in McFerrin's inimitable and indescribable way, would strangely stir his hearers; the women would come to his help, a fresh impetus would be given to the subscription, and a great victory would be achieved and recorded. A characteristic incident took place on the occasion of his visit to Louisville on this business, accompanied by Dr. Young and the writer of these chapters. The matter of his mission in behalf of the Publishing House had been presented with encouraging success to the Walnut Street and Broadway congregations. On the following evening a similar presentation of the matter was to be made to the Chestnut Street people, McFerrin to lead off and make the principal address, and his two associates to follow in brief talks, as the occasion might demand. The weather was bad, and the audience rather small. McFerrin had been taking a late supper, and made a hurried walk to the church to avoid being tardy. After preliminary religious services, he began his speech. It was evident that for once he was making a failure. His mind did not seem to act; he floundered along, pointless, languid, heavy. "What is the matter with McFerrin?" whispered Young. "I never saw him in such a plight before. He is making the poorest speech I ever heard from his lips." On he went, still limping strangely. "There is only one way to save him: we

must make him mad," said Young; "that may rouse him."
Acting upon this notion, Young asked him some question designedly impertinent. "What did you say?" demanded McFerrin, turning sharply upon his questioner.
The question was repeated. He stood a moment, pon-
dering, and then, in his most sarcastic tone, said: "Did
you ever hear such a silly question from a Doctor of Divinity? You ought to be ashamed of yourself," he continued, "to interrupt a speech with such foolishness as
that;" and then for a few minutes he poured upon his
venturesome friend such a torrent of sharp but good-
natured satire as he had scarcely ever heard before.
"All right," whispered Young; "he will go now." And
he did. There was no more halting or dragging; all
his mental resources seemed to come into full play; his
wit was never finer, his humor more irresistible, or his
exhortations more moving. He made one of the very
best speeches of his life, after that bad start, and his
bonds had a lively sale with the amused and delighted
audience. When some time afterward he was told of
the means used to rouse him, he looked half angry and
half pleased, but said nothing. If he considered the
liberty taken of doubtful propriety, the happy result
palliated the offense. This was one of many instances
in which a seeming impediment was made the means of
larger success. Woe to the antagonist in a debate who
interrupted him when under full headway! Instanta-
neously he turned and bore down upon him with all the
momentum he had acquired, and down he went under
the shock. It might be said of him, as it was said of
Stephen A. Douglas: he was never worsted in a colloquial encounter of this sort, though he met his match on
the hustings in Abraham Lincoln.

So the work went on. Wherever McFerrin went preachers and people were stirred by his appeals; confidence returned by degrees; the bonds were taken more and more freely; confidence rose into enthusiasm; despair gave way to renewed hope, and hope to certainty that the Publishing House would be saved, the honor and good name of the Church maintained, and a grand demonstration made of the denominational fealty and latent power of the Southern Methodist people. To the whole Church belongs the honor of this achievement, to its entire ministry and his immediate official co-laborers, much credit is due; but to McFerrin's wonderful hold upon the confidence and affection of the Church, and his masterful leadership, more than to what was done, or could have been done by any other man, must this deliverance be ascribed. He was the providential instrument specially adapted to the great work. The fact that he was at hand when the crisis called for him furnishes a ground for the pleasing conviction that God means good to us as a Church, and that the Publishing House is designed by him to bear no mean part in the task of supplying the rapidly multiplying millions of this great republic with a wholesome Christian literature.

" LET HER ROLL!"

D R. McFERRIN was perhaps the most original, and certainly one of the most notable, figures in the Methodist Ecumenical Conference, held in London, in 1881. He magnetized the body in the inexplicable way peculiar to himself, and left an impression so vivid that it abides. "He was a wonderful man, just such a creature as we never saw before," said a Welsh newspaper, in a notice of the notabilities of that remarkable gathering of Methodists from all parts of the world. He was one of three Americans who seem to have made a peculiarly distinct personal impression—Dr. McFerrin, by his unique individuality and magnetic quality; Bishop McTyeire, by his unconventional cutaway coat, "foghorn" voice, and weightiness in word and presence; and Bishop Peck, by his behemoth-like proportions, English ways, and parliamentary tact. On his way to London two incidents occurred that drew out McFerrin in most characteristic style. Arriving at New York *en route*, he attended a fraternal meeting held at John Street Church, the cradle of American Methodism, on the evening of August 5. The Rev. Dr. Crawford, of New York, delivered an address of welcome to the delegates, quite a large number being present. Dr. McFerrin made the principal speech in response, in which he referred briefly to the origin of the Methodist Church in America, its progress, and its divisions, especially to the division of

(368)

1844. He alluded briefly to the controversy that followed that event, in which he took an active part, being the editor of one of the Church papers in the South. He also referred to the late Civil War between the North and the South, saying he was a native of the South, that he sympathized with the South, and took sides with the South. He did not bear arms, being too old and a minister of the gospel; but he marched with the soldiers, ministered to the sick and wounded, preached to the well, and prayed for all. He rejoiced in the victories of the Southern armies, mourned at their defeats, and was sad at their final overthrow; yet all the time he believed in the providence of God, holding that he is the God of nations as well as the maker and ruler of the material universe; and when the Southern armies surrendered he accepted the situation, went home, and honestly tried to be a good citizen. He had kept his pledges. In the recent fraternal movements he. had been among the foremost. He had visited Round Lake Camp-meeting, in the North, had "made friends" and shaken hands with the brethren, and had all unkind feelings expelled from his heart. He was now on his way to the grand Ecumenical Conference, where he expected to greet the representatives of all the Methodist bodies in the world, and he anticipated a joyous time. In this strain he spoke about forty minutes, with frequent applause, at the conclusion leaving the whole of the vast auditory in a fraternal and spiritual glow. While giving his pedigree as a Methodist there was a little colloquial by-play between him and the Rev. Dr. J. M. Buckley that was sharp and witty on both sides, and which the friendly hearers greatly enjoyed.

On board the steamer " City of Berlin," in which he

24

embarked, there were over two hundred cabin passengers, many of them delegates to the Ecumenical Conference. They were from the North and from the South—Methodist Episcopal, Methodist Episcopal Church, South, Methodist Protestant, United Brethren, and several Negro Bishops. The company was select, and the voyage pleasant. On Sunday morning the English Church service was read; in the evening the Rev. Dr. George R. Crooks, of New York, preached an excellent sermon. On Monday evening the delegates and friends organized a fraternal meeting, electing Dr. McFerrin chairman. The Rev. Dr. A. C. George gave a lucid statement of the origin, progress, and design of the Ecumenical Conference. The next evening, by request, Dr. McFerrin addressed the meeting. He must have been in his happiest mood. The large and elegant saloon was crowded. After a hymn and a prayer, the speaker was introduced. No written report of his speech can do it justice. An outline of it can be given, and only those who have heard McFerrin when he was in one of his moods of alternating audacity, humorousness, and pathos can imagine its effect. After a few general remarks, he said he had been out on the upper deck of the magnificent steamer, had been marking the track of the vessel, and wondering if John Wesley and Francis Asbury had sailed that way. He had looked diligently, and he could see no signs or way-marks of their voyages across these waters; all had been swept away by the rolling billows; not a track has been left behind. But not so on the soil of America; there they had left impressions which a hundred years, with all their changes, had not erased. Nay, those impressions were deepening with the roll of time. Through Wesley and Asbury

and their co-workers and successors, God had wrought
wonders in the New World; millions had been brought
to Christ, and the work was still going on with increasing power. Their followers had branched off into different families, but they were all working to the same great
end—spreading scriptural holiness over all lands. They
had reached the Canadas, gone to the Gulf of Mexico,
swept over the Rocky Mountains, and reached the Pacific shores. On the tops of the lofty hills and in the
vales below the name of Jesus had been praised, because
the followers of Wesley and Asbury had heralded the
cross of Christ through these lands. "We are going up
to London to report progress. I imagine ourselves in
the City Road Chapel, the home of John Wesley, the
scene of his early and earnest labors. He is in the chair,
and the representatives of all the Methodist families are
around him. I arise to speak, and address 'Father
Wesley.'

"'Who are you, and what have you to say?'

"'I am John McFerrin. I come from the great Valley
of the Mississippi, lying in North America. I belong
to the Wesleyan family, and have come up with my
brethren to report what God has wrought.'

"'And what have you been doing, my son?'

"'Why, Father Wesley, we have had hard times in
many respects. Our country was new and rough; we
had in our early days to penetrate the wilderness, swim
rivers, scale mountains, sleep on the ground, and feed on
such food as a wild, new country could afford. We had
no bridges, no ferry-boats, no turnpikes, no railroads, no
steam-boats; we had to blaze our way through the woods,
and preach the gospel as best we could, under trees in
the forest, and wherever we could get a hearing.'

" ' Well, what has been the result? '

" ' Well, Father Wesley, we have great reason to thank God and take courage. We have grown to be a numerous people; we have nearly nine hundred thousand Church-members, about four thousand traveling preachers, five thousand local preachers, and five hundred thousand children in our Sunday-schools. We have missionaries in China, Mexico, and Brazil, and among the Germans, and on the borders of civilization. We have about five thousand Indians in our Church. We have universities, colleges, high schools, and academies for males and females. We have a large Publishing House, where we print and from which we send forth yearly millions of pages of sound Christian literature. We have six Bishops, or General Superintendents, and a host of doctors, editors, and professors. We have taken into the Church the rich and the poor; governors, judges, and senators, and one of the ex-Presidents of the United States, have held membership in our Church.'

" ' Well, really, my son, you seem to have had great prosperity.'

" ' Yes, Father Wesley, indeed we have reason to thank God and go forward. But there is one other item I wish to mention: We did a great work among the colored population in the slave States. Our preachers went into the rice, sugar, and cotton plantations, and preached to the poor slaves, and thousands of them were converted. They have been greatly elevated. You English, Dutch, and other Europeans, went into the wilds of Africa, captured the poor creatures, sent them in ships to our new country, and threw them upon our shores savages, but a little above the orang-outang, degraded almost to a level with the beasts of the forest. We took them and civilized and Christianized them, and now we bring them back Bishops in the Church of God [pointing to the Negro delegates in their midst, amid laughter and applause], to take part in the Ecumenical Conference. Father Wesley, we have had our trials. We got into a dispute with our Northern brethren, and for awhile Ephraim vexed Judah, and Judah tormented Ephraim, and we had a sore time of it. But it is all over now. We have met and shaken hands, and now we are here as a band of brothers to represent the great Methodist family of the United States of America. We feel that we are on board the old ship of Zion, with all the Methodist sailors, steering for the shores of the heavenly Canaan, and our cry is, *Let her roll!*'"

Here the audience became excited, and responded, "*Let her roll! let her roll!*" The words were taken up on all sides in a storm of pleasant excitement. That was an Ecumenical prelude. The music is still in the air. "LET HER ROLL!"

McFerrin soon got the ear of the Conference, and his short speeches spiced its proceedings in a way that whetted the appetite of the body for more of that curious compound of shrewdness, quaintness, devoutness, and strange power that now for the first time exhibited itself in mighty London. There was mutual wonder. The scene was all new to McFerrin, and he was a new type of Methodist ministerial manhood to those fraternal but inquisitive men who came up from all parts of the earth to look each other in the face. This occasion furnished a supreme test of that indefinable power by which some men assume practical chieftainship among their fellows. There were in the Conference men more learned, men more logical, more eloquent, according to the ordinary standards, but none who surpassed him in the elements of a popular leader. He was there, as everywhere, the great tribune.

The steel-engraved likeness which is placed as the frontispiece of this book is from a photograph of Dr. McFerrin taken in London while he was in attendance upon the Conference. It is the picture chosen by his wife as the best and most characteristic of any of which he is the subject. It represents him in his seventy-fourth year, when time and toil and griefs and grace had done their work and left their marks upon his frame and his features; when the Boanerges of the pulpit and the corypheus of the polemical arena had ripened into the serene wisdom of a sage; when what was lost in vivacity was gained in dignity and benignity of bearing and expression; when, in a word, the thoughts he had cherished, the objects for which he had lived, and the affections he had cultivated had been inwrought into all the organs of expression, and his mental and spiritual nature had received all except the final touches preparatory to his translation to another sphere. It is the picture of the McFerrin whose life we have traced from his happy boyhood and youth to robust young manhood, to the maturity of his powers. There he is, with his still robust frame, with a head that was a puzzle to a phrenologist, narrow between the temples, forehead long and sharply receding, bulging above the ears, and narrowing at the top, with immense driving-force behind; large Roman nose; mouth wide; lips mobile, yet firmly set; chin rather pointed, yet giving the impression of power and fixedness of purpose; eyes steel-blue and deep-set, with lashes rather heavy, but not shaggy; hands rather small, with slender and flexible fingers; feet also small; his gait that of a man who was going somewhere by the most direct route; his large features in repose, a little severe in expression, but with a suffusion of benignity, like sunshine on the face of a cliff.

D R. McFERRIN was beyond question the most
venerable figure in the Centenary Conference of
American Methodism, held in Baltimore in December,
1884. "He was the belle of the occasion," playfully
said a noble Christian lady, who certainly strained a figure in that expression. From the first day of the session
he was recognized as the patriarch of the body. His
seat in the chancel of the Mount Vernon Methodist
Episcopal Church was the focus of kindly and curious
observation. He and Dr. James E. Evans and Dr. Jesse
Boring, of Georgia; Dr. Andrew Hunter, of Arkansas;
and Dr. J. M. Trimble, of Ohio, were the sole survivors present of the General Conference of 1844, and
they were regarded as heroes who had come down to
this generation from that which had fought the great
battle which resulted in the two Episcopal Methodisms
in America, but which in these happier times had come
together in a gathering that revived the hallowed memories of the past, unsealed the fountains of brotherly
love and started its streams to flowing through all these
lands. It was a ten-days' love-feast, and McFerrin rode
its topmost wave. His heart had long been tuned for
the occasion, and he struck the right chord in the first
speech and every speech he made during those ten days
that typed so beautifully the promised perfection and
blessedness of the unified Church of the Lord Jesus
Christ. He went there magnetized by the divine touch,
and he in turn magnetized the whole body. His very

looks, in connection with his history, spoke of swords
sheathed, hostile banners furled, a new era, and an ac-
celerated movement of the hosts of American Methodism in their victorious march. That he should speak at
the meeting of welcome on the first night was a matter of
course. Who so ready, witty, original, and pathetic as this
old platform king? Few eyes were dry when he ended
with these words: "Last year I was very near the gate
of heaven, but God has allowed me to come back to
witness this grand Centenary of Methodism; and when
I have witnessed this I may say, with one of old:
'Now, Lord, lettest thou thy servant depart in peace;'
and I am going to carry up with me the news that all
Methodists are one in heart, and are carrying out the
apostle's injunction, 'LITTLE CHILDREN, LOVE ONE
ANOTHER.'"

At the reception given by the Mayor of the city it
was Dr. McFerrin's speech that wreathed every face
with smiles and warmed every heart with the glow of the
Christian neighborliness expressed in his quaint yet apt
and telling phrases. If a dozen delegates were on the
floor when he rose, all were ready to give way to the
old man who, by common consent, embodied in himself
the genius of that Centenary Conference. The spectators in the crowded galleries leaned to catch his words,
and the delegates cheered all his speeches with a hearti-
ness that was inspiring to one who possessed the true
orator's temperament, that kindles into a fresh blaze
when it feels the breath of popular applause. "Listen
how they applaud Dr. McFerrin!" exclaimed a delegate
in a good-natured way. "If he were to rise and recite
the multiplication-table, I believe they would cheer him!"
The echoes of his words at the Round Lake Camp-

meeting and at the Ecumenical Conference at London
were in the air at Baltimore, and with them the magic
of his presence, that never failed to catch and hold the
ear and heart of any assemblage in which he was permitted to speak.   The brilliant and imperial Bishop Fos-
ter; the polished and fine-grained Bishop Andrew; the
quick and incisive Dr. Buckley; the genial and scholarly
Dr. Pierce, with Boston culture and Methodist fervor;
the saintly Dr. Merrick, of Ohio, whose speech was like
the breaking of an alabaster-box of precious perfume;
the militant and manly Dr. Arthur Edwards, of Chicago;
the meditative yet wide-awake Dr. Fry, of St. Louis;
the learned and thoughtful Dr. Miley, of Drew Theological Seminary; the munificent and modest Dr. Gou-
cher; the ebony Demosthenes, Dr. Pierce, of North
Carolina; the sunny and clear-brained Dr. Scott, of
Pittsburgh; the princely layman, Cornell, of New York,
in whose face beamed a benediction to all humanity; the
electric and brilliant Gen. Clinton B. Fisk, whose wit is
as unfailing as his benevolence, and whose rhetoric has
a soul as well as a sparkle; Dr. Briggs, of California,
fluent, polished, and strong; Prof. Little, of Dickinson
College, a word-painter and a thought-dispenser, whose
essay on the " Methodist Pioneers " took the Conference
by storm; Dr. D. A. Whedon, kinsman of the great commentator, and of the same fine, scholarly, Christian metal;
Bishop Bowman, a typical Methodist preacher, who has
the tongue of fire in the pulpit, and the flavor of the old
Methodism everywhere—all these, and many more not
less worthy, were there from sister Methodist bodies,
besides Dr. McFerrin's own colleagues from the South,
of whom no special mention can be made here. Among
them all the central figure was the old man who sat there

in their midst, bridging the distance between McKendree and Roberts and Simpson and Pierce.

A characteristic episode took place one day, when the relation of children to the atonement and to the Church was under discussion. The debate took a wide range, and Dr. McFerrin, who always felt a special interest in that question, strained his hearing to catch every word that was said. One of the speakers—a colored delegate of remarkable sprightliness and fluency—stressed the importance of Christian culture, and drew a picture of the good angels and evil spirits contending for the mastery in the heart of a child until at last the good angels triumphed. Dr. McFerrin, who thought the speech smacked of heresy, was on his feet instantly when the brother sat down. "Mr. President, I want to say a word right here," he said, and there was at once an ex-pectant and respectful hush. "The brother seems to think that Christian culture is all that is needed for the salvation of children. He says nothing about conver-sion. Culture! culture! culture!" he continued, raising his voice. "Is culture enough? Do you begin with culture? Is that the way you read your Bible? Cult-ure! No, brother, you don't begin there. A lady once said to me what you have just said. I said to her: 'Let us see how that will work. Take a wild crab-apple tree, place it in a good place in your garden, cultivate it, and see if you can make it bear pippins. Spare no pains; give it faithful and skillful culture for ten years, and then what sort of apples will you find growing upon that tree? Crab-apples, madam, and no other sort! If you want pippins or russets, you must graft in a new branch.' Culture! That is not the starting-point. Jesus settled that question when he said: '*Except a man be*

born again, he can not see the kingdom of God.' First,
the new birth, and then the culture and the growth.
The brother," he continued, "drew a picture of the good
angels and devils fighting for the possession of the soul
of a child, and he made it so vivid that it seemed to me
I could almost see them clawing and biting one another.
But while he was talking I thought of the poor man
who had a legion of devils, *and Jesus came along and
cast them all out at once!* That's his way. That is
the good old way of our fathers. Better stick to that,
my brother."

As he sat down the Conference broke forth into general applause, and no more was needed to be said on that
side of the question. The fluent advocate of "culture"
tried to explain, but showed plainly that he was beaten,
and was more reticent for the remainder of the session.

Another episode of the Conference was the dramatic
scene that took place at its close between Gen. Clinton
B. Fisk and Dr. McFerrin. It was a fitting climax to
an occasion such as no one present could ever witness
again. The venerated Dr. Trimble was conducting the
exercises of the Conference love-feast, and as one after
another of the brethren in brief and burning words related their experiences the feeling become more and
more intense, until it seemed that all the streams of fraternity that had been open for a hundred years of Methodist history had met in the gracious baptism of that
hallowed hour. At length Gen. Fisk, surcharged with
emotion, rose, and said:

"It would take two hours for me to tell all that is
crowding upon my heart. This meeting is the remarkable hour of my life. First, I am happy in the Lord.
I am glad I am a Methodist. I am glad to see the work

of this meeting. It will be twenty years in a few months since when, at the close of the war, when the smoke and flame had died away, to my quarters in Nashville—where I was clothed with more responsibility than generally comes to me, and more than I desire—there came two men. One of them was J. B. McFerrin, and the other was A. L. P. Green. At the mention of that last name how many hearts throb with gratitude to God that ever such a good man lived! We sat down and talked together, and the talk was a religious one. We talked about Methodism—not about organic union just then, but about a better state of things, and about fraternity. I said to them: 'Do you think the time will ever come when there will be a better state of feeling?' And this good old man [placing his hand on Dr. McFerrin's head] turned to me and said: 'Why, bless you, you will see them all sitting down together in a love-feast yet!' And here we are! I was in a difficult place, and with most difficult work on my hands out there in that portion of the country, and from the President down no man gave me so much help as this good man upon whose head my hand now rests."

With irrepressible emotion Dr. McFerrin rose to his feet, and in a moment they were locked together in fraternal embrace. The effect was thrilling. The whole body rose to their feet, and with tears and swelling hearts burst forth into the song:

> Together let us sweetly live,
> Together let us die,
> And each a starry crown receive,
> And reign above the sky.

The effect of the Centenary Conference was most happy. It started American Methodism on its second century in a frame of devout gratitude to God, with brotherly love and joyful hope abounding. No delegate who was there could fail to be more brotherly forever after. Not one of the millions represented could fail to catch something of the gracious glow that radiated from it. Its concrete result was embodied in a paper offered by Dr. McFerrin on the last day of the session:

Whereas we, the delegates of the Methodist Centennial Conference, held in Baltimore, December 9-17, 1884, have found the occasion one of great personal interest and spiritual profit; and believing that it has strengthened the bond of brotherhood between the various branches of the Methodist family represented in the Conference, and with a desire to utilize and make permanent the benefit already gained, and to extend and widen its influence in the future; and, whereas we desire to acknowledge, reverently, the goodness of God in thus bringing us together on the *hundredth* anniversary of our ecclesiastical family life, and especially for the peace and harmony which have pervaded all our meetings; therefore,

1. *Resolved,* That we return sincere and heart-felt thanks to Almighty God, both for the occasion and for the marked prosperity he has vouchsafed to us as a people for the past century.

2. That we part to return to our respective fields of work and life with sincere and deepened affection for each other, and with a holy purpose to consecrate ourselves anew to the great work for which our Church was, as we believe, raised up of God—to spread scriptural holiness throughout the world.

3. That, with the spirit of true brotherhood, we will seek more than ever to co-operate together in every practical way for the accomplishment of this end.

4. That we respectfully commend to the Bishops of the episcopal, and the chief officers of the non-episcopal, Methodist Churches represented in this Conference to consider whether informal conferences between them could not be held with profit from time to time concerning matters of common interest to their respective bodies.

5. That we shall be greatly pleased to see these bonds of brotherhood and fellowship increased and strengthened more and more in the future.

6. That any occasion that may bring our respective Churches together in convention for the promotion of these objects will always be hailed with profound satisfaction.

While the vote on this paper was being taken Dr. McFerrin's face was radiant with joy. Did another hundred years of marching and of song pass before him in prophetic vision? and did he anticipate the more resplendent glory of the next centenary of American Methodism?

HIS LAST GENERAL CONFERENCE.

B Y the votes of his brethren Dr. McFerrin's name was placed at the head of the Tennessee delegation to the General Conference which convened at Richmond, Virginia, in May, 1886. As he sat, half blind and half deaf, in front of the chancel of the church in Columbia, during the balloting, he was like a father among his children, and his election was as creditable to them as it was gratifying to him. The older members of the body had nothing in their gift too good for the old chief who had so long marched at their head. McFerrin's name headed their ballots, as usual; he was first in their affections as he was first in the length of his service to the Church, and there was a smile of satisfaction on their bronzed and wrinkled faces when, on counting the ballots, his name stood first. He took this action all the more kindly as he knew that it was rather exceptional in its character. There was a time when elections of this kind went largely by seniority in most of the Conferences, but now younger men are pushed, or push themselves, to the front in the active competition of an age when aggressive energy rather than wise conservatism is the passport to honor. The old men are permitted to rest from official labors and linger as spectators of the arena in which they were victors in their prime. The pathos of such superannuation no one can know who has not felt it. The men who bow to it in unmurmuring submission thereby crown their heroic lives with fresh glory. Those who at first chafe and rebel are often men

(384)

of the finest metal: like the blooded horse that will keep its gait until it drops dead in its tracks, they want to die in the harness. McFerrin was the only really old man in his delegation. At the Conference love-feast on Sunday morning he was the first speaker, and this is what he said: "I have been a Methodist seventy-one years, and a preacher of the gospel sixty-six years, and I am still at work for the Church. I enjoy daily communion with God, and this has been the happiest year of my life." The tremulous tone, tearful eyes, and his shrunken and enfeebled frame, as he stood there before his brethren, caused a thrill of tender emotion throughout the congregation, and the old men gathered around him, embracing one another, and weeping together.

Dr. McFerrin's colleagues in the General Conference of 1886 were: Revs. R. A. Young, D. C. Kelley, R. K. Brown, J. W. Hill, T. J. Duncan; and E. W. Cole, Thomas B. Holt, B. J. Tarver, S. E. H. Dance, W. H. Morrow, and B. W. Macrae—a strong array of ministerial talent and business capacity. Dr. McFerrin's deafness caused him to take a seat in the chancel, that he might be near the presiding officer and the Secretary's desk, and thus be able to hear what was said and done. As the patriarch of the body, by common consent he was recognized as being properly placed in this position. There was no keener listener or more vigilant Church legislator among all the members of that august ecclesiastical assemblage. He was often on his feet. Any measure that he did not like he vigorously opposed, and any business which his impaired hearing prevented him from understanding clearly was arrested by his challenge until it was explained to his satisfaction. At times, when the debate became warm, he struck fire as in former

25

years; but though his heart was as courageous, his arm did not wield the battle-ax with the same strength. He was at a disadvantage in not being able to catch fully the spirit of all that was said, and he lost in some degree the stimulus that came to him from the echoes of his own forensic shots in the way of repartee or applause. He spoke against all innovations of whatever sort, and voted "No" on most of the changes proposed in the Discipline. The debate on a proposition to repeal the law making it mandatory upon pastors to read the General Rules to their congregations sprung him. His whole soul rose in arms against it. During the debate a courtly Doctor of Divinity said that the declaration found in the Discipline, that "these General Rules were such as the Holy Spirit writes on all truly awakened souls," was an unwarranted assumption. "Spiritual things are spiritually discerned!" retorted McFerrin, quickly, but in a manner so grave that he seemed to be unconscious of the sarcasm seemingly involved in the remark. He spoke and voted with the majority on that question, though able and plausible speeches were made on the other side by men of high standing in the Church.

He stood with the minority on another question that excited him profoundly. The Ritual for Infant Baptism was changed so as to substitute the words "being delivered from thy wrath" by "being saved by thy grace." He fought the change with great earnestness, and when it was made entered his protest in the following paper:

PROTEST OF J. B. McFERRIN AND OTHERS.

I protest against this action, because the change of phraseology and the transfer of words from their proper place in the Ritual for Baptism indicate and foreshadow a strike at the doctrine of original or birth sin. J B. McFerrin.

By permission of the Conference the following names were added to this protest: P. II. Whisner, A. S. Andrews, H. P. Walker, T. G. Slaughter, J. E. Ryland, W. W. Stringfield, W. T. Harris, A. W. Newsom, John S. Martin, Anson West, T. R. Pierce, Asa Holt, R. A. Morris, S. K. Cox, W. I. McFarland, Benoni Harris. A smile of grim satisfaction rested upon the old Doctor's rugged features when his protest was read to the Conference.

So deeply was he pained by this action that he insisted on entering his protest against it on the Journal. It was evident that he felt he was a breakwater against a tide of innovation that, unrestrained, might sweep away the most cherished landmarks of the Old Methodism he loved so much. He was keenly watchful. No motion was allowed to pass the body until he had heard its every word read. He magnified his office as a Church legislator. And who shall say that his watchful and pugnacious conservatism was not needed then and there? He might in some cases have leaned too far in that direction, but with so many new men ready for new experiments, this arch-conservative old preacher was not out of place as a balancing influence in the General Conference. "But he was a hard man to handle," said one of the younger men of the body. "He was so firmly set in his positions that only the hardest blows made any impression on him; and yet, if you hit him too hard, his age and venerableness caused your blow to recoil upon you." One afternoon he got into a regular colloquial tussle with a number of the delegates after the fashion of his earlier days, and such ready and strong debaters as Dr. John E. Edwards, Judge J. Wofford Tucker, and others, found that the old swordsman had not lost his cunning in fence, while the members of the grand body and the crowd of visitors were delighted to have one more exhibition of his powers on the arena in which he might often have been outargued and outvoted, but never worsted in a rough-and-tumble conversational debate in which quickness of repartee, skillfulness of manner, and impetuosity of attack are the conditions of victory.

No one question more earnestly engaged the thought of this General Conference of 1886 than that of Dr. McFerrin's relation to the Book Agency. It had been announced by him more than a year previous that he was not looking to a re-election to that office. At the session of the Baltimore Conference, held in Salem, Virginia, in March, 1885, he had distinctly affirmed that that was his last official visit to that body. To the writer of this biography he declared more than once that his purpose was to retire. But for some months before the meeting of the General Conference it was evident that his mind had changed. He said but little, but what he did say left the impression that he would not decline the office if re-elected. "I don't want to be voted for as a favor or as a compliment to me for past services. I am no hanger-on or pensioner. I am able to live without a dollar from the Church, and am ready to do so. Let no friend of mine vote for me unless he thinks, all things considered, it is the best thing for the Church." Thus he spoke, and beyond this he was silent. When the election came on the members of the General Conference scarcely knew what to do. Their veneration, gratitude, and affection for Dr. McFerrin prompted them to cast their ballots for him. On the other hand, he was nearly eighty years old, disabled by deafness, blindness, and difficulty of locomotion. Besides, it was known that a number of distinguished ministers were spoken of for the place, as was the able layman who had been Business Manager under his administration. What shall we do? was the unanswered inquiry in the minds of the delegates. "The tellers will proceed to take the vote," said the presiding Bishop. Whereupon, Dr. McFerrin rose from his seat within the chancel and, walking slowly down the aisle, took his place at the head of the Tennessee delegation. As he did so his sixty years of arduous and effective service passed before the minds of the brethren; they remembered that when he entered upon the work of the Church as a Connectional officer his stooping form was erect, his gray locks were dark, and his dimmed eyes were bright and clear, and a wave of feeling, silent but profound, rolled over the body, and when the ballots were counted John B. McFerrin's name had a majority of all that were cast. This election has no parallel in the history of the Church. The record of the man put him beyond the possibility of formal superannuation. This case will not be pleaded as a precedent. As the Church has had but one McFerrin, so it is not likely to have another instance of the election of an octogenarian to a Connectional office.

But why the change in Dr. McFerrin's mind with reference to the Book Agency? The explanation is worth recording, and is given in his own words: "I had fully made up my mind that it was time for me to retire and give way to a younger man, and so said to my friends. My purpose to do so was fixed. But as the time for the election drew near *I could not rid myself of a feeling that if I did so disaster would result to the Church.* I can not account for this impression, but it was so solemn and so abiding that I dared not disregard it." This is a curious bit of inner history, concerning which the reader will form his own conclusion. Dr. Mc-Ferrin's manner, when he spoke of the matter, was so subdued and reverential that it left no doubt that he believed it was a divine impression upon which he had acted. Why not? To be led by the Spirit is to be responsive to just such impressions that come to a true servant of God in the decision of questions that involve the interests of the kingdom of Christ. Dr. McFerrin was no mystic, sentimentalist, or fanatic. He was not addicted to visions, dreams, voices, or presentiments. He took a common-sense view of things, and expected to reach right ends by the use of right means. This experience of his concerning the Book Agency was therefore invested with all the more significance, both to himself and the friends to whom it was made known. Experiences similar to this are not unfamiliar to the readers of Christian biography. How often good men and women are unconsciously helped and guided in the minor affairs of life by the gentle yet sufficient movings of the Divine Spirit will be known to them only when the books shall be opened at the last judgment. Our twofold prayer should be: Lord, make us responsive to every gracious touch of thy Spirit! Lord, save us from the hardness and blindness that would cause us to mistake self-will for thy will!

An episode of this session of the General Conference was a sermon by Dr. McFerrin at the Soldiers' Home, of Richmond. The room was crowded, the Governor of Virginia and other notable men being present. The simple pathos of the venerable preacher, who had slept with the soldiers in camp and ministered to them on the battle-fields and in the hospitals, melted all hearts. Gov.

Fitzhugh Lee was seen to wipe away the tears from his face, and at the close of the service he pressed with warmth the hand of the preacher, amid a general commotion among the audience, whose sensibilities had been roused by his discourse.

When the General Conference adjourned *sine die*, at eleven o'clock at night on the last day of the session, the doxology was sung, and the benediction pronounced, Dr. McFerrin was in his place; and then, leaning on the arm of a brother, he made his way to his lodgings, having attended his last General Conference.

GROWING CHARITY.

I N the South the result of our Civil War hardened
some and softened others. Professed Christians,
whose faith in God was shallow-rooted, were shaken or
upset. They became bitter, cynical, skeptical, or sunk
into the apathy of despair. Those whose faith was
deep-rooted stood the storm. They did not conclude
that, because their plans had failed, God had failed.
They reconstructed their plans of life, but made no
change as to their principles of action. They clung to
God, to the Bible, and to the Church. Not only so,
but their natures were enlarged and sweetened by the
rough lesson they had learned. They accepted the truth
that the ways of God are often past finding out, and still
trusted him in the midst of their wrecked fortunes and
shattered hopes. Their religion was not surrendered at
Appomattox, for it was beyond the reach of human con-
tingencies. No sublimer spectacle has been witnessed in
the history of the world than that which was presented
by evangelical Christianity in the Southern States as it
came out of the war with its faith unshaken and its lines
unbroken. The Southern people staked all their earthly
fortunes on the conflict, but Southern Christians had been
too well taught, and their faith in the God of their fathers
was too firm, for them to adopt the shallow notion that
success or defeat in a contest of brute force must always
be accepted as an unerring indication of the right or
wrong of a cause. They had not so read the Book that
reveals the crucified Christ, nor the history of the Church,

(392)

that may be tracked by the blood of its martyred saints.
But the horizon of their mental vision widened under
the new conditions following the war. With the new
era came new ideas and new experiences. They set
about the work of re-adjustment with alacrity, and pursued it with a steadfast patience born of unconquerable
faith in the God to whom they had prayed in the agony
of their struggle, from whose goodness they yet hoped
to obtain larger blessings than those they had lost, and
under whose guidance they hoped to reach a grander
destiny than that for which their heroes had bled and
died. The conservative force that held society in the
Southern States together after that awful cataclysm, the
force that so quickly crystallized its apparently irreconcilable elements into social and civic order, the force that
propelled the reorganized South in its career of unexampled progress in the midst of extraordinary perils and
disabilities during the little more than two decades between 1865 and this year of our Lord 1888—this conservative, crystallizing, propulsive force was Christianity. It was not wise statesmanship, for the lack of it
was most conspicuous. It was not new secular leadership, for the men that led before the war and during the
war still led the Southern people. It was not a new
sociology or a new political economy, but rather in spite
of the vagaries of impractical theorizers, the blunder-
ings of ignorance and the rashness of bad men. It was
the gospel of Christ, and that only, which wrought these
wondrous results; and the Church that had been planted in the South by Asbury and McKendree and their
fellow-laborers and successors—the Methodist Episcopal
Church, South—which had carried the gospel to all
classes, rich and poor, white and black, bond and free,

bore no inferior part in the glorious work which had thus been accomplished. It had touched society at all points through the agency of a system of evangelization not surpassed by any other in its effectiveness. In the light of these later times we may see where they erred in judgment or failed to do all their duty; but they made a record of which their spiritual descendants will never be ashamed, and left them an inheritance for which they should never cease to be grateful.

Dr. McFerrin did not acidulate or despair under defeat and disaster. His faith never wavered for a moment. He needed no reconstruction as to his religious convictions, and he adjusted himself to the great changes that had taken place with the resignation of a Christian, the good faith of a true patriot, and the hopefulness of a man whose optimism was rooted in an undoubting belief in a good God who rules in this world and all worlds, who brings light out of darkness, and makes all things work together for good to them that love him. No more hopeful or courageous man came forth from the fires of the great conflict. Such a man could be no small factor in the restoration of pacific feeling and fraternal intercourse between the alienated sections of the American Union. Gen. Clinton B. Fisk, who was in military command at Nashville after the close of the war, bore strong testimony to the fact that Dr. McFerrin's large influence was exerted to soften asperities, to promote forgiveness, and to prepare the way for the happier time and grander destiny to which God was leading the nation by a way it knew not.

At the great fraternal Methodist camp-meeting at Round Lake, New York, held in 1874 and 1875, Dr. McFerrin gave expression to the fraternal sentiments that glowed in his heart toward his brethren of the North. What a surprise and delight he was to the Northern men and women who there saw him for the first time! His hearty hand-clasps, his ready adaptation to all occasions, his rare humor and quaint expressions, his sermons attended with the strange power that none could resist, completely captivated them. " If this is the sort of men we have been fighting down in the South," said they, " we want to know more of them; we are ready to strike hands with them in fraternal covenant, and to take a fresh start with them in a new era of peace, good-will, and progress, with the night and tempest behind, and the dawn of the brighter day illumining the eastern sky."

On the occasion of Dr. McFerrin's second visit, his old friend, Bishop Janes, was there in gracious mood, and opened the fraternal special service with the words: "Next to the fellowship of God is the fellowship of saints, and nothing but our spirit of love to God will transcend our love of one another in the spirit world. God is love, and all who are like God are filled with the love of God and love to their brethren. And what is true as it respects individual Christians is equally true in a more general sense as it respects the different branches of the Christian Church. We are just as much interested in the prosperity of every branch of the Christian Church as we are in the spiritual welfare of every member of that Church. Consequently, it is a great pleasure for us to understand the condition of these different branches of the Church; and we have met this morning to spend a little time in inquiring after each other's welfare, and to hear from each other respecting our spiritual condition as Churches."

Among other responses, that of Dr. McFerrin was notable for its powerful effect upon the vast audience. After telling them that the Methodist Episcopal Church, South, then embraced thirty-seven Annual Conferences, with eight Bishops, a membership of seven hundred thousand souls (being an increase of three hundred thousand in ten years), four hundred thousand Sunday-school scholars, and that the missionary work of the Church was making progress, he said: "Before the war we had a great work among the colored people. In 1860 we had one hundred and twenty-five thousand of them in full communion with our Church, and we had a large number of preachers who devoted all their time to the work of evangelizing them. [Bishop Janes: 'I know that.'] You know that, Bishop Janes; you appointed men there to that work. Planters sometimes wrote to the Bishop, requesting him to send a missionary to their plantations, and promising to support him. Sometimes two or three united in the request and promise of support, and we were devoting a great part of the missionary money and labor to those people; and to-day these missionaries sleep in the swamps of the South. I want you to understand that I have preached hundreds and thousands of sermons to these people, and have witnessed demonstrations of the power of God among the sons and daughters of Africa." After reciting other facts with regard to the work of the Church in the home and foreign fields, he said: "With regard to spiritual religion, I think our people love Jesus. We hold on to the grand old Methodist doctrines of justification by faith, regeneration by the Holy Ghost, the witness of the Spirit, and holiness of heart and life. There is no department of Methodism where the ministry hold with greater pertinacity the peculiar doctrines of Methodism than in the South. By the grace of God we intend to maintain the old doctrines, to carry forward the old standard." With regard to fraternity between the two Churches he made a most emphatic affirmation of his position, closing with this remark: "I am not much of an enthusiast, but just enough to love Jesus and every Christian, and especially every Methodist, the world over." Then came this farewell touch: "Now, brethren, I bid you good-by. I met an aged friend yesterday who extended his hand, saying, 'I want to shake hands with you; I have been reading your sermon.' I said to him: 'When we get to heaven come and shake hands, and tell me we met at Round Lake.' So I say to you all, when we get on the other shore come up and say: 'How do you do, Brother McFerrin?' and tell me we met at Round Lake. It will add to my happiness in glory." There was scarcely a dry eye in the congregation when he sat down.

Dr. McFerrin's sturdy denominationalism never sunk into actual bigotry even in the most pugnacious period of his life. He was a stalwart Methodist, but he was more—a robust Christian. "I love my neighbors, but I love my own family more, and I love my own wife better than any other woman on earth. So I love the whole body of Christians of all denominations, but I love the Methodists a little more than others," he said, with kindly frankness, in one of his speeches before a mixed multitude of hearers.

Favored by peculiar circumstances, the ministers of a certain Church had succeeded in proselyting a number of Methodists in Middle Tennessee and North Alabama, among them a preacher of some note. At the session of the Tennessee Conference, held soon afterward in

Huntsville, Alabama, these facts were brought out before the body, and a young preacher, burning with resentment, cried out:

"Dr. McFerrin, what do you think of proselyting?"

"What do I think of proselyting?" he replied, rising
to his feet. "That depends on one condition: if the
proselytes are coming this way, it is all right; but if they
are going that way, it is *b-a-d!*" giving the last word
his inimitable nasal intonation. The Conference laughed,
and the young brother said no more.

This playful remark was not intended as an expression of approval of proselyting, nor was it so understood.
He only meant that he was willing to give and take in
fair denominational competition, and that the Methodists, who had made such vast acquisitions from the ranks
of other religious bodies, should be the last to whine over
a few perverts now and then. The answer was manly
as well as witty. Methodism disclaims proselyting, and
its genius and history are opposed to the ugly practice;
but it is one of the paradoxes of ecclesiastical history
that this very absence of the proselyting spirit and exclusive assumption has been one of the chief factors in
its marvelous success, attracting to its communion and
holding in its genial fellowship the men and women who
are constitutionally adapted to it. Elective affinity asserts
itself in this matter. As a rule, people go where they
belong. Proselytes wrenched from their proper affiliations by undue influences are elements of weakness
rather than of strength to a Church. Whenever Methodism becomes a proselyting rather than an evangelizing
agency, it will have no good reason to live a day longer.
May that time never come!

There was a steady growth in Dr. McFerrin's frater-

nal love toward his brother Methodists of the North.
He was willing to bury the dead past. "There are a
few people," he said at Round Lake, "who write for
newspapers, North and South, that try to stir up strife;
but don't take an ill-natured letter as an index to the
heart of the people. Our statesmen and politicians are
coming together. The other day the General commanding the post was out with our people to decorate the
graves of Confederates that were buried near Nashville,
and two days afterward the Governor and his staff went
to the Federal Cemetery and took part in strewing flowers upon the graves of your dead. I tell you they are
coming together in feeling, and I don't envy the heart
of the man who cherishes bitterness." This feeling
deepened to the close of his life, and found expression
on all occasions. When he died the white flag of peace
was afloat.

In the winter of 1881 the Rev. Loren Webb, a superannuated minister of the New York East Conference of the Methodist Episcopal Church, lay dying in
the railroad depot in Nashville, Tennessee. To Dr. Mc-
Ferrin, who had hastened to his side, he said: "I want
a place to die; I sent for a Methodist preacher; *we are
a band of brothers everywhere.*" The Doctor replied:
"Brother, we are one in love; and here we, in the hour
of trial, know no North, no South." A Northern Methodist preacher (the Rev. E. Warriner) thus put this affecting incident into verse:

"WE ARE A BAND OF BROTHERS EVERYWHERE."

The watchman stood in silence on the tower,
    For want of strength to sound the clarion call;
He only watched for the appointed hour
    His station to resign on Zion's wall.

The summons came; the faithful herald heard;
   God gave him strength for one more bugle-blast,
And whispered in his ear a thrilling word
   To utter—it should be his best and last.

The watchman put the trumpet to his mouth;
   Webb's dying words rang out upon the air:
"John Wesley's legions know no North, no South;
   We are a band of brothers everywhere."

No bickerings pollute the dying breath,
   No thought of latitude when heaven is near;
In sorrow, trial, loneliness, and death,
   "We are a band of brothers everywhere."

The bonds of holy brotherhood are strong,
   A common name and heritage we share,
Sections and feuds can not estrange us long;
   "We are a band of brothers everywhere."

No pass-word, grip, or signal we require;
   Distress may come, but with it tender care;
Kind arms encircle us when we expire:
   "We are a band of brothers everywhere."

O'er the wide world it may be ours to roam,
   And we may fall—it shall not matter where—
Some helper we shall find, though far from home:
   "We are a band of brothers everywhere."

Let each in charity act well his part;
   All harsh upbraidings let us hence forbear;
This watch-word carry in each loving heart:
   "We are a band of brothers everywhere."

Pass the word along the Methodist lines all around the world. We *are* a band of brothers everywhere! The day is coming when some bard, inspired by the same spirit, amid the still happier conditions that will bless the Church of God as it nears its final triumph and promised glory, will sing a still nobler song with the same sweet refrain: "WE ARE A BAND OF BROTHERS EVERYWHERE!"

CLOSELY following some rough encounters and stinging criticisms that caused him no little pain, in 1884, Dr. McFerrin had a long illness. This experience marked a transition period in his life. It disclosed to him by anticipation what would be the posthumous verdict of his fellow-men concerning himself. It also revealed to him more clearly than ever before his personal relation to the solemn facts of death, the judgment, and eternity. The eminent physicians in attendance upon him gave him up to die. But he lived on day after day in defiance of all the known laws of life. Night after night it was said he could not live till morning. The news of his illness spread throughout the country, prayer was made for him in the churches, and a profound concern was felt and expressed among all classes of people. The secular as well as the religious press reflected the popular feeling concerning the venerable sufferer. Letters and telegrams of inquiry and sympathy came from the North as well as the South, and when read to him in his lucid moments moved him deeply.

By some mistake, not at all surprising under the circumstances, the announcement went forth in the press dispatches that Dr. McFerrin was dead. The report flew with the rapidity of lightning over the land, and there was a universal expression of sorrow mingled with the most grateful and appreciative tributes to his genius,

character, and services. This report reached his intimate friend, Bishop Pierce, at his home in Georgia.
"There must be some mistake," said the Bishop. "I
have felt from the first that this sickness is not unto
death; he will live, and not die." So saying, the Bishop
went into his study, shut and locked the door, and knelt
in prayer before God. It was perhaps an hour before he
came out, and then his face wore the peculiar radiance that
many have seen upon it when he was fully under the divine afflatus in the pulpit. In the meantime the daily newspaper from Atlanta had come with a fuller account of the
death of his friend. "Dr. McFerrin is surely dead," said
the Bishop's wife; "here are the particulars." The good
Bishop was staggered for a moment, but, rallying promptly, he said, with solemn emphasis: "There must be some
mistake; he is not dead. *I have prayed and gotten the
answer.*" The answer! it came farther and quicker and
surer than any telegram from Nashville or Atlanta; for
true prayer touches God, and God touches with instan-
taneous response the heart of faith. Not always does
the answer come thus in direct and literal bestowment
of the thing asked for in intercessory supplication, but
it does come in conscious benediction to the trusting soul.
In the lives of most men and women who live close to
God, and whose prayers are the breathings of unselfish
desire and unwavering faith, there will be experiences
like this of Bishop Pierce, when the suppliant hears by
the inner ear the gracious whisper of the Still Small
Voice: "Be it unto thee even as thou wilt." They who
are thus favored are the holy ones whose humility is the
channel for this blessing, which is withheld from such
as might trample the pearl under their feet. A letter
from Bishop Pierce modestly refers to this incident,

and expresses his grateful joy that his friend was yet alive:

SPARTA, December 10.

Dear Brother: Bless the Lord, O my soul! How glad, how thankful I am! When I heard you were ill I went to prayer, and received the impression that you would not die. It has remained with me. When you were reported *dead* I told my wife I did not believe it. I told my wife it was a mistake. I hoped and believed the Lord would spare you to your family, friends, and Church. Even so it has come to pass. God be praised! I am just starting for Alabama. Have been to Tennessee, Virginia, and Georgia. The Lord is in the Churches. He walks among the golden candlesticks, and his angels are on the wing again. The reports will cheer you. The centenary year dawns brightly, hopefully. Hope we shall meet in old Baltimore—Christmas, 1884.

I have not written to you before for reasons you will understand; but you have been in my heart and thoughts all the time. You have seen how the Church loves you, and what the world thinks of you. We will all receive you now as one from the dead, and we will glorify God in you. Grace, mercy, and peace be with you! Love to all yours from all mine. Affectionately,

G. F. PIERCE.

To the friends who visited him during this illness Dr. McFerrin spoke freely concerning his Christian experience, and, when his strength permitted, joined devoutly in the prayers that were offered at his bedside. A friend who visited him often, and talked freely, opened to him a subject on which Dr. McFerrin spoke seldom, but felt deeply. It was a sharp criticism in one of the *Christian Advocates* pointed with raillery. Though three or four years old, the wound still bled. That it came late in life made it none the easier to bear. His friend heard, and spoke thus: "Doctor, let me interpret to you this unpleasant passage in your history." "Go on," he replied; "thy servant heareth." The friend continued: "You have been, and are, a popular man. No man has more friends than you. Perhaps you idolized human friendship, made too much of it, leaned too much on it. The Lord lovingly rebukes you. As a Father he chastens, and would 'perfect that which concerneth you.' Your truth, honesty, purity, and uprightness have not been assailed; but you have, nevertheless, been keenly criticised on a surface-matter of character. Be thankful you have been by grace kept from giving more serious occasion of criticism. Accept the rebuke, and profit by it. Let 'All my springs are in thee' be your language." The sick man lay still, musing awhile, and then added: " Thank you. It may be so; it may be so. Thank you. I will try to give it that turn, and profit by it. The Lord permits it for my good." This heart-searching question to a dying man is one which living men would do well to consider. Popularity involves peril; human praise may become too dear to the truest soul that does not watch and pray. What discoveries were then made to Dr. McFerrin's soul we know not, but it was a faithful hand that thus flashed the light into the recesses of a brother's heart.

Dr. McFerrin at this time enjoyed a privilege accorded to but few persons—that of perusing his own obituary literature. In a most wonderful manner he rallied, and recovered from this attack. In the meantime the report of his death had gone everywhere, and elicited expression of the grief and sense of loss felt by his fellow-Christians of all denominations and his fellow-countrymen of all shades of political opinion. It was touching, and also a little amusing, to see how he was affected by the reading of these funereal tributes to himself. He read with smiles and tears. No one had a quicker perception of the ludicrous side of any incident, while he was one of the strong men who readily melted into tears when his sensibilities were touched. It was evident that he was not without curiosity to know what was said of him as a dead man, and that he appreciated the anomalous circumstances that placed him as it were among the spectators at his own funeral, and enabled him to view himself posthumously. Among these kindly expressions none affected him more deeply than that of the General Missionary Committee of the Methodist Episcopal Church, which was in session in New York when the report of his death reached that city. For sacred reasons this action is recorded here:

FRATERNAL RESOLUTION.

Resolved, That this General Committee have heard with great sorrow of the death of the Rev. J. B. McFerrin, D.D., for some time Corresponding Secretary of the Missionary Society of the Methodist Episcopal Church, South. We highly appreciate the true manliness and exalted Christian character of our departed brother in Christ; we remember with gratitude his kind and fraternal spirit; we knew his power as a preacher of the glorious gospel of Jesus Christ, and as an advocate of Christian Missions; and, as a memorial of all this and much more, we mournfully make this minute upon our record.   J. M. REID

                                                              C. H. FOWLER.

Please furnish a copy of the above to the Corresponding Secretary of your Missionary Society, and also to the family of Dr. McFerrin. It was unanimously adopted by our General Committee to-day. By order of the Committee.

                                        BISHOP J. F. HURST, *President.*
J. N. FITZGERALD, *Secretary.*

Doubtless the human heart that was in him was soothed by the almost universal outburst of admiration and affection, but he had just heard too distinctly the solemn murmur of the Infinite Sea to be much affected by human applause.

While he was reading or hearing what was said of

him by others who had thought him dead, we may not doubt that Dr. McFerrin himself reviewed his whole life—its ruling motives, its public acts, and its hidden secrets, known only to God and himself. It would be profitable for every one of us, from time to time, to apply the perspective to ourselves, and as it were by anticipation take a posthumous look at the records we have made.

After this sickness his step was feebler, his voice softer, his face more spiritual in its expression, and his whole appearance and manner chastened and refined. The fires were hot, but he came forth as gold.

DOWN-GRADE AND UP-GRADE.

IT was now down-grade and up-grade with Dr. Mc-Ferrin—down-grade with his body, up-grade with his soul. Day by day his steps grew feebler and his sight and hearing declined. "The old Doctor is failing," said many a kindly voice. He went in and out among his brethren as aforetime, but it was seen by all that the strong man was breaking down under the weight of increasing infirmities. His once robust frame was bent; he grew thinner, and still thinner. But he made a manly resistance to his growing disabilities. At times, when fully roused in the pulpit or on the platform, the old fires would burn within him, and his voice would ring out clear and strong, his frame would become erect, and there again stood the old McFerrin, the master of the arena. But it was only for a little season. When the inspiration of the moment passed away he was spent. These spurts of energy were followed by physical reactions that were alarming to his family. This steady decline of his strength was unsuspected by those who read the articles which he continued to publish in the Church papers and saw him only in public. The mental energy displayed by him on occasions that fully roused him was astonishing. The memorial sermon for Bishop Pierce, preached by him at McKendree Church, in Nashville, was a marvel of lucid statement, compact arrangement, and minuteness of detail as to facts and dates. Not a line had he in the way of notes or references. "A marvelous octogenarian," exclaimed a distinguished secular journalist who was present. "I know of no living man of his years who has such a grasp on facts and whose memory is so exact."

At a District Conference, held at the Alex. Green Chapel, near Nashville—so named in honor of Dr. A. L. P. Green—McFerrin, one hot Saturday afternoon, gave the body a surprise by making a speech which, for impassioned energy, inimitable drollery, and cutting yet good-natured satire, was equal to his best efforts in that line in his prime. His object was to rouse the Nashville Methodists to aggressive effort to meet the demands of the hour, and especially to carry forward certain needed enterprises in the way of church-building. After some playful hits at McKendree, the leading Church, and a protest against the cramped quarters of the North High Street congregation, and an appeal to the stronger Churches in its behalf, he pictured an intelligent stranger from the North on a visit to Nashville, taking a glance at the city, in company with a Nashville Methodist. Passing up Church Street, they come in sight of McKendree Church. "What church is that?" asks the stranger. "That is McKendree, the old mother Church of Nashville Methodism," is the answer. "A very respectable edifice," says the gratified visitor. A little farther on the Watkins Institute is passed and complimented, and then reaching Broad Street the beautiful stone Custom House, the elegant new Baptist Church, and the Moore Memorial Presbyterian Church are all viewed and praised in turn; and just as the stately towers of Vanderbilt University become visible to the delighted visitor, his attention is attracted by an ugly, weather-beaten, forlorn-looking frame building on the corner of

Broad Street and Belmont Avenue. "What building is that?" asks the stranger. The embarrassed Nashville Methodist blushes, hesitates, and says: "Excuse me, sir; I would rather not tell." "Why not? I would like to know," urges the visitor. "Well," says the Nashville Methodist brother, reluctantly, "that is the West End Methodist Church, and I was hoping that it would escape your notice as we passed it." "The *West* End!" exclaimed McFerrin, in his shrillest note, "the *West* End! I call it the *l-a-s-t* end of Nashville Methodism, and a disgrace to the rich Methodists of the city. Yes, sir, a disgrace to every one of you!" And then such a philippic of the rollicking order as he poured forth was never heard before by the now wide-awake and delighted audience, who winced and laughed and cheered, and resolved in their hearts to build a new church for West End. "The speech of his life!" exclaimed an old preacher, who had laughed until he cried under that extraordinary outburst. McFerrin had so often made "the speech of his life," according to the judgment of men who were under the spell of his oratory, that this remark was rather a matter of course. This was perhaps the last thoroughly characteristic, *impromptu* speech of this sort from the old tribune. The fires of his genius flashed forth from time to time, but never so brightly again, for he was on the down-grade physically, and, like a volcano that had spent its force, these bursts became fewer and feebler as the months went by. It was touching to note how he dreaded total blindness as his eye-sight failed more and more. He shrunk from that trial with human weakness. Again and again would he revert to the subject as if it had a sort of evil fascination for him. His deafness did not seem to trouble him much so long as he could see the faces of his friends and where to plant his feet in walking. His mother went blind in her later years, and that was probably the cause of his painful fear for himself. With resolute purpose, however, he would grope unaided from room to room of the Publishing House, straining his vision and listening intently to catch the sounds that reached him so imperfectly, with his right hand shading his eyes, and the look that was on his wasted features making a pathetic appeal as he stood waiting to hear the voices of those he could no longer see. In walking the streets he submitted to the use of the arm of a friend, but at first with evident reluctance. This was no light cross to the strong, self-acting man who had so long been accustomed to lead and to be leaned on by others. His mental energy and love of work kept him going, but his vital forces were nearly used up. The down-grade was unmistakable.

This was on the physical side only. Spiritually his movement was upward. His very features were chastened into a serener and softened expression. As he ceased to fret against these disabilities, accepting them as the will of God, the submission that was in his heart was reflected in his face. The reader, if he has ever visited an asylum for the blind, has noticed the expression of pathetic patience worn by these children of affliction, showing that they have accepted their sad lot, realizing but not rebelling against it. There was now something of the same look in Dr. McFerrin's face as the world of sense was being shut out from him more and more; and as the sights and sounds of earth were dulled and dimmed, the inner vision was more open to God, and the inner ear quicker to catch his voice. There was a tenderer and more solemn tone in his preaching,

and often an overwhelming pathos as he spoke of his
old friends to glory gone and of his expectation that he
would soon join them on the eternal shore. His prayers
in his family worship breathed more fervor and sweetness, and the spiritual meanings of the sacred text seemed
to unfold themselves more readily to his mind. To all
the members of his household his bearing was marked
by a solemn tenderness indicative of the fact that he
knew his stay with them was to be short. The little
children that nestled about him seemed to feel instinct-
ively that there was a benediction in his presence. There
was another sign that he was on the up-grade in his religious experience. In a newspaper discussion which
he had with his friend, the Rev. R. N. Price, of the
Holston Conference, there was a moderation of tone
and a gentleness of expression that showed that the
sharper angles of the puissant debater had been rounded
off by time and pain and abounding grace, and that while
his intellect was astonishingly vigorous for a man of his
age, his spirit was growing more child-like, and therefore more Christ-like. His pulpit testimonies were always strangely powerful, but now they seemed to be
doubly so. Back of his tremulous words were more
than sixty years of Christian experience and ministerial
service; just before him were the realities of eternity;
the savor of the old times of Methodistic simplicity and
power was in his words and ways; and the power of the
world to come seemed to rest upon him as he bore testimony for his Lord and magnified the power of the
gospel to save sinners. How the people wept under
these talks! And how they would gather around him
as he stood in the chancel, to clasp his hand once more
and to receive his blessing! Never did he preach more

effectively, if we may judge from the visible effects. His weakness was his strength. The pathos of the bent and wasting form, the failing voice, the dimmed vision, and the halting step compensated for the loss of some of the old power that had shaken the multitudes in his earlier ministry. Rather, it was power in a new form— the weaknesses of the body transmuted into spiritual force by the alchemy of grace. The down-grade movement of the frail and perishing body was accompanied by an up-grade movement of his soul. As the outward man perished, the inward man was renewed day by day. From the date of the sickness that came so near being a sickness unto death began a gentle descent to the grave and a more rapid upward spiritual movement.

SUNSET FLASHES.

LIKE the flashes of lightning in the western sky at
the close of a summer eve were the coruscations
of Dr. McFerrin's genius in his last days. His interest
in the living religious questions of the times was as intense as ever. He read the current literature of his
Church and of the Christian world in general, and was
as ready as ever to express his opinion and to controvert error whenever it crossed his path. As aforetime,
if in his own ecclesiastical circle there was any outcrop-
ping of error he quickly dealt it a blow.

Many old men continue to preach, and preach well in
an automatic way, making no new thought, but running
smoothly in the grooves of their former thinking. Like
a neglected fruit-tree, a man of this sort becomes barren,
and dies mentally before his time. The old preachers
who cease to preach are apt to become morbid and sink
into a gloomy senility.

Dr. McFerrin's unfailing popularity caused a demand
for his services in the pulpit as long as he could stand
on his feet and articulate audibly. His family and friends,
fearing the evil effects from the reaction following the
mental and physical exertion to which he was thus subjected, vainly sought to restrain him. But he persisted
in preaching, astonishing everybody by the frequency
and force of his pulpit utterances. Perhaps he was
right in so doing. It may have been a wise instinct that
warned him that if he once stopped immediate collapse

might follow. " You do not know how feeble he is,"
said his wife, who saw him as he was at home, when the
inspiration of the pulpit was absent and the energy of
his remarkably strong will was in some degree relaxed.
So he kept going and speaking, and was everywhere
listened to with wonder and delight.

At the Sea-shore Camp-meeting, near Biloxi, Mississippi, he preached to a great concourse of people on
the Sabbath-day, and at the close of the sermon there
transpired one of those scenes that so often characterized
his ministry. In the discussion of his subject he had
been led to draw a contrast between Christianity and infidelity, presenting the peace, comforts, and hopes of the
one, and the emptiness and gloom of the other, in his own
peculiar way, and with powerful effect upon the intelligent and responsive audience that hung upon the words
of the venerable servant of God who told them that
he had been a preacher of the gospel and a witness to
its divine power for over threescore years. " They ask
us," he said, " to surrender all the blessings and hopes
of Christianity; and what do they offer to give us in
return? I have at Nashville a house that belongs to
me, not a modern house it is true, but an old-fashioned
dwelling, large enough for my family—a comfortable
home for us all. A fellow calling himself an architect
comes along, tells me that my old house is very badly constructed, lacking many of the conveniences and adorn-
ments of modern architecture, and proposes to build me
a better one. He draws me a plan of the new house
on paper, and says he is ready to begin it. Whereupon
I set fire to the old house and burn it to ashes, leaving
my family and myself without a shelter, with nothing
but a house on paper! And of what use to me or my

family is a house on paper, when we have no place to live in? If I were to act that way, would not everybody call me a fool? And wouldn't I be a fool to do so? Yet that is just what infidelity is asking you to do. It would take from you the deepest joys and sweetest hopes you possess, and offers you nothing in return— nothing but the dreary negations of unbelief or the certain doom of annihilation. Are you willing to accept their offer? Are you willing to give up your belief in God, your trust in Jesus, your hope of the resurrection of the dead, your expectation of a glorious immortality? All of you who this day purpose in your hearts to hold on to the Christian religion until infidelity offers something better in its stead, rise and stand upon your feet."

As by a simultaneous impulse the vast crowd arose, one of the first to rise being Jefferson Davis, ex-President of the Southern Confederacy, who occupied a place near the speaker. The effect was electric, and infidelity was at a heavy discount that day among the thousands of worshipers by the sea-shore.

A similar scene was witnessed on the occasion of his preaching at a camp-meeting near Jackson, Tennessee, in the summer of 1886. He was at his high-water mark in his sermon on Sunday, and the pathos of the fact that it was the last time his face would be seen among his old friends in West Tennessee was felt both by the speaker and the immense concourse of hearers. He spoke of the old times, and of the old comrades of his earlier days who had crossed over the river; testified to the sufficiency of divine grace to convert, cleanse, and keep believers; told them that his journey was nearly run, and that he was happy in God and joyful through hope; and with streaming eyes and tremulous tones called on all within the sound of his voice to meet him in heaven, closing amid such weeping and shouting as is seldom witnessed more than once in a life-time. That camp-ground will be associated with McFerrin's name as long as the men and women who heard that sermon remain and the tradition of it will go down to their children.

A little later, during the same season, he was present at the dedication of a new church at Brentwood, not far from Nashville. He was so very feeble just then that it was feared he would be unable to preach the dedicatory sermon, and other preachers were present ready to proceed with the service in case he should break down. It was with obvious difficulty that he ascended the pulpit steps, and he had to avail himself of the services of his brethren in the reading of the Scripture lessons and announcing the hymns for the occasion. It was a very warm day, and the house was crowded. He began the sermon in a weak and husky voice, his trembling limbs apparently scarcely able to support his shrunken frame. The sympathies of the congregation were excited by the appearance of the venerable man, and as he stood there among his kindred and old friends a great wave of tender feeling swept over the audience. A hundred eyes grew moist at the thought that his familiar form would soon be no more seen and his voice no more be heard among them. His subject was "The Church: Its Origin, Nature, and Destiny," and the discourse was remarkable for its simplicity, spirituality, and power. There was not one ornate passage or rhetorical flourish in it, nor the least straining after oratorical or emotional effects; but his old-time power was present. The heaving bosoms and tearful faces of the people showed

that their heart-strings had been swept by a master hand.
As he came to the peroration his form became erect, his
voice swelled forth with wonderful clearness and strength,
his soul caught fresh fire, his thought took wing, and the
tremulous old man was transformed into a pulpit thun-
derer whose eloquence shook that temple on the hill at
Brentwood. The old commoner was surely himself
that day. Of the hundreds who heard him there for
the last time not one could fail to remember him as he
was that hour. The pathos of his parting words, when
he testified to the goodness of God and the blessedness
of the Christian life after an experience so long and so
varied, left an impression which no force or subtlety
of argument could have equaled. Many a saint took a
fresh start for heaven at that dedication, and how many
sinners were convinced will be known in "that day."

There was a little flash of another sort, but not less
characteristic, in the autumn of that year, 1886. He
had debated the question whether or not he would attend
a certain Annual Conference to which he had made
many official visits, and from whose members he had
received many expressions of confidence and affection.
In view of the distance and other considerations, he had
determined not to undertake the journey, when a rather
sharp criticism of certain features of his administration
of the affairs of the Publishing House appeared in the
local Church paper patronized by the Conference in
question. When the article was read to him he listened
attentively to the end, and then said, emphatically: "I
am going to attend that Conference, and I will reply
to that attack on the floor." He went, and he made the
reply and such a defense of his official acts as satisfied
and silenced everybody. His defense was, of course,

27

rather caustic and aggressive—a flash of the old fire that so quickly kindled in a debate.

During the autumn and winter of 1886, against the protest of his family and friends, he attended the sessions of a number of Annual Conferences in Texas and Arkansas. Though more than half blind, quite deaf, and heavy in movement, he undertook these long journeys alone, trusting in God and in the courtesy and kindness of his fellow-men. So universal was his acquaintance that he never lacked for a friendly arm in getting on and off the trains and in going to and from his lodging-places. After reaching the town or city in which a Conference was in session he had as many guides and helpers as there were persons in attendance, for all felt it to be a pleasure to minister to him on this "round," which they rightly believed would prove to be his last. Never on any former tour did he more mightily move the hearts of the thousands that listened to his pulpit and platform talks. Feeling himself that he was taking his farewell of the brethren, his own soul overflowed with a solemn tenderness that affected all hearts, while there was a spiritual power in his words that awed and thrilled the weeping assemblies to which he spoke and with which he left his fatherly benediction. It was a singular thing to witness: the almost helpless old man who groped his way feebly about supported by a friend, roused by contact with exciting occasions and expectant crowds, retaining his never-failing tact, and inspired by the supernatural energy of the Holy Ghost—the master of assemblies, as in the days of his fullest strength. Every sermon was a triumph of will-power under the reign of grace. It was sadly evident, however, that these were indeed sunset flashes, and that the setting was near.

SAFELY LANDED.

LIKE unto a great ship rounding to in the harbor after a stormy passage, weather-beaten, with sails torn and cordage loosened, but full-freighted and with pennant flying from the topmast, McFerrin neared the end of his long life-voyage. The harbor was at hand, but the winds were wild and the waves rolled high.

During the winter of 1886–7 it became evident to all who saw him that the old traveler's journeyings were nearly ended. His infirmities grew upon him rapidly, and it was only his extraordinary will-power that kept him up. It was pathetic to see how the faithful old servant of the Church clung to his work, and yet it was at the same time a little amusing to see how the old war-horse would rouse up at the sound of battle, when he heard the clash of swords in polemics or caught the tramp of the marching hosts of the Church. Unable to see to read or write, he secured the willing service of his beloved brother, the Rev. A. P. McFerrin, as a sort of private secretary, and through him he maintained communication with friends and kept up official correspondence. The two brothers were very unlike—the one a magnetic, fluent, aggressive, versatile, popular leader and master of the platform; the other a quiet thinker, an intellectual philosopher, who liked to dig down to the bottom of great questions, but whose modesty kept him silent when men far less knowing were ready to talk. Sharply contrasted as they were in tem-

perament, the basic element in their moral constitutions
was composed of the same granitic rock, and they were
equally sure to stand any degree of pressure in their devotion to a principle or an opinion. The writings of
A. P. McFerrin—notably a volume of sermons published in 1885—stamp him as a real thinker and a master of the sermon-making art. Whether these sermons
will be read by another generation we can not say, but it
may be safely affirmed that they are worthier of such
posthumous recognition than are many books whose popularity is based on elements of transient interest or the
tricks of style that tickle the literary palates of contemporaneous readers, but which in truth contain nothing
that will make it worth while for posterity to save them
from the oblivion that engulfs alike trashy trifles and
harmless mediocrity. His "Sermons for the Times"
may go down to other times than these, for the themes
he discusses are of eternal interest, the thought is robust,
and the style is simple and pure. His little volume of
sacred poems has so much of melody, Christian thought,
and spiritual fervor that the reader recognizes in the
author a finely-tuned soul that barely failed to take a
place among the singers in the choir led by Charles
Wesley, whose songs are girdling the globe. The two
brothers cordially appreciated each other. The unselfish and unconscious way in which the one consented to
be obscured by the other presented a pleasing illustration of the power of divine grace to hallow and exalt
human affection. And it was scarcely less delightful to
see with what glowing satisfaction the elder and more
famous brother greeted any expression of admiration for
the genius and character of the younger. Under the
reign of grace human nature rises to altitudes of moral

grandeur prophetic of its sublimer future destiny, and preparatory for the higher fellowship to be attained by the whole family of God.

There was no surprise when Dr. McFerrin failed to make his daily visits to the Publishing House and the announcement was made that he was very ill. But the popular solicitude was intense. "How is the old Doctor?" was the question on almost every lip. Christians of all denominations and citizens of all classes and races in Nashville manifested the liveliest interest in his condition. His symptoms indicated malarial fever, with nervous prostration and the usual signs of the breaking up of a strong physical organization. He steadily sunk from day to day until he was at the very point of departure. There he stopped, the tide of life feebly ebbing and flowing, at times scarcely the least breath or pulse being perceptible. He was a patient sufferer. There was a solemn tenderness in his speech that impressed every person who entered the room and looked upon his sunken and pallid features. After lying thus for some days, to the surprise of all, he again rallied, his wonderful constitution making a final effort to repel the assaults of age and disease. The absolute serenity of his mind was a notable factor in the case; he expended no vital force in anxieties or complainings. He declared his perfect resignation to the will of God, inclining to a desire to depart and be with Christ. "Hitherto in my sicknesses," he said, "I have not felt that I was going to die, nor have I desired to go. But now I feel differently. My work is done. My eye-sight and hearing are nearly gone; my temporal affairs are all arranged; my family are all provided for; the Publishing House is safe; my way is clear, and I am ready to go."

There was one day a slight depression of his spirits, caused, as we believe, by a final assault of Satan upon the suffering servant of Christ. The writer of this biography visited him while he was thus cast down, and before leaving was requested to pray with him. After reading the concluding paragraph of the eighth chapter of St. Paul's Epistle to the Romans, prayer was made at his bedside. His faith rallied, the cloud lifted, and he rejoiced in the God of his salvation. In a little while his nephew, the Rev. Dr. John P. McFerrin, a devout man and a sweet singer, came in, and sung the hymn :

> And let this feeble body fail,
> And let it droop and die.

The aged sufferer, in faltering accents, joined in the song, his eyes swimming in tears, and his face beaming with the holy joy that now filled his soul.

As he lay thus poised between life and death, the saintly William Burr, of the Tennessee Conference, lay dying in a suburb of the city. They were intimate friends and beloved yoke-fellows in the gospel. Dr. McFerrin had presided at the Quarterly Conference at which Burr was licensed to preach, in 1839. The two friends remembered each other in their affliction, and held a telephonic correspondence that was like the signaling of storm-tossed mariners as they neared the long-sought haven:

BURR TO McFERRIN.

How are you, this morning? I trust you are better. I am still very sick, and don't know what the result may be; but, living or dying, my whole trust is in Jesus my Saviour. If I should be called to his kingdom, I trust you will meet me there. You brought me into the Conference, and watched over me like a father. Pray for me to the last. Glory to God in the highest!

WM. BURR.

McFERRIN'S ANSWER.

Dear Brother Burr: Your welcome message received. I am improving, and may recover, but the will of God be done. For me to live is Christ, to die is gain. Thank God for your faith and victory over the fear of death! Hold to Jesus. He is able, and will save you. We have long been friends on earth; we'll meet in heaven. The Lord be with you. Glory to God in the highest! Yours affectionately,   J. B. McFERRIN.

BURR TO McFERRIN.—NO. 2.

Dear Dr. McFerrin: I am still alive, but do not know how long I can stay here. I am still trusting in the Saviour, and am happy in his love. I have great confidence in our Methodism and in the Church generally in the world.   WM. BURR.

McFERRIN TO BURR—NO. 2.

Dear Brother Burr: You are on the rock. Jesus is the sure foundation. Methodism is Christianity in earnest. We can adopt Mr. Wesley's language: "The best of all is, God is with us." Christ says: "I am with you alway." I rejoice in Christ. Praise the Lord!   J. B. McFERRIN.

Burr first obtained the prize. He died April 3, 1887, and Dr. McFerrin attended the funeral of his friend on the afternoon of the 5th, at Hobson Chapel, and took part in the solemn services of the occasion. The sorrowing people were awe-struck at his appearance. The pallor of death was on his face, and it bore the traces of the intense suffering he had undergone, while it was lit up with the strange illumination that at times comes over the features of dying saints. A spell was on the hearts of the people as he spoke. It was a bright afternoon in the early spring; the warm south wind gently stirred the peach-blooms, and the birds were singing in the trees—all nature attuned to the spirit of the hour. When, after speaking of the true nobility, saintliness, and fruitfulness of the life of his friend and son in the gospel, Dr. McFerrin said in trembling tones, "William,

farewell!" and sat down overcome, the strongest men
present wept. At the close of the services, by an irresistible impulse the people pressed forward to touch his
hand, and, unable to repress the emotion which had been
so deeply stirred at seeing him once more, some of them
gathered him in their arms and wept aloud. They
greeted him as one who had risen from the dead, and
the solemnity and tenderness of the meeting were intensified by the conviction that they would see his face
no more until they met him in the world of spirits.

The flame of life flickered up fitfully for a few days,
and then he was again brought to his bed, to rise no
more. The details of the physical struggle would be
painful, but the triumph of his faith was graciously
complete. "He will be likely to suffer much before he
dies," said Dr. Hardin, the skillful physician who attended him with a devotion that was almost filial; "the
very strength of his magnificent constitution necessi-
tates a hard struggle in its dissolution. His frame is
strong at every point; he has never exhausted his vital
forces by any evil habits, and this sickness is therefore a
general break-down of his whole organism." One organ
after another was attacked—his lungs, his stomach, his
heart, and at last his brain. "O Lord, give me a peaceful moment in which to die," was a prayer whispered
by him at midnight, as the watchers sat and waited for
the end. His devoted wife kept her place day and night,
taking little time for sleep or rest, the silent tears showing the anguish of her faithful heart. His children—
Mrs. Anderson, Mrs. Bryan, Mrs. Sowell, Mrs. Yarbrough, the Rev. John A. McFerrin, and his sons-in-
law, James Anderson, J. H. Yarbrough, the Rev. P.
A. Sowell, and W. R. Bryan, were with him, ministering

to him with unwearying watchfulness and tenderness. They all felt and expressed special gratitude that he was permitted to die at home, having had painful apprehensions that he would come to his death while on one of his distant journeys. His thoughts were given to the Church to the very last, a smile of satisfaction spreading over his features at any brief item of good news from the preachers or any department of the Church's work. When told from day to day that all was right at the Publishing House, and that good news was coming in from the laborers in all parts of the Church, he thanked God in whispers as he lay there laboring for breath. This ruling passion of his life expressed itself in the remark made to his preacher-son, who had staid by his bedside all the week until Saturday morning: "My son, I feel a little stronger, and you had better return and fill your appointment to-morrow. If while you are away, John, I should happen to slip off, you know where to find me." In his delirium, toward the last, his wandering speech was about what lay nearest to his heart. He spoke of the Publishing House that he had borne as a burden for so many years, then he imagined himself to be pleading for Missions in the West, and then he would be talking to his dear dead son, Jimmie, for whom he had never ceased to grieve. Who will say that the tender words were lost in empty air? Who can say what invisible presences thronged that chamber whence the great soul was about to take its flight to God? A little after midnight, May 10, 1887, as the watchers sat or stood waiting in silence, without a struggle, he died, and upon the soul of John B. McFerrin, the great commoner of Southern Methodism, burst the mystery and glory of immortality.

DR. McFERRIN'S FUNERAL.

The funeral of Dr. McFerrin took place at McKendree Church, Nashville, at 10 o'clock A.M., Wednesday, May 11, 1887. The great concourse of people present showed the profound veneration and affection felt for him in the community in which he had lived so long. Every seat in the spacious auditorium was filled, and the vestibule and aisles were also crowded with citizens, who stood during the whole of the solemn and impressive services. The pall-bearers were: Judge James Whitworth, L. D. Palmer, Esq., Dr. William H. Morgan, Samuel J. Keith, Esq., Rev. W. C. Johnson, D.D., John A. Carter, Esq., T. D. Fite, Esq., Judge E. H. East, John McFerrin Hudson, Esq., Chancellor L. C. Garland, and N. Baxter, Jr.

Bishop H. N. McTyeire, Bishop A. W. Wilson, Bishop R. K. Hargrove, Rev. J. D. Barbee, D.D., Rev. O. P. Fitzgerald, D.D., and Rev. Charles Taylor, D.D., took part in the services. It was a special request of Dr. McFerrin that the exercises should be simple and unostentatious. "Give me," he said, "the burial of a Methodist preacher. Let no solo be sung at my funeral. Let old Methodist hymns be sung to the old tunes familiar to our people." His wish was followed, and the hymns that he himself had used in burying a great company of the holy dead who had gone before him were sung. By his special request the hymn beginning, "Come, let us join our friends above," was "lined," and the vast congregation swelled the melody of the old tune whose sacred associations powerfully affected many hearts. The Scripture lessons prescribed in the solemn Ritual of the Church were read, and extemporaneous prayer was offered. The hymn beginning,

"And let this feeble body fail," was sung to the familiar tune hallowed by the use of the fathers.

Christians of all denominations and all classes of citizens united in this memorial service. It was noticed that an unusually large number of aged persons were present—gray-haired men and women, who had come with sad hearts to pay the last tribute of their love and gratitude to their early friend.

A long procession followed the body to Mount Olivet, and it was laid to rest on one of the main avenues, to await the resurrection. It is a beautiful spot, looking eastward, catching the first beams of the rising sun, where among the oaks and poplars the winter winds sigh their requiems and the spring birds warble their melodies.

THE MAN ALL ROUND.

As a preacher McFerrin takes rank among the first. If eloquence in the pulpit is to be measured by the effects produced, no one will deny that he possessed that precious gift. The popular verdict was that he was a great preacher, and the people never fail at last to assign each man his proper place. They never forgot his sermons. His texts, his arguments, and, most of all, his illustrations, clung to their memories. His quaint sayings and homely apothegms circulated among them freely. The tremendous effects of his special efforts on popular occasions were the wonder of his contemporaries, and will furnish thrilling traditions to their descendants. But how happened it that a man so audaciously unconventional, so full of humor, and often so irrepressibly and irresistibly droll on the platform, was clothed with so much spiritual power in the pulpit? The form of the question furnishes the answer: he possessed genuine spiritual power. The plain truth of the gospel, with the attesting energy of the Holy Spirit, was his sole dependence. He never took a fanciful text, nor strained after a fanciful interpretation of a text. Repentance toward God, faith in the Lord Jesus Christ, a new heart and a new life, the witness of the Spirit giving the consciousness of a present, full, and free salvation, growth in grace, victory over sin and death—these were his themes. He preached the gospel; the Lord worked with him, and confirmed his word with signs following. He did not aim to preach great sermons. He had no weakness for rounded periods, tricks of alliteration, adjectival floridness, or mere epigrammatic smartness of expression. The place was too sacred, the business before him too solemn for any lightness of that sort. Never did a man who bore himself so independently toward men bear himself more humbly toward God. He exhibited that fear of the Lord which is the beginning of true wisdom, that profound and unfailing reverence and humility which abides with him who has seen himself as a sinner in contrast with the Holy One in whose sight the very heavens are unclean, and in whose presence the angels veil their faces. His prayers were the breathings of a soul that lay low at the feet of his Lord and voiced its wants and its praises and thanksgivings in the simplest words. His prayers were spoken to the prayer-hearing God. He never orated or exhorted on his knees. His power in prayer was great because he really prayed. A real prayer is a great thing; it moves heaven and earth. The power that was in his prayers was the power that was in his sermons, and it was supernatural. He prayed and preached in demonstration of the Spirit and of power. The gospel, as preached by him for more than sixty years, was the power of God unto salvation— to how many redeemed souls will be known only in the day that shall declare all things.

As a writer, it is not easy to define the quality and value of Dr. McFerrin's work. He wrote much, and effectively. The doctrines of Methodism, the living issues of the day in the religious world, and sketches of travel in his frequent journeyings, were the subjects that most employed his pen as an editor. The value of his controversial writings consisted not in the display of re- markable scholarship, nor in the originality of his ideas, or the force of his logic; but rather in his homely, direct presentation of his side of all questions in the vernacu- lar of the people. He never weakened his cause by in- geniously forcing a doubtful text to do doubtful service for a dogma or a notion. He used only guns that had been tested, and that did execution only at their muzzles. His proof-texts were such as had been proven. He kept the beaten path, and so never lost himself or his readers in a chase after novelties. Metaphysics he despised. They were wasted on him, and he did not waste them on oth- ers. He was apt to bring down any knight who came at him mounted on a metaphysical charger or walking on rhetorical stilts. He did it by hitting him hard with a well-tried Bible text, or by a shrewd puncture of an inflated sentence, or by a sharp assault on some unguard- ed position, or by a facetious allusion to some unwise or indefensible saying. So he fought over all the ques- tions that were debated in his circle in his day. The mass of his Methodist constituency thought him invin- cible, and he agreed with them. If his logic was not unanswerable, his spirit was unconquerable. When

McFerrin was at the front the Methodist forces felt
secure. Men of superior scholarship in these more
peaceful times might easily be led to undervalue his
services as the champion of his Church. His methods
were eminently successful; the cause he defended rapidly gained strength, and held what it gained. He lived
to see the organization that was fighting for its life.when
he joined it the strongest of all in the vast region where
he labored and led the advancing columns of Methodism.

The methods of his life were not favorable to book-
making, even had he been ambitious of achievement in
that line. He was a man of action, and though he did
much hard work as an editor he could never be held
down to the writer's desk. He must travel, he must
preach, he must mingle with the people. He was not
intended to be a recluse, a book-man, or a " literary " man
in any strict sense of the word. He had it in his heart
to write a book on Methodist doctrine which would be
a breakwater against heresy after he was dead. But he
never found time for it; or it may be that he concluded
that the work had been so well done by others that he
had no call to undertake it.

The " History of Methodism in Tennessee " was his
one achievement in book-making. The value of this
work can be fully appreciated only by one who is specially interested in the historical facts that lie scattered
here and there throughout the wide field of Southern
Methodism, of which Tennessee Methodism was a radiating center. The opening chapters contain interesting and valuable historical and geographical information
of a general character, and the narrative of the introduction and spread of Methodism is told in a straight-
forward way, and the chronological unities are well

preserved. Liberal use was evidently made of the General Minutes, while his own extensive and minute personal knowledge of men and events imparted special interest and guaranteed fidelity to the minor as well as the larger facts of history. Of the philosophy of the movement and its wider relations he says but little. To him Methodism was simply Christianity on the march, with a glad gospel for all men, and he only wished to tell what was done and who did it. The men who shall hereafter write or study Church history will not pass by these volumes thrown off as a labor of love by a busy man who made more history than he wrote.

As a platform speaker his influence was extraordinary, as his power was almost, if not altogether, unequaled. It has often been said that he was the best platform speaker in the United States. If this were asserted here, there would doubtless be many to rise up at once and contest the claim. At the mere suggestion of the matter, what a galaxy of brilliant names flashes before the mind! Among his contemporaries were such men, among politicians, as Clay and Corwin and Wise and Colquitt and Vance and Prentiss and Breckinridge and Choate and Yancey and Phillips and Douglas and Lincoln and Andrew Johnson and Hill and Baker and Hendricks; and, among preachers, Beecher and Simpson and Pierce and Curry and Palmer and Vincent and Jones and Moody and Hoge and Hall and Deems and Wilson, and others whose genius was the admiration of their fellow-countrymen, and some of whom achieved international renown. But take John B. McFerrin when in the right mood—and he was seldom in any other mood so far as readiness for the platform was concerned—and put him up before a promiscuous audience, with a topic

that "sprung" him, and he would capture the occasion,
carrying the crowd and making himself the hero of the
hour.   How quickly did the assembled representatives
of the Methodisms of the world at the London Ecumenical Conference recognize in him a master of assemblies!   And so it was at the Centennial of American
Methodism at Baltimore, of which he was by common
consent the electric center.   When the brilliant and erratic Henry Ward Beecher lectured on "Evolution" in
the Masonic Theater in Nashville, in 1885, Dr. McFerrin sat in the gallery and listened to that remarkable
effort, which was a compound of crude science and back-
slidden theology.   "I would like to have had fifteen
minutes in which to reply to him," said the old Doctor
next day, and the battle-blaze was in his eye as he spoke.
Such a reply as he would have made to that lecture before that audience would have been worth hearing.
The mental verdict which a large majority had already
pronounced against the unproved hypotheses and far-
fetched presumptions of the recalcitrant son of Lyman
Beecher would have been emphasized in a way that none
present could ever have forgotten.   Beecher and McFerrin! the one a comet flaming in lurid and lessening splen-
dors into the deepening night; the other a fixed star that
will shine on in its place in unfading refulgence.

The personal influence of Dr. McFerrin was extraordinary.   His range of personal friendships was wide,
and his positive character indelibly impressed itself even
upon casual acquaintances.   What multitudes of persons, young and old, felt his touch socially, and were
the better for it, none can tell.   He never laid aside
his ministerial character, nor lowered the dignity of his
sacred office   The language of St. Paul might have

been used by him without immodesty or presumption: "Now thanks be unto God, which always causeth us to triumph in Christ, and maketh manifest the savor of his knowledge by us in every place." (2 Cor. ii. 14.) But while he deported himself as became a minister of the Lord Jesus Christ, he was as far as possible removed from all sanctimoniousness and morbidness and asceticism and repellent gloom. His religion was of the hearty, wholesome sort. It had, if the expression might be allowed, a natural flavor—that is to say, it was the normal expression of a hearty nature, whose natural sympathies were refined and intensified by grace abounding. His rare social gifts were laid upon the altar of Christian service. In ordinary conversation he had the happy art of interjecting quaint apothegms that embodied an ethical or spiritual truth in its practical bearings, or of making a hortatory suggestion so pertinently that it could not be evaded, and yet so pleasantly that no offense could be taken. At the bedside of the sick and the dying he exhibited the true pastoral instinct, and none knew better what to say and how to say it in the presence of suffering and in prospect of death. His prayers, always characterized by simplicity, directness, and fervor, on such occasions were specially noted for their brevity and effectiveness, taking the straightest line to the Lord Jesus Christ as the only and sufficient Saviour of sinners. The name of Jesus was to him the name of power, and it was oftenest on his lips in prayer and speech. The music of that name soothed and cheered the spirits of many a dying saint to whom he ministered the true consolations of the gospel. In hundreds of families and with thousands of persons he had thus in seasons of sickness, death, and sorrow, formed

28

relations that gave him a sure and sacred influence for good which he used with unfailing tact, fidelity, and success.

In his family life his faithfulness and force of Christian character were graciously rewarded. He saw the desire of his heart—the conversion of his children and that of almost all of his extensive family circle. The inmates of his home loved him, revered him, and believed in him. Children are keen-eyed; they are discerners of spirits; their instincts tell them where to look for kindness and goodness. They loved Dr. McFerrin, and to every one of his grandchildren who was old enough to remember him as he was in his later years the image of his benignant face and the remembrance of his tender caresses and loving words will be a life-long benediction. Among the photographs of him taken in his later years there was one that represented him sitting with a little grandson on his knee, which impressed the beholder as the ideal embodiment of patriarchal tenderness and infantile trust. It would make a picture worthy to be put on canvas by a great painter.

Of the quality of Dr. McFerrin's work along all these lines of activity and influence the reader of these pages has, it may be hoped, some proper conception. To get an idea of the extent of these labors we must bear in mind both the extraordinary length of his ministerial service and the almost unexampled energy exhibited by him in performing his work. A quenchless zeal worked through an almost tireless body. In the more abundant labors of his ministry he was a true successor of the great Apostle to the Gentiles and of the founder of Methodism. He was moved by the same constraining power—the love of Christ.

BISHOP McTYEIRE'S FUNERAL SERMON.

Text: "For David, after he had served his own generation by the will of God, fell on sleep." (Acts xiii. 36.)

MORE than sixty years ago God gave to this Church and to this people a servant to serve you in your best and highest interests. After proving himself good and faithful, he has fallen on sleep, and we meet to mourn and to bury him.

Forget not to be thankful, for this gift, and that God endued him with such grace and spared him to you so long. Few of this vast congregation had been born when he whose body lies before us began his active ministry. He received the parents of many of you into the Church, baptized your households, and buried your dead. In the power of the Spirit he has preached repent-ance and pointed to the cross of Christ. He has promoted good and restrained evil; reclaimed the erring, comforted the mourner, and instructed the ignorant. In every form, by wise precept and by spotless example, he has shown unto you the way of salvation. In perplexity you sought him for counsel; in trouble, for sympa-thy; in want, for help. His exceeding common sense and great kindness of heart never failed you.

While he has gone to give his account to the Master, we may well take account of our loss in such a servant.

He laid himself out for the benefit of "his own generation;" and this, and the way he did it, we may well believe, was accord-ing to the will of God. He lived not for himself, neither did he project his benevolence so far into the uncertain future as to die a debtor to the age he lived in. That man best serves the gener-ation following, starts it off upon a higher plane, who serves well his own. Providence indicates herein where duty lies. The gifts which suit one age may not suit another. The peculiar talents with which his Maker endowed our deceased brother he used, and none others. He was always himself, and not another man— unique, original, strong, and fresh to the last. Thus he made ex-

(435)

actly the contribution to the welfare of the world that was needed —a contribution that other generations may not need in the same form or degree, but of which they will ever be the beneficiaries.

John Berry McFerrin was born in Rutherford County, Tennessee, June 15, 1807, and "fell on sleep" at his home in Nashville, in the bosom of a loved and loving family, at 12:55 o'clock A.M., May 10, 1887. He was of Scotch-Irish descent. His grandfather was a Revolutionary soldier, and his father, James McFerrin, served well under General Jackson in the War of 1812. Converted about the same time with his son, James McFerrin became a minister and a member of the Tennessee Annual Conference two years before him; and after efficient service died in the prime of life. His mother, to whom he owed, and delighted to acknowledge, much, died a few years ago at the advanced age of ninety-three.

By request of the Conference, Dr. McFerrin preached in October, 1875, a semi-centennial sermon during the session at Shelbyville, where, in 1825, he had been admitted on trial. The beginning of his spiritual life, and its principal stages of activity, were thus stated by himself in that discourse:

On the 20th of August, 1820, I was converted at a Methodist prayer-meeting in Rutherford County, Tennessee. Two weeks afterward, in company with my father and mother, I united with the Methodists. This was a surprise to our neighbors, for they regarded the family as Presbyterian. Soon after we connected ourselves with the Methodists I was called upon to pray in public. When about sixteen years of age I was appointed a class-leader. My father having removed to Alabama, and erected a meeting-house and camp-ground on his land, a large Society was soon raised up, and I was put in charge as the principal leader. August 1, 1824, I was licensed to exhort by William McMahon, presiding elder of the Huntsville District, my father being the preacher in charge of the circuit. On October 8, 1825, I was licensed to preach. The next month I was received on probation into the Tennessee Conference, which convened in Shelbyville, Bishops Roberts and Soule presiding. I was appointed, with Finch P. Scruggs, to a circuit embracing Tuscumbia, Russellville, and the counties adjacent. [The Tennessee Conference then extended into North Alabama.] My second year was to the Lawrence Circuit, embracing Courtland, Moulton, Decatur, Somerville, and the counties around—Alexander Sale being my senior. At the end of this year I was ordained deacon by Bishop Soule. My third and fourth years were devoted to missionary work in the Cherokee Nation. At the end of my fourth year I was ordained elder by Bishop Roberts, and appointed, with W. L. McAlister, to the Limestone Circuit, embracing the country west of Huntsville, in Madison County, and the whole of Limestone County, Alabama. My sixth year I was appointed to the Huntsville Station; my seventh year (1831) I labored in the Nashville Station, as the colleague of L. D. Overall. My eighth year I was Agent for La Grange College. In 1833 I was sent to Pulaski Station, where I remained two years. I was then returned to Nashville; then to the Florence District; then two years to the Cumberland District, embracing Gallatin and Clarksville; back again to Nashville; and in the autumn of 1840 I was elected Editor of the *Christian Advocate.* In that office I was continued till May, 1858, when I was elected Book Agent. This office, with the appointment of missionary to the Army of Tennessee, I held eight years. Since 1866 I have been Secretary of the Board of Missions. Thus, three years on circuits, two years among the Indians, six years in stations, three years presiding elder, nearly eighteen years editor, eight years Book Agent and missionary to the army, and nearly nine years Secretary, make out my fifty years.

The General Minutes for 1825 show, in other Annual Conferences of the Connection, such beginners for that year as George C. Cookman, Levi Scott, Charles M. Holliday, Eugene V. Levert, George M. Roberts, Edgerton Ryerson, and others, who, after obtaining a good report through faith, have been so long dead that they seem to belong to another generation. Bishop Soule, who submitted the name of the unknown young man to the Conference for acceptance, was then on his second episcopal round. This semi-centennial sermon takes us a little farther back:

When I united with the Methodists they had not a denominational school in operation in the United States. In 1819 the first Missionary Society was organized in the Methodist Episcopal Church in America. The next year (1820), the year I joined the Church, the receipts were $822.24. In 1874 the two divisions collected nearly $900,000, besides the hundreds of thousands collected in other bodies of Methodism in America.

In 1820 there were in North America 904 traveling preachers, 256,881 white and colored members. This included Canada. I have lived to see the time when the same Church, in her two grand divisions, leaving off Canada, numbers: Traveling preachers, 14,330: local preachers, 18,062; members, 2,262,285.

These items help us to realize the important historic space covered by this man's life and ministry. He was no idle spectator of what was passing, but had a hand in making up the record of those eventful years. Beginning with that held in Cincinnati, in 1836, he was a member of thirteen General Conferences consecutively; also a member of the Convention of 1845.

On his first coming to Nashville (1831) the Church here had four hundred and two white members and three hundred and five colored. At the same time F. A. Owen was stationed in the village of Memphis, on the Chickasaw Bluffs; Robert Paine was for the second year "Superintendent of La Grange College;" David O. Shattuck was at Brownsville, A. L. P. Green at Franklin, and

Fountain E. Pitts on the Nashville Circuit—the two last named having entered Conference a year before him. Referring to contemporary events, Andrew Jackson was in the stormy period of his first presidential administration; James K. Polk was a rising young Congressman; and Andrew Johnson, the great commoner, having learned to read and cipher on the tailor's board, had just been elected mayor of the village of Greeneville. The waters of Cumberland River were occasionally stirred by a steam-boat, affording rapid transportation to New Orleans within ten days. Not a mile of macadamized turnpike existed in the State, while railroads and tunnels were not dreamed of.

That John B. McFerrin was an important factor in the moral and material development of his native State none will question. In three potent ways he wrought, for sixty years—by the pulpit, the press, and the platform—most potent of all ways; and he was forceful in each. Such a ministry, it is readily seen, must directly and permanently influence the *moral* character of the public. Its material development is also promoted indirectly, but none the less powerfully, by the same agency. Where public opinion is right; where honesty, truth, and social purity dwell, there life and property are safe, there the rewards of industry are sure, there commerce is nourished and population gathers. It is impossible for such a man to leave the world no better, no richer, and on no higher plane than he found it.

He has not merely lived, but acted through two generations of rapid transformations—inheriting the sturdy strength, the simple manners, the energy and sagacity of the first, and taking on no small degree of the breadth and culture of the second. To the end he was employed in great trusts. There had been no intermission, no superannuation. Such was his diligence that he was always gaining influence; and so steady and prudent was he, he never lost any. No Tennessean was more loved and revered, at home or abroad. The people claimed him as one of themselves. His style, address, and mode of thought were to their liking. He impressed them as an honest man; they believed what he said; they felt his sympathy; and they followed where he led. If a politician, he would have been unequaled as a stump-speaker; if a demagogue, he would have been dangerous; in either character, invincible. If a man of worldly business, he would have been thrifty. But, by the grace of God, he was none of these. All his zeal, hopes, labors, and aspirations were in the Church and for the Church. He turned not aside to the right hand or to the left. He was simply a Methodist preacher, drawing all his cares and studies this way.

Of large frame, heavy features, and standing squarely upon his feet, John B. McFerrin was the typical Western man, regenerated by Christianity. His education began in the old-field schools of boyhood, and was continued by books and object-lessons through life. His cast was practical, not poetical or rhetorical—unlike his eloquent contemporary, Pitts. He saw things as a whole, not in their component parts, and judged of their relations as by intuition. Abstract thought was a weariness, if not an impossibility, to him. The power was not his of considering the single properties and qualities of things apart, of analyzing and then combining them to new forms, thus leading to invention. He was, therefore, slow to admit changes of any sort. In these respects he was unlike his great contemporary, Green. He was against all "new-fangled notions," and constitutionally conservative—perhaps to excess. He preferred to work the old plans and to get the best results out of them. An innovation must be clearly safe and very clearly an improvement before he could accept it. He could hardly conceive of it until he saw it in operation. Woe to the antagonist whom he encountered when defending "Old Methodism!"

His attitude toward every material modification of Church economy among us has been, first, that of suspicion, if not of down-right opposition at its introduction. When adopted, he put it on trial and watched its working; then, if it worked well, he espoused it, and became a wall of defense against any who would disturb it. That caution of Solomon he habitually observed. "Meddle not with them that are given to change."

Who will say that such a contribution to ecclesiastical legislation was not valuable in this nineteenth century?

The confidence of his brethren in his honesty, his intuitive sagacity, and the safety born of his conservatism, was well illustrated in this city during the General Conference of 1858. A new departure was inaugurated in Publishing House matters, by the committee in charge of that interest. The member who led in the proposed scheme was bold and inventive, but slightly *doctrinaire*. Various depositories were to be established, and agencies here and there, to enlarge and expand the circulation of religious literature for the benefit and on the credit of the Church. The measure passed, and it was generally understood that the author of it was to be Book Agent to carry it out, and that certain others were to occupy subordinate places. But, as they thought over what they had done, members became afraid of their plan; and when the election came on, and ballots were counted, the whole slate was broken by the majority of votes being cast for J. B. McFerrin as Book Agent. On adjournment, I exchanged views with a venerable member on the unexpected result, and his remark may be taken as representative: " Well, I voted for that plan, but the more' I thought on it the less I liked it—too complicated. It may do finely, and then again it may ruin every thing. But McFerrin, we know him. He can pull, and if it's necessary he can hold back powerfully, and he *will* hold back if there's danger."

A strange sight that was—the General Conference correcting, modifying, and almost nullifying its dubious legislation by putting one man in charge of the business for the four years following.

It was much the same case at Atlanta in 1878. We had lay delegates then to help us—a help we had not twenty years before. But after fullest investigation of liabilities and assets, and the best legislative contrivance, there was painful suspense as to the fate of the Publishing House. Again, McFerrin to the front. Not that he was fertile in invention, but he could be relied on to carry out whatever an able Book Committee, with enlarged powers, devised. When Mr. Nathaniel Baxter, Jr., of that committee, took me aside and opened the four per cent. bond plan, on long time, I first saw light. The United States Government had already adopted the plan and made it popular and familiar to the people. But—how to place the bonds for $350,000! Creditors were clamorous, and the sheriff was at the door. The Church could not repudiate just debts. Her voice, ever after, in preaching justice, honesty, and truth, would be like a cracked bell. To sacrifice present assets, and leave liabilities unprovided for, was to entail worrying collections throughout the Connection for years, and so to disgust and drive away the public from our churches. The prospect was gloomy enough.

With a well-matured plan Dr. McFerrin went forth. Now was his power with the people seen. He opened the campaign at the Western Virginia Conference, then one of our smallest and weakest. I heard him state nis case and present his plea, and watched the effect with an interest I can not describe. It was soon evident that he had the jury. But did the jury have the money? He rang the changes on old Methodism and what it had done for them and for their fathers; touched up their patriotism by allusions to losses and damages through the war, his client being a sufferer in common with themselves; showed that relief was possible, and failure would be shameful. He enlivened the discussion with anecdote and clinched it with argument, and at the opportune moment offered his bonds. Two generous farmers (brothers) on the south side of the Ohio took a thousand dollars' worth at par. Others followed with less sums; and the preachers, as they always do, came up promptly with twenty and fifty and a hundred. When the hand-shaking was over, the speaker looked like a victor, and so he was. From that day I never doubted that the bonds would go and the House be saved. He pursued the campaign, going through the Conferences until the work was done. Who that saw and heard can ever forget that dramatic scene, in which he represented the Bishops and superannuated and other preachers and their wives, and the official members, all assembled on the Public Square of Nashville, and the crier, with "one, two, three—l-a-s-t call"—swinging down his hammer upon the Publishing House of the Methodist Episcopal Church, South? Those who heard and laughed and wept said, "No, that must never be;" and they took the bonds.

Under his administration as Missionary Secretary a debt was paid that was heavy and depressing for those times. And yet, the least success of his life was during the years he was at the head of the Missionary Bureau. The position was not suited to him. Enterprising new fields, and selecting, from untried men, proper agents for opening and occupying those fields, involved experiment and adventure; and he was not adventurous. The changing aspects of times and places, in those unsteady years from 1866 to 1878, required new measures and expedients to meet exigencies; and, as he lacked the analytic faculty, invention was not his forte. True, he was strong on the platform; his speeches at missionary anniversaries were popular; he lifted large collections. But imitation is the homage unconsciously paid to genius, and the imitators of Dr. McFerrin's speeches, though numerous, were no successful or edifying. A broad and steady missionary movement in the Church must be based on a quickening of the public conscience; on information, rather than on entertainment. Not one worker that crowds a house upon announcement is wanted, but thousands of earnest men and women must be put to work systematically for the cause where no applauding audiences greet the advocate of Missions. When a plan was devised to apportion the old war debt among the several Annual Conferences, according to an accepted ratio, he took the field and worked it so well that the missionary debt was paid.

As a public speaker you know how ready and effective he was. The substance of discourse was sometimes premeditated in paragraphs, but not the words or style. Stimulus rather than preparation was what he required for success. His resources were at command. He took hints from the occasion, and the suggestion of circumstances was his main reliance. Who ever saw him, when pressed in debate, at a loss for a reply? The more he was interrupted the more he was at himself. Those who injected questions at him on the floor made nothing by it, so easily could he turn every thing that happened, and every thing that was said, to his own advantage. Whether in social discussion or in deliberative assemblies, his power of repartee was formidable. Cicero's famous treatise, *De Oratore*, puts this among the "peculiar gifts of nature"—"a talent," says the master of Roman eloquence, "which appears to be incapable of being communicated by teaching." Cicero, after discoursing on this rare, quick, and terrible weapon of the orator through several chapters, and making on the reader the impression that he coveted the .gift for himself, adds: "It is one of the things in which, unless the orator has a full supply from nature, he can not be much assisted by a master." If John B. McFerrin could not meet an argument, he parried it so skillfully that the crowd felt that he had met it, and cheered accordingly. A look, an attitude, an inflection of the voice did the work effectually. A facetious remark, or pathetic play on collateral issues, was unanswerable. Sharp wit, overwhelming drollery, unfailing humor, cheapened the adversary or broke the force of a logical lance. While he could see and appreciate the strong points of his cause, and could strongly urge them, he did not always resist the temptation to win victory by lighter and natural auxiliaries. But he never used that dangerous weapon maliciously. Often his own hand was first to pour in oil where it had made a wound. He was naturally cautious and modest, and yet a consciousness of this gift made him bold.

His ministry of the gospel was faithful and fruitful. The mission among the Indians was like a golden thread of poetry worked into his early life. At Chickamauga and Ross's Landing, where Chattanooga now stands; at the junction of Etowah and Oostanaula Rivers, where Rome, Georgia, now is; and at Gunter's Landing, were his principal appointments. I remember that once we ascended Lookout Mountain together, and he pointed out, with vivid reminiscences, some scenes of his mission life among the Cherokees. The chief, John Ross, he baptized and received into the Church, doubtless with the same simplicity that he performed the like offices for ex-President Polk a quarter of a century later. We traveled together through the Indian Nation some years ago, visiting the Missions west of the Mississippi. A night was spent in a Cherokee home. The mother of the family, who was also a grandmother, was drawn into conversation. Her maiden name was Gunter, born on the Tennessee River. The names of her father and brothers were given, and of the missionaries who had preached to them before they left the "Old Nation" for the Western Reservation. The conversation drew on to the climax of mutual recognition. "Katie Gunter," said the Missionary Secretary, "don't you know me?" "No, sir." "My name is John B. McFerrin." The Indian woman rested her hand on his knee for a moment, gazing intently into his face, and then, in an abandon of joy, fell upon his neck and wept aloud. She was one of his converts, and still maintained her integrity.

As chaplain in the army he was very useful. A stump or a wagon served as his ready pulpit, wherever the soldiers halted to rest or camp. In the hospital, or on the march, he was pastor, friend, nurse. Many seals to his ministry bear the date of those sad years. He introduced me at one session of an Annual Conference to two ministers, efficient and promising men, saying: "These are two of my boys, converted while Confederate soldiers; and there are a heap more of 'em. Hallelujah!" His final ministerial service was at the funeral of the late Rev. William Burr, whom he had licensed to preach forty-odd years ago. It was a race between them, like that of Peter and John, which should first reach the sepulcher. They lay on their death-beds, sending mes-

sages of love and Christian confidence to each other by telephone.
The saintly Burr reached the grave first, and his aged companion
rallied to bury him. "There is a natural body, and there is a
spiritual body," saith St. Paul. I entertain myself with thinking
of the great hand-shaking that has been going on in paradise since
Brother McFerrin left us, as he greets on the other shore the
thousands who have been awakened, converted, reclaimed, edified,
by his ministry, and helped on their way to that better country
where now he has joined them. His old companions and his
spiritual children are there to welcome him into everlasting habitations. White people, Negroes, Indians, the small and the great,
are there enjoying with him their release and " full felicity."

He was one of the few men whose preaching improved with
time. Borne up by a wonderful constitution and will-power, he
went around attending the Annual Conferences, at the rate of
ten or twenty a year, selling books, making collections, and throw-
ing off those inimitable speeches on various Church interests, of
which the brethren could never get enough. There was an increasing unction. Even an ordinary business notice, in his latter
days, often left the Conference in tears and raptures, because of
the spiritual peroration that unconsciously attached itself to a talk
about plain dollar-and-cent accounts. Men observed that he was
ripening for heaven. Some of his sermons at the Conferences,
these last dozen years, were extraordinarily melting. He kept up
the habit of the fathers—mixing experience with the exposition.
His stock themes were sin, repentance, faith, regeneration, and
salvation for all, through Jesus. They were good enough for him;
and his exactness of definition and distinction on these divine top-
ics was to the last a grateful surprise to those who crowded to
hear him. In theology he held that what was new was not true,
and what was true was not new; it was a revelation rather than a
science. Without relaxing diligence in earthly things, he was
coming daily more and more under the influence of things invisible and eternal. The attraction of the world to come grew evidently stronger; his speed quickened as he drew near the end. The
personal Saviour, the love of the Spirit, and his own deeper experience of grace, were themes he most readily fell into conversation about.

I have spoken of him as a Tennessean, because his native
State, I dare assert, has not produced a man better known, more

beloved, and for rare combination of moral and mental power and wealth of character his superior. But far beyond the lines of his State and Conference he was esteemed. In the great synods of the Church he was watchful and eminent. He represented American Methodism in the Ecumenical Conference which met in London in 1881. At the Centennial in Baltimore in 1884 Southern Methodism had in him her most eminent representative. No figure in that body of five hundred holy and picked men was more honorably conspicuous, no voice more eagerly heard, and no presence more respectfully greeted than Dr. Mc-Ferrin's. He was selected to respond to the address of welcome, and met that and every occasion—whether of counsel, discussion, banquet, devotion, or farewell greeting—with prompt and felicitous address. To him it was a joyous occasion. His soul overflowed with its bountiful fellowship.

We mourn not alone. In the North as in the South, in Canada and beyond the seas, in the Foreign Mission stations and along the wide frontiers, they weep with us to-day.

He grew old gracefully: a hard test. It has been well said that old age is itself a kind of day of judgment. Now begins the reaping of what has been sown; now begins the harvest of youth and middle life. The selfish are left without friends, the penurious are devoured by full-grown avarice, the meanly ambitious are embittered by disappointment, and all evil passions and habits consume their victim in a helpless old age. Pitiable sight! But not so with one who has not lived to himself. "At evening time there shall be light." The temper mellows; peace flows as a river; children and friends crown the hoary head with love and reverence; temperate habits, chastened passions, and Christian hopes smooth the present and throw their light on the future. Even those alienations caused by conflicting interests and honest differences of opinion with our fellow-men find an end in the vindications of time, for "when a man's ways please the Lord, he maketh even his enemies to be at peace with him."

Our deceased brother had a happy old age. "I will not, the Lord helping me, become sour and sore-headed," he once said to me, on observing the case of a friend who acidulated as he aged. Then, bending half down, removing his hat, and showing the full crown of his bald head, "Do you see any sore place there?" If he spent a few days as the Conference guest with a family, it was an era with that household, including children and servants.

The Lord blessed his servant in his home life. In 1833 he was married to Miss Probart. Their married life was blessed with six children, three of whom survive. Mrs. McFerrin died while her husband was attending the session of the General Conference in Columbus, Georgia, in May, 1854.

He was again married to Miss McGavock, a member of the family of McGavocks so well known in Virginia and Middle Tennessee. Of this marriage were born two daughters. These five children, with nineteen grandchildren, made his domestic life complete. In 1880 the oldest son, James W., was suddenly killed in a railroad accident. He was a noble young man. The father was visiting a Conference in Texas when the sad news reached him. The "stroke was heavier than his complaint." In the last few delirious days he was overheard talking with "Jimmy." All his children and grandchildren of twelve years and upward are members of the Methodist Church. Wife and children, sons-in-law and daughters-in-law within the fold; all his business wound up and papers signed; the new church under roof where his family worship; the Publishing House safe; and seventy-five thousand members added to the Church this year—he was ready to say, with Simeon: "Lord, now lettest thou thy servant depart in peace."

Over a year ago he was sick, as was thought, unto death. When doctors and nurses gave him up he persisted that though it might be so that he was going to die he did not feel as he had supposed a dying man would. His work was not yet done. He strangely recovered. But when this last sickness came he held a different language. "My work seems to be done; my eyes and my hearing fail; the old tabernacle is giving way." The Master was closing the doors and shutting the windows, thus saying to his servant: "Arise and depart, for this is not your rest." He took the warning kindly. The prospect was unclouded. Indeed, he remarked to me that his trouble now was to keep from being impatient to go. The language of his soul was: "Now, Lord, what wait I for? My hope is in thee."

I found him one day rejoicing over a portion of Holy Scripture that had been read to him by a preceding visitor (fourth and fifth chapters of Second Corinthians.) "I understand it better than ever. Portions of the Bible come back to me that I had forgotten." And he fed on that word.

At another time I found his son reading hymns to him out of the Unabridged Hymn-book, and he would have me read a few that he indicated by subject or title. Among them:

> Lo, on a narrow neck of land,
> ' Twixt two unbounded seas I stand.

And this:

> Rise, my soul, and stretch thy wings
> Thy better portion trace.

Then, gathering in the family, he asked that

> And let this feeble body fail,
> And let it droop or die,

be sung to a familiar tune. It was done, his nephew leading. At the conclusion of the stanza,

> Give joy or grief, give ease or pain,
> Take life or friends away—
> I come to find them all again
> In that eternal day,

he praised God and exulted. "Nothing like our old hymns," he exclaimed. "I hope the Committee [on Revision of the Hymn-book, then in session] will spare those dear old hymns on doctrine and experience that the Wesleys gave us." This charge he gave me, with emphasis: "Those little songs about 'Sweet by and by,' and 'Shall we know each other there?' and the like, may all be very nice, but don't you let any of them be sung at my funeral."

His last sermon was preached in Arkansas, near his mother's grave, to which, with filial piety, he had made pilgrimage. (Text: 1 Cor. xv. 58.) He has helped to build and pay out of debt many churches for others. His last begging speech was made in this pulpit, for help to build the church in which he and his family worship. His last contribution to the press was an article in the *Christian Advocate*, insisting on the value of a systematic statement of theology and vindicating creeds. He has been as an anchor to many who were ready to drift before every wind of doctrine. Eminent service he rendered his generation at this point. May there be no need of such service in the future!

I have spoken of him as a Methodist. In a high sense he belonged to all Christ's people. With Charles Wesley he could say:

And fellowship with all we hold
Who hold it with our Head.

He loved Methodism, her creed and polity; but he loved, and was beloved by, members of other Churches as few men have been.

May 2 he called his son-in-law, the presiding elder of the Murfreesboro District, to his bedside to receive a last message to the Tennessee Conference:

"Tell them to hold fast to our articles of belief—justification by faith, the witness of the Spirit, and holiness of heart and life.

"Tell them I forgive all who may have injured me at any time, and I ask forgiveness if at any time I have wounded a brother. Evil may have followed where evil was not intended; if so, I ask forgiveness.

"I love the Tennessee Conference. I die in peace with them and all men, and in the faith of the Lord Jesus Christ, and in the love of God, and in expectation of eternal life." Again: "Tell the brethren I love every one of them."

His words two weeks ago to his son, who has charge of a circuit twenty miles away, and had been summoned to see him die, are most expressive of character: "My son, I feel a little stronger, and you had better return and fill your appointment to-morrow. If, while you are away, John, I should happen to slip off, you know where to find me."

He has gone, my friends and brethren; we shall behold him no more in this world. He has gone; we ne'er shall see his like again. John B. McFerrin has gone; BUT YOU KNOW WHERE TO FIND HIM. Amen.

www.ingramcontent.com/pod-product-compliance
Lightning Source LLC
Chambersburg PA
CBHW031058110726
47900CB00003B/973